SALT CREEK

SALT CREEK

A Novel

Phil LeMaitre

Salt Creek: A Novel by Phil LeMaitre Copyright © 2019, Second Edition 2021 Published by Salt Creek Tales-Phil LeMaitre, Rockledge, Florida

ISBN:978-1-7379585-2-9 (Paperback)
ISBN: 978-1-7379585-3-6 (eBook)

Cover photography by Phil LeMaitre

phillemaitreauthor.com

Dedicated to everyone who has lived or is still living within the Salt Creek community ....GO OILERS!

1

August 25, 1984

Near Midwest, Wyoming

In the warm and cloudless August Saturday morning in central Wyoming, Tim Savolt pushed through shoulder high greasewood bushes and waist-high sagebrush growing along the banks of Salt Creek. It was his first morning off from coaching football in the last two weeks as two-a-day football practices ended the day before. He now took advantage of his respite by doing something that he truly enjoyed.

Tim had walked this path multiple times, not just over the summer but over the last 18 months, and his repeated footfalls made a rough trail along the creek's northern bank.

Separated by only a mile, Midwest and its sister town of Edgerton were the only settlements left in a once-booming region of Wyoming. Over the years, the Salt Creek Oilfield had produced more petroleum than any other like it in the United States. Midwest received its name after the Midwest Refining Company, which pioneered oil production in the Salt Creek field. The company built the town to house employees. On the other hand, Edgerton had once served as the nighttime entertainment center for the region boasting over 10,000 residents. As of 1984, the Salt Creek area had little over a thousand people. Even Wyomingites looked toward this community with little more than an afterthought like many other boom and bust towns across the massive state.

Tim stopped his hike long enough to retrieve his canteen off of his hip, and he took a sip of water. While standing there, he looked down at his heavily worn cowboy boots that used to be a deep brown hue. But now, tan patches of undyed leather highlighted the abuse the boots had taken over the years. With his canteen in one hand, he bent down toward his feet and used his free hand to pluck out a dozen or so of the needlelike cheatgrass seeds that had pierced through his wranglers above his cowboy boots. The pesky seeds had irritated him with each step over the last hundred yards or so.

Under his backpack, his faded brown University of Wyoming t-shirt was soaked with sweat. But, notwithstanding the heat, the effort, or the annoying cheatgrass, Tim Savolt was in his sound mind and peace. Being outdoors allowed him to think, and hiking along Salt Creek gave him the perfect excuse to enjoy the sights and sounds of the countryside.

The serenity is short-lived by the sound of squeaks and yawns from thousands of pump jacks in the surrounding treeless valley. They incessantly pumped oil out of the ground, 24 hours a day- every day. Some of the pumps were located on the very edge of town.

Tim then looked westward toward Interstate 25. When he thought of the travelers on that highway, he wondered whether any tourists from back east knew or even appreciated where the gasoline and oil in their motorhomes were produced?

He lifted his tattered King Ropes hat off his head and wiped his sweaty brow with his shirt sleeve. All around him, the air sagged heavily with a smell of sulfur that came from a nearby flare. The burn stacks combusted unusable gas bi-products from oil production or injection water cooling ponds throughout the valley.

Savolt had long known that the injection well hot water came naturally from formations located deep below ground. It was then piped into the oil formation to efficiently bring the petroleum out of the sands and rock. Water was then collected into cooling ponds, which released naturally occurring sulfur into the air. At one time, the same hot water was used to heat homes in Midwest and was also used to heat swimming pools in Midwest and the forgone town of Lavoye nearby.

Because of the water's geothermal properties, the smell was not unlike the geyser basin in Yellowstone National Park. Still, visitors to Midwest reacted much differently to the odor here than they do while watching Old Faithful erupt. Tim recalled what his father always used to say when driving by an oilfield: *it is the smell of money*, and the memory brought a slight smile to his face.

Savolt adjusted his hat once again and then heavily sighed. The following week would begin the 1984-1985 school year, which meant he would also start his fourth year of teaching junior and senior high school science. His employer, Midwest School, was an oddity since 300 students from Kindergarten through Seniors were educated within the same building.

Students came from Midwest, Edgerton, Linch (in Johnson County), and local ranches. Savolt further marveled that the school itself served as the community's centerpiece that intimately bound the area residents into a large family. Another interesting fact was that the lives of nearly everyone in the Salt Creek area revolved around the school's activities, especially during football season. Additionally, secrets were nearly impossible to keep within the community because most residents knew one another where everyone's victories and struggles in life were public domain. It was this essence of community that endeared him even more toward the area where he found an innate sense of belongingness.

During the school year, Tim Savolt was very popular amongst the students who found him engaging and caring. He made science fun and understandable to everyone. However, he was a target by the single women in the area, especially a few unwed teachers. They viewed him as the best available bachelor. He had been propositioned and tempted many times, yet he remained a strident bachelor. Tim secretly vowed to push off serious commitment while searching for that special someone for as long as possible.

He stood 5' 9" tall and weighed a trim 165 pounds with chestnut brown hair and matching eyes. Though he always viewed himself with average looks. However, people seemed drawn to his kind nature, humorous wit, and intelligence.

Tim lived in an apartment complex owned by the Natrona County School District. His employer also rented many other homes on two streets in Midwest for teachers rather than commuting two hours roundtrip daily from Casper.

Earlier that morning, as he left his apartment, Tim found a note pinned to the door frame from his next-door neighbor, Karen Connelly, who taught home economics. Karen moved to Midwest five years ago from Maine. She hoped to catch a dashing cowboy but turned her focus to Tim when she realized that oil workers outnumber cowboys in Midwest by a 10 to 1 ratio. Her note read:

"Hi Timmy, I hope you like me calling you that? Anyway, we are forming a bowling team of teachers to play at the bowling alley in Edgerton during the league season that starts in September. I hope you will join us, and I can even make the team shirts, but I need you to come over for a proper fitting. How about maybe supper, is tonight good for you? You could bring some wine if you want. I can't wait!

Me

P.S. If you are going on one of your "little walks" today, let me know, and I will go with

Drawing her note out of his pocket and re-reading it again, he noted that the exclamation point at the end included a heart. Karen had left at least twenty messages on his door within the last year. It was not that the teacher was unattractive; instead, she had light brown hair, blue eyes, and a full figure. To Tim, however, it was just that she was so over the top with everything, and the last thing he wished was to hurt her feelings or feeling trapped. He also knew that the two of them came from two very different backgrounds. Their combination could be just as volatile as a chemistry experiment gone awry.

Shortly after finding the note earlier in the morning, Tim decided to make his getaway as fast as possible without making a sound rather than risk an awkward confrontation with Karen. So Tim snuck down the apartment complex stairs as quietly as he could and made it out to the sidewalk without her noticing.

After his get away, Tim had waited next to the building for an additional 15 minutes for one of his students, Josh Anderson, to accompany him on the trek. However, Josh never showed. Still, he guessed that the boy had slept in, which was easy to forgive. Moreover, Tim thought it was fortunate that Josh had slept in since Karen would surely hear the boy tromp up the stairs.

His escape from the apartment complex would have been nearly perfect if not for a fellow teacher, Doug Pierson. His colleague spotted him while walking his Irish Setter in the vacant lot behind his house near the corner of Lewis Street and Teachers Row. Tim fully understood that word travels fast in this town, and Karen would know about his evasion before he even returned home.

Tim grew up in Thermopolis, Wyoming, known for its famous hot springs, which accustomed him to the same familiar sulfur smell found in Midwest. As a Thermopolis Bobcat, he earned second-team All-State honors in football. He was also an accomplished wrestler and had placed third in the State Wrestling Championships twice. However, his childhood dream of wearing the brown and prairie gold jersey of the Wyoming Cowboys football team vanished when he failed to receive even a walk-on tryout.

Without other scholarship offers and not wanting to take on massive college loan debt, he opted to enlist in the United States Army for four years and then used his GI Bill to pay for school.

The regimented Army life suited Tim well and offered him a chance to mature beyond his high school peers. Following basic training, he became a combat arms range official since he already had an ingrained knowledge of firearms and was an expert marksman. Then while serving in Germany, his parents died in a traffic accident within the Wind River Canyon while returning home from a trip to Casper. Being an only child, Tim had to learn to cope with holiday leave and having no place to go home. Two years after the funeral, Tim left the Army and started his degree work to teach science since it was his favorite subject in high school.

Tim Savolt's real passion in life, aside from teaching, was seeking answers through scientific study. He caught the bug of conducting studies due to the long hours he spent in the science lab at Montana State University. It was there that he majored in secondary education with a minor in science. He also appreciated each field study that took place within Yellowstone National Park just south of Bozeman, Montana, but on the Wyoming side of the border.

As a teacher, Savolt utilized his school breaks throughout the school calendar to make hikes across open country in the local area. The rewards of his many treks were on display in a glass case in his classroom. He then used the fossils and the geodes as tactile learning aids.

But, two years ago, Tim discovered an odd rodent that resembled what everyone thought to be the extinct Wyoming Long-tailed Rock Mouse. The small mammal was living on the edge of an oilfield near the Rattlesnake Mountains west of Casper. He immediately reported his discovery to the federal Fish and Wildlife Service, which confirmed that it was the same species that many experts had thought vanished long ago. However, as environmentalists triumphed his discovery, those in the energy industry despised it since the oilfield soon closed. He was then labeled a "tree hugger," but in reality, Tim just did what he felt was the right thing, all politics aside.

The Salt Creek now served as Savolt's object of study since it flowed through an active oil field. So naturally, he was curious about the oilfield's environmental impact on plants, aquatic animals, and other wildlife. So aptly named, Salt Creek naturally possessed high amounts of salt and hard water, which contained measurable quantities of sodium, chlorine, and carbonate. The headwaters began 20 miles to the southeast of Midwest from the drainages and springs that swept down from the Pine Ridge. Then the creek ended another 20 miles to the north, where it emptied into the Powder River. Salt Creek traversed over land that many would assume to be a wasteland of nothingness. The square top mesas that bordered the valley floor served as the area's only redeeming natural features.

Tim had made his way downstream to a point adjacent to the football field, where he knelt to fill up a sample cup of creek water. It was then that he thought he heard a vehicle pull up behind him and come to a stop. Rather than turning around to see who was there, Tim continued to take his sample.

"I wouldn't drink that if I were you," said a familiar voice from behind him that was laden with humor.

Without turning around, Tim said, "hey Reed, what was that about drinking?" Tim asked.

Reed served as one of the custodians at the school and was sitting behind the wheel of a school district pickup truck on the bypass road just 15 yards from the bank of the creek. It was apparent to him from looking at the new yard stripe machine in the truck's bed that Reed planned to paint the borders on the football field a little over a hundred yards away.

The custodian also had a dubious reputation as a loner. He was pleasant and friendly though he mostly kept to himself while he attended to his duties. Nobody at the school or the community knew anything about Reed, or even if Reed was his first or last name. Ironically, in every school yearbook, the caption under his photo listed his name only as "Reed."

Like Tim, Reed joined the school staff a few years ago and was also a fellow bachelor. Rather than living in the apartment complex, Reed bargained with the school to fix the one-time office in the maintenance building into a quaint little bachelor pad. The custodian immediately took a liking to Tim since they shared the same passion of following the Denver Broncos. Then one fall Sunday, Reed showed up at Savolt's apartment unannounced to watch the Broncos on television, and they continued the tradition ever since.

Reed repeated to Tim, "I wouldn't drink that water from the creek because only God knows what is in it. I hear it is toxic, just like everything else about this place."

"Actually, I have, but the water is too salty for me to stomach it," Tim said with a laugh.

"You are a crazy man!" Reed said with a chuckle, but then something caught his attention in the water behind his friend. "Tim, I think I just saw a fish; I didn't know that they could live in that water?"

Savolt turned his head and saw four small minnows dart upstream from shadow to shadow.

He then turned toward Reed and said, "yes, Salt Creek has some fish in it, though they are mostly small. If you go further downstream, I have seen some species of Chub that are six inches long."

Caught in surprise, Reed reached up with his hand and adjusted his hat, and questioned his friend, "I thought that the creek was dead?"

"I know what you mean. Everyone told me the creek was polluted too when I moved here. But, one day, I was walking along this same road and stopped at this very same spot. It was then that I saw some minnows too. I got to thinking about it, so I decided to begin a study on the creek."

The two men looked at each other in silence until a thought had passed through Reed's head.

He warned, "hey, even though you are on public land, I would keep an eye out for any MERP trucks. I say this because the company might take notice of you snooping around in the creek and doing your little experiments."

Reed took a quick look around them and surmised that no one else saw them talking. He then continued, "you didn't make many friends over that mouse deal in the Rattlesnake Mountains, especially with the oil field companies. I overheard some guys talking in the Corral Bar that they are worried about what your study will turn out, so just know that this study of yours has rubbed folks the wrong way."

"Thanks, Reed. I will keep my head on a swivel."

MERP was the acronym for Midwest-Edgerton Resources Production. This company owned the Bureau of Land Management (BLM) lease and managed all the production activity within the ten-mile-long and five-mile-wide field. The Salt Creek Oil Field production dates back to the late 1800s when drilling struck oil north of the present-day Midwest.

Tales and folklore abound that it was Native Americans who first discovered oil seeping out of the ground in multiple seeps in the valley. Rumor also has it that they sold oil to U.S. Calvary units making their way from Fort Laramie in the south toward Fort Fetterman to the north. Finally, some say Native Americans sold it to travelers on the Bozeman Trail to the east.

Other historians claim that it was early prospectors who first found the oil seeps. Then, after their discovery, the prospectors sold the oil as wagon wheel lubricant for travelers on Oregon, Mormon, and Californian immigrant trails near old Fort Caspar.

Regardless of who found oil first, the field had produced more petroleum than any other like it in surrounding states. The Salt Creek Field alone accounted for one-fifth of all the oil exported from Wyoming.

Reed then placed the pickup in gear, rumbled off down the road, and turned into the football field parking lot. Meanwhile, Tim resumed his meandering march downstream. Shortly afterward, he stopped again at the confluence where Castle Creek joined Salt Creek to take another water sample.

Tim then bent over like many other times that day, filled a little plastic jar, labeled it, and placed the sample into his backpack. He also wrote down some field notes in his tiny green pocket-sized notebook. After making the annotations, the notebook found its usual spot in the back pocket of his Wrangler jeans before trekking onward.

Once at the bridge, Tim walked up and over Gas Plant Road and then down the other side, making way to the following sample point. When he reached the bottomland again, a mule deer doe and her fawn spooked out of the sagebrush. Tim instinctively dropped to one knee to watch the spooked animals just like he would do if he were out hunting. The doe soon settled down as she was unsure where Tim disappeared and then looked over to her fawn. Unfazed as well, the fawn rejoined her mother as if nothing happened.

He then noticed that the deer suddenly fixated their attention on another noise coming from the road. He turned his head toward the deer's focus and saw a pickup truck with a MERP logo on the door, followed by a vacuum or "vac" truck with the same paint scheme. The two vehicles drove north on Gas Plant Road toward the one-lane bridge that spanned the creek that led to the western edge of town. The maroon and white paint on the trucks matched the school colors that showed visible solidarity with the community.

Just then, Tim remembered Reed's warning about being seen conducting his study on the creek. So he remained hidden in the sage until both MERP trucks disappeared up the hill on the edge of town. Looking at the deer once more, he told them, "just three more samples, and then it is back to the apartment for lunch."

Minutes later, Tim took sample eight where Salt Creek made an inexplicable sharp turn to the south and then a quick turn to the north toward Powder River country. After standing up again, he stretched his aching back after making many stoops that day. Then looking up, he observed a large hill advertising an enormous "M" painted white. As it was known, M-Hill notified any visitor, or any rival school for that matter, that they were in Oiler country. The hill also reminded the teacher that the upcoming Monday, all incoming Freshmen would repaint those bricks with the supervision of this year's Senior class as part of an annual tradition.

Thirty minutes later, Tim crossed over Highway 387, where the bridge traversed the creek, and he began working up the opposite bank on the west side of the stream. Later, he abruptly stopped near one of many uncharted small oil seeps in the oilfield, bent down, pulled up a few grass samples by the root, and then placed them into another labeled bag. The seeps fascinated him the most because, despite all the oil production over the last 90 years, oil still oozed up naturally out of the ground.

As he continued another half-mile north along the creek, Savolt stepped around Jackass Springs, which was perhaps the most famous of all the oil seeps in the entire oil field. But this was not the object of his search; instead, his next sample point awaited him another ten yards further downstream.

Tim then spotted his target and got down on all fours to creep up to the edge of a bathtub-sized pool of hot water. The source of the small hot spring came from a trickle out of the hill just above the creek. He once again took a water sample and a specimen. Then he made the last field note annotation for the day. Afterward, he stood up and retraced his steps back toward Midwest.

But, something just didn't seem right to him, as if having a premonition of something terrible about to happen. It became such a troubling thought that he could not shake it from his head for the next 150 to 200 yards. Then his premonition came to fruition.

Suddenly, Tim heard what he thought was a single loud woodpecker knock on a piece of tin with a distinctive "pa-ting" sound. The odd noise came almost instantaneously as the sharp bee sting sensation he now felt in his left shoulder. He stumbled backward and lost the grip on his notebook, which fell precipitously into the large sagebrush near his path. Looking at his arm, he spotted a dark stain on his sleeve and a few droplets of blood that dropped off his fingers. Momentarily stunned, Savolt heard another "pa-ting" sound and another bee sting, but this time on his left ear lobe.

With nary a thought, he ran and bounded over the small oil seep with a giant leap. It was then that Tim's years of Army training took over as if his mind flipped a switch. Instinctively, he made his way into the tall greasewood and crawled out of sight, just like a wounded deer or pronghorn antelope.

Within the shadows of the greasewood, Savolt assessed his wounds. With his fingers, he found a small injury that entered his shoulder and an exit wound on his back the size of a dime. He knew from experience that only a small-caliber, high-velocity bullet could make that type of wound. Additionally, he found that a second bullet took a half-moon chunk out of his earlobe instead of completely blowing it off.

While scrambling away once again, Tim began a rolling conversation in his head. *"What was that noise?"* It didn't sound like a rifle shot, not that it would be an unusual sound outside of town at any point during the year. Then it hit him; that *pa-ting* sound he heard was a bullet fired through a muzzle suppressor. As an Army range official stationed in Germany, he'd grown accustomed to that distinctive sound. Then he asked himself, "*why are they shooting at me?*"

"*Just breathe,*" he told himself, and soon his respirations normalized. Then Savolt began to listen around him. Seconds later, he thought he heard something, but wasn't sure, so he laid down prone and peered through the lower branches of sagebrush toward the east across the creek. Tim then caught a glint of sunlight reflecting off the windshield of a dark green pickup an estimated 800 yards away.

Tim's first thought was that whoever shot him must have driven it, but he still couldn't see a shooter. Listening carefully, he picked up the sound of footfalls snapping and breaking dry sagebrush branches on the opposite bank. Moments later, he heard the voices that accompanied the footsteps.

"I know I got him at least twice," the first man said.

The other man replied in a commanding voice, "we need to find him and finish this, or the boss will have us for lunch."

The first voice asked, "We'll find him, but I don't understand why we were assigned to this detail anyway. I mean, he is just a science teacher?"

"If this guy lives and publishes his study, it could blow the lid off this oilfield, and the bosses can't have that, can they? Let's get him before anybody sees us," the second voice demanded.

Trying hard to keep quiet and gain distance from the men by low crawling through the brush, Tim struggled to stave off shock from losing blood. Finally, sensing the seriousness of his predicament, he stopped behind a thicket of tall sagebrush and removed his backpack. Once open, Tim now remembered that his Colt M1911A1 .45 caliber pistol was left in his apartment, which was usually with him if a rattlesnake was in the path. Despite the disappointment, he continued to search his backpack for anything he could use as a weapon. Still, all he found was his collection of samples and a nearly empty canteen of water.

He told himself, *"just keep moving by using whatever cover possible."* Tim then continued to crawl when the cover was close to the ground and stoop walked when the taller vegetation was available as he retraced his path toward the highway.

Then he came to an abrupt stop. Ten feet ahead of him, the tall sagebrush gave way to a bare patch of ground that would leave him exposed. He had to decide whether to fight or flight, but his selection became clear without a weapon. But, his next question was which way to run?

Tim could easily see Highway 387 and the bridge directly in front of him, but there were 500 yards of open ground between the edge of the sage and the blacktop. Another option was to go uphill toward the oilfield road about 150 yards above him. Still, that would be slow going and left him an easy target for the shooters. In contrast, another option was to cross the creek and hide the reeds and bushes on the north side. But, the deep mud on the edges of the stream would slow him down, or even worse, the muddy bank would stop him in his tracks entirely. His only choice was to make a break directly away from the killers.

Suddenly it occurred to him that this is about his research study on the creek, but why? He shook his head from side to side because there was no time to reason with himself. Instead, Tim reached behind him with his right hand and removed his backpack, and went back into the tall sage to find a place to hide it. He then found a small abandoned section of a metal culvert discarded long ago by some project on the road above him and stuffed his backpack into it. He reasoned he could always come back for the pack, but he could also run faster without the added weight.

While he caught his breath before he made his dash across the open ground, the thumping of his heart drowned out almost everything else. Tim's break was only short-lived when he heard the footfalls and the sound of denim scraping against the sagebrush coming up from behind.

Within moments, he knew they would indeed find him by following the sloppy trail left behind along the bank.

Tim made up his mind that it was time to go, and with a sudden rush, he darted for the highway. He sprinted in a zig-zag pattern hoping to make himself a challenging target. But the last thing he heard before his world went suddenly black was an audible "pa-ting" sound.

* * *

2

Later that night, Josh Anderson sat in the Rialto movie theater in downtown Casper to watch *Red Dawn*, a newly released thriller. Josh was about to enter his senior year at Midwest High School. Aside from being an honor roll student and an athlete, he was also the son of one of the school's teachers. Josh also worked part-time between practices, and his summer job ended the day before since school will begin next week. Like all teenagers, he truly enjoyed being in the company of his friends.

The product of the two-a-day football practices that he endured over the last 14 days had left him feeling exhausted. Plus, his sore muscles made it even more challenging to find a comfortable position in his theater seat. Football was Josh's favorite sport, where he played tight end on offense and linebacker on defense. Typically, on any night like this, fellow senior Ricky Fleming would be next to Josh. However, Ricky was grounded in the house by his parents.

As the scenes changed on the screen, the light illuminated the faces seated to the left of Josh as fellow seniors Pete LaRoche and David Proctor; and juniors Carlos Mondragon and Steve Otten.

The movie *Red Dawn* was perfect for a group of Wyoming teenaged boys for two reasons. First, the plot implied that teenagers could thwart Communist invaders on their home turf. Secondly, the setting of the movie highlighted a small town at the foot of the Rocky Mountains. For these reasons, the boys easily connected with the story.

Dressed in typical Wyoming chic for the day, each boy wore a t-shirt that bore either a Midwest Athletics logo or a rock band concert from earlier that summer. The rest of their ensemble included Levi's button-fly 501s and a pair of the previous year's basketball shoes. Glaringly absent on the boys- because it was still summertime-was their distinguishable maroon and white letter jackets that they rarely left at home.

After the movie, the boys filed out of the theater and onto the sidewalk. They followed Josh to what the boys referred to as the "banana" car, a yellow, four-door, 1969 Plymouth Fury III.

Steve said it first, "man, that is an ugly car. It is almost embarrassing to ride in it!"

"Man, why don't you buy something newer with all that money you made working for the school district over the summer?" Pete asked without hiding his sarcasm.

Carlos jumped into the exchange and said, "come on, give Josh a break. At least he has a car that is big enough for all of us to ride in." Carlos then retorted back to Steve and Pete, "I want to know why neither one of you have a car with all that money you both made working as roustabouts over the summer?"

"I made the house payments, you jerk; you know my dad got hurt last spring and can't work yet," Steve sternly replied while Pete remained utterly silent on the issue.

"Cool it, guys, let's go get something to eat," barked David and thus ended the conversation abruptly.

David Proctor held the reputation as the toughest kid in town. Though not overly big by football standards, his 5' 10" frame carrying 185 pounds combined with his quickness and tenacity made him a formidable offensive lineman and middle linebacker on defense.

David had moved to Midwest as an infant of a bi-racial couple from Elizabethtown, New Jersey. His parents, Joe and Toni Proctor regaled their story that they faced incredible bigotry and intolerance when they had married. But, unfortunately, it was the so-called enlightened college students who attended nearby that gave them the most grief.

The boy's parents also informed him that race riots broke out all over New Jersey soon after he was born. They then decided that it would be better to find a fresh start in a place where race didn't seem to matter. So after reading an advertisement soliciting for oil field workers in Wyoming, David's father took a chance and moved his new family to Midwest.

Despite being the only African American in the area, Joe Proctor quickly earned respect from co-workers as a hard worker. Still, his background never became an issue. Hence, David grew up fully aware of his bi-racial status. However, he was lucky in one aspect: people saw him as another oilfield kid. Yet, he could not fully empathize with others like him, who faced racial disparagement in other parts of the nation.

The boys bounded into the yellow car, and Josh steered it out of the parking space and onto Second Street and headed toward the mall, where there were multiple options of fast food to choose.

"How about Hamburger Stand," Steve suggested?

"Come on, the last time we ate there, I had Montezuma's revenge for a week," pleaded Pete.

"Is that supposed to be some kind of Mexican joke, Pete?" demanded Carlos, who took offense.

Carlos Mondragon was the Oilers quarterback. He had dark hair and dark eyes and was smaller than his friends, but he possessed the top-flight speed that propelled him to third place in the State Track finals as a sophomore. He could throw the ball well, but the team's offensive strategy was to pound the football with the running game and passed the ball when it posed no significant risk.

The boy also represented the fifth generation of his family in the Salt Creek area. His ancestors came from Mexico to Wyoming before it was even a state. They settled upon 5,000 acres of ranchland eight miles northwest of Midwest. His family, however, was land rich and cash poor, like many ranchers and farmers throughout Wyoming. The

Mondragon Ranch now leased some of their property for cattle grazing to help pay annual taxes.

Carlos' father, Art, hired out his services as a welder, whom many in the valley considered the best in his trade. His income helped keep the ranch solvent at a time when more ranchers sold their holdings and moved into the nearest city. Nonetheless, Carlos remained proud of his Spanish heritage and had little to no tolerance for disparaging remarks.

"No, it is just an expression. Lighten up, Carlos, you are just *OFT* just like all the rest of us, including the teacher's kid Josh" chimed David.

Bewildered, Carlos asked, "what is *OFT*?'

David explained, "OFT stands for oil-field-trash. All our parents work in the oilfield in some way or another, including the teachers. Some have deep roots in the oilfield, just like Pete, whose great-grandfather lived and worked in French Camp outside of town."

After a breath, Proctor continued, "the Salt Creek oilfield is the reason for Casper's very existence, but do you think anyone in Natrona County would acknowledge that fact? All of you know how people here in Casper look at us when we are in town when they see our letter jackets with 'Midwest Oilers' written on our backs? *OFT* is what they think. But, at least they are consistent since they treat all of us the same regardless of what we look like- it is almost as if we bring the smell of the town with us."

David had a point. During the previous school year, David, Josh, and the rest of the yearbook staff went into Casper to sell yearbook ads. They heard townspeople say things like: "I didn't know there are three high schools in Natrona County," or "Midwest still exists," and even more egregiously, one shopkeeper suggested that "all of the Midwest students should be bused into Casper every day and forget about maintaining the school."

Josh nodded in agreement with David's assessment. Then he replied, "*OFT*, I like it! Maybe we should make that our motto when we are warming up before football games, you know, shouting out *M-I-D-W-E-S-T-O-F-T* while doing jumping jacks or something like that."

"I like it too, but we can add another *F* into it as in Oil Field F*&^%$# Trash," Pete suggested. Then he leaned forward and immediately apologized to Josh. "I am sorry for using that word around you, buddy. I know your family never curses around your house."

Josh acknowledged Pete's apology with a head nod.

Then Steve inquired from the backseat, "how come it is that you don't cuss Josh? I mean, I get the whole religion thing, but you hear this stuff from us almost every day, and I want to know why you don't do so yourself?"

Josh slowed his car to a stop at a stoplight and then thought about what Steve said for a long moment. Finally, he revealed as the light turned green, "I read one particular scripture when I was 12 years old, and it gave me a little more wisdom on the subject."

"Okay, Mr. preacher man, feed us sheep then," David chided.

Josh cleared his throat and said, "Ephesians teaches us to refrain from using foul or abusive language. Let everything you say be good and helpful so that your words will be an encouragement to those who hear them."

The boy's words brought an instant silence inside the car as his friends contemplated the message. Josh then continued, "I am not trying to be holier than thou, but I just don't see the point in using curse words to replace plain language."

As he continued down Second Street in silence, Josh finally asked, "How about Burger King for a bacon double cheeseburger?"

His suggestion initially generated a carload of moans that somehow metamorphosed into a unanimous agreement. The truth was that the boys would always intimate that they wanted to eat somewhere different. Still, they nearly always ended up at Burger King. But if Ricky were with them, he would have suggested Little Big Man Pizza on CY Avenue on the west end of the city, which was their second favorite place.

After turning off of Second Street, Josh parked outside of Burger King, and everyone exited out of the car. The boys soon made their way inside and stood behind four other teenagers waiting at the counter. The youth standing nearest to Josh and his friends wore a Kelly Walsh High School Football t-shirt, who turned his body around to see who just came in behind him.

The teen with the Kelly Walsh t-shirt asked with a look on his face that spoke trouble, "where are you guys from?"

David whispered to his friends, "watch this," and then he turned to the Casper boy and said, "we are from Midwest, and yes, we already know, we are oilfield trash."

David stood defiantly in front of the boy in a match against wills. David's physical build made him look a lot larger than he was, which did not go unnoticed by the Casper youth, who sized him up quickly and wanted nothing to do with David.

What came next was the Casper boy's bemused reaction that would become legendary for years to come. Oddly, the boy just stood there with his mouth agape and not knowing what to say back. Deflated, the dumfounded boy simply turned around to the counter, grabbed his take-out bag, and headed out the door to his awaiting friends.

"Dude, that was awesome. *OFT!*" exclaimed Josh.

Fifty minutes later, the boys made their way home with their bellies filled while driving north of Casper on Interstate 25. So, naturally, they began a rolling replay of the movie *Red Dawn*. But then the discussion delved into an even more in-depth back-and-forth about what they would do if the Russians ever invaded Wyoming as portrayed in the fictional town of Calumet, Colorado.

"You know that Midwest and Edgerton would be prime targets for Russian paratrooper drops because of the Salt Creek Oilfield. Plus, the Naval Petroleum Reserve south of town would be a target too," offered Pete from the backseat.

Steve shook his head in disagreement. "I think you are mixing that up with the news report that the Navy field is a target for Russian nuclear missiles."

Josh looked back at Steve and Pete through the rear-view mirror and said, "maybe both are true, but if anything like that happens, where would we go? At least the Eckert brothers had the mountains close by."

Carlos squeezed himself forward from between Pete and Steve in the back seat and suggested, "we could go to the Bighorns. I know an area west of Kaycee that my family has hunted on for years, and there are plenty of elk and deer up there to feed us."

David listened intently to Carlos while he chewed on the end of the drinking straw. He then removed it from his mouth and asked Carlos, "what about Hole-in-the-Wall west of Kaycee? I mean, that was a good enough hideout for Butch Cassidy, and it may be good enough for us too?"

"But if we go through Kaycee, we could always pick up some girls to take along with us. I mean, there are so many of them there," Pete shouted from the backseat.

Pete's observation was accurate since Kaycee High School possessed a 3 to 1 ratio of girls to boys compared to the 1 to 4 in Midwest. Since the two towns were less than 30 miles apart, Midwest and Kaycee proms were typically held on separate weekends in the spring because several teens were dating someone from the other school.

"Speaking of Kaycee, you guys know that I went to their prom with Annie Crawford last year. But, did I tell you that Chris Ledoux played during the dance" inquired Josh?

Chris Ledoux was a Wyoming Country Music icon and former World Champion bronc rider who made his home outside Kaycee. Many of his songs spoke to the heart of what it meant to live under the vast Wyoming skies. Chris produced many albums in the 1970s and 1980s that were marketed at rodeos throughout the Rocky Mountain region and then he later toured with Garth Brooks in the 1990s. His life prematurely and tragically ended twenty years later when he succumbed to cancer.

David rolled his eyes and said, "yes, you have told us all about the prom probably a thousand times."

Pete sensed an opening to interject and leaned forward toward Josh's right ear. He asked, "what I want to know is what happened between you and Annie after the dance," which brought forth a round of laughter throughout the car.

Momentarily embarrassed, Josh adjusted in his seat and then explained, "you guys know she is a preacher's daughter. Do you think I would do anything that her dad would disapprove? And, if anything did happen, do you think I would tell you about it?"

"I tell you about every girl, don't I," Pete said with a chuckle.

Josh nodded and met Pete's eyes in the rear-view mirror. "Yup, and it is too much information. I also know full well that you would evoke the two-week rule on me if Annie and I were actually going out and then broke up. This would be especially true if we actually did anything."

"What is the two-week rule?" Carlos asked inquisitively.

Josh explained further that the two-week rule is where Pete waited precisely 14 days after a break-up to ask the ex-girlfriend out. But, if he knew she was sexually active, then there is no waiting time for him. As a result, Josh nor the other boys ever told Pete anything about their dates or girlfriends."

David grinned and shook his head slightly. Then he quipped, "Annie's dad is not who I would worry about- it is your dad! Last year he caught me looking at my notes during a math test and pulled me into the hallway to discuss what I had done. All I have to say is that when he is upset, he puts the fear of God in you!"

Laughter again broke out, and within a few moments, a quiet hush enveloped the car.

Josh then exited Interstate 25 and onto Highway 259, a cut-off to Midwest and Edgerton that reduced the drive time by five minutes instead of taking the second exit to Midwest a few miles north.

The silence broke when Pete requested that Josh would turn on the radio. Josh obliged by turning the knob until the radio signal from 95 FM KTRS came in crystal clear out of the car's speakers.

Suddenly, Steve pushed forward from his seat and pointed at the radio, "this is the new song I was telling you guys about that I saw on Night Tracks last night."

Night Tracks was a music video show that aired every Friday and Saturday night on WTBS out of Atlanta. Though every household in the Salt Creek area had cable television, MTV was not a part of the cable package of 12 stations. Instead, the area teenagers kept abreast of all the latest videos through shows like Night Tracks.

Josh complied with Steve's request and turned up the volume on the radio. Then Twisted Sister's *"We're Not Gonna Take It"* thumped loudly out of the speakers and through the frame, the tires, and into the pavement.

Soon, the boys spied the signage for the United States Naval Petroleum Reserve #3, which was notoriously known as Tea Pot Dome oilfield. That oilfield established its infamy by being tied to the significant scandal and downfall of President Warren G. Harding.

Then at the top of *40-mile Hill*, the lights of Midwest danced in the distance. The oil field was easy to see at night due to the half dozen gas flares burning that resembled orange-yellow balls from that range.

David turned to look at the guys in the backseat and asked, "so what is everyone doing tomorrow afternoon? Want to come over to my house and hang out?"

"I can't. I have to move hay tomorrow," Carlos replied regretfully.

Pete shrugged his shoulders and said, "sure, I'll be over," while Steve added, "me too."

Turning toward Josh, David asked, "what about you?"

Sheepishly, Josh looked over at his friend and said, "I have to go to church in the morning. Then tomorrow afternoon, I am expected to be with my family at the faculty picnic for the new school year. I'm sorry, I can't."

"Better you than me, Josh. I don't want to even think about school or teachers for a few more days other than playing football," Steve replied.

The car passed over Salt Creek, which demarked the outskirts of the town of Midwest. At the intersection ahead, Highway 259 ended and became Highway 387 toward the northwest to connect with I-25. To the east, Highway 387 joined the Salt Creek Community with the town of Wright 45 miles away.

Josh turned right at the intersection toward Midwest's sibling town of Edgerton, one mile east of the junction. As he the town, Josh turned off the highway onto Howard Street, where he stopped at Pete's house to drop him off. Steve also got out of the car too since he lived just around the corner on Main Street.

But suddenly, Pete stopped on the sidewalk and walked back to Josh's window. Then he said, "maybe you can get lucky with Miss Connelly tomorrow," with a wink of his eye. "You know how she flirts with all the boys!"

Quick with a comeback, Josh asked Pete, "is there any female too young or too old that you wouldn't try something with?"

Just as quick, Pete replied, "too young, yes, but a woman is never too old for me," and on cue, he spun on his heels and turned up the sidewalk toward his house.

Carlos shook his head. "That guy has too many hormones exploding inside him."

David agreed. "And that is why we are his buddies, you know, to keep him out of trouble."

After heading back to Midwest, Josh came to a complete stop at the stop sign at the junction. The year before, the boy early lost his driving privileges when he received a ticket for failing to stop at the junction. In that particular instance, Josh heeded to the goading of his friends, who proclaimed, "no cop, no stop." However, tucked in the shadows of the relic oil derrick sat the town deputy, who quickly pulled the boy over and ticketed him.

Josh soon crossed the intersection and cattle guard and into Midwest. He looked over at the teacher's apartment complex to the right of Lewis Street and felt a pang of guilt for not helping Mr. Savolt collect samples that morning. It wasn't that he overslept: he was just too sore from the two-a-day practices to get his body moving that morning.

Next, the yellow Plymouth turned left onto Ellison Street and then right onto Stock, where David lived a few houses down from the Post Office on the south side of the street. After stopping, David hopped out of the car with only a simple "see ya," to his friend. Carlos then moved to the front seat for the short ride to Josh's house where he left his mother's car earlier that afternoon. Afterward, Josh turned back onto Ellison to the north, and, at last street, turned west onto Navy Row. Then at #6, he pulled into the gravel driveway on the side of the house. Just like David, Carlos got out of the car and said, "see ya" over his shoulder and instantly left in his mom's car for the drive out the ranch.

* * *

3

Sunday, August 25, 1984

#6 Navy Row, Midwest, Wyoming

The morning sun pierced the curtains on the window of Josh's room, but it was not the light that woke him up; it was the sound of his dad stirring his coffee. For as long as the boy could remember, his father followed the same distinctive pattern to stir his coffee, which made a unique clicking sound of the spoon as it hit the inside of the cup. The chorus of clinks always rose to a crescendo when the elder Anderson struck the utensil on the edge of the cup with three hard raps to remove the excess droplets of coffee. For Josh, the coffee ritual also served as an alarm clock of sorts.

While he rolled out of bed, Josh was reminded of his aching hamstring tendons in both legs from the overuse over the last two weeks. Still, he was healing and would be 100% for the season-opening game the following Friday.

Josh reached down alongside the bed and grabbed a pair of grey sweatpants, and pulled them over each of his aching legs. As he stood up, he briefly looked out his bedroom window that overlooked the front porch. The boy then reached into his closet and grabbed a clean t-shirt from the top shelf, and pulled it over his head. Josh noticed that his shirt sleeves were a little tighter on his biceps, attributed to hitting the weight room every day after work over the summer. That morning, Josh stood 6' tall and weighed 175 pounds with dark brown wavy hair and blue eyes. It was readily apparent to everyone that he was beginning to resemble his father in looks and build.

Before Josh left his room, he looked into his mirror and noticed two prominent cowlicks of hair that stood out like horns on top of his head.

He tried to flatten them out with his hand to no avail and decided he would need to wet his hair down in the bathroom.

Josh was the oldest of two children to Rob and Sara Anderson, with his sister Cindy being two years younger than him. Rob and Sara Anderson moved to Midwest in 1974. Before that, they lived in Holyoke, Colorado, which was Rob's first teaching job following his and Sara's graduation from the University of Northern Colorado in Greeley. Rob Anderson grew up in Akron, Colorado, where his father owned and operated a small lumberyard. Sara was also a Colorado native and grew up on a small farm in Logan County along the banks of the South Platte River.

In Midwest, Rob taught junior high math and pre-algebra. He also coached the high school girls' volleyball and basketball teams with his daughter, Cindy, as the budding star following her freshman breakout in both sports. Sara Anderson also worked at the school as an administrative assistant in the elementary school office.

Josh stumbled to the kitchen and spooned himself a bowl of Cream of Wheat left for him on the back burner of the stove, and then he poured himself a glass of milk for breakfast. He walked over to the dining room table and set down his bowl. After taking a seat, he turned his head to watch the Sunday morning news on KTWO Channel 2 out of Casper, which was already playing on the television.

The breaking story reported a massive flash flood in the western Wyoming town of Stinson following a thunderstorm that dropped a record seven inches of rain in just over two hours. The scene depicted an overly dramatic reporter who explained that six people died, and thirteen people were still missing from the freak flash flood. The camera then panned over the scene to show the devastation. Cars were cars stacked atop one another as if a child had played with them and left them in the middle of the living room floor. Josh's face turned to shock at the news, and he contemplated what it would look like in this town if it had rained like that here.

Rob looked up from his Sunday edition of the *Casper Star-Tribune* and said to his son, "Wyoming is a wonder, isn't it? We haven't had any rain for three weeks, and Stinson receives half of its annual rainfall in one fail swoop. Imagine if that happened here two years ago before the streets were paved Midwest and Edgerton?"

It was true. Before pavement the massive paving project in the Salt Creek community, residents used to refer Midwest as "Mudwest" as the dirt streets turned into a sloppy soup of mud with any form of precipitation. Houses in the area had mudrooms for practicality rather than adding charm and character to homes that future generations desired.

"People died, dad," Josh remarked back without hiding an ounce of his disdain.

"I know, son, but out here, you have to prepare for the unexpected. It is hard to imagine a storm like that one happening, but that was the lesson learned in Cheyenne after the tornado destroyed the city's north side back in July 1979. My point is this: the land we live in will consume anyone that is not prepared."

"Yes, dad, I get it, and that's why you make me carry a shovel and snow chains in my car even in summertime," Josh quipped surly.

The boy went back to his breakfast, and when he finished, he rose from the table, walked his bowl over to the kitchen, and placed it into the sink. As he passed his father, who was still seated at the table, Josh offered, "maybe we can take up a collection at church and maybe start a relief drive in the rest of town?"

Rob looked up from his newspaper and gave his son a wink and a nod indicating his approval.

Suddenly, at a volume of just under a shout, Sara instructed from the master bedroom, "the two of you need to get cleaned up and get ready to go soon since it is our turn to set up the church. Oh, and Josh, you need to call Mr. Savolt and apologize for not meeting with him yesterday."

Rob and his son turned their heads and said in unison, "yes, ma'am."

Thirty minutes later, the Andersons walked up Navy Row to the Community Church at the end of the street. Regular attendance was sparse by standards of larger churches in Casper. Still, the 70 parishioners represented nearly 10% of the population in the Salt Creek area. However, on Easter and Christmas, two packed services were the norm.

Rob and Josh quickly set up the rows of chairs, which took all of five minutes, while Sara settled in at the piano bench and began warming up for the service's planned hymns. However, Rob's attention to his wife's playing was interrupted when he heard the tires of Pastor Roberts Jeep Wagoneer pull into the church's gravel parking lot. The elder Anderson then turned his body to meet the Minister.

Pastor Roberts actually lived in Buffalo but traveled to the small Wyoming towns of Midwest, Sussex, and Story every Sunday in staggered meeting times to shepherd to his three flocks.

Soon after the arrival of the pastor, other parishioners began to show up and filed inside to take their usual seats awaiting them. Josh found a seat next to his friend and teammate, Scott Merino, a senior. Scott played offensive and defensive tackle and was a two-time state wrestling champion.

The boy was also the middle child of nine siblings, and his parents were stalwarts in the community. For example, the Merino's hosted a weekly youth group bible study in their home. Additionally, the clan always pitched in to help with just about any community project. For example, in 1976, with supplies provided by MERP, the family voluntarily painted the pump jack at the entrance to town in red, white, and blue colors to commemorate the nation's bicentennial. None of the Merino children, however, got into trouble, and teachers at the school often left a Merino child in charge of the classroom if they had to step out for a moment.

During the service announcements, Josh stood and delivered a plea for a unique collection as a relief fund for the citizens of Stinson. The church then collected $150 on the spot. Walter Merino, Scott's father, stepped forward to take the funds to the bank in Edgerton in the morning. Then he planned to draw a cashier's check and forward it to a sister church in Stinson.

Pastor Roberts then came forward and delivered an eloquent sermon on having an attitude of Christ, as seen in Philippians Chapter 2. What got Josh's attention, and Scott's, too, was the Apostle Paul's example that a successful athlete puts on a winning attitude. The Pastor further implored that an athlete possessing the right attitude will sharpen the focus of his eyes to see clearly in any adversity. Plus, from the depths of his heart will come forth inexhaustible endurance. In summation, Pastor Roberts asked a lasting question to the congregation, "what is your attitude in Christ?"

* * *

4

Three hours after returning home from church, Josh and his father loaded up the car with potato salad, fresh home-grown zucchini bread, and a Coleman cooler full of pop. In Wyoming, very few people said "soda" or "soda pop." Instead, Wyomingites call it just "pop" or a "Coke." In some cafés and restaurants in the state, when someone ordered a Coke, the waitress will ask, "what kind?"

Soon afterward, the Andersons headed to the house of another teacher, Bill Crooks, who taught civics. Bill and his wife Lois had recently purchased a home on Ash Street in nearby Gas Plant. The couple then volunteered to host the annual back-to-school barbeque for the faculty, school employees, and their families as a housewarming gesture.

Years ago, the township began as a Midwest Oil Company community adjacent to the nearby gas plant. Then, a few years ago, Gas Plant was finally incorporated into a part of Midwest.

At the stop sign, Rob Anderson turned the car south on Fitzhugh Road, which became Gas Plant Road as the street descended toward the one-way bridge spanning Salt Creek. Then, at the entrance to the span, they waited for a MERP truck to traverse the bridge. When the vehicle cleared, Rob then took his turn. However, they had to stop once more at the exit of the crossing to allow a herd of thirty Pronghorn Antelope to cross the road.

While most students would do anything to get out of attending a faculty picnic, Josh didn't have that luxury. After all, he was a teacher's kid and knew gatherings like this one came with the territory.

Upon arrival at the Crooks house, Josh hauled the cooler to the back yard and immediately spotted Ricky Fleming, who lived just down the street from him at #10 Navy Row. Ricky had the build that everyone could identify as an athlete. While only 5'8" tall, he weighed as much as Josh and was even faster than Carlos and was the reigning State Track Champion in both the 100- and 200-meter events.

Ricky also sported a new haircut with close-cropped hair on the top and sides in a conservative length, but the hair in the back was long enough to touch the top of his shoulders.

Shocked with the fresh style, Josh asked, "So what's up with the doo?"

Ricky quickly turned his head to a profile and back toward Josh, "like it? Sheila cut it for me on Friday night...it is the new thing, you know."

Josh nodded. "So that is why you haven't cut your hair since, what, last Christmas, so you could grow out the back?"

Ricky smiled widely. "That was my plan all along. You see, I saw a couple of guys on music videos wearing these, so I thought I would give it a try."

"What does your dad think about it?"

"He can't stand it and keeps telling me that I will be lucky if someone doesn't tackle me by my hair."

Ricky's dad, Alan, was the Principle in the Elementary School and was also the head high school football coach. He was a big man even amongst other large men, and he gave an imposing presence.

Alan Fleming grew up in Lyman, Wyoming. He later graduated from the University of Idaho, where he became a standout center for the football team. Following graduation, the Dallas Texans of the up-start American Football League drafted him to play professionally. Unfortunately, Alan only played for two years when a severe knee injury forced him to retire from his career. It was then that he decided to go to graduate school at the University of Wyoming, where he obtained advanced degrees in Education. But, while attending school in Laramie, Alan met Ricky's mother, who worked at the Albany County Public Library at the time. After graduation, Fleming's first job in education landed them in the Wyoming town of Greybull before he moved the family to Midwest in 1973.

A year after that, Josh moved onto Navy Row, and he and Ricky have been best friends ever since. Tonight's mandatory family gathering for both boys remained barely tolerable to them only because misery loves company. The boys also shared mutual friends. On any given day, the foursome of Josh, Ricky, David Proctor, and Pete Laroche were always together.

While the minutes seemed like hours to the boys, soon, other teachers and their families began showing up to the picnic. To the boys' surprise, even the handful of teachers who lived in Casper had also made the forty-five-minute drive north.

Once the food line opened up, Josh and Ricky quickly grabbed their plates and found a quiet spot to eat atop the backyard fence made of old drilling pipe. In between bites of food, Josh confided in Ricky that he dreaded meeting up with Coach Savolt that night for failing to show up the day before.

Ricky shook his head in disagreement. "Dude, relax, I'm sure Coach Savolt will understand. Besides, he knows you were sore from two-a-day practices like everyone else."

"I know. I don't like feeling that I let Coach down," explained Josh.

"Josh, you always worry about other people's feelings, which is good, I think, but sometimes you worry for nothing."

"Yep, I have heard that before."

Later, while leaning on the back fence near the gate, Josh and Ricky shared an entire bag of potato chips that Ricky snuck off of the table. Aside from eating, the boys compared observations about the people who made up the faculty and staff. The boys noted who amongst the faculty smoked, cursed, or consumed too much alcohol. Most shocking to the boys was when the new art teacher and her husband parked their small car behind them. Josh and Ricky turned in unison to watch the couple exit their vehicle and walk through the gate. After the couple passed by, Josh asked Ricky, "what is that smell?" Ricky grinned but did not immediately answer Josh.

But, Tim Savolt's nonappearance became glaringly apparent to all of those attending the picnic. Not only did Josh and Ricky notice, but the boys also overheard many of the faculty members question why he wasn't there. They even overheard Ms. Connelly talking with the First-Grade teacher Mrs. Paul.

While Karen Connelly nervously peeled the label off of a Coors Light bottle she held, she told Lisa Paul that she believed that Tim Savolt shacked up with some "bimbo" in Casper. Mrs. Paul then tried to console Ms. Connelly. However, Karen insisted on knowing why Tim Savolt would dare to look elsewhere when his soulmate (speaking of herself) lived just across the hallway from him. Yet, to the boys, at least, Karen's display looked faked and impetuous.

Yet, all around them, the boys saw, heard, and even smelled things that most students never got a chance to observe about their teachers. Growing up as they did, Josh and Ricky saw other faculty members as regular human beings replete with likable and flawed characteristics alike.

Not long afterward, Rob Anderson walked over to the boys, who still sat on the back fence. As if out of empathy, he told the boys it was okay for them to go home. However, Josh would have to take his sister Cindy along with them. Ricky and Josh gave the senior Anderson a quick nod and waved Cindy to follow them to Ricky's car.

Ricky owned an old Volkswagen Beetle that was so ancient that it received the nickname: grub. Their friend Pete reasoned that Ricky's car had not grown up to become a modern-day beetle. Notwithstanding, the boys soon left Gas Plant behind with Cindy in tow for their short trip back to Navy Row.

But as soon as they turned onto Gas Plant Road, Ricky exclaimed, "Wow, did you get a load of the new art teacher smelling like she just rolled out of Spicoli's van?" Ricky's utterance referred to the movie *Fast Times at Ridgemont High*, a film that both boys had watched at least a dozen times together.

Josh's face suddenly changed from a broad questioning expression back down to his natural shape once he connected that the odor he smelled with marijuana.

Then he said to Ricky, "I know, man, that is crazy. Isn't it weird that we get to see teachers as 'real' people and not how David, Pete, Steve, or Carlos ever gets to see them?"

Ricky nodded. "So, how was the movie last night?"

"It was awesome. I wish your dad hadn't grounded you." But then Josh suggested, "maybe next Saturday you and I can go to town, and I can watch it again with you?"

"We'll see. My dad is still pretty torqued off about me sneaking out of the house Friday night to go over to Sheila's. It wouldn't have been a big deal if I hadn't got caught in her room by her mom." Ricky then allowed Josh's reactionary laughter to subside, and then he continued. "I just don't know what the big deal was, I mean, we were both dressed, and we were just sitting on Sheila's bed talking when her mom walked in. My dad grounded me for a week, but I still have the car to get around in at least."

"Thankfully, you both had your clothes on, unlike most times you sneak over there."

"Whose side are you on, mine or theirs?"

Josh assured, "well, I'm on your side naturally. But I think you might have to put yourself in your parent's shoes for a minute and think about what your reaction would have been if you walked into your own daughter's room and found a boy sitting the bed?"

"Dude, can you sound more like my dad or what?"

"He is the marrying kind," Cindy chimed in from the back seat, and the boys looked back at her as they had almost forgotten she was there.

"What are you talking about?" Josh questioned his sister.

"You have a rep, you know. I overheard a couple of senior girls in the locker room last year saying they thought you were cute. But, they thought you were not someone to date because you are the marrying kind of guy and not the kind of guy to date and have fun."

Ricky laughed and instantly stored the information for later when he would talk to his girlfriend, Sheila. He knew his girlfriend would gladly verify if there were any truth to Josh's reputation.

Ricky and Sheila had dated each other exclusively since their Freshman year. Now, as Seniors, they represented one of the power couples amongst others in the school. Though Ricky made time with his friends, everyone else observed that neither Ricky nor Sheila were independent. The rumor was that they scheduled everything to include time for hanging out with just their friends or with other couples. But lately, it seemed all that they did was fight.

After Ricky's car chugged up the hill from Salt Creek and had entered into town, Josh pointed ahead of them and requested, "Ricky, turn right onto Lewis Street."

"Why, what's going on?"

"Please, Rick, just do as I say."

Ricky turned onto Lewis Street as asked. Then the trio rode in silence until the teacher's apartment complex came into view, to which Josh asked Ricky to pull over and park in front of the building.

Ricky asked, "what are you doing?"

Josh answered, "I am going to go knock on Coach Savolt's door and apologize for not meeting with him as we had agreed."

Ricky met Josh's eyes and wondered aloud, "I don't get you, Josh. I mean, you could have called him, or you could just wait until tomorrow at football practice. Why does it have to be now?"

"I did try to call him, but he didn't answer his phone. So I was going to talk to him tonight, but he didn't show up at the picnic either. Please, Rick, give me a few minutes so that I can apologize to Coach right here and right now."

Ricky nodded and Josh quickly exited the car and walked up the front sidewalk. Then he stepped inside the landing, and climbed the flight of stairs to Savolt's apartment. Next, Josh knocked on the door and received no response, so he knocked again, but still no answer. The boy then turned and trotted down the steps, and instead of going directly back to Ricky's car, he turned left and went around to the back of the building. As he rounded the corner, Josh saw Savolt's pickup parked where it always remained. Confused, Josh asked himself, "where is he?"

Soon afterward, Ricky became impatient and honked the horn on his car that emitted a weak "beep, beep" sound. When he heard the horn, Josh emerged around the side of the building and soon re-entered the vehicle.

"Was he there?" Cindy asked from the backseat.

"No, sis, he wasn't. I don't know where he is?"

Ricky turned in his seat and asked, "can we go home now?" and with an affirming head nod from Josh, Ricky pulled away from the curb and made his way back to his house on Navy Row.

Upon arrival at Ricky's house, Cindy climbed out of the backseat in a rush and then ran down to the Anderson house. Meanwhile, both Josh and Ricky remained idling next to the car.

Josh broke the silence when he said, "this is our final year together. Next year, we will both be in college, and all of this will start to become a blurred memory."

Facing his friend, Ricky bent down and picked up a rock, which he threw across the street and into the vacant lot on the south side of Navy Row. He then looked back at Josh and said, "I don't even want to think about next year since we still have our senior year ahead of us."

Josh chuckled.

Ricky asked, "what is so funny?'

"Oh nothing, it is just that for the last three years, we just couldn't wait until the next year of school. Remember last year after we lost to Cokeville in the State Football Championship? All we kept saying is wait until next year. Well, next year is now, and what do we have to look forward to, college?"

Ricky shrugged. Though different than himself, he always quietly appreciated Josh's innate ability to think deeper on any subject. Ricky also admired his friend's drive to delve into things that just didn't immediately make sense to him on the surface. For example, during Trigonometry class the year before, Josh kept asking the teacher to give examples of where and why he would use certain theorems and formulas for a given situation. The teacher, however, could only insist that one just knew instinctively when to use a particular equation for a specific problem. Surface-level learning was never good enough for Josh, and Ricky wished at times that he could be more like his buddy and dig deeper rather than just going along with the flow.

After a short pause, Rick remarked, "first, stop thinking so much, and secondly, we will take State this year....I just know it."

Josh nodded and then realized, "I almost forgot, David calls all of us 'O-F-T,' which stands for oil field trash. At Burger King last night, he got one of those looks from a kid wearing a Kelly Walsh t-shirt. You know how those Casper kids look at us? Anyway, when the kid asked where we were from, David said that we were from Midwest, and yes, we know that we are oil field trash."

"What did the kid say?"

"Nothing, he just stood there looking stupid, and then he left."

"David came up with that?"

"I think we can use *OFT* as a chant or something when we are warming up before games or something, maybe to give us a little psychological advantage somehow."

"I like it." Ricky then begrudgingly announced, "well, I had better go inside and give Sheila a call before she starts to think that something is wrong. My dad grounded me from the phone as well, so if I want to talk to her, I had best do it before he gets home."

"Do you want to ride with me tomorrow since I doubt your car can make it up M-Hill?"

"Okay."

"I will see you at 9 a.m., just walk down and knock on my window," Josh replied and then turned for his short walk home.

An hour later, Josh's parents arrived home, and he jumped off the couch and helped his father retrieve things from the car. He then dumped the left-over ice and water from the cooler in the backyard and took the container to the garage. Afterward, Rob Anderson re-joined his son on the couch to watch whatever show Josh had on the television.

The boy then looked up at his father and asked, "dad, don't you think it was weird that Mr. Savolt wasn't there tonight?"

Sara interjected as she passed by her husband to take a seat next to him, "Josh, did you call Tim Savolt as I asked?"

"I did, mom, right after we got home from church. We also stopped by his apartment on the way home tonight too?"

"He wasn't there?" Rob asked his son.

"Nope, and the weird thing was his truck was parked out back too."

Rob nodded and saw the worried look on his son's face. Then, finally, he assured his son, "well, if he isn't at work tomorrow morning, then we will know that something is up. But, how about we do not worry about it until then, okay?"

Josh nodded that he understood. He leaned forward to stand up, but his father motioned for him to remain seated on the couch.

"Josh, as a teacher's kid, you are exposed to a lot of inside information like seeing a graded test of one of your friends sitting out on the table at night. Tonight is no different. I know that you saw some of the faculty members doing things outside of your experience with them. All I am asking is that you keep your observations to yourself and not your friends."

"Come on, dad, you know that I follow the rules and won't say anything."

While he entered his room, Josh recalled the memory from last year when he learned at the kitchen table that his friend Steve had failed the mid-term final in his dad's algebra class. The low grade resulted in Steve becoming ineligible to play basketball for the rest of the season. Unfortunately, Josh kept all of that information from his friend until his father had the opportunity to tell Steve himself.

It was also common for Josh to overhear discussions between his parents concerning a particular teacher, and sometimes, the talk was not very flattering. It was hard at times for him to reserve and withhold such things from his friends. Still, Josh knew that he would never betray his father, nor would he put himself in any situation that would bring his father to discredit or dishonor.

When Josh reached out to close his bedroom door, his mother called out, "goodnight, son."

Josh turned and offered "goodnight" in return and closed his door.

* * *

5

Monday, August 27, 1984

In the morning, Josh awoke suddenly alarmed by the sound of loud raps on his window, and he realized that he had overslept. Josh jumped out of his bed wearing nothing but the track shorts he conveniently forgot to turn in last spring and went to the front door to let his friend into the house. Ricky was not annoyed but rather amused that his normally responsible friend had shown a little chink in his armor by oversleeping. Saying only "morning," Ricky plopped onto the couch and turned on the television as if this were his own house.

Meanwhile, Josh returned to his room, dug out a pair of Wrangler jeans, and put them on. Usually, he and his friends wore Levi's, but they didn't hold up at work or in the countryside. He then grabbed his cowboy boots, an old t-shirt, a pair of socks, and his faded orange University of Texas baseball cap. Finally, he re-joined Ricky in the living room to finish dressing.

As he tugged on his second boot, Josh asked Ricky, "I am going to grab a glass of orange juice for a quick breakfast. Do you want anything?"

"No, I'm fine. I just ate a bowl of cereal before I came over."

Josh stood and then walked into the kitchen, but when he reached for the refrigerator handle, he saw a note from his father. It read:

I know you are going up M-Hill today, and I want you to use common sense and make sure that nobody gets hurt. Also, make sure you go out to the garage and fill up the water jug to take with you, as I don't want you getting dehydrated before football practice this afternoon.

Dad

The note reminded him of an infamous incident a few years ago. Back then, some seniors thought it would be funny to toss all of the bricks down to the bottom of M-Hill, and then have the freshmen haul the blocks back to the top. Unfortunately, one freshman girl got hit in the head by one of those tumbling bricks. Back then, the event was school-sponsored and took place on the first day of school. Regretfully, the injured girl spent two weeks in the hospital for a fractured skull, and her parents lobbied the School Board to end what they felt was a systemic hazing of students.

As a result, students from the following years organized an unsanctioned event to happen the day before the school year began. Members of both the senior and freshmen classes now received notices and invitations by word of mouth with a strict warning that anyone doing anything other than painting the bricks would not be acceptable. Subsequently, no injuries or anything that constituted hazing had occurred since.

Josh yelled out to Ricky, "Give me another minute; my dad left a note telling me to go out to the garage and get the water jug for us to take with us."

His friend laughed. "Ah yes, the dutiful son. Why can't you be the prodigal son occasionally?"

"Very funny. I will be right back."

After exiting the house via the back door, Josh soon opened the side door of their garage and walked over to where they stored their camping gear. The water jug was not hard to find since he had to look for a Coleman label. Then, it occurred to him that his family could start their own Coleman outlet store. His family owned the company's 8-person tent, cooler, white gas stove, two lanterns, five sleeping bags, a five-gallon water jug, and the smaller 1-gallon jug as well.

The boy grabbed the one-gallon water jug and went to the backyard to fill the vessel from the garden hose on the house's side. Afterward, Josh yelled to Ricky from outside the living room window that it was time to go. Then his friend begrudgingly turned off the television and walked outside.

The duo then drove over to Edgerton and picked up Pete. However, when they arrived back in Midwest, the boys briefly stopped, picked up David, and soon went north toward Highway 387. When they reached Light Plant Road and Highway 387 intersection, Josh turned left and quickly crossed over Salt Creek's bridge. But then, they exited the black-top highway and onto an oilfield road toward the south.

From there, getting to M-Hill mandated knowing which nearly identical oil field road to turn onto, but with each turn, the boys made their way further south from the highway.

The boys soon spotted their destination dead ahead, as evidenced by the dozen or so parked cars near the bottom of a steep hill. Other students were already walking to the top. Instead of parking below, Josh powered his old Plymouth up the ridgeback incline on a trail better suited for a goat than a vehicle. It wasn't Josh's driving skill or the power of his car that allowed him to climb to the top: it was economics. Since the boy could only afford to own one set of tires, he opted to keep the deeply treaded snow tires on the rear wheels during all seasons.

Once atop M-Hill, Josh set his emergency brake, and the four boys exited the car only to find the contemptuous face of Mrs. Ridgeway. She was the mother of one of the freshmen boys. She made it known that she would observe that none of the seniors were too rough on the underclassmen. Fortunately for all concerned, the heavyset Mrs. Ridgeway remained seated in her brown and gold Jeep Renegade, which was ironically a vehicle envied by most of the boys in town.

Minutes later, 21 seniors alongside 37 freshmen started the task by squaring up the bricks into four-foot-wide by 10 feet long lines to form a gigantic "M." Then, the teens added a more minor sized "85" to the left of the "M" to pay homage to the senior class. Finally, everyone involved began painting each brick with a fresh coat of standard white paint. The last task lasting for another two hours.

By 1 p.m., the students had finished, and more importantly, nobody got hurt. Ricky then trudged to the top of M-Hill and sat on the ground with his back against the old yellow Plymouth. Silently, Josh handed the boy the water jug, and Ricky expertly finished off the dregs of the water within. Then he wiped his mouth on the sleeve of his t-shirt.

"I bet you are glad we brought that water now, aren't you," Josh remarked with an ample amount of sarcasm.

Ricky cracked a small smile. "Listen, I just did my part to keep you out of trouble. I know your dad would find out one way or another whether you actually took that thing or even drank from it."

From behind them, they heard David say, "why don't you two OFTs come over here and take a look at this."

When the duo moved around to the other side of Josh's car, they found David sitting alongside Pete in the only shade on the hillside.

Josh looked at Ricky and said, "there he goes with the *OFT* stuff that I told you about," and then he added, "I still think it can be our mantra."

Pete looked up at Josh and asked, "what kind of foreign language are you speaking when you say 'mantra'?"

Ricky jumped into the conversation. He then explained to Pete that *mantra* meant a motto or a slogan. Though the look on Pete's face indicated that he still didn't get it, so Ricky summed it up in a perfect deadpan voice, "it's a saying, you moron."

The boys sat quietly and soaked in the vista of the treeless grass-covered hills, the deep sagebrush choked draws, and the multiple herds of Pronghorn antelope grazing around them. The only trees the boys saw were Cottonwoods that grew sparsely along the creek and the town's streets. The only exception was the Ponderosa Pines that grew along

Pine Ridge about 15 miles east of Edgerton. Still, from that distance, the trees looked like small pixelated black dots.

The Salt Creek valley looked like the entire landscape had collapsed upon itself from this vantage point, forming a discernable bowl shape. Additionally, the high perch gave the boys a great view of the town of Midwest and the freshly striped football field well below.

Pete suddenly broke the silence. "Who owns that dark green Ford pickup?"

"Where," Ricky inquired?

Pete then pointed with his right hand. "Just down from the Corral Bar and across from the store."

The Corral Bar sat on the west end of Ellison Street. At the same time, the eastern end of the street became bookended by two white monolith buildings of the Mason Lodge and the abandoned Midwest Club. Still, the structures formed the two most significant buildings in the town, except for the school. Also in view was the Midwest Grocery Store that split the distance between the Corral Bar and the Mason's Lodge. In addition, the street bordered precipitously against the edge of a cliff that rose 75 feet above the football field to the south of town. During home football games, tailgaters parked bumper to bumper from the Corral Bar to the Mason Lodge along the cliff edge to watch the action as if they were sitting inside a large stadium.

David shrugged his shoulders and looked at the others, "I don't know. It could be somebody new to town who just found work in the oilfield."

"Whoever it is, they must know Mr. Pierson because it looks like they are talking to him," Pete determined.

Josh shook his head. "How do you know that is Mr. Pierson? I can't make anything out from this distance?"

Pete nodded. "It is him alright because I can see his red dog, and the Piersons are the only people in town with a dog like that."

Josh squinted again and could not make out the details, but he didn't doubt his friend's innate ability to see things far away. During hunting season, everyone wanted Pete along because his eyes were just as good as a set of binoculars. An additional benefit was the boy never complained about helping to drag out harvested animals.

"The truck is leaving, so I think the dude must have asked for directions or something," Pete surmised finally.

It was then that Josh looked down at his wristwatch and said, "guys, we need to get back home, we have practice in two hours, and I am starving."

Prompted by the mention of food, the boys quickly loaded into Josh's car. After starting the engine, Josh then released the emergency brake and put his car in gear, and inched forward on the ridgeback road and over the crown of M-Hill. For a brief moment, Josh panicked when the trail vanished from view. However, it was short-lived. When the car's nose dipped, only then could he see well enough navigate down the south side of the hill.

Once back on an established road, the boys rolled down their windows in hopes of dispelling the heat trapped within the car. Unfortunately, by that time of day, the temperature had already crept over 90 degrees. So instead of going through another labyrinth of connecting roads to get back to Highway 387, Josh drove further south and caught a main east-west road that ended on Gas Plant road.

Once inside Midwest again, Josh first dropped off David and Pete at David's house, and then he and Ricky returned home. But before going inside their homes, the boys made plans to walk to football practice together rather than drive as they have done all through two-a-day practice sessions. Walking was a practical decision because even if the boys took a shower after each session, it was common for both of them to continue sweating for another hour. Thus, in this arid climate, the walk home allowed the boys to air dry.

Later, while eating a bowl of ramen noodles, Josh opened the newest issue of the Midwest-Edgerton News and took out a pair of scissors, and cut out the football schedule. Then, he got up from the table and moved to his bedroom, where he thumbtacked the list of games on his bulletin board.

The schedule pitted the Oilers up against other 1A schools of Big Horn, Wright, and Hulett. However, the five remaining games were against much larger 2A schools of Guernsey, Moorcroft, Sundance, Upton, and Tongue River.

* * *

6

At 2:50 p.m. that day, Josh stepped out of his house, and before heading down to get Ricky, he turned around to look west to M-Hill to admire the work from that morning. The freshly painted "M" stood out in stark contrast to the land around the hill and could be seen from miles away.

Josh then turned and walked a few doors down and arrived at Ricky's house. But before he opened the gate to knock on the door, his friend burst out of the door and jumped off the porch and onto the sidewalk. The two boys then walked across the vacant lot south of Navy Row and then across Peake street and south along Ellison. Once at Lewis Street, the boys turned east and walked toward the school.

Because the only unlocked door in the entire school was the high school parking lot entrance, it forced the boys to walk around the Elementary School wing. They soon passed by the playground fence and then the recently completed Library addition. But, rather than the sight of familiar cars and pickups of their teammates in the parking lot, the boys were greeted by the presence of two Natrona County Sheriff Chevy Blazers and the Ford Bronco of the Midwest Police Chief Wyatt Traynor.

"Something is up," Josh said, which Ricky acknowledged with a simple head nod. Then, they proceeded into the school and the locker room located directly across from the outside door.

The boys entered the locker room door and weaved around the rows of lockers toward the varsity room in the rear. It was then that they looked through the glass windows of the coach's office to see Coach Fleming talking to the unfamiliar Sheriff Deputies and Chief Traynor.

But before the boys could ask, Carlos Mondragon walked up to them and said, "this is all about Coach Savolt. Didn't you guys hear that he went missing?"

Josh shook his head. "No, we were up on M-Hill most of the day," but then he asked Carlos, "when was the last time someone saw Coach?"

"I dunno; I heard about it about at noon today when one of our hired hands returned to the ranch after going to Jones Hardware in Edgerton to pick up a spool of barbed wire. He said everybody in the area is talking about it."

In reaction to the news, Josh pushed through other players toward his locker in the rear of the room and quickly dressed out into his shorts, half shirt, and a pair of socks. He then decided to walk down to his father's classroom to speak to him before volleyball practice began.

He exited the locker room into the hallway and turned right at the administration office. Moving swiftly, Josh walked past the science lab and the two science classrooms on his right. At the same time, on his left, he passed the faculty lounge, the home economics room and finally entered his dad's classroom at the end of the hallway on the left. Once inside the room, he found his dad sitting behind his desk.

"Dad, what is going on with Coach Savolt?"

The elder Anderson shrugged. "He did not show up for the faculty meeting this morning, so Dr. Gaines asked Bill Crooks and me to go over to his apartment to roust him out of bed. But, when we got there, he didn't answer the door. The odd thing is that his red pickup is parked where he always keeps it behind the apartment complex."

Before Josh could ask a follow-on question, his father continued, "Crooks and I came back and reported it to Dr. Gaines, who, in turn, called Chief Traynor to do a welfare check on Tim. Reed, the custodian, met the police at the apartment since he holds all the spare keys to every school district home."

"What did they find?"

"The same thing Crooks and I found- nothing. But, Reed reported to Chief Traynor that he last saw him on Saturday morning when they spoke together along the creek near the football field. So now, the police are questioning people in what is becoming a missing person's case. Considering that his truck and all his belongings are intact, the police speculate that it unlikely that Savolt left town in a hurry. Right now, we just have to wait and see."

Josh's face flushed into a pinkish hue, which was his poker tell for being upset. Rob got up from behind his desk and gave his son a quick one-armed hug, and ensured him that everything would be okay.

Then the Rob instructed, "now, get to practice, and we will see you at home after I get done with volleyball."

Josh started to turn away but suddenly changed his mind. "Dad, I was supposed to help Coach Savolt Saturday morning, but I was too sore. Maybe if I were with him, he would be okay and here today....do you think?"

"Son, I am thankful that you stayed home since I would be more worried about you being missing than just my friend. So, stop worrying; I am confident Tim will show up and have nothing more than a funny story to share. Now, off to practice!"

Leaving his father's classroom, Josh trotted down the freshly waxed hallway in stocking feet. The fresh coating on the floor nearly caused him to slip outside of the faculty lounge, which forced him to extend his right arm out against a hall locker to regain balance. Simultaneously, Ms. Connelly existed in the teacher's lounge with cheeks streaked with a mascara line from a previous flood of tears.

With one hand still on the wall locker, Josh asked her, "are you okay, Ms. Connelly?"

Without a word, Karen Connelly stepped in and hugged the boy tightly in a full-body press, released him, and then headed toward her classroom. Too shocked to move in the afterglow of the unsolicited embrace, Josh's attention focused upon the voice of Chief Traynor. He could hear the Chief questioning someone behind the faculty lounge door.

Upon returning to the locker room, Josh was relieved to find that the Sheriff's Deputies had departed. Still, the locker room was still abuzz with whispers and conjectures of what happened to Coach Savolt. He then quickly put on his remaining pads, football cleats and then grabbed his helmet to walk down the hill from the school to the football field.

Once the entire team made it onto Oiler Field, every conversation contained plenty of conjecture and what-ifs concerning the whereabouts of Coach Savolt. Some boys speculated that he stepped into a pool of quicksand along the creek. In contrast, others thought someone took offense to his field study, while some of the freshmen opined aliens abducted him. Josh then sharply rebuked two other freshmen players engaging in a dialog where someone could hide a body in the area.

The practice was a haphazard and chaotic affair, with everyone's attention being on something else. Players moved in half-speed and showed half-interest in what they were doing. As usual, Coach Fleming worked alongside Coach Jim Orton with the lineman. However, Coach Savolt's absence was felt most with the backs and receivers, who occupied themselves without coaching oversight.

Instead, the team's junior quarterback, Carlos, took over for the absent coach in conducting drills. Unfortunately, he found it challenging to throw passes that connected with anyone. However, for any ball Carlos did deliver on target fell precipitously to the turf.

One hour into the practice, Coach Fleming noted his error in leaving the backs and receivers alone and assigned Coach Orton to work solely with the lineman. While he walked across the field to the other group, he noticed a glaring absence of discipline that affected the entire team. The coach then stopped abruptly in the middle of the football field and blew his whistle. He instructed everyone to form up in two lines, one for the lineman and all others along the 50-yard line.

Once Coach Fleming got the full attention of his team, he said, "I know we have a distraction today that has taken away everyone's focus, so now we will run some wind sprints."

The instruction was met with a chorus of moans and groans, to which he responded with, "men, other teams are going to die tired chasing us because we are in such good shape."

The first group toed the line, and with a prompt by a short tweet of the coach's whistle, they sprinted to the goal line and back to the 50-yard line. Both groups completed ten sets of wind sprints when Coach Fleming blew a long and hard whistle, which signified the end of the conditioning portion of practice. He then instructed the team to get a drink of water from the garden house behind the concession stand and then reassemble on the bleachers afterward. After each mouth watered, all 35 boys sat down in rows with their helmets on top of their laps.

Coach Fleming walked to the front of the team and began his address. "Men, I think we should have started today's practice with sprints instead of just assuming that we could continue with our normal routine. That is my fault. I accept full responsibility."

He continued, "in a close-knit community such as ours, it is hard to remain unaffected when something tragic or when something out of the ordinary happens to one of our own. However, all we know is that Coach Savolt is not accounted for, and there is no reason right now to suspect anything else. So if you want to talk about this topic, get it out of your system tonight, because tomorrow we start planning for our game in Guernsey on Friday. The Vikings are big and average 225 pounds across their front line, so don't think we can shove them around like we did last year."

Abruptly, Coach Fleming turned and walked a few paces up the cinder track with his hands on his hips to gather his thoughts. Then, with an audible sigh of resignation, he turned back toward the team.

"I am canceling the rest of practice today, and we will resume tomorrow after school. I expect that each of you will process your emotions and put them into their place. I don't know much about what is going on with Coach Savolt than you do. But, when you step foot on my field, I want you to think only about football, or somebody is going to get hurt."

Lastly, Coach Fleming reinforced that his team understood his message by shouting, "are we clear," as if he were a drill sergeant.

Without hesitation, the boys en masse projected a corresponding, "Yes Sir," which indicated they heard and understood the coach correctly.

Then all 35 boys hurried back up the hill to the locker room, where they would shower before heading home.

With his mind clearly elsewhere, Josh quickly rinsed himself off in the shower, hastily dried himself with a towel, and quickly got dressed. However, his hair remained dripping wet, and his t-shirt had stuck to his damp torso. He then exited the locker room and waited impatiently in the hallway for Ricky to emerge to walk home together. However, when his friend exited the locker room, the boy informed Josh that his dad wanted him to ride home with him. Instead, Josh nodded and walked into the main gym only to find it was empty, which meant that volleyball practice must have also ended early too.

Instead of retracing his route to school earlier, Josh walked out the back door between the office and the Industrial Arts room on the other side of the trophy cases since all the school's locked doors open from the inside. Then, he strode across the freshly paved courtyard toward the cafeteria that bookended the complex and crossed over Lewis Street to pick up the middle sidewalk on the east side of town.

When Josh was about ten yards from the alley when he saw a dark green Ford pickup barreling westward down the aisle toward Ellison street. With the dust still lingering in the air, he ran up and looked down the alley. However, the truck had already disappeared from view. He then looked east to where the pickup had come from and saw a plume of dust that still lofted in the air, beginning at the apartment complex to the east.

Then it hit him. The truck was similar to the one he and his friends spotted from atop M-Hill earlier that day. But as the dust settled, Josh spoke to himself, "whoever was driving, they are driving too fast and may run over one of the Folds kids that always played in the alley."

A few minutes later, rather than opening the gate outside his house, Josh vaulted over the fence, and with three long strides, he rambled across the lawn and jumped onto the porch.

"You are home early," remarked his mother, Sara.

"Coach cut practice short because of the news about Mr. Savolt going missing."

"Your dad did the same thing at volleyball practice. But I am sure everything turns out fine, and everybody is just overreacting. Just have faith, Josh." Then, with a short pause, she asked him, "could you go out back to the garden and tell your father that supper will be ready in 15 minutes?"

The boy answered curtly, "sure, mom," and then promptly walked out the backdoor and into the backyard. There he found his father in the garden holding a half dozen red ripe tomatoes.

"Dad, Mom says supper is in 15 minutes."

"Okay, I will be right in. Come here, take these tomatoes into the kitchen, and I will bring in some squash."

Josh returned to the house and placed the tomatoes next to the sink, and in doing so, he noticed a pile of dirty dishes that reminded him it was his turn to wash them that night.

Later, the Andersons sat down for dinner, which seemed precipitously more quiet than usual. It was as if nobody wanted to talk about the apparent major event of the day; instead, everyone ate quietly and then placed their empty dishes on the counter. Afterward, Josh positioned himself in front of the sink and mumbled that he wished they had a dishwasher that plugged in rather than one named *Josh* or *Cindy*.

When he finished the dishes, Josh retired to his room, where he listened to a cassette of Night Ranger's *Dawn Patrol* album. Finally, he laid back onto his water bed and stared at the ceiling.

His mind turned over the many scenarios that hovered about Coach Savolt's disappearance. Josh rejected the obvious ones about his coach being in another town or that he had just simply quit teaching and coaching. Yet, in his heart, he knew that something had happened to his friend, and it had to be because of his field study as it was the only scenario that made sense to him.

When additional answers to his many questions finally ceased, Josh got up, turned off his light, pulled the covers back on his bed, and crawled in between the sheets. In the dark, he then began to think of a way that he could start retracing Coach Savolt's steps and, by doing so, discover what happened to him.

* * *

7

Tuesday, August 28, 1984

Josh and Ricky arrived for their first school day together in the "banana" car. When they reached the parking lot, they found a space next to Carlos' beat up and barely drivable Dodge Power Wagon with a faded "Rafter M" brand stenciled on the doors. The emblem represented the Mondragon Ranch.

The boys entered the school through the main high school entrance, turned right down the hallway, and went directly to their lockers near the end of the hall. Lockers were only assigned to Freshmen or new students because everyone kept their same storage space throughout high school. Interestingly enough was that none of the locker doors were affixed with combination locks because there was no need for them. Similarly, area residents did not lock their front doors for two reasons. First, people respected each other's space. Secondly, nearly every resident in the community possessed at least one firearm.

Josh had chemistry for his first-period class with Mr. Savolt but was apprehensive about what to expect if Savolt's absence became extended. The rest of his schedule included: Literature, History, Student Publications (newspaper and yearbook), Lunch, Calculus, and finished as a teacher's aide in Physical Education.

A few minutes later, he found a seat in the science lab next to David Proctor. As Josh sat, the tardy bell rang, which indicated that the school day had officially begun. Then all the students stood and recited the pledge of allegiance in unison, and, afterward, they listened to the morning's announcements. Dr. Gaines took the microphone next and welcomed everyone back to school, and professed that this would be a great and memorable school year. But, the chemistry class was still absent a teacher, and most of the 14 students, except for Josh and David, engaged in a whole dialog about Mr. Savolt's disappearance.

Suddenly, the science lab door opened, and an abrupt silence hushed over the room. Dr. Gaines entered along with Shannon Isom, who was a regular substitute for elementary classes.

Dr. Gaines quickly introduced Mrs. Isom to the class. He also announced that she would temporarily look over all of Mr. Savolt's classes until he comes back or until the school finds a permanent substitute teacher. Finally, Dr. Gaines assigned the class to work on a research paper about alternative energy resources outside of fossil fuels until such time.

David whispered to Josh, "don't look now, but I think that next week, we will have to go out and hug a few trees," which brought a smile to his face.

Josh and his friends completed the rest of the class period in the library researching the paper. It was evident to everyone that Mrs. Isom, who openly displayed her apprehension with teaching science, let alone chemistry, was relieved most of all. The intercessory bell was her only reprieve though she privately dreaded the four other science classes to cover during the school day.

After walking the short distance from the library to the classroom, Josh, along with Ricky, David, and Pete, slid into their seats in Literature class to start the second period. It was then that Pete turned in his seat and asked Carlos if it were possible to hunt deer in October on the Mondragon ranch versus resigning to hunting on public lands like he always did.

Carlos replied, "I will ask my dad if it is okay."

However, Shelly Pierson, the Literature teacher, overheard the conversation and interrupted the boys. "I find that hunting is a barbaric and murderous activity that only keeps Wyomingites from evolving into citizens of a civilized nation."

Pete replied, "well, I do not since my family eats everything we harvest. To us, hunting is a way of life."

Mrs. Pierson folded her arms across her chest and asked Pete, "but can't you just go to the store and buy your food like people everywhere else?"

Pete was about to say something in return, but the bell rang, and Mrs. Pierson spun on her heels and walked to the front of the classroom.

For the first fifteen minutes of the class, Mrs. Pierson explained the rules and assignment expectations in excessive detail. During one point, she described the process of turning in assignments as if reading a flowchart of "if yes" or "if no" courses of action.

Oddly, Mrs. Pierson rarely ever looked directly at someone while she spoke; instead, she either glanced at the ceiling or would look over the top of a student to the back wall. To Josh, at least, Mrs. Pierson's aversion tendencies spoke to a deep-seated character issue.

At the grand finale of her speech, Mrs. Pierson revealed 15 copies of George Orwell's novel *1984*. She instructed three of the students to pass out the books to the rest of the class.

"This semester, I thought it would be neat for us to read this classic since we are in 1984 after all," Mrs. Pierson announced.

Josh, however, shook his head in disbelief. Then he raised his hand, and when acknowledged, he asked, "but what if I have already read this book?"

"You have read *1984*?"

"Yes, ma'am, I have a copy of it in my room at home, and it is one of my favorite books."

The teacher placed her hands on her hips and then looked out of the window when she challenged, "prove it."

The boy shrugged. "Prove it, ma'am? I am not sure what you are asking me to do?"

"You said you have read the book, so tell us all about it."

Josh replied, "*1984* is a warning to all of us. The book depicts an overbearing government that gains incredible power and authority when the citizens refuse to question its motives. One of my favorite quotes in the book is this: *There are no heroes in the face of pain.*"

Mrs. Pierson furrowed her brow in confusion and then tilted her head to one side and stated, "I don't remember that quote in the book...."

Josh cut her off by providing another quote, "what about *doubles-peak,* which I believe Orwell coined the term himself?"

"What is *doublespeak* as I'm not familiar with that term, either?"

From behind him, Josh heard Ricky whisper to David that maybe she should read the book before assigning it, though he prayed that Mrs. Pierson couldn't hear the comment.

Josh shifted in his seat. Then he calmly explained, "*doublespeak* is, and I quote Orwell: '*the power of holding two contradicting beliefs in one's mind simultaneously and accepting both as truth.*' For example, you say that hunting is a murderous activity. But, just last Sunday at the faculty picnic, I saw you eating a hamburger. Whether you know it or not, cattle are herded into a tight chute, killed with a bang stick to the head, then butchered, but that isn't barbaric to you? A hunter, however, works to get his meal by walking miles, then stalks his prey, harvests the animal, and packs it out on his back. Wouldn't you agree that the two things do not juxtapose each other since killing an animal is central to both examples? In my mind, both activities are justified since humans need to eat, don't you think?"

Momentarily stunned, Mrs. Pierson stared blankly ahead with her mouth agape. Then she sighed heavily and threw her hands up in resignation, and she turned back toward her desk. But just before reaching her desk chair, Mrs. Pierson grabbed another book of the shelf and tossed it onto the desktop in front of Josh.

Turning the book over, he saw a copy of *The Lord of the Flies* written by William Golding.

"Josh, you will read that book instead and be prepared to write a book report on it at the end of the semester."

He smiled and looked over at both David and Pete and winked. Then he whispered to them one last Orwell quote, *"the best books are those that tell you what you know already."*

The rest of the morning went by innocuously and mundane. However, lunchtime gave Josh the chance to be with his friends in the cafeteria. While eating, David, Ricky, Pete, and Scott Merino regaled in retelling the tale of how Josh outwitted Mrs. Pierson for the benefit of Steve Otten and Chet Harrison since neither was in the classroom. On cue, Josh provided his quotes from 1984, which brought the boys into a loud round of cacophony.

The laughter, however, drowned out the sounds of the loud clicks of Rob Anderson's heels that struck rhythmically upon the cafeteria floor in the direction of Josh and his friends. David was the first to see Mr. Anderson coming toward them and leaped up from the table, which caused all the boys except Josh to look up and move back.

Rob then leaned over and whispered into his son's ear from behind and ordered him to follow with an audible "now," which Josh quickly abided.

He dutifully followed his father through both the elementary and junior high wings of the school to his classroom. Once there, Rob slammed the door abruptly behind him. If Josh didn't know already, his father was upset with him.

The elder Anderson got straight to the point, "just what were you thinking in challenging Shelly Pierson like that in her class? Did you not think for even one second that at her first opportunity, she wouldn't drag me along with her into Dr. Gaines' office to file a complaint against you?"

Josh raised both of his hands waist high and pleaded, "Dad, all I said was that I had already read *1984,* and she challenged me to prove it."

Rob brought his right hand up and placed it upon his forehead. "I gave you that book from my college days for you to expand your mind and not for you to use it as a means to make someone else, let alone one of my colleagues, look stupid."

But before Josh could reply, Rob motioned for his son to remain quiet. "According to her version, you grandstanded in her classroom to what she describes as you 'impugning her authority' and 'challenging her credentials.' Then, according to her, you called her a hypocrite for eating meat and not supporting hunting. Are you out of your mind, son?"

"But dad, all I did was give her direct quotes from the book. She brought up the topic of hunting by trying to make me and Pete feel uncivilized for talking about hunting on the Mondragon ranch. I used her words to illustrate the concept of Orwell's doublespeak because it was obvious to me that she has not read the book. If you don't believe me, ask my friends, they saw it all."

"I am not interested in what your friends might say..." and in a momentary pause, Rob regained his composer and looked at his son. His gut told him that his son spoke the truth. He also reminded himself in a situation like this that reality is often distorted by one's ego, especially from the view of the offended.

Rob tried in vain not to grin, though his eyes told Josh quite the opposite. Once again, the father placed his right hand on his forehead, and when he lowered his hand, he said to Josh, "tell me what I have always said about correcting people?"

He knew that his father was referring to the lessons in the book of Proverbs about dealing with foolish people. So once Josh retrieved something from memory, he lifted his head and looked into the senior Anderson's eyes and recited: "*Don't correct the simple-minded, because he will not get you. Don't correct the fool because he will ignore you. Don't correct the mocker because he will hate you. But do correct the wise because he will thank you.*"

Rob gave his son an approving nod and then asked his boy, "which of those do you think applied in your Literature class this morning?"

Josh smiled and said, "probably the first three."

The elder Anderson smiled. "I tell you what, son. How about we go down to Dr. Gaines's office, and you can tell him your version of what happened in class. But, promise me that you will not aggravate Mrs. Pierson any further. Is that a deal?"

Josh replied with a quick "yes, Sir."

In the moments that followed, he recalled the specific events of his exchange with Mrs. Pierson with the Principal. At one point, Dr. Gaines guffawed aloud but adroitly regained his composure. The meeting ended with a cautionary provision that sometimes it was better to let things go rather than stand upon principle just because you know you are right.

When the 3:15 p.m. bell rang, which signified the end of the school day, Josh was already in the locker room putting on his football pads. One of the advantages of being a P.E. aide during the last period was that he could change into practice gear for football or any sport for that matter at the end of class.

Once they donned their pads, Josh, along with Ricky, exited the back door of the small gym to make their way down to the football field. However, standing directly in their path was Doug Pierson with his red Irish Setter on a leash.

The teacher then said, "I heard that you were challenging my wife in class today. I also know that both your father and Dr. Gaines spoke to you about it too. I find it appalling that you posture yourself on the same intellectual level as my wife or I."

"You mean *me* instead of *I*, don't you, Sir?" Josh asked.

"What? What are you talking about?"

"Sir, I think you meant to say 'posture yourself on the same intellectual level and my wife and me?"

Doug Pierson didn't know what to say. While he remained temporarily dumbfounded, Josh added, "respectfully, Sir, I didn't mean anything by it with your wife."

Ricky interceded by grabbing Josh by his shoulder and partially drug him toward the football field. At the same time, three more players erupted out of the gym door, putting much-needed space between Mr. Pierson, Josh, and Ricky.

Pierson shouted at them from behind, "this isn't over, and I will be watching you!

Josh heard the comment but looked at Ricky instead and said to him, "just like Orwell's Big Brother, I bet."

"Let me guess. I will find that in the book, too, won't I?" Ricky asked. He nodded. "Yes, you will. The book paints a picture that is much worse than you think. Imagine that your every word, thought, and action being monitored, judged, and then scrutinized by people with assumed authority over you."

Ricky shook his head as if being overloaded by information. He said to Josh, "all I know is that it is a good thing that neither of us has Business or Typing class with Mr. Pierson because that guy is a tool."

The execution of football practice went much better than the day before. The team completed all drills with a crisp purpose. True to their promise, every player also abstained from any talk about Coach Savolt's absence. Next, Coach Fleming ran the team through plays from the offensive game plan against a reserve defense comprised mostly freshmen and sophomores.

The lone exception was defensive tackle, Brian Agee, who was only allowed to play defense. However, players like Ricky, Josh, David, Carlos, Steve, and another six teammates played both offense and defense, plus all special teams.

As a junior, Brian belied his 5 feet 10 inches in height by carrying a sturdy frame of 245 pounds of solid muscle. The boy's only downfall was that he only had half of a right foot due to a chainsaw accident six years ago. Although Brian moved well in a straight line, still, he had limited lateral movement, making him a significant offensive line liability.

He was also the team's kicker as Brian self-taught himself by watching video footage of professional kicker Tom Dempsey. The latter gained notoriety for having a half foot like Brian and for kicking the longest field goal in the National Football League's history. Brian, too, had a tremendous leg, and his kicks boomed with incredible distance. However, his accuracy was inconsistent at best.

The practice ended following the first-team defense lining up against the same formations that Coach Fleming expected Guernsey to run against them. At the final whistle, all of the team members gathered around David in the center, who shouted out, "one, two, three," and then the team members, in unison, yelled out, *"O-F-T!"*

* * *

8

Early in the evening, Midwest Police Chief Wyatt Traynor held a puzzle in his mind. Tim Savolt's disappearance was his lone major case to work on, but there were very few answers for all the questions he possessed.

That morning, he had coffee at the Edgerton bowling alley with the mayors of both Midwest and Edgerton and the Edgerton volunteer policeman. The latter only patrolled the streets on Fridays and Saturdays, looking for drunk drivers. During the meeting, the Chief withstood a barrage of questions from the two civic leaders about this incident surrounding Savolt's disappearance.

Chief Traynor considered it a missing person case, but that didn't satisfy the officials who demanded that he apply every resource available to the situation. While he patiently listened to the elected officials, he could not help but think of the juxtaposition here. Traynor wagered that the mayors in either Casper or Cheyenne would not become intimately involved in a missing person's case. But, in this tight-knit community where actual felony crime was low, anything outside of the ordinary became a big deal.

He looked over to the file cabinet in his office. Counting Savolt's case, it contained only three active or unsolved investigations. One of the cases occurred three years ago, involving a dead cow found dead under the Cottonwood trees where the annual town picnic took place next to the football field. The cow was one of four such creatures found dead in the area for two years. Additionally, the Mondragon Ranch found one of their prized bulls dead in its stall, plus two steers on the Lauren ranch east of Edgerton met the same fate. The ranchers' cattle shared the same oddity as the cow found dead within town limits: they all died from apparent mutilation. Investigators from the states, both Wyoming and Colorado, arrived and removed the carcasses. This sort of phenomenon had plagued ranches along the border between the States as far back as the mid-1970s. However, the case was still classified as "open" since there was not a resolution.

The only other open investigation consisted of multiple instances of vandalism involving MERP company property, like slashed tires on two occasions and one report of someone adding sugar to the fuel tank of a backhoe.

While seated at his desk, Chief Traynor once again opened the SAVOLT case file. He hoped by reviewing it that he might find another lead. He re-read his notes that indicated the exact time he received a phone call from the school last Monday. In that phone call, Dr. Gaines had requested a welfare check on the absent teacher. Upon arrival at the apartment, Reed, one of the custodians, opened Savolt's apartment door with a spare key. The Chief vividly recalled his relief of not finding Savolt dead in either the bed or bathtub-unlike some welfare checks upon a few elderly residents in town.

He looked at his notes once again. He was baffled still over the fact that it didn't appear that the teacher left Midwest in a hurry since his tidy apartment looked as if nothing was amiss. He also recorded Reed's response when asked about the last time that he saw Savolt. Reed admitted that he talked to Savolt on the previous Saturday morning around 9 a.m.

Also, in the file was the report from the Natrona County Sheriff's office that detailed their area search for Tim Savolt. One deputy rode on horseback along Salt Creek from Edgerton to the bridge where Highway 387 crossed over the stream to the north and west of Midwest. However, the officer reported zero findings and no traces of Savolt. Another Deputy also failed to find any evidence of the teacher while driving along oil field roads south and west of town.

Traynor abruptly pushed away from his desk and closed his eyes while he thought about the size of the search area. Finally, he agreed that the search parameter was adequate because nobody knew how far downstream to look. When he opened his eyes, he sat forward to the desk and took out a pen and a paper pad from his drawer.

He drew two columns on a blank piece of paper. In one column, he labeled it "left town" and labeled the other column "deceased" along with a subheading of "suspects." At this point, Reed was the only suspect because he was the only one so far that saw Savolt between Saturday and Monday last.

Wyatt Traynor grew up in Edgerton and had graduated from Midwest High School in 1969. He still possessed an athletic build that defined him in high school when he played football, wrestled, and participated in track as a distance runner. It was rare that Traynor had to use his physicality. Still, when needed, he did not have any problem subduing a suspect. He also wore a hat almost invariably because the top of his head was nearly bald. However, the covering helped keep his secret from everyone, except for his wife.

Three months after High School graduation, Traynor received a draft notice and went into the U.S. Marine Corps. Then he served two tours in Vietnam before returning home to the states. Considering all the combat that Traynor experienced, he only had two scars on his back. The injuries happened when a Soviet-made rocket-propelled grenade exploded outside the showers in base camp. The explosion sent two chunks of shrapnel through the thin shower walls only to become embedded into his back just under his right shoulder blade.

Upon discharge, Traynor found work as a provisionary police officer in Mills, a small community bordering the city of Casper. He later achieved full status upon completing the State of Wyoming Law Enforcement Academy in Douglas, Wyoming. After that, the Chief spent another three years in Mills, followed by two years on the Casper PD.

Then he applied for the vacant Chief of Police position in Midwest. That year, 1984, marked his eighth year on the job. Additionally, Traynor was married to his wife of ten years, Debra, whom he met while working in Mills.

But, Deputy Cory Isom was a completely different story. Chief Traynor hired him because Cory was the only applicant for the job. Although trained as well at the academy, the deputy was still more inept than capable. His best abilities resided in patrolling the town and sitting either underneath the old steel oil derrick or parked next to the red, white, and blue painted pump jack opposite of one another at the junction of Highways 387 and 259.

Deputy Isom was married to Shannon Isom, who Chief Traynor quietly referred to as "the brains of the outfit." Shannon had a heart for kids, and the Isom's had four children of their own, three boys and one girl. She also substituted at the school and wanted to become an elementary educator full time, but only possessed an Associate Degree from Sheridan College.

Looking down at his newly created list, Traynor knew that there were challenges to consider. Just two days ago, after entering Tim Savolt's apartment, he called Deputy Isom for assistance to guard a potential crime scene. But, he had to leave Reed, the school custodian, on guard outside the door because Cory was home alone with the kids while Shannon was over at the grocery store in Edgerton. Deputy Isom arrived on the scene fifteen minutes later to relieve Reed and quickly sealed the exterior of the apartment door. Then, since the area's Deputy Sheriff was on vacation, Traynor requested the Sheriff to provide help to search for Tim Savolt.

Traynor took the notepad out again and circled his entry about a statewide all-points bulletin. To date, he had yet received any confirmation of Savolt's appearance somewhere else in the State of Wyoming. Then the Chief dropped his eyes back onto the file in front of him and read that the teacher had no known relatives other than his deceased parents from Thermopolis. He found it sad that nobody was to mourn Savolt's absence other than Karen Connelly, who called him six times, asking for updates on the case.

He shook his head. There was nothing really to go on in the current case. There was no probable cause or physical evidence that pointed to something evil like murder. Tim Savolt had just vanished.

Then a thought occurred to Traynor; perhaps he could interview some of Savolt's students and maybe close some loose ends as to what the teacher was doing along Salt Creek in the first place. He knew who he would interview first, and that student lived just a hundred yards away from his office.

* * *

9

Ablock away from the Police Station, Josh Anderson appreciated that normalcy was slowly returning to his life as he joined his family for supper. The Andersons ate every meal together at the dining room table, where they also prayed before eating. He had no idea that his family's routine was unique until he observed a mealtime at David's house. Everyone at the Proctor home ate whenever and wherever they wanted.

Rob stopped his fork halfway to his mouth and said, "son, you will be home by yourself this Friday night after you return from Guernsey. We will be home late Sunday since your mom, Cindy, and I will be in Sundance Friday and Saturday for the season-opening volleyball tournament. We will then spend Sunday night with your Aunt Sue in Gillette."

He replied, "I know, dad, I will be fine," feeling placated.

Sara changed the subject to ask her son how his Literature class was going and how Mrs. Pierson treated him?

Josh looked down at his plate. "Fine," he said curtly since he secretly wished to avoid that topic. But, unfortunately, Mrs. Pierson had since ignored him with her apathetic and silent treatment toward him.

However, he did say, "she is ignoring me, which is far better than her husband."

Rob stopped eating and looked at his son. "What about her husband?"

The boy shrugged. "He confronted Ricky and me outside the small gym yesterday before practice to let me know that he didn't appreciate me belittling his wife."

"He did what!" exclaimed Sara.

Josh nodded. "Mr. Pierson met us on the backside of the school like I said, and he even had his dog with him."

Rob's face began to radiate bright red just like a thermometer does as it reacts to a rise in temperature. Sara stared her husband down and sternly warned him, "don't even think about engaging him; rather, I think it best for you to have a talk with Dr. Gaines instead and let him handle it. Please?"

"Okay. I will speak to Doc in the morning. Right now, I wish that I wasn't a fellow teacher and just a regular parent."

"Why is that, dear?" Sara asked.

"That way, I could be over at his house now kicking his butt down the street," Rob thundered.

She tried to calm her husband's justified emotions by reminding him that the Pierson's have always placed themselves on their pedestal and treated others inferior.

After a short pause, she emphasized her point with an example. "Just last Sunday at the barbeque, Shelly flat out said that religion is for fools or the weak-minded and that believers are all controlled under some mass dissolution. She even quoted Lenin by saying that 'religion is the people's opium.' But, it wasn't what she said that infuriates me; it is how she said it by adding the words 'we all can agree' and 'we all know' to preface her statements."

"What did you say, mom?" Cindy asked after silently listening to the entire exchange.

Sara turned her head toward her daughter. "I told her that millions of people around the world worship God, and in this country, it is our right and privilege to do so."

Rob then asked, "What did she say then?"

"I never gave her an opportunity; I simply walked away from her and went inside to help Lois Crooks clean up in the kitchen."

Rob looked at both Josh and Cindy and reminded them of the house rules about what was said at home-stays at home when it comes to other teachers. Josh and Cindy nodded in agreement and cleared the dishes from the table together.

Suddenly, a knock on the front door interrupted the evening. When Rob opened the door, he found Chief Traynor standing upon the porch.

Rob greeted him, "well, hello, Chief, what can we do for you?"

"I was wondering if I could talk to Josh for a few minutes about Mr. Savolt? But don't worry, I would like you and Mrs. Anderson to sit in on the discussion as well," explained the Chief.

"Okay, well, come on inside. Do you want a cup of coffee?"

"Sure, if you have any already made, I would hate to put you out."

Rob dispelled the notion with a wave of his hand. "We always have a coffee pot going in this household, so it is no problem."

The senior Anderson led Chief Traynor to the dining room table where Josh had already sat. But then Sara excused Cindy from washing dishes temporarily and asked her to go to her room while they talked with Chief Traynor.

Chief Traynor cut to the chase by explaining that he was investigating further into the mysterious disappearance of Tim Savolt. He reported to the Andersons that Savolt's whereabouts were still unknown. However, he had no evidence to believe that Tim met any ill will.

He opened the questioning with Josh. "It is common knowledge that you and Mr. Savolt have a good relationship. I also know that you often accompany him on his treks along Salt Creek. Still, I am wondering about what you two were up to?"

Josh eagerly explained, "Mr. Savolt has been working on a study about Salt Creek. Specifically, he wanted to determine what was in the water from the creek's source, through the oil field, and to its confluence with the Powder River."

"But everyone in this area knows that Salt Creek is hazardous...." the Chief tried to say, but Josh cut him off.

"I hate to correct you, Sir, but the creek supports a variety of different fish and other wildlife. The water, though, is bitter with salt from the limestone at its source. Yet, I don't know whether Mr. Savolt proved whether there are any toxins in the water. Nor do I know if the creek is half as harmful as everyone assumes it is."

Meanwhile, Rob and Sara Anderson sat quietly, listened to the exchange, and appreciated that Chief Traynor asked them to sit in on the questioning.

The Chief asked, "how long has Mr. Savolt been involved with this study?"

The boy replied, "the study began during the summer break of last year. Since then, Mr. Savolt has collected water and vegetation samples that he analyzed in the science lab. I think he was very close to begin working on the technical paper to publish his results."

"What is the location on the creek where he conducted his study? I mean, where did he start, and where did he stop?"

Josh shrugged. "The start is easy since I have gone there twice with him. He always begins just south of the Edgerton Grocery Store. On both occasions, we ended at Highway 387 bridge west of town. But he has told me many times that he went further downstream near the Jackass Springs oil seep."

Traynor appeared confused. "Jackass Springs? I have heard about it but have never seen it. I always thought that was something of a legend."

But, during the brief pause, he made a few notes in his notebook, then focused his eyes on Rob and Sara. "Did Tim Savolt have any serious disagreements with any of the faculty members?"

They stared at each other briefly. Then Rob offered, "Chief, I am not aware of any serious disagreements. But I know of a few instances where he exchanged words with a couple of other teachers. But then I would be talking out of place in discussing a personnel matter. So why don't you stop by the school and ask Dr. Gaines about that."

Chief Traynor scribbled notes furiously, paused to think for a moment, but didn't identify any follow-on questions. So instead, he finished his cup of coffee in one gulp. The Chief then thanked the Andersons for allowing him to intrude upon their evening. Afterward, he got up from the table and made his way toward the door, with Josh following behind him.

Just as he gripped the doorknob, another thought occurred to him. He turned and asked Josh one last question: "did Mr. Savolt keep notes of his study?"

Without hesitation, Josh said emphatically, "yes. Mr. Savolt took copious notes in his field book and kept a box full of other notations related to the testing of the water and the plants in his classroom."

With that, Chief Traynor wished the Andersons a good night, and he exited the door.

After leaving the Anderson home, Chief Traynor drove east on Navy Row and turned right onto Shannon Street toward the school. As he passed by Watson Street, his attention became fixated on the brake lights of a dark vehicle backing out of the parking area to the rear of the teacher apartment complex. For some reason he could not explain, he felt the need to investigate.

Turning right into the alley that also served as a driveway to the apartment parking lot, the Chief looked west for the tail lights of the unknown vehicle but spied none. He then pulled his Bronco into the last parking space, shut off the engine, extinguished his headlights, and waited. He hoped that the mysterious vehicle would appear passing by the front of the building on Lewis Street.

After a few moments, Chief Traynor determined that the vehicle had gone somewhere else, so he exited his Bronco and walked around to the front door. The complex had two apartments downstairs and two upstairs, with Tim Savolt's pad on the upper left. Ascending the stairs, the

Chief discovered that the tape seals over Savolt's door were broken and dangled lifelessly to one side of the doorframe.

A rush of adrenaline coursed through his veins, and his heart began beating with a thumping rhythm. Then he deftly retrieved his revolver off his right hip and held it squarely in front of him. As Traynor slowly approached the door, he saw no apparent marks around the lock that indicated a forced entry. Then the Chief reached down to try the doorknob with his left hand. He found it unlocked. Then he slowly opened the door and swept the living room and saw no movement, and turned on the light switch next to the door. Instantly, the living room lights revealed a mess of books, papers, and upturned boxes in the center of the room, which was precisely the opposite of how he found it two days ago.

Stepping carefully around the pile, Chief Traynor searched the kitchen and the bedroom to rule out any hidden intruder. After he found the apartment empty, the Chief used Tim Savolt's phone to call his deputy. Specifically, he ordered Isom to come to Savolt's place to secure it as a crime scene. In the morning, the Chief would install a padlock shackle on the door frame.

Deputy Isom soon arrived and parked his cruiser on Lewis Street directly outside the only entrance to the building. Chief Traynor instructed his deputy to remain there until midnight, when he would return. Then told the deputy to come to relieve him promptly at 6 a.m.

Back at the police station, Chief Traynor called Dr. Gaines and informed him of Tim Savolt's apartment finding. He asked the Principal if Reed could install a hasp and paddle lock on the apartment door in the morning. Traynor also requested that the keys stay in Police custody since the place was officially a crime scene due to evidence of a break-in. Additionally, he asked for a meeting with Dr. Gaines the following morning as he had a few questions he would like to ask him. Gaines relayed that 10 a.m. would be okay.

Taking out the Savolt file again, Chief Traynor added his notes from the evening. It bothered him that things were happening around him that didn't connect, at least not yet.

* * *

10

Friday, August 31, 1984

Midwest High School

Just before the end of the fourth period, the intercom squawked inside the school. The message informed the football team members, the cheerleaders, and the coaches that the bus would leave for Guernsey in 15 minutes. Josh and the other players quickly got up from their desks, made their way to the locker room to retrieve their equipment bags, and placed them inside the storage compartment under the bus.

While exiting the school, he could already hear a cacophony of different and loud voices emanating from inside the bus. It seemed that most of the players, especially the younger ones, were anxious to get going on the trip. When he stepped onto the bus, Josh noted the unspoken hierarchy of seating with the cheerleaders in the front, including Ricky's girlfriend, Sheila. Then there were two rows reserved for coaches, and followed by rows of freshmen. Finally, even the sophomores, juniors, and seniors seemed to sit in order toward the bus's rear.

Josh and Ricky sat together in the second to last row with David Proctor, Steve Otten, Pete Laroche, and Scott Merino, claiming the entire back row. Chet Harrison sat across from them, the unofficial disk jockey, who had already turned on his stereo. Upon the seat next to him sat his cassette case full of music and enough extra batteries to last both legs of the trip.

The bus departed the school parking lot at 1:45 p.m. and headed south on Highway 259 toward Casper. However, before the Salt Creek Oil Field disappeared from view, Ricky was already fast asleep. That left

Josh to his thoughts while looking out the window. The pump jacks in the oilfield eventually gave way to sagebrush-covered hills and a sea of grass. Then suddenly and dramatically, Casper Mountain came into full view.

Eventually, all talk inside the bus dampened to a low murmur except for David and Carlos. They renewed a discussion about the movie the boys watched the night before. For two years now, the same group of boys met the evening before each game to watch game film on their opponent, but this year, David added the Tom Cruise movie *All the Right Moves* to their night. He liked the similarities between the blue-collar steelworkers in the film with those in the oilfield.

Meanwhile, Chet Harrison kept the music playing. He deafly jockeyed a mixture of rock albums from groups like Journey, AC/DC, Kiss, Ratt, Night Ranger, Van Halen, and Scorpions, to name a few. His music selection soon became the only noise on the bus, except for the constant hum of the tires.

An hour and a half later, the Laramie Mountains, and the 10,200-foot Laramie Peak, dominated the view out of the right side of the bus. At the same time, the North Platte River shadowed the left side. As the motor coach passed by the upper reaches of Glendo Reservoir, Josh took note of the road sign for "Elkhorn Creek" next to a bridge, and he looked down to see that the creek was dry as usual. It seemed silly to him that the highway department would go through all the trouble of putting up a sign for a stream that never had any water in it.

Not long after crossing the dry creek, the bus pulled over at the rest area, and none too soon as Steve Otten jumped up and ran down the aisle with Pete right behind him. When the driver opened the doors, the duo sprinted to the men's restroom. The dozen or so empty cans of Coke around their seats explained the reason for such haste.

Upon return to the back of the bus, Pete announced to everyone that Steve now held the new record for the longest urination. So naturally, this remarkable yet dubious distinction became the topic of conversation, especially amongst the younger boys.

Ricky suddenly sat up as the bus turned off Interstate 25 and onto US Highway 26 toward Guernsey. Josh looked at his friend and spotted a few stray sleep line indentions on the boy's face. It made him smile.

"I can't believe that Pete would time someone taking a pee. Isn't that a little odd to anyone?" Ricky asked.

David leaned forward to Ricky and said, "you know those two, they compete against each other over everything, like who can eat the fastest or the most. It is just what they do."

"That might be normal to them, but it is weird to us," remarked Carlos.

Ricky changed the subject by turning his head toward Josh and asking, "what do you think happened to Coach Savolt? Do you think he left town, or something happened to him while he was out on one of his walks?"

Suddenly, everyone seated in the last two rows of the bus turned their attention toward Josh, awaiting his answer. The sudden movement in the back of the bus caught the attention of Coach Fleming. He always preferred to sit sideways in his seat to keep an eye on his team. But, after a moment, the coach dismissed the boys' actions since he assumed that the players were talking about tonight's game, girls, or both.

Josh shrugged. "All I know is that he asked me to help him walk the creek, and now he is gone. But maybe he tripped, fell, and hit his head and didn't wake up?"

Ricky nodded. "Maybe that or he got stuck in that soupy mud along the edge of the creek. Kind of like what happened last year when we pulled that deer out of the bog just below the football field?"

Meanwhile, Steve sighed. "Maybe Coach just quit, but I didn't get the feeling he would do that."

Then Pete suggested, "I think he hooked up with some woman in Casper or somewhere else."

David waved his hands and stopped the conjecture. "All I know is that Coach Savolt wouldn't have quit, and even if he did meet some woman, he would've been at practice last Monday."

Steve added, "well, maybe we should help find out what happened." Then the boy shifted in his seat uncomfortably. "I hope we get to Guernsey soon because I have to pee again!"

"Again?" Ricky questioned.

On the road ahead, the bus rounded a bend in the road, and the North Platte River came back into view and, with it, the town of Guernsey. As if on cue, Chet Harrison inserted a new cassette in the stereo. He aired the Kansas song *"Play the Game Tonight."*

Guernsey was a popular stop for tourists following the famous nineteenth-century pioneer trails along the North Platte River. Nearby stood Register Cliff and wagon ruts carved into stone by tens of thousands of passing wagon wheels. Guernsey was also home to the training center for the Wyoming National Guard. On any given weekend, hundreds of guardsmen infiltrated the town for their obligated drills.

The team arrived two and a half hours ahead of game time as planned, and the bus stopped at a local diner with a large private room in the back already prepared to feed the team. The coaches, cheerleaders, and nearly every reserve player ate hardily, the other players ate lightly. Instead, the starting players focused more on hydrating since the night game would still be hot, even for Labor Day weekend standards.

After dining, the team loaded back up on the bus for the short ride to Guernsey High School. When they reached the facility, the boys exited the bus, grabbed their equipment bags underneath, and followed their coaches into the locker room.

Inside the entrance, banners and flyers that cheered on the hometown Vikings greeted the visiting Oilers. Like most small schools with only two locker rooms, Midwest utilized the Guernsey girls' locker room.

Inside the room, Coach Fleming barked out a warning, "do not touch anything in here other than your clothes, your gear, and your towel. Everything else is off-limits. Above all, be respectful."

The warning was not without merit because two years before, the coach caught Pete LaRouche in Sundance attempting to pull a pair of girl's underwear through a small gap of a locker.

Later, during warm-ups, Carlos Mondragon began throwing passes to the backs and receivers on the field. Then, while waiting their turn to run another route, Josh and Ricky sized up the other team, where over 30 of them were stretching and doing calisthenics.

"They don't look that big. My dad must have been trying to get us to work harder to prepare, that is all," proclaimed Ricky.

Josh nodded. "I agree, they don't look as big as I expected, but...." His remark trailed off as he realized the numbers on the Vikings jerseys were only back and receiver numbers. Just then, the hometown crowd cheered, and twenty more players ran onto the field, all of them were big, and all of them wore traditional lineman numbers.

Ricky turned back to Josh, unfazed, and said, "okay, so they are big, but we are better."

Ricky's statement turned out to be more than just macho bravado. It was a prophetic truth. The game kicked off at 7 p.m. under ideal conditions. Still, after each team had the ball on offense once apiece, the skies turned dark, and a thunderstorm impacted the rest of the first half, with Midwest winning with a score of 8-0.

The second half saw a constant drizzle of rain and steady wind. Though Midwest scored two more touchdowns, its defense prevented the larger Guernsey team from crossing the 50-yard line all game. After each long gain on offense or after each crunching tackle on defense, Oiler players repeated their new mantra to one another *"OFT."*

David led the team in tackles, caused one fumble, which Josh recovered, and opened running lanes for Ricky and Carlos, who scored the teams' touchdowns.

Dr. Gaines, who also attended the game, later reported that the Oilers' impressed some of the partisan home crowd. He recalled overhearing expressions like: "they are not so big, but they are fast and hit hard." To the Oiler players, it was a great compliment.

Following showers and packing up the equipment, the players filed into the bus once again. Before leaving Guernsey, the bus driver pulled over at the convenience store on the edge of town so that the teens could get some snacks and drinks for the long ride home.

Inside the convenience store, Josh turned to Ricky and David while standing at the cashier. Then, he suggested, "tomorrow morning around 10 o'clock, why don't we go down to Salt Creek and begin walking the route that Coach Savolt would have taken?"

David nodded. "I like your idea, and maybe we will find something that will solve this puzzle." Ricky, meanwhile, listened to both of his friends and nodded too in silent agreement.

Once they took their seats on the bus, all talk seemed to suspend for the rest of the trip home. Josh and some other boys took a much-needed nap, while others sat quietly listening to the ever-present music echoing from Chet's seat. His music selection for the ride home included songs from the group Alabama and a few from local legend Chris Ledoux.

* * *

11

Saturday, September 1, 1984

Josh awoke to a strangely quiet house. He slowly rolled out of bed and walked into the kitchen. While he poured a bowl of corn flakes for breakfast, the phone in the kitchen rang. Answering the phone, he said, "hello."

"Hey, son, I just wanted to say hi and to tell you that we received word last night that you guys won your game," Rob Anderson said to his son.

"Hi dad, we played well even though it rained most of the game. The wind was so bad that Guernsey even had a punt that didn't cross their line of scrimmage."

"So, tell me, how did you play? Did you score?"

"Ricky had two touchdowns, and Carlos ran in another off of a triple-option play, but I did catch a two-point conversion. I also recovered a fumble and had five solo tackles on defense." Then he asked his dad, "so how is the volleyball tournament going?"

"We played two games yesterday, won both of them, and we are in the semi-finals against Big Horn this afternoon. If we win, we will face either Kaycee or Sundance in the final. You would be proud of your sister who served up three aces in a row, made two diving saves, and had three spikes in the game against Upton," Rob reported.

Josh smiled and replied, "tell Cindy that I am proud of her and good luck this afternoon and tonight."

"So, what are you going to do today?"

"I will probably just hang out with Ricky and David."

"Okay, but two things: one, the lawn needs mowing, and two, your mother and I expect you to go to church tomorrow even though we are not there. Okay?"

Josh nodded. "Okay, I will, and I will see you tomorrow. Tell Aunt Sue 'hi 'for me," offered Josh.

"I will. Goodbye, Son."

"Bye Dad," Josh said and hung up the phone. Then he picked up his bowl of cereal and walked to the couch to watch television while he ate.

No sooner had he sat down when the phone rang again. Josh sighed loudly. Then he set his bowl on the coffee table and trotted back into the kitchen to answer the phone hanging on the kitchen wall.

After snatching the receiver off of the cradle, he said, "yes, dad?"

"I'm not your dad rube," and Josh suddenly recognized David's voice on the line.

"Oh, hey David, what's up?"

"Do you still want to take that walk today?".

Josh emphatically replied, "absolutely, but I have to mow the lawn first, so how about I grab Ricky and meet you at your house at 11:00 this morning?"

"Cool, I will see you then."

After hanging up with David, Josh called Ricky's house and relayed the plans. Josh now stared at his bowl of unappetizing corn mush and decided to throw it out and make a new bowl.

Josh did as his father instructed by mowing the lawn, which took him until 10:30. Then, he went into the house, changed into his cowboy boots, retrieved his Winchester pump-action .22 rifle from the closet, and placed it on his bed. Josh nearly always carried the gun with him in the oilfield because it was frequent to encounter rattlesnakes. He hated them most of all creatures. Like Josh, almost every golfer in the area took a loaded rifle in their golf bag when playing on the sand green Salt Creek Country Club on the edge of town. It was common for golfers to encounter the serpents sunning themselves on the greens or in the shadows of the tee boxes.

Minutes later, Josh drove a few houses down Navy Row and watched Ricky come out of his house and take his usual place in the passenger seat. The boys then went down to David's house to find him waiting on the front porch. As David rose from the porch, the boys noticed a Ruger Blackhawk .45 caliber pistol sitting snuggly in a western-style holster on his hip. Then, without a word, David climbed into the backseat.

"Hey John Wayne, are we ready to chase after them rustlers," chided Ricky about David's pistol.

In his best John Wayne impersonation, David replied, "well, ah, we will get after them rustlers right after I round up your mom pilgrim."

Josh turned and looked at David in the backseat. His friend reacted by holding up both hands and defending himself when he said, "what? Is it too early for a mom joke?"

Josh grinned and looked over at Ricky in the passenger seat. "That was a good one, huh?"

However, Ricky didn't find the joke funny. Though, in truth, the boy rarely passed up the opportunity to pick on someone with a mom joke of his own.

David then reached up from the back seat and playfully smacked Ricky on the back of the head. "I'm sorry, momma's boy." Then he asked his friend, "where is your gun?"

Ricky turned in his seat. "What am I supposed to bring, my BB gun? You both know that my mom won't let any real guns into the house."

As they approached the outskirts of Edgerton, Josh drove past the grocery store and then down the dirt road to the bottom of the hill that placed them a short distance from the creek. Josh grabbed his .22 rifle and exited the car, followed by David and Ricky. Next, he pumped the action of his rifle and loaded a live round into the chamber. Then led the other boys down to the start of the path that he'd walked before with Tim Savolt. When they reached the stream, it didn't take long before the boys picked up the distinctive footprints of a pair of cowboy boots, just like the teacher wore.

Josh said, "one good thing about not having any rain is that we can still see Coach Savolt's tracks, and I would bet that if we follow them, then we can see where the tracks stopped."

Ricky grunted, "well, let's hope that he didn't walk to the Powder River because it is already getting hot out here."

Josh ignored Ricky's remark and continued down the path. From David's vantage point behind Josh, he too could discern between the recent and the old tracks. The boys even found one spot where Savolt's knee made an impression in the ground where he had knelt to take water samples in at least two places. Also plainly visible on the trail were wildlife tracks of rabbit, coyote, deer, and antelope dispersed amongst the remnant boot heel impressions of Savolt's.

Meanwhile, Josh patiently and continuously trudged ahead and looked for even the slightest change in the trail. Notwithstanding, David and Ricky felt as though they were just along for the ride. So, they shifted their attention from the path to the landscape around them. At one point, David stopped on the trail to pick something up at his feet when Ricky, who wasn't paying attention, walked directly into and knocked him to the ground.

"Hey, watch where you are going, you moron!" exclaimed David.

Ricky stammered a reply, "what do you mean, watch where I am going? I think you need a set of brake lights on that big butt of yours to let someone know you are stopping."

David started to laugh, and as he rolled back up onto his hands and knees, and he saw something peculiar sticking out of the gray soil. He reached out and grabbed the object and pulled gently to retrieve a nearly perfect arrowhead.

"This is why I stopped, dork," he said while holding up the point in front of his friend's face.

Overhearing the commotion behind him, Josh doubled back on his steps and spotted the object in David's hand. Then he said, "hey, let me see that."

The arrowhead was nearly perfect with just a tiny piece of the tip broken off, but if affixed onto an arrow shaft, the point was still sharp enough to do its job.

As Josh held it up, Ricky looked at the point and then asked, "what tribe do you think this came from?"

David shrugged. "I like to read stuff about Native Americans. From what I remember, the Arapahoe, the Shoshone, the Crow, and even the Sioux claimed this area as hunting grounds. So, take your pick as to who made this arrowhead."

"It is too bad that we can't take this to Coach Savolt for him to look at it. I am sure he would have been interested in it, too," suggested Ricky.

As the boys trekked further, they kept their eyes concentrated on the trail for the teacher's tracks and any other artifacts they could find. Finally, still leading the way, Josh rounded around a sizeable red ant mound and pointed it out to David immediately behind him.

Suddenly, Ricky called out, "Hey guys, come back here and check this out."

Josh turned and looked at David, and they walked back to where Ricky was squatting near the anthill as he picked up what appeared to be tiny flat slivers of rock. When Ricky saw his friends approach, he stood up and held out his hand holding the objects.

He then said, "right after we moved on from the arrowhead, I got to thinking about something Coach Savolt told me in class last year. He insisted that you will find fossilized shark's teeth if you look into the spoils of ant hills in this area. So now, look at these," while holding his hand open for the other boys to see.

"Wow, these do look like shark teeth, but just smaller!" exclaimed David.

Josh inspected the tiny shards and nodded in agreement that they were fossilized shark teeth. Josh then uttered the word: "amazing."

Ricky asked, "what is so amazing?"

Josh chuckled. "I am amazed that you paid attention long enough in science class to remember anything, considering that you sat next to Sheila. She can't stand it if your attention is on anything else but her at every moment."

David laughed so hard he started coughing, but Ricky's face turned a shade of red, not in rage, but embarrassment because it was true.

Then he offered in consolation, "it's okay, man, we were just poking fun, no harm meant by it."

Resigned, Ricky said, "I guess it is funny from your perspective only."

"Tell you what, I will lay off of Sheila just as soon as I get off of your mom," joked David.

Ricky spun around and put a faux headlock on David in a half gesture wrestling spar, and as soon as it started, the jokes ended, and the boys continued on their walk.

As the boys reached the Highway 259 bridge spanning the Salt Creek, David suggested they walk back to his house to get something to drink and then go back for Josh's car. Though comforted that they failed to find Coach Savolt's body on the trail, Josh couldn't shake his innate concern for his missing teacher, coach, and friend.

The boys quickly walked under the bridge and up the northern bank and across the open field toward Teacher's Row on the eastern edge of Midwest. By that time, the wind had started to blow into a light breeze in Wyoming standards. Though the same 20-mile per hour wind was considered a gale anywhere else in the county. Just then, several pieces of paper caught by the breeze captured the boys' attention. Ricky looked westward and traced one leaflet coming from the lidless trash can behind Mr. Pierson's house.

"Start grabbing those papers, will ya," barked out David, and on cue, the other two complied.

While bending over to pick up a page, Ricky grumbled, "you would think that they would pay attention to putting a lid on their trash. We always put a rock on our lids at home."

But then, just as Josh reached down to pick up a piece of paper, he noted a peculiar design on it. As he drew it closer, he saw the sheet had a single green leaf printed on it with the word *LEAF* in the center, and at the bottom had the words:

Next meeting, Thursday, September 13
307 East 2nd Street in Casper

The wind gusted again, and another piece of paper stuck on the leg of Josh's jeans, so he quickly folded the paper he held and placed it in his back pocket. Meanwhile, all three boys darted back and forth in the open field, collecting all the loose items they could. Then, as the boys approached Pierson's trash cans, Doug Pierson bounded out the back door himself and trotted to the back fence.

"What are you kids doing going through my trash?" Pierson demanded.

Josh spoke up, "hey, Mr. Pierson, we saw all of these papers from your trash can blowing across the field and thought we would clean them up for you."

Pierson grimaced. "It looked to me from the kitchen window that you boys were rifling through my trash."

Ricky shook his head. "Honestly, Mr. Pierson, these papers were blowing out of your trash can. Maybe you could put a rock on the lid just like we do to keep the wind from blowing it off."

"Thanks, I take that as advice from a future trash collector," Pierson snickered. Then the man asked, "just what are you miscreants up to anyway with those guns you are carrying?"

Josh looked down at the weapon in his hand and shrugged. Then he curtly replied, "we were just out walking along the creek."

Pierson huffed and asked, "why would you do that?"

"Because we want to, Sir, it is our right and freedom to do so," argued David.

The discourse only infuriated Rob Pierson further, and all he managed only to say was, "just put those papers back in the trash can and go away!"

The boys did as the teacher requested and placed all their collected trash back into the trash can without a word. After that, David put the lid on top, and Ricky set a fractured chunk of cinderblock on the cover for good measure.

They walked in silence down Lewis Street and then turned left down the alley separating the school cafeteria from the first house beyond the school. Only then did the boys speak.

"What a douchebag!" exclaimed Ricky.

David said, "you got that right, I mean, we pick up his mess, and he treats us like we are scumbags."

Ricky inquired to the others, "did you guys happen to see what was on those papers? From what I saw, it was some crap about saving the planet, planting more trees, and saving the whales."

David shook his head. "Nah, I didn't see anything like that. The papers I collected looked like old tests and quizzes from English class that Mrs. Pierson was probably throwing out."

Josh suddenly realized that he still had the first piece of paper, which remained folded and tucked safely away in his back pocket. So he reached into his back pocket and unfolded the piece of paper.

Then he said to his friends, "I almost forgot; I picked this up first and put it in my back pocket. I looked at it for only a second, but I wonder what it means?"

The boys stopped outside the old tennis court, and each took a turn looking at the apparent meeting flier that Josh filched. Then, when neither boy could make anything more out of the leaflet than Josh could, the group resumed their short walk to David's house.

Later, while Ricky and Josh sat on the front porch in the shade, David emerged from his house with three cans of pop and the keys to his mother's car. He suggested that they go and retrieve Josh's car outside of Edgerton instead of retracing the way on foot.

David then added, "I called Steve, and I will pick him and Pete up after I drop the two of you off." He then looked at Josh and said, "I think that if you and Ricky drive over to the bridge off Highway 387 northwest of town and start walking upstream, me, Steve, and Pete will work our way downstream to meet you."

Josh nodded. "That would save a lot of time, good idea."

Ricky offered, "and then after we finish, how about we all come back here tonight to watch the game film? And maybe we could go over to the store and get some frozen pizzas too?"

David looked at Josh, and the two boys shrugged their shoulders and said, "okay."

* * *

12

A few blocks away, Chief of Police Traynor watched a college football game on television while relaxing on his couch. He loved football season and couldn't get enough of the sport, whether watching high school, college, or professional games. But then his phone rang.

He picked up the receiver and greeted the caller. "Hello, this is Chief Traynor."

"Just what kind of hillbilly hell do you oversee here that it is allowable for delinquents to walk around the streets with firearms, Chief?" the caller asked.

"Excuse me, but I didn't catch your name; who is this calling?" Chief Traynor requested.

"This is Rob Pierson over on Teacher's Row, and I just saw David Proctor, Ricky Fleming, and Josh Anderson messing around my trash cans."

"Well, Rob, may I call you Rob?" Chief Traynor asked, to which Rob Pierson cut him off by saying, "no, you may not Wyatt, you may call me Mr. Pierson in deference to my position at the school."

"Okay, I will call you Mr. Pierson, and you may address me as Chief Traynor in deference to me being the senior law enforcement officer in this community. Now that is settled, what is your complaint again about these boys?"

"I just saw Ricky Fleming, David Proctor, and Josh Anderson messing around my trash cans. David was wearing a pistol, and Josh was carrying a high-power rifle, and though I didn't see a gun on Ricky, I am sure that he had one hidden on him somewhere too. So, Wya..., I mean Chief Traynor, what are you going to do about it?'

"Mr. Pierson, I'm not sure that there is anything to do about it. Did you see them commit a crime?"

"No, but they are walking around armed, and if that isn't a crime, it should be. Is Wyoming so uncivilized that it can't apply a simple moral code of decency of keeping guns off the streets?"

Chief Traynor paused momentarily and let out a huge sigh, then asked, "Mr. Pierson, you said the boys were messing around your trash cans. What were you trying to tell me?

"I saw them holding papers that they claimed were blowing out of my trash can. I asked them what they were doing, and they gave me some lame excuse that they were cleaning up the vacant lot. They also said that they had been down by the creek, which I also find highly suspect."

"Well, Mr. Pierson, there are a couple of things here that I need to tell you. First, I know those boys, and every one of them is a good kid. Secondly, carrying a firearm is not illegal, and if the boys went down along the creek to just shoot or even hunt a few rabbits, then they are within the law to do so."

"While you think they are good kids, however, I get to see them at school every day, and I find them all just a notch above reprobates. Don't you or their parents understand that guns kill people?"

"Mr. Pierson, guns don't just magically go off and kill people indiscriminately. Rather it is people killing people and not the gun."

Rob Pierson started to object further when Chief Traynor cut him off. "I know those boys come from good families, and I had all three boys in my hunter's safety class last year, and they demonstrated to me the proper handling of firearms."

Chief Traynor paused briefly and then added, "and, one more thing, Mr. Pierson, regarding the trash can, I suggest you place a rock on top of your trash can lid to keep the wind from blowing it off."

Traynor then waited for a response from Mr. Pierson, to which there wasn't one, so he hung up the phone.

As planned, David dropped off Ricky and Josh at his car near Edgerton, and then he picked up both Steve and Pete. Meanwhile, Josh and Ricky drove back toward Midwest. They then turned right at the junction to continue on Highway 387 toward the bridge northwest of town.

About a hundred yards shy of the overpass, Josh turned off the highway and onto another oilfield road that led them to an operating pump jack just yards away from the creek. Josh parked his car alongside the pump, and the boys exited the vehicle. From there, Josh and Ricky walked down toward the waters' edge. They immediately picked up the same tracks left by Tim Savolt further upstream.

Then Josh looked at Ricky and asked, "instead of walking back toward David and the others, why don't we continue following these tracks heading north along the creek?"

"That'll work," offered Ricky.

The pair followed the trail up to the bridge, ascended the berm, walked across the blacktop, and descended the other side. The boys, however, did not find any boot tracks on the other side.

Finally, Ricky suggested, "why don't we go back up and cross over the bridge. I bet Coach Savolt crossed to the other side of the creek here since greasewood and willows have choked this side."

Josh nodded. "Good idea."

The boys quickly crossed over the bridge and continued their search on the other side. Immediately, Ricky's intuition paid off as Savolt's boot tracks could be seen again, and the boys followed them along the creek's edge. They diligently followed the remnants of Tim Savolt's boot prints for about half an hour until, as Josh observed, that the footprints seemed to double back upon themselves.

Josh waved at Ricky. "Over here, I think Coach Savolt went further downstream and then walked back over his tracks."

Ricky looked down and agreed with Josh's assertion, "yup, that is what it looks like." Then he added, "how about we turn around carefully and let's see where the return track takes us?"

The boys tracked another 20 yards, but the trail suddenly veered away from the Salt Creek to the west. However, when Josh rounded a shoulder-high clump of greasewood, he saw something out of place in the smaller sagebrush. Then he reached down to retrieve it.

"Whatcha got there Josh?"

He stood up and looked at his friend. "I think it is Coach Savolt's field book?"

They squatted in the shade greasewood and began pouring over the notebook. It contained many field notes, though some annotations appeared as if in code. Plus, the booklet included acronyms unknown to the boys. Finally, Josh flipped to the last entry bookmarked by two microscope slides bound together with a rubber band. He then raised the small glass plates, and both boys saw a noticeable dark green smudge in the center. Josh re-opened the notebook and then showed his friend the annotation left by Savolt. It read:

Location #24- H2O temperature still hot and obtained another sample of the specimen- I can now finish my research

"Josh, what is that stuff on the slide?"

"I dunno, but I think we need to study the whole notebook for it all to make some sense. Why don't we get back to town and find David and the others and look over what we found?"

Ricky suddenly stood up. "No arguments from me; I'm still spent from last night's game and am ready to sit and do absolutely nothing."

The boys soon abandoned the foot trail along Salt Creek. Instead, they decided to walk along the more direct route along the bottom of the hillside that eventually emptied into a wide flood plain.

With Ricky in the lead, Josh abruptly whispered, "do you see that dark green pickup on the other side of the creek?"

The boy reacted by turning his head ever so slightly and then he replied, "I see him."

"Do you know who they are?"

Ricky shook his head. "No, but how about we find out?"

The boys stopped, turned, and watched the pickup drive slowly along a path about 100 yards away. Though they could see two people in the cab, the distance prevented them from recognizing the truck's occupants. As the boys continued to watch, the driver suddenly turned the truck to the east toward Light Plant Road.

After a few minutes, Ricky asked, "I wonder what they wanted? Have you ever seen that Ford before?"

Josh shook his head. But in a moment of sudden clarity, he pointed toward the truck and said, "that is the same truck I told you about that barreled down the alley like an idiot."

Ricky shrugged. "Whoever they are, they creep me out."

Within seconds, the skies darkened, and thunder erupted in the distance. Ricky pointed to the sky, which Josh followed his finger. The friends exchanged a quick look, and then began a quick dash up and over the berm of the bridge, over its span, and down on the other side toward Josh's car.

Inside the dark green Ford, as it sped away from the eastern side of the creek.

The passenger looked toward the driver and asked, "I don't get it; why are we out here and fully exposed?"

The driver gave his partner a stern look. "They hired us to do a job. It includes making sure nobody finds out what happened to the teacher or where his body is hidden. I predict that these rubes up here will get spooked and stop looking if they view us as a threat. I mean, come on, these are just stupid oilfield kids and town cops we are dealing with here."

"That is what I don't get; I mean, we are in the open?" the passenger asked.

In a sharp rebuke, the driver chastened his partner, "we are under orders from the boss to finish this job. So now, unless you want to become disappeared, I suggest you buck up like the trooper I know you to be."

As lightning began to crash around them, Josh and Ricky sprinted across the open field to Josh's car. As they closed each car door, the clouds opened up, and rain fell upon the parched ground like a garden hose pouring onto dry concrete.

Within minutes, Josh maneuvered his car back up onto the highway and then turned right onto Fitzhugh Road that brought them back into the west side of town. The rain was still coming down in sheets when he turned off of Fitzhugh and onto Stock, where he instantly spotted David, Steve, and Pete jogging along the street. He quickly pulled over and loaded his friends into the car.

"Where is your car?" Josh asked as he looked at David in the rearview mirror.

"We decided to leave it at my house and walk down to the creek by the football field to see if we could pick up Savolt's tracks, which we did."

"How far did you get?"

"We made it as far as to the bottom of M-Hill when we saw the thunderstorm brewing, so we got out of there as fast as we could."

But when Josh turned off the street to park, he spied Chief Traynor's Ford Bronco sitting next to David's mom's car. Additionally, the Chief stood on the porch and waited for the boys to get under cover before he spoke.

"Hey boys, I heard the news about your football game last night, great job. He paused for a few seconds and then asked, "what have you boys been up to today?"

Josh spoke up first. "We've been walking along the creek," though he parsed his words carefully because he didn't know if what he and his friends were doing was wrong or not.

Chief Traynor then asked, "did you boys find anything unusual?"

David stepped forward and said, "Here, take a look at this arrowhead we found," and placed the artifact in the palm of the police chief. Then, taking David's cue, Ricky retrieved the handful of shark's teeth and said, "we found these as well."

Traynor examined the pieces in his hand and said, "these are good finds, boys." As he handed back the items to David and Ricky, he got down to the purpose of his visit. "Boys, I received a call from a concerned citizen that you were running around town, and I quote, 'heavily armed.' Now, I see that you have a sidearm on you, David, are any of the rest of you carrying weapons too?"

Ricky, Steve, and Pete shook their heads no, but Josh answered, "yes Sir, my .22 rifle is unloaded and is in the trunk of my car. Would you like to see it?"

The Chief thought about it for a few seconds and then said "no," but then asked David, "mind if I have a look at your pistol?"

To which the boy promptly handed over to him butt first. Traynor looked over the piece and inspected the cartridges, and counted them.

"David, I appreciate your loading only five bullets and leaving the hammer on an empty cylinder."

"Thank you, sir, but I just did what you taught us last year in firearms safety class."

Chief Traynor then replied, "can I ask all of you boys another question?" The boys nodded affirmatively. Then he continued, "what were you doing in the field behind Teacher's Row today?"

Josh answered, "we were walking up from Salt Creek and heading here to get something to drink when we saw that the wind was blowing a ton of trash out of Pierson's trash can."

David stepped forward and interrupted and said, "ya, we gathered everything up and put it back in their trash can, and Mr. Pierson came out of his house and started yelling at us. But, Chief, all we did was pick up his trash, and instead of saying thank you, he gave us crap for his own mistake."

"I see, well…. okay then, boys, I will let you get back to whatever your plans were, and please, say hi to your parents for me."

As he reached the door of his department vehicle, Chief Traynor called out to the boys, "good luck this season. You know, I watch every football practice of yours from the top of the cliff. I think you boys have the makings of an exceptional team."

* * *

13

After Chief Traynor left the Proctor residence, he turned onto Lewis Street instead of returning home. He knew that Rob Pierson had wholly misrepresented the situation with the boys concerning his trash cans. However, he was completely satisfied that the boys were not up to ill will, especially after his talk with them. Nevertheless, to be sure, Traynor thought it would be a good idea to look around the field behind Rob Pierson's trash cans to check out their story.

After he parked his Bronco behind the Pierson home on Teachers Row, Traynor stepped out of his rig and walked over to the trash cans and removed the piece of cinder block that held down the lid, and looked inside. What he found was as he had expected: hundreds of sheets of paper and bits of grass that must have come from the field where the boys picked it all up. Traynor then replaced the lid and walked due east into the open area.

About 20 yards from his vehicle, he spied a wadded piece of paper stuck in some knee-high grass, so he bent over and picked it up.

After he carefully opened the paper, it revealed the word *LEAF* in gold lettering printed in the center of a green symbol that resembled the shape of an aspen leaf. Underneath the tree leaf were the words:

Next meeting, Thursday, September 13, 7:00 p.m.
Natrona County Public Library
307 East 2nd Street in Casper

Traynor pocketed the notice and looked across the field again for any other trash. After finding none, he turned back toward his truck. However, as the Chief approached his vehicle, he found Rob Pierson standing next to his back fence.

"I am glad to see my tax dollars at work by you helping to clean up this town," the teacher snickered.

Traynor shook his head at the remark. "Well, Mr. Pierson, there's the problem, isn't it?"

Pierson furrowed his brow. "What problem are you referring to, Chief?"

"The problem is that you are not, in fact, a 'taxpayer' that pays my salary. I know that you rent your house from the school district, so how is it then that your non-existent property taxes pay for the police department?"

"It is a figure of speech," Pierson said as he threw his hands up in a what can I do manner.

Traynor's face suddenly hardened. "Mr. Pierson, I looked into your complaint against those boys you mentioned. It turns out that none of them violated anything by carrying firearms. You see, Wyoming is an open-carry state, after all. The high-power rifle was nothing more than a .22 caliber used to hunt small game or target shooting. Furthermore, I find it comforting that those boys were courteous enough to pick up your mess without anyone asking them to do it. Maybe next time, you should thank them."

Pierson's face quickly narrowed into a viperlike point. Then he hissed, "those boys and every other child in this town get my appreciation every single day. They get it by my willingness to provide them with the only quality education that they will ever receive out here in Hicksville, U.S.A."

"Well, that may be true, Mr. Pierson, but I think you are barking up the wrong tree with those boys. I mean, two of those boys have fathers that are colleagues of yours?"

"Don't be serious; you cannot put me in the same category as a couple of coaches."

"Well, Sir, that is for you to consider, but I must be going. Have a good day," Chief Traynor said in resignation.

He turned and then entered his Bronco to drive back to his office. Once there, he annotated Rob Pierson's complaint, the investigation, and the resolution in the department logbook.

Meanwhile, at the Proctor house, David already changed into dry clothes and had loaned Steve and Pete some of his t-shirts and sweatpants. They all noticed that Pete looked like a little kid playing dress-up since he wore a t-shirt and sweat pants three sizes too big for him.

Seated on the couch in the basement, Josh asked David, "did you guys find anything along the creek?"

"Nope, just a set of footprints that continued to head in your direction."

Steve then interjected, "tell them about the MERP guy."

David replied, "we were walking along where the creek gets close to the road when a guy in a MERP truck pulls up and tells us that we shouldn't be messing around in the oilfield. The weird thing is that I know most of the guys that work for MERP since my dad does, but I haven't seen this guy before."

Ricky asked, "so what did you guys do?"

"Nothing, we walked back up on the road until the truck turned south and went over the bridge toward Gas Plant. Once he was out of sight, we went back down along the creek," Pete explained.

Steve then asked Josh, "did you guys see anything?"

Josh and Ricky recalled where they parked and how they thought the same thing that David did by looking for Savolt's tracks heading downstream. They explained that they found a place where Savolt's footprints had doubled back on themselves and then told them about finding the notebook. Finally, they also described that they were going to follow the footprints going the other direction. But the thunderstorm forced them to run for the car.

David nodded. "I bet those tracks are long gone now with all this rain....so let's see this notebook."

Josh rolled his body over to one side and pulled the notebook out of his back pocket. Then he handed it over so the other boys could examine it. As the boys poured over each page, Josh sat back and began to think about what their next move should be. Then, the telephone rang, and someone upstairs answered it.

David looked up from the pages and asked, "so what is this thing wedged here in the last entry?" as he held up the bounded microscope slides.

Josh shrugged. "I don't know what that is, but my guess is it's a sample of something he found growing in the water. Other than that, I don't know."

"It looks like a grease smudge to me, or it is a sample of a turd," Pete stated, which instigated a round of laughter from the others. However, the boy thought he offered valuable input.

"Josh, why didn't you tell Chief Traynor about this notebook when he was here? David asked.

Once again, Josh shrugged. "I thought about it, but we don't know yet if this has anything to do with why Coach disappeared. But then again, if I had handed this over to the Chief, I don't think we would ever find out more about the study."

Steve asked, "but, Josh, you went with him a few times, didn't coach say anything to you during those times?"

"No, all he said is that he was conducting a study, which I naturally assumed had to do with the water quality of the creek. This inquiry is probably the thing that has so many MERP folks upset considering that the company could be held responsible for any pollution."

Though inside his mind, Josh felt terrible that he wasn't more forthcoming with Chief Traynor and his omission began to tug on his conscience.

All conversations abruptly stopped when Toni Proctor called downstairs from the kitchen. She informed Pete that his mother had called and wanted him to return home to watch his little brother while she went to work at the bowling alley.

Then Ricky bounded to his feet and asked to borrow Josh's car to give Pete a ride home, justifying that he could also swing by his house and pick up the game tape from the last night. In response, Josh dug out his car keys and handed them over with an ample measure of trust.

On the other side of town, Chief Traynor was about to leave his office when a thought occurred to him. He walked back over to his desk, and he called the Natrona County Sheriff Deputy assigned to assist with the Tim Savolt case. Unfortunately, the Deputy revealed that he hadn't received any additional information on Savolt's whereabouts.

Traynor hung up the phone and then decided to call his friend, Ken Hopkins, at his home in Cheyenne. Agent Hopkins worked for the Wyoming Department of Criminal Investigations. The two of them had met years ago when they attended the state law enforcement academy together in Douglas. They have remained good friends ever since.

When the call went through, Traynor said, "hey, Hop, it is Wyatt."

"I thought it was you. I could smell the oilfield coming through the phone," Hopkins said with a belly laugh. Then asked, "to what do I owe this pleasure of your call, Wyatt?"

"I need a favor, Hop."

"Sure thing, what can I do?"

"I need you to help me locate a teacher that has gone missing up here in Midwest."

"Wow, I didn't know about this.... either Natrona County is tight-lipped about it, or they don't have much to go on to feel the need to involve us here at the state level."

"That is why I am calling you Hop. The consensus in the county is that Savolt just walked away from his life. Still, my hunch is the opposite because this guy is so ingrained with the kids from coaching football and teaching. Also, I found no evidence of foul play when I entered his apartment on a welfare check. I mean, everything I found was neat, tidy, and in its appropriate place as if he was returning right away."

"I think you might be onto something, Wyatt, but I have seen cases where someone just didn't come home. Was there any other evidence to support your hunch?"

"Yes, shortly after the welfare check, this guy's apartment got tossed."

"Well, that would get me to thinking too. But, did this guy have any enemies to speak of?"

"Enemies? No. But some of the oilfield workers here have openly grumbled about a field study that the teacher was conducting, so maybe somebody was motivated by the fear of what he might publish?"

"Wait a second. This teacher wouldn't happen to be the same guy that found some rare insect near Casper? I heard the oilfield was closed because the area became a protected habitat."

"It was a mouse, actually, but yes, it is the same guy. So, in truth, all Savolt did was make the discovery and then reported it to the feds."

"Well then, if I were in your shoes, I would look around and see if any of the workers up there took matters beyond just a simple disagreement."

Traynor nodded in agreement. "Thanks, Hop, that was just what I was thinking too."

"I tell you what, Wyatt, give me his name, and I will run it across the wires to Colorado and Nebraska to see if we get a hit on his whereabouts."

"Great, his name is Timothy Savolt. The last name spelled 'S-A-V-O-L-T,' but I would also include Montana because Savolt graduated from Montana State.

"Okay, I will get back to you when I find something."

"Thanks again, Hop. I owe you one!"

"You owe me many, so I will just add this to your growing list, Wyatt."

Chief Traynor hung up the phone, rose from his desk, and left his office for home.

* * *

14

Sunday, September 2, 1984

#6 Navy Row, Midwest, Wyoming

Josh awoke again to a strangely quiet house absent the ever-present clinking of his father's coffee cup. As he rolled over onto his side, his stomach started to hurt a little. Perhaps it was due to overeating on the frozen pizzas the night before, since David's mother insisted the boys eat more than a fair share.

While he stared at his bedroom wall, Josh started to put together the other events of the last evening. First, they watched their game film from the previous Friday. But, when Ricky returned to David's house, Sheila was with him too. Soon afterward, two of Sheila's friends, Dana Barber and Tammy Winslow, arrived.

At first, the group dynamics were acceptable while watching the game film since the boys were engrossed in critiquing their play. But, as soon as the game film ended and a movie started playing, the dynamic changed. David became engaged in Tammy. Likewise, Steve and Dana snuggled up together, and Sheila and Ricky already existed in their reality. Rather than being a third wheel, Josh said goodnight and went home.

Josh got out of bed and retrieved the Sunday copy of The Star-Tribune off of the front porch. He sat down in his father's chair and quickly removed the sports section. The University of Wyoming football team dominated the sports headline with the Cowboys defeat of South Dakota 31-13 in Laramie.

He skipped to the next page that provided coverage and write-ups of most high school football games. He then read about his Oilers' defeat of Guernsey the previous Friday and read a preview of their upcoming matchup against their rival Big Horn. Additionally, Josh read an article about the Denver Broncos season opener against Cincinnati later that afternoon. Josh rarely, if ever, missed a game on television.

After breakfast, Josh got dressed for church and walked down the street to assist in setting up. As the service started, he noted the number of empty seats since only nine people were in attendance. Pastor Roberts pointed out the sparseness of the congregation as well. However, the Minister excused the absence of many since it was Labor Day weekend, which marked the last weekend of the summer.

The comment made Josh think about how September snow was not unexpected, either. Instead, it was a norm throughout the State. Early snows melted just as quickly as they accumulated. As a result, fall was as spectacular as it was brief in Midwest, with warm days and cold nights. By Halloween, parents would have to figure out costumes that fit over a down coat, hat, and gloves for their trick-or-treaters.

Pastor Roberts finalized his message about seeking God. He emphasized that the more one pursued God, the greater the number of blessings would come as a result. The pastor used several biblical scriptures to make his point, but one stuck out to Josh in the Gospel of John: *Then you will know the truth, and the truth will set you free.*

The last passage caused Josh's thoughts to drift toward the disappearance of Tim Savolt and then about the teacher's quest for truth in his field study. Finally, he looked out of the window next to the seat in the rear of the church and said to himself, *"perhaps seeking the truth of the study will also find the reason he disappeared."*

As he walked home after church, Josh thought about driving back out to where he and Ricky found the notebook the day before. Still, with the rain yesterday, all the roads in the oilfield would have turned into a soupy mess. Josh felt a slight chill in the air, and it seemed to him that yesterday's rain brought in a weather front that dropped the temperature 20 degrees. In truth though, the boy secretly loved this time of year and wished the weather stayed at this temperature year-round, minus the low seated clouds.

After lunch, Carlos called Josh on the phone. He asked if it would be okay to come over to watch the Bronco game that started at 2:00 p.m. since they didn't have clear television reception out on the ranch. Josh told him it was okay if he wanted to come over, and in truth, Josh welcomed the company because he would typically watch the game with his father. His other friends, i.e., Ricky, would be with his girlfriend, and David often worked in the MERP shop on Sundays to fix truck tires.

After changing out of his church clothes, Josh sat on the couch and began pouring over Savolt's notebook. Soon, he was able to make sense of Savolt's entries and the underlying context. He set the notebook aside and started retracing the teacher's route in his mind. Then he could pictured each place where Savolt his samples. Then an idea flooded his brain and he opened his eyes.

He picked up the field notes again and turned to the last entry, and there it was: the final location wasn't a sample after all. Instead, it identified something that Savolt called a *specimen*.

Josh left the couch and went into his room to retrieve a blank spiral notebook. Upon returning to the couch, he began copying Savolt's notes. But, at two other places in the field book, Josh noticed the word *specimen* too. So, he went back to the very first entry of the unique usage of that word. He found it logged under the previous January notes. It read:

I saw steam rising out of the bank above the creek and found a pool of collected water. About 4" below the surface, I found a type of algae growing on the sides and bottom. I obtained a specimen to test later

Next to the second entry for specimen, Josh saw a curious name scribbled in the margin. It read *T. Brock,* and he noted the person's name in his notebook. Once all of the relevant parts were copied, the boy determined that it was the right thing to do by turning over Savolt's field notes to Chief Traynor. Then he would have to disclose where he and Ricky discovered it.

He looked up at the clock, which read 12:45, and surmised that it was enough time to walk over to Traynor's house on Peake Street to give him the notebook and return home in time for the football game.

Chief Traynor was washing dishes in the kitchen when heard the doorbell ring. Then he walked through the house and found Josh standing on his porch.

"Good afternoon, Josh. Is everything alright?"

Flummoxed momentarily, Josh didn't know what to say. He knew that his conscience couldn't withstand another day of withholding information to Chief Traynor about the notebook he found.

Josh looked down at his shoes and inhaled deeply, and he lifted his head and said, "Chief, I found something along the creek that might be a clue to Coach Savolt's disappearance."

Chief Traynor's face hardened a little but invited the boy into the living room, nonetheless.

Once they seated themselves on the couch, Traynor asked, "what is it you want to show me?"

The boy pulled the small green notebook out of his back pocket and handed it over to the Chief without a word. Confused, Traynor didn't know what to say initially, so instead sat back in his seat and quickly scanned the pages of the notebook.

"What exactly is this you are giving me?"

"This is Coach Savolt's field book that he made notes about his current study."

"Where did you find it exactly?"

"Ricky and I were about 1/2 of a mile north of Highway 387 bridge on the west side of Salt Creek; I can show you where if you like?"

The Chief looked deeply into Josh's face and then replied, "I would appreciate that. But it is too muddy today. Are you doing anything tomorrow since it is a holiday?"

"Yes, sir, I can do that, and I will bring Ricky too since he was with me when I found it."

"Great, why don't the two of you walk across the lot from your houses to my office at 10:00 tomorrow morning, and you both can show me where you found this book."

Josh nodded in agreement.

Then Traynor thumbed through the book once more and found the microscope slides with a dark blot of an unknown substance pressed between them.

He held it up toward Josh and asked, "what is this?"

"I don't know, Sir? I think it is some kind of sample that Coach took."

Traynor now sat back and rubbed his eyes with the palms of both hands, then sat forward and addressed the boy once again.

"Why didn't you tell me about this yesterday?"

Josh knew the question would come eventually, but he determined that truth would relieve the guilt he had felt ever since their meeting the day before.

"I'm sorry, Sir, but I wanted to look at the book on my own. I needed to get a hint as to what Coach was up to with the study. I admit my omission of not telling you about this clue, but I justified my action because Coach Savolt was more than a teacher or a coach to me. He was my friend too. So, again, I just wanted more time to look for something or anything that could explain what happened to him."

Chief Traynor's face softened, and he relaxed back into his seat. "I appreciate your honesty even if it is a day late. I also appreciate that you want to find out what happened to Mr. Savolt." Traynor observed Josh's appearance and knew that the boy indeed regretted the omission.

The Chief then added, "I tell you what, Josh, since you and Ricky will take me out there to the location tomorrow, I will keep your omission between the two of us. You have my word."

Relieved, Josh said, "thank you, Sir," and then asked, "Sir, would it be okay if I bring my .22 rifle with me?"

"What for?"

"I don't like snakes, and I rarely go anywhere along the creek without my gun."

Chief Traynor cracked a smile and said, "Okay, son, you can bring it."

After leaving Traynor's residence, Josh then walked over to Sheila's house on Peake Street. As he anticipated, Ricky's car was parked out front. He opened the gate on the fence and then knocked on the front door. A few seconds later, Sheila answered it. When Josh asked to speak to Ricky, she immediately demanded to know why? Before he could say anything in reply, Ricky came to the door and stepped out onto the porch.

"What's up, dude?"

"I just turned over the notebook we found to Chief Traynor."

"You did what? What did you do that for?"

"I got to thinking about Savolt's disappearance and that notebook that what we found is a clue, and I also know that we should have turned over yesterday when we had the chance."

Ricky's eyes widened. "Oh, I get it. This is about that conscience of yours, isn't it?"

"Yes, it bothers me that I didn't tell the Chief about it yesterday and because I know it was the right thing to do."

"Is the Traynor gonna tell our parents?"

"No, but instead, Chief Traynor asked that we take him to where we found it tomorrow morning at 10 o'clock."

Irritated, Ricky blurted out, "I suppose I don't have any say so in it, do I?"

"Nope."

A short moment of silence ensued, with both boys looking at one another. Josh broke it up, "I'll come by in the morning to get you, and we can walk over to the Chief's office together."

He did not wait for Ricky's reply, so, instead, he spun on his heel, walked down the sidewalk, and headed home.

Ricky, meanwhile, watched his friend walk away and around the corner. He remembered an incident five years ago when the two of them took turns hitting a baseball in the lot across the street from their homes. Josh had fouled off one of Ricky's pitches, and the ball spun up and over C Street and into Mrs. Fortney's kitchen window. He recalled how his friend waited for Mrs. Fortney to return from Casper and then promised her that he would pay for the window. Ricky felt the same way now that he did then and resigned that his best friend will always do the right thing, even to a fault.

A few minutes after arriving home, Carlos showed up moments before the kickoff of the game. Broncos quarterback John Elway had performed well during the game and had Denver up 13-3. But just before halftime, he took a hard hit that separated his left shoulder. Instead, the boys watched in horror as Cincinnati made a comeback and scoring two touchdowns in the fourth quarter to take the lead 17-13. But, the Broncos' backup quarterback, Gary Kubiak, who was ineffective for much of the second half, led the Broncos on the game-winning touchdown drive, and the Broncos won 20-17.

During the breaks in the game, Josh quickly caught his friend up on the events of the day before that culminated in finding Savolt's notebook. He also told Carlos about the boys' interaction with Mr. Pierson and his trashcan. Finally, Carlos suggested that if they wanted to search further downstream along the creek, he could bring in a few horses to make it easier.

In the early evening, Josh's folks arrived home just as his friend was leaving. Josh immediately helped his parents by bringing in the luggage. However, he left his sister's oversized and overstuffed bag for her to deal with it.

Later, over a quick supper of tuna noodle casserole and canned green beans, the family talked about Josh's game, all of Cindy's games in dramatic detail, and about their visit with Aunt Sue in Gillette. But uncharacteristically, Josh said nary a word about his exploits, nor did he mention what he found along the banks of Salt Creek.

* * *

15

Monday, September 3, 1984

It was lucky for Josh that he didn't need to make up an excuse for why he had to leave the house that morning. His mom and dad announced at breakfast that they would go into Casper to shop for groceries and wouldn't be home until later in the afternoon. Likewise, Cindy left the house after getting a ride from her friend's mother to spend the day in Edgerton. Nonetheless, Josh waited until everyone left the house before entering his closet to retrieve his .22 rifle. Then walked up a few homes on Navy Row to retrieve Ricky. As planned, they walk across the vacant lot to Chief Traynor's office.

Inside the Police Station, the boys found Deputy Isom engrossed in a copy of *The National Inquirer* spread out over his desk. He scarlessly looked up at the teens and told them that the Chief would be right out.

Chief Traynor overheard the discourse from his office just a few feet away and walked out to greet the boys. He then instructed them to go ahead and load up into his department Bronco parked outside.

After the door shut, Chief Traynor looked over at Isom and told him, "I need you to hang out here near the radio because I might need you."

Traynor then spun around, and walked outside to join the boys.

As he turned north onto Fitzhugh, Traynor asked Josh where he should park.

Josh suggested, "go over the top of the bridge and then turn right onto the first oilfield road. That road is above where we walked, and it will make it easier to go down by the creek."

Chief Traynor liked Josh's idea and nodded his approval. Three minutes later, Traynor turned off Highway 387 and onto the dirt road still soft in spots from the recent rain. After he observed four-tenths of a mile tick off on his odometer after leaving the highway, he pulled his rig as far off the road as possible and parked it.

Josh and Ricky led the way from the Bronco and trudged up and over a short hill, and in doing so, spooked three mule deer bucks and seven does out of the sagebrush. The trio stopped in their tracks and watched the deer bound away like pogo sticks toward the distant, abandoned electric plant barely in view to the north.

The boys then zig-zagged their way down to the bottom along the creek and led Chief Traynor toward the exact area where they found the notebook.

Suddenly, Traynor saw something shiny just to the left of Ricky's foot. He barked, "stop, Ricky, don't move." The boy immediately complied and remained as frozen as a statue.

The Chief reached down and picked up the object and rubbed the end of it with his fingers.

Ricky pleaded, "can I move now, Sir?"

"Oh, I am sorry, yes, you can," he said with a chuckle and amazed at the boy's compliance.

Josh walked up to the Chief and asked, "what did you find, Sir?"

Traynor recognized immediately that the object was a shell casing even before he picked it up off the ground. He looked at the primer end and saw that it was a .223 caliber but also noticed a unique marking on it and murmured to himself, "*I haven't seen one of these in a while.*"

Josh reiterated his question, "did you find something, Sir?

The Chief suddenly realized that Josh had spoken to him twice and replied, "sorry, son, I was just looking at this rifle casing." Then he asked the boy, "do you know if Mr. Savolt carried a .223?"

Josh answered his question with a question of his own, "what is a .223?"

"It is a small caliber and high-velocity bullet that doesn't drop much over long distances. I've had experience with the round when I was in the Army, but I found that the wind plays hell on that small bullet. Of course, you boys have heard of an M-16, haven't you?"

Ricky nodded. "I've heard of it, but what would an M-16 be doing out here?"

Traynor answered, "an M-16 is a military weapon, but there are a few manufacturers, like Armalite, that sell predator rifles that are chambered in .223 as well."

"Back to your question, Sir, no, I never saw Coach carry anything other than that old .45 semi-automatic pistol," Josh replied.

Chief Traynor pocketed the brass and motioned for the boys to keep going forward. Josh took the lead and navigated the party another 50 yards downstream when he stopped and motioned for Chief Traynor to come along.

"Sir, we found the notebook in that sagebrush right there," and Josh pointed to a sagebrush plant four feet in front of him.

Chief Traynor motioned the boys to back away from the scene and diligently looked all around the area for any other sign or clue left by Savolt. Finally, he stood up and sighed. "There isn't anything here, boys, but how did you know to look out here in the first place?"

Josh explained that he had been with Savolt a couple of times, and in both occurrences, they ended at the bridge. He also recounted how easy it was to follow Savolt's boot prints all along the creek and even found them on the north side of the bridge. Traynor looked around again and thought he could make out what looked like a boot heel, but the rain had pretty much washed everything out. The trio pushed further downstream for another hundred yards when Chief Traynor spoke up.

"Well, boys, I think we should be getting back. Unfortunately, the rain has washed out anything useful to search further."

Unhesitatingly, Ricky turned around and led the trio back toward the truck.

But then, unexpectedly, Ricky stopped short and froze in his tracks. Josh looked around Ricky's legs and spotted a colossal prairie rattlesnake already coiled to strike. It lay no farther than two feet in front of Ricky.

Like Josh, Ricky also hated snakes more than anything else in the world and was now living out his worst nightmare. Even worse, it seemed that the noise of the snake's tail drowned out everything else around them.

Josh grabbed his nearly petrified friend by the shirt collar and slowly pulled him back away from the snake. He then pumped the action of his .22 rifle and chambered a birdshot round. Josh had pre-loaded his weapon with six birdshot cartridges and carried 20 Hornet rounds in his left front pocket. With Ricky out of the way, Josh turned and fired a quick shot into the snake.

He then turned to his friend and asked, "are you okay? Did the snake get you?"

"No, he didn't get me, but he could have since he was only two feet away from me."

Before Josh said another word, Ricky's eyes doubled in size as his attention focused on something behind him.

As he turned to see what alarmed Ricky, his friend screamed, "it is still alive and trying to crawl up into that culvert above it!"

Chief Traynor scrambled in front of the boys and drew his .357 Magnum revolver out of his holster. He took careful aim and fired. The magnum load let out a loud *BOOM* that left both boys with a painful ringing in their ears. Traynor's shot, however, struck the snake directly behind the head and decapitated it.

Josh looked over at Ricky and said, "It is dead now." Then he asked him, "do you want the rattle?"

Before the still terror-stricken boy could answer, Josh pulled out his pocket knife and grabbed the still wiggling snake. Its nerve endings continued firing long after the snake's heart stopped beating. After cutting off the rattle, he looked up above the snake and spied an old culvert concealed by grass and sagebrush. However, what caught his attention was what he spotted inside the tube.

"Chief Traynor, come over here, please," demanded Josh as he reached into the large conduit and retrieved the familiar-looking backpack. The boy then turned the pack around and looked at the flap, and on it read:

PFC SAVOLT 0399

"Josh, isn't that Coach Savolt's old Army backpack?" Ricky questioned.

He ignored his buddy for a second while noting several dark spots on the green canvas. Then Josh wondered whether or not it was Coach Savolt's blood. Chief Traynor also saw the red streaks, and suspected the same thing. The boy delicately handed the backpack over to the Chief, who also wore a look of shock on his face.

Next, Traynor opened the backpack very cautiously to avoid touching the bloodstains on the outside flap. Meanwhile, Josh curiously looked in closely over the man's shoulder. The bag's contents held at least 20 water sample containers and a few plastic bags that contained grass and other vegetation samples. The inside pocket of the pack only included a pencil, four clean glass microscope slides, and five rubber bands.

Chief Traynor then sent Ricky back to the Bronco for two things: first, he wanted a large clear plastic evidence bag out of the back of the unit. Secondly, he also wanted the boy to call Deputy Isom on the radio and have him come to this location.

When Ricky arrived back with the bag, he explained to the Chief that successful in reaching the Deputy. Then, while the boys held the plastic bag open, Traynor carefully placed the backpack inside and sealed it.

As they walked back up the hill and toward the Bronco, Chief Traynor asked the boys, "have you boys seen an odd 1970s model of a dark green Ford F150 around here?"

Josh nodded. "I saw it a few days ago speed past me down the alley between Lewis and Watson Streets. But we also saw it on Saturday too on the other side of the creek right after we found the notebook."

"Did it look like that one creeping along slowly on the other side of the creek right now?" The boys followed Traynor's finger that pointed across the creek and up on the shelf above.

"Yes, Sir, that is what we saw in the same place!" Ricky exclaimed.

When Deputy Isom arrived at the Bronco's location, he found the boys leaning against the vehicle. However, Chief Traynor remained standing at the top of the hill. The dark Ford had already sped off to the east, and from his high vantage point, he could see it turn left onto Highway 387 and then disappear.

The deputy parked and got out of his car.

"Isom, get up here!" ordered the Chief.

The Deputy quickly walked to the top of the hill and stood in front of the unhappy Chief.

Traynor lowered his voice and asked him, "why didn't you answer your radio on your way out here?

Deputy Isom stared blankly at his boss. Then he explained, "I didn't turn it on. I figured it didn't matter since I was already coming to your location.".

The Chief rolled his eyes skyward and then focused them back onto Isom.

"We just saw a 1978 or a 1979 dark green Ford F150 who was watching us out here. It was the same vehicle that shadowed the boys two days ago in this exact location. I was trying to alert you to pull over the suspects so that we could question them, but because you didn't turn on the radio, they got away."

Isom's face flushed in embarrassment, and he stammered to offer an apology.

Instead, Chief Traynor held his hand up in front of the deputy's face to stop him. "I have a specific order for you. Do you think you can handle it?

"Yes, Sir, anything you say, Sir."

"I am going to take the boys home, secure the evidence in my office, make some phone calls, and then I will come back out here. You will stand right here and make sure that nobody steps foot upon the area from the bridge down to the draw to the north, do you understand?

"Yes, Chief, I can handle it."

"I will be back here shortly."

Chief Traynor loaded up the boys and the evidence and made a three-point turn to turnaround to head back toward the highway. When the Chief came to the intersection with the pavement, he only glanced left and then right, and entering the road without stopping. Traynor then sped into town and came to a skidding stop outside his office. He quickly opened the back door and grabbed the evidence bag, and started toward his office.

But he stopped as if he were in an absentminded moment. Then the Chief turned toward the boys and said, "thank you, boys, for your help, and if it weren't for you two, we might not have this new clue if it does turn out to be Savolt's blood."

The boys echoed, "you are welcome, Sir," and turned to go home.

Chief Traynor turned again and went inside his office. Once there, he placed the evidence bag on his desk, and picked up the phone. He called the Natrona County Sheriff's office for assistance since the scene was the county's responsibility and outside Midwest town limits. He also requested that a BOLO (be on the lookout) for a 1978 or 1979 dark green Ford F150 last seen headed east on Highway 387, who could be driving east toward Wright or south on Highway 259 toward Casper.

Ricky followed Josh into his house and plopped comfortably onto the couch while his friend put the gun away.

When Josh returned, Ricky asked, "how much can you remember from the notebook? The reason I ask is we now have no chance of looking at it again."

A Cheshire grin unfurled on his mouth and he calmly stated, "I wrote out another copy."

Ricky smiled. "I am shocked by such defiant behavior," and gave his buddy a quick shoulder punch with his first.

Josh then reacted by letting out a fake cry of pain and falling back onto the couch.

* * *

16

Later that afternoon, Ricky got up from the couch, walked around the tiny living room, and then stopped to look out the front window. He examined the damage on the wooden window framing. Ricky saw that decade's worth of stapling cardboard strips to hold the transparent plastic sheets over the window every winter had started splintering the wooden frame. The boy noted that it was much the same at his house, and he wished the school district would get around to installing new windows. On the other hand, it seemed silly to him to winterize homes like this.

While still standing near the window, Ricky turned and asked, "Josh, I don't know what to make of what we saw today?"

Josh asked in return, "what do you mean?"

"What I mean is this: #1, Coach Savolt is missing; #2, we know that his last location was along the creek; #3, we found his notebook; and, #4, today we found his backpack with what looked like blood on it. Doesn't that blow your mind?"

"It does," Josh said, and he felt a kind of remorse that rose within him. It seemed much like hearing the news for the first time that his grandfather had died. Josh chocked back his sudden realization of the grief that welled up within him.

Instead, he cleared his voice and then looked back at Ricky and said, "I think it would be best if we find out why someone wanted him to disappear."

"How are we to do that, Josh?"

"We have notes from Coach's field book."

"I know that, but don't tell us anything except 'I took sample A from Point 1,' but what I want to know is why he took those samples to begin with?"

"So, do I, and that is why I need your help."

"What can I do? I am not as smart as you. Plus, I am no help when it comes to that science stuff?"

Josh nodded. "I need you to speak up whenever you have something on your mind, whether you think your thoughts are dumb or not. You see things that I easily overlook, so I may even need you to argue against me when it comes time to form a theory."

Ricky laughed. "Why would that help? I argue with you all the time!"

Josh laughed as well, but his face turned to all seriousness and said, "you will be my sanity check to the theory." He let his remark sit for a moment and then asked friend, "do you think you could do that for me?"

Ricky nodded his head slightly and replied with a simple, "yes."

Josh rose from the couch and went into his room just off from the living room. When he returned to the couch, he held his notebook that contained all the transcribed notations from the Savolt field book.

He then shuffled to the last page of the notebook and ripped out a clean sheet of paper, and placed it on the coffee table in front of them. He motioned to Ricky to hand him the pencil sitting on top of the TV Guide magazine in the center of the table, to which the boy complied.

"I have read a few mystery novels before, and I have found that I can usually make out who did it and why if I just start jotting down random facts. Then I question why they are important," Josh asserted.

He then wrote the words *Creek Study* at the top and center of the page. Then he wrote on the left side of the page the word "*why*."

Josh turned to Ricky and asked, "why would Coach do a study on Salt Creek?"

Before Ricky could answer, the boys heard a knock on the door. Josh got up and answered the door and found David standing on the porch. Then with a simple wave of his hand, Josh asked his friend inside.

David asked, "what have you guys been up to?"

Ricky and Josh took turns to explain all the events since Saturday night. First, Josh recalled that he gave Coach Savolt's field book and the specimen slide to Chief Traynor and then described how he and Ricky led the Chief out to where they found the notebook on the creek. Later Ricky recounted how Josh shot a snake at his feet with his .22 rifle and how the Chief finished the snake off with a pistol shot.

At each revelation, David nodded and focused upon the context of what his friends told him. Though David did feel the need to mention what he thought about using .22 birdshot loads on the snake and that an ordinary bullet would have been better.

Josh grimaced and picked up the story again, carefully constructing the scene of their finding of Savolt's old army backpack.

David interrupted, "how do you know the backpack was Savolt's?"

"Good question, though it was obvious since the backpack had white block letters that spelled out S-A-V-O-L-T on it," Josh replied.

Ricky then interjected, "the thing that threw me off was the numbers on it."

"What numbers?" David asked.

"0399," Ricky answered.

"What is so significant about 0399?"

Josh explained further, "I thought it was strange too, and I asked the same question to Chief Traynor on the way back to the Bronco. The Chief said that military members label their belongings with their last name and the last four digits of their social security number in the military. He also said that he will confirm that the numbers are, in fact, the last four of Savolt's social security numbers when he was able to look up that information."

David sat back in the chair adjacent to the couch and stared down at the yellowing brown shag carpet on the floor. The silence was not awkward, nor was it unwelcomed, as the three boys seemed lost in their thoughts as they tried to sort things out.

Josh sighed and then reached to the coffee table and picked up the piece of paper, and leaned over toward David, so he could see what he wrote.

Then he explained, "when you got here, Dave, we were just about ready to start throwing ideas onto paper as to what Coach was up to with the study and why? But when you knocked on the door, I had just asked Ricky why Coach would do a study on Salt Creek?"

David blinked once and said, "Salt Creek runs through an oilfield. So, it doesn't take a rocket scientist to figure out that there could be some kind of pollution in the creek. Besides, we all know that he collected water samples up and down the banks of the stream."

Josh wrote the word pollution down, and then he asked, "why else would he do a study?"

Once again, the boys sat in silence and could not think of any other reason than the obvious.

Josh drew two more lines off of the word '*pollution* and wrote down two more items at the end of the tangents, which were the words *confirmed* and *contradicted*.

He looked up at his friends and said, "we don't know if he confirmed pollution or contradicted the opinion of everyone around here that Salt Creek is poisonous."

After a moment, Josh asked, "so, without knowing the results, who would benefit if the samples did show pollution?"

Ricky barked out, "only those people who do not like oil production."

David shook his head and said, "No, I don't buy it, dude. I mean, the oil field is the lifeblood of everyone that lives in this area, so why would Coach Savolt want to jeopardize that?"

Like David, he had the same thoughts too since it just wouldn't make sense. Many residents in Midwest or Edgerton had generational ties to the area and the oil industry.

Josh then provided the alternative question: "who would be hurt by a revelation of pollution?"

"The oil companies," growled David. "My dad owes his life to MERP and this field, and something like this could make his career go away. He told me that several MERP guys think that Coach Savolt was trying to get the oil field shut down by proving that oil production was causing too much harm to the environment."

Josh asked David, "do you believe that?"

The boy sat back into the chair again, and judging by his expression, it seemed that two invisible forces were pulling him apart inside.

Then David's face softened with a fresh perspective and offered, "if the study proved pollution in the creek, wouldn't that possibly jeopardize Coach Savolt's job as well? I mean, if the oilfield shut down, families would have to move away, and the kids that are left would end up bused to Casper, don't you think?"

Ricky nodded and said, "ya, I get what you are saying. It is kind of like that old saying that a dog never pisses on his own bed."

Josh nodded in agreement and then repeated the first question, "so who would be hurt the most if the creek is clean?"

After a few beats, Ricky answered, "tree huggers," and grabbed the pencil from Josh's hand and made that note on the paper.

Josh then got up and went into the kitchen, opened the refrigerator door, and retrieved three pop cans. He returned to the living room and handed one to each of his friends.

He opened his can and took a sip, and then sat back down on the couch. Josh picked up the piece of paper, looked at it, and then set it down and wrote out the word *other* in the margin on the right side of the sheet of paper.

Then he said, "there are a few other things that just don't add up, like the Ford pickup."

"You mean the one we saw from on top of M-hill that day?" David asked.

Josh responded, "yes, it was the same one that ran down the alley...."

Ricky cut him off and said, "and it was the same one that Josh and I saw right after we found the notebook and the same one that showed up after we found the backpack with Chief Traynor."

Josh wrote *dark green Ford F-150* in the space on the right of the page.

Ricky's eyes widened, and he asked Josh, "do you remember what Chief Traynor also found yesterday? It was that rifle casing with .332 or something stamped on it."

"It was a .223 round," clarified Josh, then added, "Chief Traynor also remarked that it had a military-grade marking on it too."

Josh jotted down *.223 round* in another space on the right side of the page.

David asked Josh, "what gun shoots .223 caliber?"

"Chief Traynor said that the military's M-16 is chambered in .223 but also made it sound like the caliber isn't very popular around here. I mean, the guns we have in our house are a .308, a .30-06, and a .35 Remington plus my .22, but I hadn't heard of a .223 caliber until the Chief picked up that shell casing."

Ricky picked up the pencil again and circled the note "*.223.*"

Meanwhile, David had lifted the notebook of the transcribed field notes. He continued to listen to Josh and Ricky's observations and looked over the field notations.

Finally, David inquired, "Josh, why did you circle the word *specimen* at least three times in your notes?"

Josh sat forward and explained, "I noticed that Coach Savolt made a note of his collections and where he used the word *sample* repeatedly. But he only used the word *specimen* for three entries."

Ricky questioned, "but couldn't the word specimen describe the grass and other plant samples that we saw in the backpack?"

"I've thought about that, but the numbering was off."

"What numbering?" David asked.

Josh used his right index finger to point out several examples in the notebook. "I noticed previously with Coach that he labeled each bottle with a #1, #2, or# 3 according to the corresponding location. I know that #1 was the first spot near Edgerton, and the highest number I saw in the backpack was #23."

Josh leaned forward and picked up his pop can off of the coffee table, and he took a drink. He turned back to David and said, "If you look at the very last entry, you will see that the word *specimen* follows after the annotation of sample #23."

Once again, Josh took up the piece of paper off of the coffee table and wrote the singular word *specimen* on it.

The boys sat in silence and thought about whether or not there were any other things that they could add to the list of the unexplained. But then Josh jumped up from the couch and dashed into his room, and when he returned, he announced, "I want to know what the heck this is?" Then he handed over the piece of paper that he had folded and tucked in his back pocket that he retrieved from the open field near Mr. Pierson's trash can.

Ricky and David looked at the paper, and each possessed the same equal confused expression.

Ricky then spoke, "What is *LEAF*?"

David couldn't resist the opportunity to tease his buddy and quickly taunted him with "a leaf, like what is on that tree over there, you dope!"

Ricky retorted back to David, "I know what a leaf on a tree is, you jerk! However, I think this is different. Why would it be written in all capital letters over a symbol that looks like a leaf? Doesn't anyone else find that weird?"

Josh nodded. "Yes, that is weird. But I think that might be an acronym for something else."

After he said it, he noticed the confused looks of both friends, and then realized that they weren't following him. He calmly said, "I think it is an acronym like MERP, or OFT is what I am saying."

David nodded that he understood. However, Josh grabbed the pencil again and added a new word, *LEAF*, onto the piece of paper. The boys gazed at the meeting notice and worked different things in their heads.

Moments later, Ricky asked, "so now, what do we do?"

Josh replied, *"Seek ye the truth and the truth shall set ye free."*

"Do you honestly think a bible verse will solve this?" Ricky challenged.

Josh replied, "yes, I do because when we seek the answers to our questions on this piece of paper, then we will find the truth of what happened to Savolt." Then, he stood up and held the paper at shoulder level and continued, "all of these things we have identified are connected, and by seeking them out, we will know the truth."

David shook his head and cautioned, "this isn't something we can do very quickly. Remember we only have a small part of our weekends to work on this because of school, and most importantly, because of football."

"You're right, David," Ricky acknowledged.

Josh remained stoic in thought when David tapped him on the chest. Finally, he lifted his eyes to meet the intense set of his friend.

Sternly, David implored, "I want you to stay focused, not on this mystery, but the team. Last year we got to the championship by getting lucky at the right time, but I know we can beat them all if we keep focused on what we are doing this year. I understand how much Savolt meant to you, but right now, we need you to focus."

David's pep talk was interrupted by the sound of a car pulling up in front of the house.

Ricky told Josh, "take these papers and hide them in your room," which he grabbed and disappeared into his room. When Josh returned, he went outside and met his parents, along with Ricky and David. The boys grabbed as many paper bags as they could handle and carried them into the house without prompting.

Sara grabbed David by the arm and said, "thank you, and you too, Ricky. You didn't have to help out."

David smiled. "It is okay, Mrs. Anderson, we are over here enough and eating your food. It is the least we can do by helping out a little bit. Besides, Josh always helps my mom the same way when he is over at my house."

Rob overheard the conversation and echoed his "thank you," and invited the boys to stay for dinner.

* * *

17

Later that evening and well after dark, Chief Traynor parked outside his office and turned off the ignition switch on his department Bronco. In the sudden quiet, the engine ticked as it cooled in a rhythm, much like a metronome sitting atop a piano. Traynor was dead tired, and he looked into the rear-view mirror with the stray light from his office door. What he saw were baggy and bloodshot eyes that made him look much older than he was. As he reached for the door handle, Deputy Isom pulled up next to him. Dogged tired, both officers walked up the sidewalk and entered their tiny office.

"Isom, after you hang up your jacket, make us a pot of coffee, please. I think we will be here a while. Then call your wife and let her know that you will be missing supper."

The Chief realized that he, too, needed to call his wife, so he picked up the phone and dialed *4422* to connect him with his home. Of course, to outsiders, it would seem odd only to dial four numbers. Still, for residents in the Salt Creek area, all phone numbers shared the same prefix of 437, so they only had to dial the last four digits of the phone number to call locally. Moreover, phone calls within the state's 307 area code only required dialing a 1+ the rest of the seven-digit phone number.

Chief Traynor got up from his desk after informing his wife that he would be home late, which devolved into a discussion about the number of hours at work versus the hours spent at home. He kept the conversation short, though he wished he had the courage someday to stand up to his wife and tell her that the only reason she wanted him home was to cook and clean for her. But discretion won out over valor, as it always had before, and he reserved his comments for himself only.

The day had been taxing one for Traynor. It began with Ricky Fleming and Josh Anderson leading him to the spot where the boys found Tim Savolt's field book that contained notes of his samples along the creek. Then he and the boys found Savolt's backpack, and then Traynor was forced to call the Sheriff's office for help.

The county dispatcher sent out four Sheriff Deputies. She also notified the local deputy, Eddie Crandall, who was fresh off of vacation, to help secure the scene. Unfortunately, Traynor failed to expect and would regret later that the Sheriff himself would show up unexpectedly.

Sheriff Doan was not a fan of any part of Natrona County that existed 10 miles beyond the city limits of Casper. He especially despised all of the small-town police officers in the county like those in Midwest, Bar Nunn, and Alcova. The Sheriff treated all of them with equal amounts of arrogant disdain. Despite the exceptional credentials and training that Chief Traynor possessed, the Sheriff always spoke to him like he was a trainee.

What riled Traynor most about the Sheriff's visit was that Doan parked his department Chevy Blazer midway across the Highway 387 bridge spanning Salt Creek. Then, a few seconds later, a television news crew from Casper pulled in behind him.

Specifically, the Chief disliked how Doan always acted like the prototypical western Sheriff with a crisp uniform pulled over his enormous overgrown belly. Doan completed the ensemble with a necktie and a pristine $300 Stetson. The hat always looked like it had come out of the box, and it did. Plus, the tie was a clip-on. Sheriff Doan made it a habit to carry the hat with him always. That way, he could look good in front of the camera, regardless of the site.

The news reporter interviewed the Sheriff, who described how his department "received a tip into the case of missing teacher Tim Savolt." He also bragged that "his department found crucial evidence to change the focus from a missing person case to a suspected homicide."

Soon afterward, the reporter and camera operator departed the scene. Once the news van was out of sight, Doan quickly removed his clip-on tie and opened his shirt collar. Then the Sheriff placed his fine Stetson back in the box. Afterward, Doan reached inside his vehicle, grabbed his well-used green baseball cap with the department logo on the front, and placed it upon his head. Instead of descending the bank and helping the men, Sheriff Doan took up a position on the bridge and set one foot upon the guard rail.

Earlier, while overhearing the Sheriff's comments, Traynor told himself: *funny that Doan failed to mention that my efforts produced the new evidence.* But then he reminded himself that the real investigators in the case were a group of high school boys who sought their answers.

Aided by the hardworking deputies, Traynor and the team canvased the west side of the creek from the bridge 3500 feet to the north at the site where Bothwell Draw joined with Salt Creek. Meanwhile, Deputy Isom handled traffic by ensuring that onlookers on the highway didn't form a bottleneck at the bridge.

About 1500 feet from the bridge, Chief Traynor pointed out to the deputies where the backpack remained hidden. Then, on the other side of Bothwell Draw, the Chief also pointed out where the boys found Savolt's notebook.

While the searchers walked back toward the bridge, they came upon a wide-open flat section of ground crusted with a frost of alkali. Yet, from this particular angle, the men could easily make out two distinct parallel marks in the dirt that looked as if a person had been drug. But the recent rains softened the drag marks to the point that it wasn't conclusive; still, they photographed them anyway.

When the team reached the bridge, Sheriff Doan instructed them to cross over and begin canvasing the eastern side of the creek for another 3500 feet to the north. One deputy walked next to the creek bank while the others fanned out 50 yards apart. Chief Traynor took his position along a dirt oilfield road that paralleled the creek. He reckoned it was the same path that he spotted the mysterious Ford pickup earlier in that day.

The new search resulted in finding two more .223 caliber shell casings about 3000 feet from the bridge. The bullet casings were bagged, logged, and photographed.

Now, the only thing Traynor had left to do in the office was to type out a formal report for Sheriff Doan. But first, he got up from his desk and poured himself a cup of coffee and picked up the handwritten statement from Deputy Isom that detailed his efforts to contain traffic.

"Isom," the Chief said, "I don't see any reason for you to hang out here. You should go home."

"I'd rather hang out here, Chief, to help out any way I can if you don't mind."

Chief Traynor had heard several times about how he and Isom resembled the fictional characters of Andy Taylor and Barney Fife from the hit television series *The Andy Griffith Show*. It didn't bother him so much because there was a lot of truth in the comparison. But tonight, he sensed that his deputy just wanted to be included in the investigation. Although Isom wasn't all too bright, he was still a devoted law enforcement officer. Traynor had reminded himself of that fact more than once and vowed to treat his deputy with respect.

The Chief offered instead, "I tell you what; I need you to take charge of finding that late 1970's dark green Ford F150. Once you find it parked somewhere, I want you to call me immediately so we can question the driver together."

Isom's posture straightened a little, and his chin lifted as well with his new important assignment. He grabbed his hat and made his way for the door, and when his hand touched the doorknob, he turned and said, "Chief, I am going to do a sweep of the town, and then I will go on home. Then first thing tomorrow, I will look around again for that pickup."

"Thank you, deputy. You are a tremendous help."

After Deputy Isom departed, Chief Traynor took off his hat and rubbed his ever-increasing bold spot. At the same time, he pondered how to write up his report. Typing was an arduous task for him, and the Chief despised every occasion that forced him to do so. As a result, he never learned the proper mechanics and techniques of typing; instead, he used his index fingers on each hand to search out each letter and strike the keys one at a time.

It took Traynor a little over an hour to type the 2-page report, and he set it aside to deliver to Deputy Crandall in the morning. He also had a box with all the collected evidence, including the backpack, the notebook, the slides, and two .223 caliber casings. Each piece was labeled correctly and stored in a separate plastic bag.

However, the other .223 casing he found earlier in the morning remained in his pocket for further inquiry. He planned to turn it over to the Sheriff's office once he either confirmed or negated his suspicions about it.

With Tim Savolt's file in front of him once again, Traynor went back through his notes and noticed that there were some things he needed to follow up on tomorrow. Most notably, he needed to go by the school and talk to Dr. Gaines. Specifically, he wanted to know whether or not any faculty members disagreed with Tim Savolt? He knew that he should have done so immediately after talking with the Andersons. Still, until now, it didn't seem all that important.

Chief Traynor got up again and filled up his coffee mug for a second time, and suddenly, he got another thought and walked back over to his desk. He pulled the middle drawer out and moved pens, paper clips, and other miscellaneous items out of the way until he found the folded piece of paper he was seeking. Traynor unfolded the paper and wrote down the four-letter word on a scratch piece of paper: *L-E-A-F.*

Maybe if he found out what the name stood for, it might be tied to something in the Savolt case, or it might not. He then looked down at the bottom of the page. Finally, he copied down the information about the next meeting into his notebook that he kept in the right pocket of his uniform shirt.

He finally sat back and contemplated further and then finished off the last of his coffee in one big swig. After a full sigh, he said aloud in the empty office, *"maybe I will send Deputy Isom on an undercover assignment to see what this LEAF thing is all about? It wouldn't be that risky since the next meeting would gather at the library. So it wouldn't be that unusual if Isom were spotted there outside of his uniform. But, of course, if Isom were in street clothes, most people would not recognize him."*

The last thought made him giggle a little, but maybe he should give this idea some serious thought.

* * *

18

Tuesday, September 4, 1984

Chief Traynor left his house that morning and drove over to the café in Edgerton to meet up with Sheriff Deputy Crandall over breakfast. Traynor arrived on time, parked his Bronco next to the Sheriff's Department pickup truck, and went inside.

Seated at the counter on a swivel topped stool, Deputy Crandall nursed a cup of coffee. Eddie Crandall was 22 years old and had served 13 months as a deputy. The deputy grew up in Glenrock, which was another oilfield community in central Wyoming, but east of Casper. When he received orders to live and work in the Salt Creek community, Eddie gladly accepted it.

Crandall was always easy to spot in a crowd because of his distinctive shade of red hair. He had heard all of the nicknames before like, carrot top or red. In addition, he had been picked upon mercilessly through grade school for having so many freckles spaced so close together that it gave him a perpetual tan. But now, he mostly ignored what others perceived or remarked about his appearance.

"Mornin' Deputy," Traynor said, to which, Crandall replied, "mornin' Chief."

"Here is the report from yesterday to take back to your department headquarters. I used carbon paper, so I could make myself a copy to keep in my files as well," he said and slid the report over to the Deputy.

Crandall looked at the document briefly and then said, "thanks for doing that. It sure saves the department a lot of time by your thoroughness." Then the Deputy added, "I didn't take typing in high school, and I hate to type out anything."

Traynor chuckled and said, "ya, me too."

Crandall sipped his coffee and then said, "Chief, thank you for helping yesterday with canvassing that area. What I mean is that I know you didn't have to do it. But as for the other deputies and me, we sure appreciated it."

Traynor brushed off the compliment with a wave of his hand. Then, he humbly replied, "don't mention it." Then after another sip of coffee, the Chief added, "I had some great sergeants when I was in the Army. What stood out to me is that they never told us grunts to do anything that they weren't willing to do themselves."

Crandall began to say something but then thought better of it and reached for this coffee cup once more.

Traynor then motioned with his hand. "I have all the evidence bags in the back of my Bronco, and I will help you transfer them into your unit once we finish breakfast."

The waitress suddenly appeared and stood in front of them. First, she took Chief Traynor's order of a slice of ham with two eggs over easy and white toast. Then she wrote down the Deputy's order of pancakes and bacon. But before leaving, she refilled Crandall's cup of coffee and retrieved a fresh mug from under the counter, and poured one for Traynor.

The waitress asked the Chief, "do you want cream and sugar?"

He replied, "no, thank you, I prefer mine black."

While they waited for their breakfast orders, Crandall took the opportunity to ask Traynor a few questions about Tim Savolt's missing person case.

"Considering that the spots on the backpack look like blood, what do you think happened to Savolt?"

"Well, first off, we need to match the blood type on the backpack to Savolt's blood. Then, I can ask Dr. McMaster over at the town clinic to provide me Savolt's blood type for a reference."

"Okay, saying that the blood does match, then what? What do you think happened to him?"

"Here is my feeling, Deputy, off the record." Traynor paused and waited for him to acknowledge the "off the record" comment. Crandall provided a quick nod of his head that sufficed acknowledgment.

He continued, "I believe that Savolt's conclusions in his study had perhaps rubbed some people the wrong way around here." Then Traynor looked around the room to make sure that nobody overheard the conversation.

Crandall followed Traynor's eyes and then asked, "you mean someone that works in the oilfield could be responsible"?"

Traynor nodded. "It is just a hunch. But, logically, wouldn't the oilfield be threatened if an environmental study came out asserting that the Salt Creek was toxic because of oil production?"

Their breakfasts arrived and provided a short hiatus in the discussion as both men focused on eating the food from their plates.

With the last forkful of pancake, Deputy Crandall asked Chief Traynor a peculiar question, "have you noticed a dark green 1978 Ford F150 around the area lately?"

"I have, and I want to find whoever is driving that pickup to question him. But I was unsure of the exact year until you just said it."

"My father drives the same truck, except his is red."

But before Traynor could ask him a follow-up question, Crandall continued. "After I left the bridge yesterday, I drove north on Light Plant Road as ordered by Sheriff Doan."

"What were you looking for?"

"The Sheriff told me to look for anything unusual, but nothing out there seemed out of place."

"But what about the Ford pickup?"

"I was just getting to that. Upon returning to Highway 387 and heading home, I stopped at Edgerton Grocery to buy milk and bread. When I came out of the store, I saw the truck drive by me heading westbound."

"Is that it?" questioned Chief Traynor.

"No. When I pulled up to my trailer near the end of Center Street just before East Street-you know where I live, don't you?"

The Chief nodded and motioned for the Deputy to continue.

"I got out of my rig and went inside and put my weapon and belt down on my kitchen table. Then, when I went back outside to get my groceries, I saw that green Ford roll very slowly by my trailer."

"What did you do next?"

Crandall shrugged. "I didn't do anything because the driver turned the corner and sped off north on East Street."

"Did you get a description of the driver?"

"No, I didn't. The window tint prevented me from seeing anything inside the cab, but I could make out that there were two people inside."

"Were they men, or women, or both?"

"I am 99% sure they were men because of their size."

Chief Traynor sat back and rubbed the sides of his head and thought about what Deputy Crandall had just said. He rubbed his head so hard he nearly knocked off his hat, which he caught himself and righted the hat to fit precisely back atop his head.

Crandall interrupted the Chief's thoughts when he asked, "what are you thinking, Chief?"

Traynor shook his head. "I think whoever is driving that Ford pickup is directly responsible for the disappearance of Tim Savolt." Then he paused and looked into Crandall's eyes. "Deputy, I trust you, and the last thing I want is for this event to become a public spectacle that helps your Sheriff get re-elected."

Eddie seemed confused by the Chief's statement, so Traynor continued. "I know what you are thinking, Eddie, that I am speaking about your boss, but this thing with Tim Savolt has shaken this area in depths that we won't even know for years to come."

"What do you want me to do, Chief?"

"I want you to work with me. But, you know, two heads are better than one kind of thing."

Crandall nodded. "Okay, I can do that."

Thirty minutes later, Chief Traynor pulled into the high school parking lot and parked his unit in a space next to the swimming pool entrance. Then, he exited his vehicle and walked over to the main door. After passing by the boys' locker room and the school counselor's office, he turned right and entered the high school office.

Edna Burrows looked up at Chief Traynor from her reception desk and asked, "may I help you?"

"Yes, Edna, you can. I was wondering if Dr. Gaines has a moment to speak with me?"

When the principal overheard his name spoken, he called out from his office for the visitor to come inside.

"It is good to see you again, Dr. Gaines, and I hope I am not bothering you?" Chief Traynor asked.

"No, not at all, Chief, please have a seat," Dr. Gaines replied while pointing to the spare chair in front of his desk.

Then Traynor said, "I don't want to waste your time Doc since I know you are busy running the school, but I have a follow-up question regarding Tim Savolt."

Dr. Gaines nodded and opened his hands to indicate, "go ahead."

"Doc, did Tim ever get into an altercation with another teacher or even have a serious verbal disagreement?"

The principal held one finger up to intimate the Chief to hold onto his thought, and then he got up and walked over to the doorway and shut the office door. Then he closed the shades covering the window. It wasn't uncommon for him to do this whenever he did not want to be disturbed.

"Sorry, Chief, I just wanted to make sure our discussion had the privacy this sort of talk requires. To answer your question, yes, Tim Savolt had a rather noisy verbal altercation with another member of my faculty in late May near the end of the school year."

"Whom was the other party?"

Dr. Gaines leaned forward and motioned for the Chief to do the same. Then he whispered the name, "Doug Pierson, my Business Teacher."

"What was it about?"

The principal sat back and continued. "I don't know exactly, but I do know it had to do with the study that Tim was conducting during his off time. Of course, I knew that he also used his classroom laboratory to conduct experiments. Still, Tim used some of those water samples as test subjects for his classes.

Chief Traynor made a few notes in his notebook. He also took advantage of the pause to come up with another question. Then he asked, "did Doug Pierson object that Savolt's study could negatively impact operations in the oilfield?"

"Chief, you are thinking on the wrong side of this. Doug Pierson is the personification of what it means to be a nouveau environmentalist. For example, suppose I don't regulate my staff meetings carefully. In that case, Doug and his wife will hijack them to recruit sympathies to their cause, but I digress. I got the impression, however, that Savolt's study was not going to reveal anything damaging to the community. I think Doug Pierson took great offense to that fact."

Traynor let that sink in for a few moments and again annotated the information in his notebook. Then, finally, he raised his eyebrows and asked Dr. Gaines, "what about Doug's wife, Shelly? Did she argue with Savolt as well?

The principal smiled. "Well, yes, of course, she was in Tim Savolt's classroom screaming at him alongside her husband."

Dr. Gaines reached for his coffee cup and took another sip before continuing his remarks. "I understand that both of the Piersons take offense too easily when anyone opposes their views. I attribute that to their elitist nature that they probably picked up in college. You see, Chief, I did not attend a liberal college as they did. Nor did I discover my need to change the status quo. Rather, I attended Texas A&M during the 1960s, where the campus culture was conservative. The Piersons, on the other hand, attended Cal Berkley, where activism is not only encouraged but also taught. I have found over time that the couple voice every grievance of theirs whether or not it has any merit."

Before Chief Traynor could ask another question, Dr. Gaines offered, "I know what you are thinking, Chief. Why do I put up with the Piersons?" To which, Traynor nodded.

Gaines continued, "Chief, it is hard to find faculty replacements. I mean, it is not easy to recruit a new teacher to work and live in such lavishness that Midwest has to offer."

"Well, thanks, Doc. I think I have taken up more than enough of your time," Traynor said as he started to rise out of his seat. But then he stopped and sat back down.

"Doc, I apologize, but I have one more question if you don't mind." Traynor shifted his gun holster so that he was a little more comfortable in the chair. Then he asked, "why is it that the Pierson's have such a negative affinity towards three boys: Josh Anderson, David Proctor, and Ricky Fleming?"

Dr. Gaines sat back, folded his hands together, and pressed them up against his chin while he thought.

He broke the silence when he offered, "well, I am not sure about David and Ricky though they are best of friends with Josh. But I know the Piersons feel that Josh is a little precocious in their view."

Traynor remained silent in hopes that Dr. Gaines would continue. He sometimes used the tactic to elicit more information, and most often, it worked during questioning.

Dr. Gaines suddenly shifted uncomfortably in his seat. Then he revealed, "last week, Shelly Pierson accused Josh Anderson of disrespecting her in her classroom. However, she cannot accept that Josh is a very bright student who has already read the book that she assigned the class for the semester. Josh responded by quoting parts of the book back to her, which became obvious that she didn't know them herself."

Gaines stopped for a few seconds to let out an involuntary chuckle about the incident. Then, he regained composure and continued his remarks. "Shelly wanted Josh's head, that is for sure. But, after I talked to both Josh and his father, Rob, about it, I was assured that the boy didn't do anything wrong. Josh is a great kid, and I hope you see that in him as well."

Chief Traynor replied, "yes, it is my experience with the boy that he is truly one of the best kids in town."

Traynor rose from his seat once more, but this time he moved toward the door. Dr. Gaines followed him through the office and into the hallway. But then Chief Traynor glanced to his left and spied a person he did not know through the open door of the science lab.

Traynor leaned over to Dr. Gaines and whispered, "who is that?" while he pointed to a young, slim, and blond female teaching the class.

"Oh, that is Kandi Kowalski, she likes to be called *KK*, and she is my new hire to replace Tim Savolt for the time being," Dr. Gaines whispered.

"But Doc, I thought you said that it was hard to recruit new teachers?"

"They are, but the Pierson's recommended her because they went to school with her. By sheer coincidence, Kandi was living in Casper. It turned out that she was working part-time outside of her field of expertise, which is microbiology. So, I thought it was a natural fit to teach science."

Chief Traynor nodded at the information and stuck out his hand to offer a handshake to Dr. Gaines, who accepted his gesture. Then, he thanked the principal for his time. Traynor also asked if he could stop in on Bill Crooks' class for a second, and Dr. Gaines nodded approval and turned and walked back toward his office.

Chief Traynor then walked the length of the hallway and stopped outside the last classroom on the right. He peered through the window and viewed a class decorated in a manner expected for a social studies room. However, this one had three different U.S. flags adorning the walls. Each contained a different number of stars in the dark blue field.

Bill Crooks was a veteran but did not look the part since he had cast off his clean-cut military appearance long ago. Instead, he now resembled a mountain man. Aside from social studies, Crooks also taught a life sports class, including lessons on firearm safety, hunting, and making fly fishing poles. On some occasions, the teacher took students afield with him to demonstrate how to appropriately field dress game animals.

Traynor softly knocked on the door and stepped inside to get Crooks' attention. Bill looked up and pointed at Scott Merino and appointed him to watch over the class while he stepped into the hallway.

"Hey Wyatt, what can I help you with," Crooks asked.

"You were involved with some 'black ops' stuff when you were in the service, correct?"

"Well, yes, I was, but if you want specifics, I could tell you, but then I would have to shoot you," he said teasingly.

"Seriously, I want you to take a look at this and tell me what you think," Traynor said and then placed the empty .223 cartridge in Crook's hand.

The teacher examined the casing and turned it up on end to see the stamp at the end. His eyes opened wide when he saw a peculiar mark on the rim just after the *.223*.

Crooks then looked at Traynor and asked him, "you know what this is, don't you?" as he pointed to the mark with his fingernail.

The Chief nodded. "I do, but I needed your expert opinion to validate it for me."

"That is the mark that snipers use to signify hot loads used in windy conditions. Plus, this other mark is indicative of special forces."

"Thanks, Bill, that is what I thought too."

"Where did you find this?"

"Near the creek on the north side of Highway 387.

"That is BLM land. Did you notify the feds?"

"You know, I hadn't thought about that until now, but I suppose I should give that man a call."

Crooks winked. "Don't waste your time; I'll take care of that for you."

"Thanks, but back to the bullet. Could someone use this to hunt antelope?"

Crooks shook his head. "No. It is illegal as hell since the round is technically too small. If a game warden caught you hunting big game with a .223, then the fine would be hefty. It is also a potential forfeiture of your rifle and hunting privileges. But the round would be legal to shoot predators though."

Bill Crooks examined the casing once again. Then he opined, "no, this little cookie here (pointing out the mark again with his fingernail) indicates it is a hot load to shoot in high wind conditions. A lot of ex-operators I know, including a few snipers, swore by this round. But it lacks enough knockdown power for me, so I always prefer a .308."

With that, Crooks tossed the casing back toward Chief Traynor.

He caught it in the air and put it back into his pocket. He thanked Crooks and suggested that they meet up at the rifle range in Edgerton to do some shooting, to which the teacher agreed.

* * *

19

Thursday, September 6, 1984

6:30 p.m.

After supper, Josh left his home to drive to David's house to watch a game film on their next opponent, Big Horn. Located near the city of Sheridan, the rival school possessed one of the finest vistas in the whole state since the football field portrayed the grandeur of the Big Horn Mountains. Though a small town like Midwest, Big Horn served as a desirable living location for those wealthy enough to pay for the gorgeous landscape.

As Josh reached out to open the door of his Plymouth, Chief Traynor drove up in his Bronco and came to a stop.

The Chief rolled down his window and said, "Evenin' Josh, where are you headin' off to?"

"Hi Chief, I am on my way over to David's to watch a game film on Big Horn."

Traynor further inquired, "you haven't seen that green Ford pickup around, have you?"

"No, Sir, I haven't, but then again, I am in school all day, then I am pretty much here at home after football practice, so I can't say I have been looking hard for the truck."

"Please let me know if you do, and don't wait. Call immediately, please."

"Chief, do you have any more leads on what happened to Coach Savolt?"

"I do, son, but they are all pretty thin or purely suppositions at this point. I need hard facts and evidence that directly links someone with what you and I both know is the crime."

"I understand, Sir, and I will help any way I can."

Traynor tipped his hat toward Josh. "I know you will, and thank you. But the best thing you can do for the folks around here is to make sure you give the Big Horn Rams hell tomorrow."

"Thanks, Chief," the boy replied, and Traynor pulled away and drove down Navy Row.

Josh arrived at David's house simultaneously with Ricky, Steve, and Pete. Carlos was there too and had arrived just a few minutes earlier.

While three boys sat on the couch, another in a chair, Josh and Ricky opted to sit on the floor. As always, David's mother graciously provided snacks and drinks for the boys. Next, David bent over the VCR and inserted the tape that Ricky had brought along with him.

Pete broke the silence and asked the group, "have you guys seen the new science teacher?"

"Of course, we have seen her. Do you think we are blind? What about her?" Josh asked.

Pete stood up and puffed out his chest, and said, "well, I think she is hot! So hot that maybe she could make me stay late after class like the Van Halen song *Hot for Teacher*."

Nobody dared to reply to his comment as it would have only encouraged him further. But David, on the other hand, stood up and walked over to the VCR and pressed the pause button and then looked at Pete with an incredulous look and said, "as if she would notice you. The closest you could get to her is if she died at old age and left her wheelchair to you in a will."

The boys erupted into laughter that was so loud that David's mother came down the stairs. She gave the boys a stern look with a resounding, "Shhhhh!" She then followed up by admonishing David, "your dad just got home from work. So please keep things in here to a dull roar."

After his mother left the room, David looked around and asked his friends to keep it down.

He warned, "the next one of my parents who will come in here to tell us to keep quiet won't be so nice because you know it will be my dad, so keep it down."

The boys settled down, and David resumed the video by pressing the play button on the VCR.

The real reason Ricky chose to sit on the floor near the television was that he could control the VCR. He would press the pause and play buttons to point out things he detected on tape. Some things were just formation recognitions, but others held significant importance. Additionally, he would intermittently pause the screen to point out items.

Ricky didn't come up with all these points himself; instead, he lived it day in and day out with his father doing the same thing to him every night.

"David," Ricky said suddenly, "I want you to watch for this," as he pointed to the Big Horn fullback on the television screen. He continued, "watch the fullback, every time the play is a straight dive, he looks straight ahead to where he has to go, now watch this," and Ricky forwarded the tape to another play. "When it is a counter, the fullback looks to the hole where the counter trap play is going to go," he explained.

David shook his head. "You are kidding me; why would he do that?"

Ricky shrugged. "I don't know, but watch the tape. The fullback does it every time. Now you, being the middle linebacker, can foretell where the play is going to go by just watching the fullback before the snap."

True to form, the fullback on tape prophesied each play by a slight turn of the head. Josh made a note of it, too, as his job as the outside linebacker was to contain cutback lanes.

Ricky then turned to the offensive strategy and pointed out Big Horn's defensive tendencies.

"Carlos, if we go into a double tight end set, Big Horn will stack everyone but two cornerbacks within 5 yards of the line of scrimmage. So, we can throw against that."

"But how am I supposed to see anything? It will be a wall of lineman in front of me!" pleaded Carlos.

"Exactly, but that is where our speed comes in. You take the snap and sprint toward the flat where you can look downfield, then set your feet, and throw to whoever is open. But don't take off and run the ball."

"Why not? I can outrun the defensive end and get around the corner," suggested Carlos.

Ricky smiled. "That is what we want the defense to think you are doing. The cornerbacks will fall off of their coverage, and Josh will be wide open twenty yards downfield with nobody around him."

Josh nodded. You know, that will work, once or maybe twice in the game, but their coach will adjust to stop it."

Ricky stood up and walked over to Josh just as if he was the coach himself. He then instructed, "you are right, but both of those times are scoring plays. I also think that our defense can hold them to one score. If we do that, then we will win the game, right?"

David took out the game film and handed the VCR tape back to Ricky to return to his father at the end of the discussion. David then inserted his copy of the movie *All the Right Moves*, and the boys sat back and watched the film for the second time in as many weeks.

* * *

Friday, September 7, 1984

Sheridan, Wyoming

"Order #26, your food is ready at the counter," sounded over the loudspeakers at the McDonalds restaurant. Josh got up from his seat and pushed his way through fellow teammates and other guests for his food.

Josh sat back down and inventoried his order: one filet of fish, one cheeseburger, one large order of fries, and two large Cokes-one to drink during the meal and one for the ride home to Midwest on the bus. On sport road trips, the school paid for meals, and if it were in a sit-down place, the team members would be responsible for providing a tip. Tonight, the monetary limit announced was $5, and Josh far under-spent that amount.

Ricky sat down opposite Josh, only for David and Carlos to follow.

Josh looked at Ricky and smiled. "You are brilliant, you know, simply brilliant. I was so wide open on that play that I could have scored with my shoes tied together!"

Ricky shrugged. "I would love to take credit, but it was my dad. I know you see him as nothing more than a hard case, but he does have a brilliant football mind. Since Coach Savolt isn't here, he has turned to me to be his sounding board. All week long, he has coached me up, so I could tell you guys because he knows you would rather listen to me."

David chimed in, "you called it too, 16-8, just like you said about holding them to one score, but who would have thought that Pete would a touchdown on a reverse?"

The boys soon finished their meals and loaded back onto the bus. Once the team settled into their seats, Coach Fleming took the chance to reiterate his post-game locker room speech. He commended Big Horn as a quality football team and praised the Oilers by beating their chief rival school.

It was true. Big Horn and Midwest had a storied rivalry in football and on the basketball court and the track. Additionally, the core of that Big Horn team would go undefeated in 1985 and win the State Cham-pionship.

The bus slugged up the ramp to enter I-90 south. Unfortunately, it took the driver fifteen minutes to ascend the infamously long and steep hill to the south of Sheridan since the vehicle could barely maintain 20 miles an hour during the climb.

Chet Harrison went immediately to work by selecting music for the ride home. In succession, he played the three George Strait albums, Strait from the Heart, Right or Wrong, and Does Fort Worth Ever Cross Your Mind. But, as fate would have it, by the time Strait's last song, *The Fireman*, began to play, the bus had turned off I-25 at Smokey Gap Junction and onto Highway 387 that would lead them into Midwest from the north.

Josh looked north out of the bus window as it crossed over the Salt Creek bridge. He could make out the thin ribbon of the stream and some of the hills and bushes in the moonlight.

Then he sat back and sighed since it seemed like months had gone by and not just a few days ago that he and Ricky were down there along the creek looking for clues to what had happened to Coach Savolt. To Josh, at least, it was yet another day away from solving the mystery that plagued his thoughts every night.

* * *

20

Thursday, September 13, 1984

Midwest High School

Josh Anderson sat in English class and stared at a personal copy of *The Lord of the Flies* during the silent reading time allotted by Mrs. Pierson. He wasn't thinking about the story since he could give an oral summation about the book on command. However, Mrs. Pierson maintained her distance from him and had barely spoken a word in his direction since their exchange over Orwell's *1984*.

Instead of reading, his mind shifted toward the Oilers' game against Sundance the next day. But then a troublesome thought hit him: he wondered whether Coach Savolt was still living or not? Josh could not shake the feeling of self-imposed guilt because life seemed to push on after the Coach's disappearance. The past weekend only exasperated his subsurface contrition.

The previous Saturday, Josh traveled to Shoshoni with his mom to watch Cindy play two volleyball games against Shoshoni and Basin. On the way home through Casper, his mom made a quick stop at the grocery store, and the two of them arrived home late, but before Cindy and Rob Anderson had arrived home on the bus.

Then, on Sunday, the family attended church like always and came back home for the early 11:00 a.m. kickoff of the Broncos and Bears game in Chicago. The game was a washout, and the Broncos looked overmatched for the entire game and even failed to score a single point. Afterward, his father had him help at the church, and together, along with the Merinos, they organized all of the donated food from a month-long canned food drive. The church served as a valuable resource during the winter that gave food away to needy families.

Josh also refrained from hiking along the creek to look for the *specimen* described in Tim Savolt's notes because the Pronghorn Antelope hunting season was in full swing. It also happened that the entire Salt Creek area was a popular area to hunt them. He balked at the idea of hiking along the creek and spooking game animals from a hunter that needed the meat to feed the family.

What Josh pined for most was a few Saturdays or even a school holiday so that he could resume his search for answers. But as fate would have it, Bill Crooks stopped by the Anderson house the night before and asked Josh to go antelope hunting with him. Considering that Bill and Rob Anderson were close friends, it was not that unusual of a request.

Josh initially hesitated at Crooks' offer since he didn't have a license. Instead, he only bought a deer tag that year, and that season didn't start until October 1st. The teacher explained to Josh and his parents that the boy could help him scout, field dress, and carry out the animals. Then he also admitted that he needed the extra help since he possessed both a primary tag and an additional doe tag and wished to fill them both in one day. Crooks sealed the deal when he offered to split some of the meat and sausage with the Andersons in exchange for Josh's help.

When Josh thought about the possibility of walking along Salt Creek north of town again, he accepted the offer.

Across town, Chief Traynor waited patiently outside the office of Derrick Bostick. The latter served as Chief Operations Officer for all MERP activity within the Salt Creek Oilfield. Then, growing impatient, Traynor stood up and looked at all the pictures on the reception area wall that well documented the Salt Creek history. Some of the photographs depicted gushers, while others of fires and still others captured the aftermaths of floods and blizzards.

The receptionist, Ruth Darnall, finally called for Chief Traynor and led him down the hallway to the last office on the left. He then entered the office only to see Mr. Bostick still talking on the phone. From the abridged information that Traynor overheard, he could tell that the discussion entailed something about a shipment of material that should have arrived from Casper that morning.

Derrick Bostick was in his mid- '50s and was dressed in Wrangler jeans, steel-toed cowboy boots, and a flannel shirt covering a bulbous belly.

Bostick grew up in Taft, California, and was a third-generation oilman. He took this position five years ago and was married at the time. Still, his wife left him because she couldn't stand the Wyoming winters, at least that was the version that Bostick told when the subject came up at the bar.

The man finally signed off on his phone call and grinned at Chief Traynor, though his mustache was so thick that one could ever discern whether he smiled or frowned.

"Good morning, Chief. What brings you here today?" Bostick questioned.

Traynor motioned to the empty chair in front of Bostick's desk and asked him, "mind if I sit down?"

"No, no, not all at....do you want a cup of coffee? It isn't bad, but then again, it isn't that good either?"

"Thank you, Derrick, but I am fine."

Traynor sat down and opened his notebook, and found his page that listed his questions. "Have you heard about the disappearance of the science teacher, Tim Savolt?"

Bostick sat back abruptly and threw his hands in the air. "Why, hell, Chief, everybody knows about that." He moved his body forward and placed his beefy hands on the desk to lean toward Traynor. "Is that what you are here about today?"

"Yes, Derrick, I am here about that. But, more specifically, I want to know what you think about why he disappeared?"

Bostick let out a huge sigh and then got up from his desk and closed his office door. He then returned to his desk, but he stood alongside it close to the Chief instead of sitting in his chair.

"I suppose you already know that many people who work in this field weren't very fond of Mr. Savolt, don't you?"

Chief Traynor nodded and motioned for Bostick to continue.

"A lot of these same folks didn't appreciate the fact that the small field over by the Rattlesnake Mountains got completely shut down over a mouse that Mr. Savolt found there. I also know all about the teacher poking around the oilfield and along Salt Creek. I was also waiting for the day that he published some reports that cast accusations of impropriety against MERP."

Chief Traynor checked off the question in his notebook. Before he asked another one, Bostick offered, "Chief, you are a reasonable man. What kind of red tape or bureaucratic crap do you think the feds and their shiny Environmental Protection Agency would do to us here in Wyoming? Huh, Chief?"

Rather than wait for an answer, he continued, "I'll tell you what they would do, Chief! They would shut down the entire operation in this valley, forcing me to lay off, probably permanently, over 100 employees. Meanwhile, those do-gooders will set up a permanent field study. That is what will happen, Chief! We are up to our eyeballs in regulations, thanks to the EPA. By the way, we fully comply with everything they stuff down our throats. Did you know that all that water we release into the creek is cleaner than we find it in a natural state?" Bostick thundered as he hammered each point home as his fist thumped the top of his desk.

Chief Traynor nodded in agreement. "I understand your position. But if something happened to oilfield operations here, I, too, might be out of a job. That is, once Midwest became a ghost town."

The Chief paused briefly, then continued, "but Derrick, I have to ask, do you know of anyone that might have taken it a step further concerning Savolt?"

"If you are insinuating that I or any of my employees had anything to do with Savolt's disappearance, then you can go piss up a tree, Chief."

Traynor shook his head and held both of his hands up with palms out. "I am not accusing you or any of your employees of any wrongdoing. I am just asking the questions that are part of me doing a thorough investigation. You know that is my job, Derrick!"

Chief Traynor went back to his notes and used the time as a calculated stall tactic. He shuffled to pages forward and then back to the current page and repeated it once more. The tactic worked before for Traynor as his non-verbal communication to Bostwick intimated that he knew more than he had let on.

Traynor finally spoke up, "Derrick, according to my notes, Savolt disappeared on August 25th sometime after 8 a.m. I now have reason to believe that the actual disappearance would have been closer to noon, but that is still speculative. What I want to know is if you have crews working on that Saturday?

Bostick replied, "yes, you know we run a 24-hour, 365-day operation here."

"Could you tell me who was on the day shift that day?"

"Why should I do that, Chief? Are you going to accuse them of something?"

"No, Derrick, I just want to interview them to see if they saw something that might help me put this whole case to bed."

Bostick sat back down behind his desk and studied Chief Traynor's face for at least 30 seconds. His face then softened a little, and then pulled the bottom drawer of his desk open and retrieved a plain manila folder. He opened it, which contained time cards for the last month.

He then looked up at Chief Traynor and said, "on that Saturday, I had three guys that drove around looking at pump jacks and water separators."

Bostick scribbled the three names onto a piece of paper and handed it to Chief Traynor. The list read: *Hank Gorman, Roger Sands, Mike Allen.*

Chief Traynor took the note and thanked Bostick for the information. Then, as he turned for the door, Bostic called out, "Chief, I hope you find out what happened to the teacher. I mean, the kids around here loved him, and I am sure that he has family somewhere that misses him."

"Thanks, Derrick, but Savolt doesn't have any family that I can find other than those same high school kids you mentioned," he said, but then turned and asked, "if you hear anything, please let me know."

"I will, Chief," Bostick replied.

Later that night, Josh took up his familiar position on the floor of David's living room. Once again, David's mother, Toni, catered to the boys with more frozen pizzas. First, the boys watched their 1983 game film against Sundance. Additionally, they viewed another Sundance game against Custer, South Dakota, which Coach Fleming obtained from his buddy who coached the Custer team. Again, it was a simple transaction in reality. Coach Fleming exchanged a 1983 tape on Upton High School for the Custer tape on Sundance.

Sundance, Wyoming, was located in the extreme northeastern corner of the state. It was the same place that Harry Longabaugh spent time in jail, to which he took on a much more famous name of the Sundance Kid. The school belonged in the larger Class 2A division and was much larger than Midwest. However, the two schools enjoyed a long history of playing against one another since they once belonged to the same conference. Midwest traveled to Sundance that year, making three consecutive road games to open the Oilers 1984 season.

Unlike the previous week, Ricky was less animated and had less information to communicate to his teammates. Each boy, however, noted a few tendencies to look out for, and they gained confidence that things would go their way the next day.

Then, for the third week in a row, the boys settled in and watched *All the Right Moves.*

* * *

21

Friday, September 14, 1984

8:00 a.m.

At the Police Station, Chief Traynor picked up the phone and called Deputy Crandall's home in Edgerton. When Crandall answered, Traynor asked for his assistance. Specifically, the Chief wanted help interviewing three MERP employees working in the oilfield at the time Tim Savolt disappeared. Crandall jumped at the opportunity to help, and the two agreed to meet at the gas pumps at the Salt Creek Inn since he needed to top off the tank in his department pickup. The meeting place worked out well for Traynor since he needed to return a movie rental there.

Chief Traynor pulled into the Salt Creek Inn parking lot a few minutes later, and he spied Deputy Crandall already filling his tank at the gas pumps.

He called out to the deputy, "give me a second, will ya? I have to return this," while holding up the VHS cassette in his left hand as proof. Crandall simply nodded in response.

As Chief Traynor entered the hotel office, it always struck him about the diversification of the business. The hotel consisted of 30 rooms mostly rented to oilmen who worked on a contract in the Salt Creek area. However, an occasional tourist would stop there as well. Inside the hotel office was a store that any convenience store chain would have admired. Here, one could buy anything from a gallon of milk to repair parts for a pickup truck. The new thing that Clare Olsen ventured into was renting movies and portable VCRs.

Traynor said, "morning, Clare, just returning this movie," and he set the cassette on the counter.

"Did you rewind it?" Olsen asked, but before Traynor could reply, the older man opened the case and looked at the reel himself.

Chief Traynor then exited the office and walked over to Deputy Crandall, who was still parked at the gas pumps and was leisurely leaning against the bed of his truck. Traynor sidled up next to him and assumed the same posture.

The Deputy spoke first. "So, who do you want to interview first?"

Traynor replied, "I want to talk to Roger Sands," but then he asked, "do you know him?"

Crandall's eyebrows raised with surprise. "Well, heck yes, I know him since he lives in a trailer two slots down from me."

"Do you know if he is home or what time he gets home after his shift?"

"Chief, he is there now. At least he was when I left my place because I saw his truck on my way over here." Then Crandall continued, "but, before we go, I have to admit that questioning a witness is something I don't cotton much. I don't have much experience in it."

Traynor assured him, "don't worry, son, I can lead the questioning, and you can ask the follow-on questions." The Chief paused long enough that Crandall acknowledged him and then instructed, "we could be, you know, the good cop, bad cop type of thing, but we are going to play it good cop versus good cop."

Crandall adjusted his cowboy hat on his head and then met Traynor's eyes. "That'll work."

Deputy Crandall led the way through the streets of Edgerton, and they soon arrived in front of Roger Sands trailer home. Crandall parked on the curb, though Chief Traynor instinctively parked behind Sands' pickup to block him in case the witness tried to flee for some unknown reason.

The officers stepped lightly on the makeshift sidewalk made from discarded 8' pine 2X6 boards that had long ago cemented themselves into the underlying "gumbo" mud. Then, finally, they reached the metal steps to the front door, and Chief Traynor sharply rapped on the door and called out Roger's name.

Soon, afterward, Roger Sands opened the door just a crack and asked, "who is it?"

Chief Traynor announced that he, along with Sheriff's Deputy Crandall, had a few questions for him.

Sands stepped out onto his small metal porch, wearing a black Aerosmith concert t-shirt, a pair of faded Levi jeans, and stocking feet. The officers noted Sands' dour appearance and refused to raise his eyes to meet theirs. Instead, he stood despondently like a child that just got caught with too many cookies.

Traynor took the lead as previously agreed upon and greeted Sands with a hearty "good morning," which was followed up with, "Roger, we would like to ask you a few questions."

Sands instantly blurted out, "I know who you are, and I know why you are here."

Confused initially by the man's unsolicited response, both Traynor and Crandall looked at each other inquisitively. Still, Traynor winked at Crandall with his right eye that Sands could not see and turned towards Roger.

The Chief allowed Roger to confess whatever he felt guilty over, so he asked, "well, Roger, what do you have to say for yourself?"

Sands raised both of his hands with his palms facing forward as if pleading for mercy, then said, "Chief, I know that I shouldn't have bought that beer for those boys because I didn't see any harm in it. I know those kids well over there." The officers turned their heads and followed to where Roger had pointed down the street.

He continued, "They promised me that they would stay home to drink it."

Deputy Crandall spoke up for the first time when he asked, "how much beer did you buy for them?"

Sands quickly answered, "only a six-pack of Budweiser."

"Refresh my memory. On what day did that occur again?" Crandall asked.

Exasperated and genuinely remorseful, the man replied, "last Saturday."

Traynor turned and stepped close to Crandall and whispered in his ear, "trust me and follow my every move here, do you understand?"

Crandall looked up as the Chief stepped back and gave him a quick affirmative nod of his head.

Traynor stepped forward closer to Roger and said, "Sands, if any other boys should come by to ask you to buy beer for them, what will be your response?"

Suddenly relieved at the Chief's question, Sands replied unequivocally, "I will say no, Chief, and I swear to it!"

Deputy Crandall stepped in as well and said, "Okay, Roger, we believe you, so don't do it again."

The man was so relieved by his immediate acquittal of his confessed crime that he sat down on the top step of his staircase. He looked up to the officers and said, "thank you guys, my job would have been in jeopardy if you guys had run me in on something as stupid as that."

"Don't mention it, Roger, but I do have another question for you," Traynor said.

Sands gave a curt response, "shoot."

"Where were you on August 24th between the hours of 8 a.m. and noon?"

"Um, let me think what day of the week was that?"

"It was a Saturday."

Sands looked toward the law enforcement vehicles and then said, "oh, I remember, I was at work checking oil wells."

Crandall asked, "where in the field exactly?"

"I was assigned to a sector north of Midwest around the old Shannon area above Coal Draw," responded Sands.

The Deputy acknowledged Sands' response with a nod and then asked, "did you happen to hear any gunshots that morning?"

Sands looked down at his feet and stared at his big toe that had worn a sizable hole through his sock. He stroked his head in thought and then suddenly lifted his head with a wide-faced expression on his face.

Traynor stepped forward and put his hand on Sands' shoulder and said, "you heard something, didn't you?"

Sands looked at the Chief and said, "I hadn't thought about it until now, but on my way back to the shop while on Light Plant Road, I had to stop and change the right rear tire on my company truck. While I was taking off the lug nuts, I heard something like a loud clap, or better yet, have you ever heard the sound that a sub-sonic .22 round makes?"

Both Traynor and Crandall nodded that they had. Then the Deputy asked, "how many of those claps did you hear?"

Again, Sands rubbed his head to remember and revealed, "two, no three of those loud claps I heard. Although, to be honest here, fellas, I didn't pay it no mind at the time. I thought that someone was shooting far off to sight in their rifle for hunting season."

"Why did you think they were sighting in a rifle?" Crandall asked.

"Because I see it all the time out there in the field since 95% of the land is public access BLM land. Folks generally go out there just to target shoot or plink rounds, but they also shoot quickly, like, BLAM-BLAM-BLAM-BLAM, but folks who are sighting in take their time."

Traynor scribbled notes at a furious pace trying to capture every word. Then Crandall asked, "how much time elapsed between the first shot and the last shot?"

Sands thought about it and said, "probably ten minutes, but I heard the first two shots close together right after I jacked up the truck, and the last shot came just as I was about to put the lug nuts back on."

Chief Traynor wrote down Sands' last words and then placed the pen in his teeth for a second to think. He then removed it from his mouth and asked, "about what time would you say it was when you changed that tire?"

Sands threw up both of his hands, palm up, at waist level, and replied, "I don't know because I didn't look at my watch when I broke down."

"Can you give an estimate of the time?" Crandall asked.

"It was definitely after 10 o'clock since I had to reset the timer on the last pump jack on my list, and I know that I set the local time at 10:00. That last well was only about 300 yards from where I changed the flat tire, so around 10:15, maybe?" Sands replied.

Chief Traynor and Deputy Crandall stepped back about ten yards and compared their observations at a whisper so that Sands couldn't hear them.

Afterward, Traynor stepped back toward Sands and asked, "did you see any vehicles north of Highway 387 or off Light Plant Road?"

With enthusiasm, Sands replied, "heck ya, I did! Just after I replaced the tire, I started back toward town when I saw a dark green 1970s Ford F150 coming fast from my right as I made my way south on Light Plant Road."

Crandall asked, "Is that all?"

Sands' demeanor changed into seriousness. Then resumed speaking, "as I said, they were coming from the right like this." He used his hands to illustrate the effect. "Then that scumbag cut right in front of me to turn left onto Light Plant Road. I don't know how the jerk didn't see me?"

Traynor interceded, "let me get this straight; you said he turned back to the north and not toward town?"

"That is exactly how it was, Chief, he cut me off, and if I didn't put my truck into the ditch on the right-hand side of the road, I would have t-boned him right in the driver's side door," Sands insisted.

"How is it possible that the driver of the truck couldn't see you? I mean, it is a wide-open and flat area out there"? Traynor inquired.

Sands shook his head and shrugged. "I saw them coming, Chief. So, I tried to make eye contact with the driver, but his head turned toward the passenger. It looked to me like they were arguing about something."

"Can you provide us a description of the truck's occupants?" Crandall asked.

Sands looked down at his big toe again. The pink-colored digit turtled out through a hole in his sock. Then lifted his head and said, "I didn't get a perfect look at them because everything happened so quickly. But I do remember that the occupants were both men, and the driver had blond hair. Though I don't remember much about the passenger."

The questioning paused for a moment, and Chief Traynor tried in vain to capture the revelations from the discourse. Then, finally, Traynor leaned over to Crandall, and the two of them exchanged whispered thoughts, and Crandall resumed the questioning.

"So, after you put your truck into the ditch, did you follow them or anything like that?"

"Heck, no, I was running late to check some other pump jacks over by Gas Plant because I wasted time changing my tire."

"Did you see the license plates?" Crandall asked.

"They were greenies; you know that green license plate they have in Colorado. I'd know that plate anywhere."

"Did you get the number?"

"Sorry, deputy, it happened so fast that all I could do was avoid an accident. Yet, when I turned around and looked out the rear window, I could see the green plate with a top border of white mountains. Though I also saw the first two letters, *U G*."

Crandall interjected, "you are sure it was Colorado plates that you saw?"

Sands asked Crandall, "where are you from, deputy? Everyone in Wyoming or Nebraska would instantly know a Colorado green license plate. I mean, you can't go to Glendo Reservoir on any weekend without nine-tenths of the license plates being from Colorado."

Traynor stopped writing and said, "wait a minute, you remember the first two letters?"

"Yes, Chief, it was such a weird combination that I could never forget. But, I mean, come on, *UG*, it was too weird not to remember it."

Then Crandall whispered to Traynor, "does that mean anything to you?"

"It sure does. You see, in Colorado, they use a numbering system on their license plates as we do in Wyoming, except in Colorado, the first two letters indicate the county. Whereas, in Wyoming, the numbers to the left of the bucking horse indicate the same. So, UG will tell us where the truck is registered."

The Deputy thought about what the Chief had just said, and it made a lot of sense to him. While he thought, he shuffled his boots on the makeshift sidewalk boards while Chief Traynor finished writing down notes.

"I have one last question for you, Sands, your co-workers Mike Allen and Hank Gorman; where were they that morning?" Traynor asked.

"Those two were working together that morning checking pumpjacks near Edgerton and over by the Rimrocks after they moved the vac truck back to the shop," Sands replied.

"Wait a minute; I thought you guys worked mainly solo when you check on wells?"

"Normally we do, Chief, but Gorman's truck had four flat tires that morning. It looked like someone stabbed them with a 'Rambo' knife."

Crandall then asked, "does that sort of thing happen a lot to you guys?"

Sands explained further, "as a matter of fact, Deputy, that sort of stuff has gotten to be a regular occurrence around here from slashed tires to sugar in the gas tanks. So now we are finding broken injection well pipes that look like a bullet punctured them."

Once again, Chief Traynor and Deputy Crandall huddled together and inquired if there were any more questions.

Satiated with the information that Sands provided, Chief Traynor looked at Roger and said, "thank you for your information, and we may need you to make a formal statement later."

Sands nodded. "No problem, guys, I'm glad to help."

Traynor started to step away but spun on his heels and said sternly to Sands, "about that other thing we talked about, don't ever do it again!"

"No problem, Chief, I will behave," and Sands turned and re-entered his trailer.

Chief Traynor and Deputy Crandall walked back out onto the street and leaned on the hood of Crandall's pickup.

The Deputy then looked at the Chief with a perplexed look on his face. He then asked, "why didn't we pinch that guy on contributing to the delinquency of a minor?"

Traynor raised his head to the sky and took a deep breath of the early fall air filled with the peculiar scent that only comes at that time of year in Wyoming. He let out a sigh and again looked at the young deputy in the eye.

He said, "that is a good question, but as to the boys that live in the trailer on the corner trailer, one of them is 19 years old, and the other one is his 16-year-old cousin. So, considering one of them is of drinking age and that we have no proof the younger boy drank himself, then we have no crime involved."

After a short pause, Traynor continued, "the 19-year-old lost his driver's license a year ago when a Wyoming highway patrolman clocked him doing 130 miles per hour.

"As he should have," Crandall added.

"But the thing was that the boy had overslept and was trying to get to Casper College to take his SAT exam."

Crandall looked flummoxed.

Traynor continued, "the kid tried to explain himself to the patrolman, but the officer had already decided that the boy's story wasn't plausible because of where the boy lived."

Crandall shook his head in disbelief, but Traynor insisted, "It is true. I talked to the patrolman myself over at the junction store a week after the judge had revoked the boy's license. He told me that he based his suspicion solely upon the fact that the boy came from the oil patch. It was improbable, to him, that the boy was telling the truth about taking an SAT."

"Chief, that is discriminatory on the patrolman's part."

Traynor nodded. "Yes, it was."

"But what is the greater point that you are trying to get at Chief?"

The Chief pointed over to the deep draw on the southside of the road, "Deputy, why does rainwater run down through that draw?"

Crandall shrugged and replied, "I guess it just flows downhill?"

"Exactly, the water follows the path of least resistance. You see, Deputy, people tend to follow the path of least resistance too. People take the easy course, whether because of a minor setback like missing an SAT or being outside their comfort zone. Some people do overachieve, while others just go with the flow. The people in this area are no different than any other larger city in that some folks succeed, while others do not. But, in a small community like this, successes and defeats are more easily seen."

"It is kind of like that, too, in my hometown of Glenrock."

Traynor rubbed his chin. "I would go easy on Roger too. He lived in that same trailer with his wife and his two little girls. The trouble was that Roger's former wife was running around on him every chance she got and even bedded down with a few of his co-workers. To top it off, the judge in the divorce case awarded her custody of the kids and ordered Roger to pay excessive child support. The man does everything he can to support his daughters financially, though he only gets to see his girls two weeks out of the summer."

Deputy Crandall broke off his gaze from Chief Traynor and turned around to look again at the massive draw and followed it southwest toward the Salt Creek.

Traynor turned around and nudged Crandall with his arm and opined, "I see it this way, and I hope that someday you will share this same wisdom given to me. I know the Sheriff's department insists that you guys remain distant from the people in your district so you can remain impartial. Still, our Creator created guys like you and me to make a positive difference in people's lives and not by simply enforcing the most mundane of ordinances."

Chief Traynor allowed his words to sink in and remained silent.

Then Crandall broke the silence, "I see what you mean, Chief, and I appreciate your taking me under your wing sort of speak. It means a lot because nobody else in my department has offered as much."

After a beat, Traynor said, "we have some more work to do. Why don't you follow me over to my office? Once we get there, we will place an all-points bulletin for a dark green 1978 Ford F150 with Colorado license plates beginning with the first two letters of *UG*. We'll say the occupants are wanted for questioning in connection to a possible murder."

"Okay, Chief, but what I want to know is this: if the occupants of that truck are directly responsible for the disappearance of Savolt, then why are they still hanging around here?"

Traynor shrugged. "I don't know either, Eddie. However, perhaps they are still around to make sure nobody finds Savolt's body? I mean, without witnesses or a corpse, we stand little or no chance of ever prosecuting the parties responsible for Savolt's demise. But, first, we have to find them."

* * *

22

Saturday, September 15, 1984

#6 Navy Row

Josh had already made himself a few peanut butter and jelly sandwiches and had filled a Thermos of black coffee when Bill Crooks pulled up in front of the house. It wasn't that he saw him. Instead, Josh heard the truck coming from the time it climbed up the hill from Gas Plant and into town on Fitzhugh and then onto Navy Row. The boy was confident that other Midwest residents had heard the truck too.

Bill Crooks drove a 1960 Willys Jeep pickup that badly needed an exhaust system overhaul. The muffler was in good shape, but holes kept opening up in the exhaust pipes on either side of the muffler. Crooks had made it a habit to patch his exhaust pipes by cutting an ordinary soup can in half, placing it over the hole, and then securing the patch in place using two hose clamps. It was apparent to Josh and everyone else that it was high time for another repair.

The boy exited his house quietly, not that the household didn't hear Crooks pulling up, but he did so out of respect and habit. Josh threw his pack into the back of the pickup next to two giant coolers. When he tried operating the handle to open the door, it didn't work. Crooks noticed that fact and slid across the bench seat to open the passenger door from the inside.

"Sorry about that Josh, it is just another thing that I need to fix on this beast."

The boy jumped into his seat and placed the Thermos and sandwiches on the bench seat between them.

It was cold that morning, and Josh took the time to look at the thermometer positioned just outside the kitchen window. It indicated a temperature of 28 degrees. Like Mr. Crooks, he was dressed in multiple layers that he could shed throughout the morning as it warmed up. Additionally, he wore a blaze orange stocking cap since regulations required hunters to wear the color while afield.

Crooks then exhaustively conducted a three-point turnaround without the aid of power steering. Afterward, he turned north onto Fitzhugh when he exited Navy Row. However, instead of crossing over Highway 387 at the stop sign, the teacher turned right instead, which prompted Josh to ask about it.

"Where are we heading, Sir?

"I have a favorite place up north of here that I like to access from the backside or the east. I've found that if you rumble up Light Plant Road in the pre-dawn hours, that every animal in the valley will pinpoint your presence and seek cover."

Next, the truck turned left at the junction of Highways 387 and 259, and they continued over the hill to Edgerton. Josh noticed that none of the instrumentation lights worked inside the cab. Mr. Crooks illustrated that fact when he turned on the flashlight sitting in his lap to illuminate the cab of the pickup long enough to see the speedometer. Then the teacher slowed down on the outskirts of Edgerton and turned left onto the gravel road that ended at the area's landfill.

Crooks interrupted the silence when he said, "we will take this old back road for about mile, or so that will bring us directly behind the ridge to the east of the Light Plant Road. We will park near Coal Draw and walk up on top where we will have a 360-degree view of the entire area."

The truck turned left as if on autopilot onto an old two-track goat path of a road, and soon, Crooks veered left again onto an even worse trail.

As they bounced and pitched down the track in the pitch-black pre-dawn darkness, rabbits, both Jackrabbits, and Cottontails took their turns of running down the trail in the headlights of the truck.

Then, while climbing over a slight rise, the vehicle's lights illuminated the distinctive color of deer eyes. Josh counted six sets of eyes that watched stoically as the truck passed by them. Seconds later, a badger suddenly appeared before them while holding a prairie dog in its mouth. However, just as quickly as it appeared, it darted off the road and into the sagebrush.

Minutes later, Crooks parked the old truck on a flat elevated table that may have been an ancient oil well location. The two occupants quietly exited the cab. They slung their backpacks and made the quick ascent up to the top of the hill to the west.

The duo arrived at Bill Crooks' favorite roost just as the eastern sky began to cast a pinkish hue. As the sun rose in the east, the land awoke as the darkness recessed into pools of shadows that shortened themselves toward the east. The day started cold with high clouds diffusing the sunlight, which cast a grayish-blue tint to the land that surrounded them.

Josh sat quietly and faced west scanning along the Salt Creek valley, while Bill Crooks pointed his body east to observe the many breaks and draws that led into Coal Draw.

After a while, Josh picked up his binoculars, scanned the creek upstream, and quickly made out objects from a mile away. Then he panned down to the all too familiar landmarks of where he and Ricky had found Coach Savolt's belongings.

Josh continued his sweep and noted where Boswell Draw merged with the creek. He paused for a moment when he observed a small herd of deer that milled around foraging on the edges of the large sagebrush choked drainage. He resumed his scan north along the creek when he glimpsed what he thought was a wisp of steam vapors that rose out of the bank immediately above Salt Creek.

He pulled his binoculars down, rubbed his eyes, and refocused on the area with the naked eye. The boy tried to estimate the distance from the steam column to Boswell draw, to which he guessed to be about 100 yards downstream. Josh raised his binoculars again and determined that it was, in fact, actual steam that rose from the earthen bank.

It was not unusual at that time of year nor throughout the winter, for that matter, for people to observe steam rising from the ground in the oilfield. It was partly due to the hot water injection wells and cooling ponds that dotted the landscape. But this steam plume had a different appearance to Josh since his additional scans of the area failed to reveal any injection wells in the vicinity.

Josh then thought back to the last entry of Coach Savolt's notebook:

"H2O temperature still hot and obtained another sample of the specimen."

Taking up his binoculars again, he scanned in vain to see the steam, but it dawned on him why: the air had warmed up enough that the vapors didn't condense so quickly. Josh made a mental note of where he had seen the mist and vowed to investigate the area after hunting season to find the exact location where Savolt took the *specimen*.

Bill Crooks broke the long silence when he raised his Ruger .270 caliber rifle and thumbed off the safety that emitted an almost inaudible click. Josh slowly turned his head toward the direction that Crooks aimed his gun and saw a fine Pronghorn buck standing broadside to them, not 100 yards away and 20 yards below them.

Crooks wetted his finger and tested the wind direction, and then resumed taking his aim.

KA-BOOM thundered across the land! The next sound heard was Crooks ejecting the spent casing and ratcheting a new shell into the chamber with his bolt action. Josh started to rise when Crooks held up his hand that signified to wait. When the teacher was satisfied that the animal remained down, he turned and gave Josh a quick wink.

The dyad made their way carefully down the hill and navigated around clumps of sagebrush that impeded a direct path to the animal. The buck was found precisely in the same spot but lying on its side.

Josh pulled out his hunting knife and slit the jugular vein on the buck to start the field dressing.

He took note of the bullet placement and asked Bill Crooks, "why did you shoot him in the neck? Because didn't you always teach us in class to aim for a heart shot?"

Crooks nodded. "I did tell you that, and for most people, I would only recommend a heart shot. However, I am an expert marksman, and hitting the neck makes it less traumatic and painless for the animal, and it saves both of the front quarters of meat. Besides, with prairie goats, you have to harvest them cleanly lest their adrenaline starts pumping, which will taint the meat."

The duo made fast and quick work of field dressing, skinning, and quartering out the animal. Next, the teacher made two bags of meat, one which he shouldered, and gave the other one to Josh. When they reached the truck, Crooks unlatched both sides of the tailgate and lowered it with his free hand. Josh, meanwhile, placed his bag of meat on the tailgate and scrambled up into the bed of the pickup. Then he quickly loaded both meat bundles into one cooler half-filled with ice to begin the cooling process.

Bill Crooks then grabbed a handful of ice from the other cooler. He turned to Josh and said, "This is my trick to antelope hunting, which is getting the meat cooled quickly. It prevents the meat from tainting into an overbearing gamey flavor that is notorious with these critters. That is why I always make an exacting shot, too, because a wounded antelope will end up tasting like garbage." He accentuated his point with a hearty laugh.

Josh smiled in return and remembered eating the tenderloins from Pete's antelope last year, which was, by all accounts, barely palatable.

While they took turns pouring water onto each other's hands to clean up from a five-gallon container, Crooks asked Josh, "so how did you guys make out in your game yesterday?"

"We won 26-0. Ricky scored three touchdowns and had like 200 some odd yards of rushing. David scored when he intercepted a pitch on an option play. It happened so quickly that the only one on the field that saw it happen was the referee, who raised his hands, indicating a score. I scored our only successful two-point conversion on a drag pattern across the middle."

The teacher nodded his approval and then added, "football, like life, is fun when you are winning, isn't it, Josh?"

The boy allowed the comment to hang suspended in the air. Perhaps that was the teacher's intention since he often used questions like that in the classroom to spark more profound thoughts from his students.

They grabbed their gear once again and climbed back up to their roost, where they would wait for the next sighting of Pronghorns. Once seated, Josh and Crooks ate their sandwiches and washed them down his semi-hot black coffee from the Thermos.

Directly in front of them and across Coal Draw, a Pronghorn doe stepped out from behind a Cottonwood tree halfway up the north slope. Failing to detect Josh or Crooks across from them, instead, the doe gently lowered her head to eat. Conversely, the hunters carefully and painstakingly lowered themselves to a prone position. Then Crooks raised his rifle again to aim. However, the instant before he thumbed off the safety on his gun, a dark green Ford F-150 pickup appeared out of nowhere and sped north up Light Plant Road toward the old power plant. The doe spooked and returned into the shadows of the tree.

For five long and highly patient minutes, the duo waited for the doe to re-emerge from the shadows, and when she did, Josh heard the safety click off and *KA-BOOM*! The doe dropped instantly and without any fuss.

As they walked downhill and across the Cottonwood choked draw, Crooks looked up at Josh and said, "word is around town that a mysterious dark green Ford F150 keeps showing up wherever you go, son."

Josh didn't know what to say, but that wasn't the expectation of the teacher. So instead, Crooks added, "I also know you and your friends are looking into Savolt's study. Plus, I know you found his field book too."

Josh nodded his head, affirming the teacher's assertions. It wasn't that the boy was embarrassed about the investigation, though he worried his father would disapprove somehow.

Crooks read the dismay on Josh's face and assured the boy, "son, I know I am not your dad, but I don't have a good feeling about that Ford pickup showing up every time you leave town. So, promise me you are never alone out here."

Josh nodded. "I promise, Sir."

"Good boy, now let's get that antelope."

With great teamwork and proficiency, the duo dressed the doe quickly. Afterward, however, the hike back to the truck was more arduous than it was with the buck since the path was straight uphill. The hunters were exhausted upon reaching the pickup; thus, it took a few minutes to catch their breath. Only then did they load up the remaining cooler with the bags of meat from the doe.

A funny thing happened while they backtracked their way toward Edgerton. The once stoic and internally thinking Bill Crooks began to chirp like a little bird and talked on many subjects.

"And I tell you another thing, Josh. I don't for one second think that there is any coincidence between that dark green Ford truck showing up and Tim Savolt's disappearance. For one, nobody saw it until after Tim disappeared, and two, like I already said, it seems like that truck is hunting you. It is as if you know something that its passengers do not want you to disclose."

"Sir, can I tell you something that I trust that you will not take back to my dad?" Josh asked.

"Depends on what kind of information that is, Josh. So why don't you start telling me?"

Josh first rehashed what Crooks already knew about him and his friends retracing Tim Savolt's path along the creek. But he also detailed how the Sheriff's department did a pretty weak job of searching for Savolt as the boys just followed the teacher's boot prints. He then told Crooks about finding Savolt's field book, the backpack full of samples, and the .223 shell casing. Finally, the boy also predicted that Coach Savolt might have found something else that would rock this area, but in a positive way.

"What makes you say that, Josh?"

"It is just the feeling I got from reading his notes. He called this one item a *specimen*, which tells me it is a living thing, and the fact that it was secret only tells me it was something miraculous." Josh also added, "I know in my heart that Coach's report was going to reveal that Salt Creek is not as polluted as everyone assumes it is, but all I have to do is to prove it."

"I understand, but I still worry about your safety." Crooks sat back and looked out his window. Then added, "I admire your passion, son, and you remind me of myself at your age, but you have the tenacity of your dad and the smarts of your mom working for you as well."

Josh let that sink in and then said, "Mr. Crooks, I just can't stand idly by and not find out what Coach Savolt intended to prove in his study plus identify why he might have died over it."

"You think he is dead?"

Josh nodded. "Unfortunately, I do. It just makes sense, Sir, because Coach hasn't shown up anywhere else."

Bill Crooks made the turn toward his garage in Gas Plant, then stopped his truck and turned off the ignition key. He then turned to face the boy.

"Son, the search for truth is never an easy one, just like what you read in your Bible. However, I'm not going to try to dissuade you from continuing your search since only you can satiate your thirst for knowledge."

"Please don't tell my dad. I don't want him to worry about me."

Crooks shook his head. "Josh, if your father asks me directly, I will not lie to him, though I promise not to seek him out and tell him either. How is that for a bargain?" Then the teacher extended his hand out for Josh to shake. The boy quickly gripped the man's massive paw and sealed the deal.

As the duo worked in the garage, Josh was amazed at how quickly the two of them butchered the animals. During this time every year, Crooks converted his garage into a first-rate butcher shop. It was complete with stainless steel tables, a washing tub, and even a bandsaw to cut up more massive animals like elk.

Crooks made effortless cuts throughout the process that trimmed just the right amount of muscle sheath off and carved excellent steaks and roasts. Then it became Josh's job was to wrap and label each cut of meat, though, at times, could barely match Crooks' pace.

The fun part for him was taking all the scraps of meat that the teacher had set aside and mixing it with fresh beef and pork suet to grind it into sausage. As Josh operated a hand-powered meat grinder, Crooks seasoned the meat at differing levels in the large mixing bowl. Once he finished grinding, the teacher inserted his large and powerful hands into the mixing bowl and slowly massaged the spices into the meat.

Crooks then taught Josh another neat trick by using an empty peach can with both ends removed to fill with sausage, accurately measuring one pound of meat. Once again, Josh's job was to wrap and label the packages.

At 2 p.m., Bill Crooks and Josh climbed back into the old Jeep pickup to take the boy home.

As the Jeep moved forward, Crooks looked over at Josh. "I appreciate your help today, and most of all, I enjoyed your company, so this bag is my token of thanks." At the same time, he pointed to the paper bag filled to the brim with select cuts and many pounds of sausage.

The boy grabbed the bag and stepped out of the pickup. Then he turned and faced Crooks again. "Thank you, but I don't know how much I helped since you work amazingly fast with that knife. I felt like that I was in the way."
Before Crooks pulled up to the curb outside Josh's home, he said, "you did fine, and you are one of my best apprentices ever."

* * *

23

Friday, September 21, 1984

Oiler Field, Midwest, Wyoming

The 1984 Midwest Oiler football team played their first home game against another Class 2A foe, Upton. As usual, it was a nighttime contest under the lights at Oiler Field. But to citizens of the Salt Creek community, playing under a lighted field meant a great deal to them historically.

Back on November 19, 1925, Midwest hosted Casper High School to play under the lights supplied by the Midwest Refining Company. This event went down in history books as the first nighttime high school football game in the United States.

The game against Upton was over as soon as the Upton kicker booted the opening kickoff. Ricky Fleming fielded the kick and sped 84 yards for a touchdown. Following Midwest's kickoff, the Oiler defense yielded zero yards to the Bobcat offense forcing Upton to punt. Carlos Mondragon fielded the punt at his 37-yard line and immediately ran to his right. He then exploded through a crease for a 63-yard punt return touchdown.

Minutes later, the Oiler defense pushed the Bobcat offense back 6 yards forcing the Bobcats to punt again. This time, Carlos caught the punt and scampered for another return touchdown. Before the Midwest offense had even taken the field, the Oilers led 22-0. Then Midwest took a half-time lead of 36-0, and Coach Fleming pulled all the starters out of the game and allowed the reserves to gain experience. Every one of the 35 Oilers played in the game, which ended Midwest 42, Upton 6.

Josh remained close to home that weekend and dared not to adventure out into the public lands since the antelope season was still in full swing. Instead, he gratefully accepted his father's suggestion to begin winterizing their cars and the house since colder weather would soon be upon them.

The father-son team completed three oil changes on the family's three vehicles. They also performed specific gravity checks on the antifreeze of the cars. Preparations like these paid dividends later as Josh had already witnessed many vehicles in the area not starting when the temperature dropped to -35 degrees Fahrenheit the previous winter.

The Andersons then turned their attention to the house. Josh went to the garage and retrieved a roll of plastic sheeting, new cardboard lathes, and tucked a staple gun in his back pocket as he carried the supplies back inside the home.

Afterward, the Anderson duo cut precise fitting sheets of semi-transparent plastic to fit over the entire window and casing. They then secured the layers in place with the cardboard lathes stapled to the wooden window frame. The simple procedure was an effective way to keep warm inside and cold air outside the old windows.

This year, though, Rob took out a razor blade, cut a small square in the plastic, and taped the edges down directly to the window. In years past, it irritated the family that nobody could see outside because of the plastic. So, then, the elder Anderson cut out improvised portals for each remaining window in the house.

On Sunday, as fate would have it, the 60-degree weather gave way to a sudden chill from the north that also brought brief and wet periods of snow that socked in the area. So, after church, the Anderson family settled in for a family day together inside their home. As usual, Josh and his father watched the Denver Bronco game on television. The Broncs won 24-14 over longtime rival Kansas City and, in doing so, increased their season record to 3 wins and one loss.

Things seemed to settle down a bit for Josh and his friends during those last two weeks of September. But, to the boys, it remained that two things: school and football were all that mattered. Juxtaposed to this routine was Ricky, whose priorities were Sheila-school-Sheila-football-Sheila, usually in that distinct order. But the boys began planning for their future as well. They had filled out and sent off many college applications during any free time aside from football and school.

Josh had applied to the University of Wyoming, the University of Nebraska, Chadron State College (also in Nebraska), and the University of Northern Colorado, which pleased his parents much. But he also completed the exhaustive paperwork to apply to the United States Coast Guard Academy located in New London, Connecticut.

Early in the school year, Bill Crooks had planted the seed in Josh's head that the Coast Guard was unlike the other service academies. For example, the Coast Guard Academy did not require the cadets to receive a U.S. Congressional appointment. Instead, the academy ranked the incoming cadets upon how well they performed on a standardized qualification test.

That was not all; Mr. Crooks had secretly finagled a Coast Guard Academy representative to visit Josh and his parents in their home in Midwest. The big meeting between the Academy and Josh would occur on the same day that Midwest played football against another Class 2A powerhouse, the Tongue River Eagles.

A few houses down the street, Ricky was also busy filling out applications. He sent them off to the University of Idaho to follow his father's footsteps, the University of Montana, and Utah State. David, too, had sent off an application to Carroll College in Helena, Montana, while also applying to Black Hills State College in Spearfish, South

Dakota. His reasoning: both schools had sent him recruiting letters to play football for them.

* * *

Saturday, September 29, 1984

Josh was home alone after the Oiler's Friday afternoon 36-0 victory at Wright High School since his sister and their parents were in Moorcroft for a volleyball game.

That afternoon while Josh lounged on the couch and watched a University of Nebraska football game on television, someone suddenly knocked at the door. He got up from the sofa and walked over, and looked out the peephole. To his surprise, he didn't see somebody standing there but instead found a cardboard box sitting on the wooden porch underneath his bedroom window. Josh walked out the storm door and went down the steps and onto the sidewalk in his stocking feet. He looked around to see who had just come to his door. However, he didn't see anyone, so he returned to the box left on the porch.

As he reached down to pick up the box, Josh noticed a folded piece of paper affixed to the top with a bit of tape. He lifted the piece of paper, unfolded it, and it read:

Josh,

This box contains all of the lab results from Savolt's study. I only trust you to make sense of Savolt's work. Do not talk about this stuff to the police or your parents because you could end up just like Savolt. There are people here that do not want the results of this study to come out.

Oddly, the note was left unsigned. The boy shrugged and then lifted the box and carried it inside to set it down next to his bed. Then he took each item out of the box to inspect. Josh had a secret hiding place that everyone in the house had overlooked. After looking at the contents, he knew he had to hide all of it. But Josh didn't have to look very hard.

Underneath his super twin water bed, the wooden box frame had separated on the corner on the far side of the bed. The small crack of no more than two inches, yet it was big enough for Josh to wedge in his hand. Over the years, he placed many things in the cubby that he didn't want his parents to see. Now his secret vault contained the new materials delivered to him.

Next, Josh picked up the empty cardboard container and carried it into the dining room, and set it down on the table. He then grabbed a pair of scissors from the kitchen drawer to begin cutting up into small pieces. Only then did he notice a label on the cardboard, it read:

To: Midwest Public Schools
ATTN: Custodial Department
256 Lewis Street
Midwest, WY 82643

A box addressed to the school was puzzling to the boy. Still, he quickly began cutting the cardboard into 4" X 4" squares and placing them inside the kitchen's trash bag. Afterward, Josh hauled everything to the trash can located behind the backyard fence.

* * *

24

Monday, October 1, 1984

Midwest Police Station

Early that morning, Chief Traynor looked over Deputy Isom's report on what he observed the previous Thursday at the Natrona County Library in Casper. Isom had arrived fifteen minutes earlier than what was advertised on the flier that Traynor had found in the field behind the Pierson house.

Isom then reported that he arrived inside the library before the meeting and pretended to browse for books. He noted that when walking by several conference rooms, he overheard some discussions in all of them. Still, Isom could not see inside the occupied meeting rooms. The deputy also reported that he refrained from opening any of the meeting room doors because he didn't want to be seen and cause any suspicions upon himself.

Traynor was a little surprised by Isom's intuition. Nevertheless, he continued to read the report that revealed that the deputy left the library and sat in his car, giving him a clear view of the front entrance.

Chief Traynor set down the report on the top of his desk and got up to refill his coffee cup when he called out, "Isom, come in here."

The deputy appeared almost instantaneously from the other room. Traynor motioned for him to sit down in the chair across from his desk, and the deputy sat down.

He looked up at Isom. "I was just reading your report, and from what I have read, you have done a great job!"

"Thanks, Chief. It felt good to be on something important for a change."

"So, who did you see coming out of the front entrance? I know it is somewhere in this report, but I just want you to fill me in verbally at this point."

Isom cleared his throat and sat up stoically. "I saw both Doug and Shelly Pierson emerge from the building, and I then observed the subjects walk over to and enter their vehicle with Wyoming plate number...."

Chief Traynor cut him off. "I don't need the vehicle information right now, but did you see anyone else from this area exit the building?"

Isom shook his head. "No. I didn't."

Chief Traynor leaned back in his desk chair and rubbed the whisker stubble on his chin. He was in a hurry that morning to get out of the door that he forgot to shave. It worried him none since the uniform regulation didn't require him to have a clean-shaven face. Instead, it was just his preference.

Traynor pitched forward again and asked the deputy, "did you see anyone else from this area at any other point while you were in Casper that night?"

Isom pulled his notebook out of his breast pocket and scrolled through his notes to the day in question. "Yes, Sir, I spied the new Art teacher, Debra Jansen, and her husband Lucas, eating a huge tray of soft tacos at Taco Johns on CY Avenue."

"Did they see you or even acknowledge you?"

"No, Sir, they ate as if they were starving, you know, head down and shoveling food in." Isom then began to demonstrate how the couple ate physically.

"Did you see anyone else?"

Once again, Isom shuffled through his notes. "Yes, Sir, I ran into Tinker Reece at the gas pumps at the Mini Mart off Howard Street in north Casper."

"Did he say anything to you?"

"Yes, Sir. He said a lot."

"About what?"

"Tinker said that we need to catch the 'scumbags' that have been vandalizing all of the MERP property. He also said that there are several injection well leaks all over the oil field that look like they were busted open with a bullet."

Chief Traynor sat back abruptly and started to connect that some things were escalating around the area and not his previous assumption that kids were responsible for the vandalism. Before excusing Isom, he instructed him to begin some random nighttime stakeouts of the MERP truck yard. He hoped to catch someone in the act of vandalizing the company's equipment.

After the deputy left his office, Chief Traynor then picked up the phone and called Deputy Crandall at his house, which served as his office, and filled him in on the latest developments. Just as soon as he hung up the receiver, his phone rang once, and he answered it by saying, "Chief Traynor."

"Chief, this is Doctor Gaines over at the school."

"Hey Doc, is there something wrong?"

"Yes, I need your assistance; somebody or some people broke into the maintenance shop and Reed's apartment last night."

"Doc, how do you know it was a break-in? I mean, that stuff doesn't happen around here much?"

"Chief, the maintenance building was locked as always. It looks like someone broke the window on the side door and let themselves in. From the looks of it, the intruder was looking for something and ransacked both the shop and Reed's apartment."

"But you said this was last night? Where was Reed at the time?"

"Yes, Chief, last night while Reed was in Casper buying groceries. He returned home around 9:00 p.m. and found this mess."

"Why didn't Reed call last night?"

Dr. Gaines let out an audible sigh. "Chief, I don't know why he didn't call you or me for that matter, but he is pretty frightened about it. All he said was that he wanted to wait until this morning to show me what happened. So, I need you to come over to take a look."

"Okay, sure, Doc, I am on my way," Traynor said and hung up the phone.

"Isom?"

"Yes, Chief."

"Grab your hat. We need to go over to the maintenance shop at the school to begin investigating a forced entry incident."

"Okay, boss, I will grab the dusting kit if we want to lift some fingerprints."

"Do it and meet me in the Bronco."

* * *

25

Thursday, October 4, 1984

#6 Navy Row, Midwest, Wyoming

On every night that week, Josh excused himself from the family around 8 p.m. and claimed that he had homework to do, which was usually finished during school hours. His regularly scheduled Thursday night meeting at David's house was the only exception to this new routine. As they had all season, the boys watched the game film, and then the movie *All the Right Moves*.

What amazed him about the movie ritual confirmed the notion he read that some athletes were incredibly superstitious. Josh thought about the example of Roger Maris, who ate "special eggs" to further his homerun streak back in 1961. By all comparison, the movie *All the Right Moves* had become the boys' superstitious obsession.

After returning home from David's house, Josh reached into his hiding spot and took out the notes, charts, graphs, and the map that he studied every night. The more the boy read, the more he grew convinced that all the data supporting the study proved that the Salt Creek was not toxic. Instead, it did have trace amounts of the bi-products anyone would expect within an operating oilfield. Josh also read Savolt's notes that challenged a 1976 water quality study on Salt Creek. The teacher wrote:

The study referenced is nothing more than an unproven hypothesis replete with conjecture where shoddy water sampling failed to prove the existence of toxins other than the naturally occurring sodium and alkali.

However, it was Savolt's hand-drawn map that intrigued Josh the most. He could easily trace each sampling point from # 1 to #24 along the creek. Furthermore, Josh visualized in his mind exactly where Savolt collected those samples. Additionally, the map plotted the location of aquatic plants, which also explained the florae found in Savolt's backpack.

But the word *Thermo* on the map also captivated him. The point was written with a pencil and not a pen, which intimated that Savolt had added this point on the map later into the inquiry.

Josh set the notes aside and laid back on his water bed. But he did so too quickly, which caused the water to splash violently back and forth within the baffle. The action resulted in a loud swoosh noise as the waves hit the side rails of his bed.

Rob yelled out, "hey, what are you doing in there?"

Josh felt embarrassed. "Nothing, dad, sorry."

The boy then heard his dad say to his mother, "it sounded like you broke your bed."

Embarrassed, the boy called out, "sorry, dad," and the resumed his thoughts of the location on the map labeled *Thermo*.

The sketch placed the spot north of Jackass Springs, which meant that it was also a little north of Bothwell Draw. Then Josh heard his voice in his head say, *maybe Thermo is referencing that steam you saw rising out of the bank when you were hunting with Mr. Crooks. It, too, was just north of Bothwell Draw.*

Josh gingerly got off of his bed to not cause another mini-tsunami and placed the map and all of the other notes into his secret vault. The next day, Josh determined to himself. He would find out what *Thermo* meant.

* * *

26

Friday, October 5, 1984

Midwest, Wyoming

The Midwest students had the day off because it was a teacher's in-service day mandated by the new School District Superintendent. Because it was unknown how long the session would take, the district gave an entire day off for students, which was different than the standard half-day in-services.

Accordingly, Josh, David, and Pete made plans on their day off to hunt for mule deer to the north of town since Hunting Area 31 opened up that same day. On the other hand, Ricky turned down the offer to go hunting with his friends so that he could spend some time alone with Sheila unsupervised.

Earlier that week, Josh had discussed his hunting plans with his parents. They did not object to his activity; instead, they merely reminded him to be home in time to meet the Coast Guard Academy representative at 4:30.

In the pre-dawn hour, Josh arrived at David's house, and then they quickly proceeded over to Edgerton to pick up Pete.

Josh caught his friends' attention off guard when he turned north onto the dirt road on the west end of Edgerton rather than driving back to Midwest and then north along Light Plant Road.

"Dude, where are you going?" David asked.

Josh explained, "Mr. Crooks showed me a back way to Coal Draw that doesn't scare everything away if we simply drove up Light Plant Road."

Pete sat up forward from the backseat and placed himself between Josh's and David's shoulders. Then he said, "I know this route. Doesn't it follow near the top of the ridge that ends in a little turnaround area?"

Josh nodded. "It is the same one."

"Well, this car can't handle that goat path, but I know a back way to Coal Draw from here that your car can handle."

Alternatively, Pete instructed Josh to follow the same path that Crooks had driven. However, Pete suggested turning onto another decent road that came out on Light Plant Road just south of Coal Draw. Josh went as directed, and when he reached Coal Draw, he parked his car on a bit of table above the road and below the lookout point that Josh had sat with Bill Crooks.

In the soft pre-dawn light, the boys carefully got out of the Plymouth and made an extreme effort not to make any noise while donning their gear and retrieving their rifles out of the car. The boys then stepped toward the slight cliff edge above Coal Draw. When they looked down, the boys spotted the notorious spot where many high school parties took place. Even in the poor light, they could begin making out the rocks that formed a circle they used as a firepit. The location was perfect for a party because anyone driving north or south along Light Plant Road could not see the bottom of the draw, even with a bonfire complete ablaze.

The only problem with that location was the entrance. The lone entrance into the party spot was via a two-track trail a little further north on the other side of the coulee. Suddenly, Josh realized that he had parked his car in that same spot before.

Josh looked at David and said, "do you remember the keg party that we had up here between our sophomore and junior years?"

David smiled. "Yep, I remember. That was the same night that you refused to give me your keys so that I could spend some quiet time alone with Monica Willis, you jerk."

Pete snickered behind them. "I remember that party because the former Deputy Sheriff busted me, Steve, and a bunch of others because we were parked down there by the bonfire. The cop car blocked our only way out."

Josh looked at Pete and said, "and now you know how me, David, Ricky got away scot-free because I parked in this same spot."

The boys ceased their conversation and took on the task of hiking to the top of the ridge and settled in upon the same place where Josh and Mr. Crooks had sat just a few weeks before. Josh led the way with David and Pete trailing behind.

Sitting atop the roost, David faced due east with a Bushnell scoped, Winchester bolt action .243 caliber rifle across his legs stretched out in front of him. Pete sat a further downhill and focused upon the copse of Cottonwood trees and Grease Wood that grew along the bottom of Coal Draw. Not surprisingly, Pete carried an open-sighted Marlin .30-.30 lever-action rifle since his eyesight was uncanny and didn't need a scope. Meanwhile, Josh took up the same position that he had before with Mr. Crooks. He then focused on any deer movement along the valley floor and upon the other side of the creek less than a mile away.

Josh was armed with a .35 Remington and chambered with 165-grain bullets. He liked the set-up of his gun that his grandfather gifted him. It had a simple Weaver 4 X 4 scope set upon mounts. It allowed him to see through them and still use the iron sights if the gun accidentally bumped against something to knock off the scope's settings.

As if on cue, a slight breeze picked up, and Josh reached up and adjusted the collar of his flannel-lined denim jacket. He noted that it was a lot colder than it was when he hunted with Mr. Crooks. The weatherman on the news had forecasted an overnight low of 26 degrees but it felt about 5 degrees colder than that.

As if a remote light switch had suddenly turned on, the surrounding area began to brighten slowly, just like the lights of a gymnasium, slow at first but steadily illuminated over time. Within five minutes, the boys could see enough command all the land around them within the grayish-blue light.

What worked against the boys that morning was the waning three-quarter moon had shown brightly and unabated by cloud cover for the last couple of nights. That meant that the deer would have been up most of the night feeding by moonlight and would have bedded back down before sunrise.

For 30 minutes, the boys sat ultra-quiet, save from the sound of David opening his Copenhagen tin. David then handed the can over to Josh, who quickly passed it directly over to Pete, who obliged himself with a huge pinch.

Josh grew dissatisfied that he could not locate any deer. He was also disappointed that he could not see the wisps of steam rising from the location that was labeled *Thermo* on Savolt's map. Josh thought that maybe they should load up into the car and make their way north to the fence line that demarked the border between the public and the private land that surrounded the old electric plant. But, instead, Josh looked north and made out the hulking form in the distance.

Built by the Midwest Refining Company in 1924, the light plant provided electricity to the entire oilfield since electric oil well pumps increased production efficiency. The plant burned a waste gas bi-product that heated huge boilers, and then steam turned the twin turbines. In addition to the oilfield, the plant supplied electricity to neighboring towns and camps as well. Sadly, the electric plant ceased operations in the 1950s and stands now as a relic of ages past. By 1984, it became a concrete barn for cows.

Over the years, Josh and many other generations of students had trespassed onto the property. On every occasion that they went inside the hulk, they gazed down into the seemingly bottom-less turbine pits containing coal-black water. Unfortunately, teenagers customarily spray-painted their names onto the concrete. Josh's mark was on the northeastern corner away from the turbine pits. So instead of his name, he painted his initials *JJA* to thwart anyone from identifying him with his trespass. Conversely, David had painted his full name two years prior. Then he received a citation from the former Sheriff's deputy, who regularly wrote down all the new entries upon the walls.

However, Josh remained restless, and just before he suggested that they should move to a new location, he caught a glimpse of movement out of the corner of his eye towards Bothwell Draw. He picked up his binoculars and saw it, the same vapor trail that had eluded him all morning in the same place it had demonstrated itself as before.

But, beyond the mist, Josh saw the unmistakable large ears of a mule deer in the sagebrush. The doe had her head down and was eating on some grass. Josh looked across the void and determined that the boys could easily walk over to that area and would be under some cover as well.

"Guys," Josh whispered.

"What?" David replied in a soft voice that exhaled a column of condensed breath into a cloud.

Josh continued his gaze. "Unless you guys are tracking a deer right now, I suggest we walk down the hill and make our way over to Bothwell Draw on foot because I see at least one doe over there."

David turned and got out his binoculars and asked, "where?"

Josh pointed in the direction, and Pete also turned his head and looked. David said, "I see one, no two does over there," but then Pete whispered, "no, there are four. Look upward about 20 yards to the right."

David shook his head. "Dang, Pete, you are right. Man, you have good eyes." Then he looked at his friends and suggested, "let us go over there because where there are does, bucks are never far behind," and then teased, "just like Pete, huh?

Pete turned around and flashed a wide smile. "Giddy-up."

* * *

27

The boys stealthily moved from their position down the hill and across Light Plant Road toward the deer they located southwest of them. Just as Josh thought, the small tables of land and sagebrush in the valley offered them just enough cover to traverse the treeless plain without being seen by the deer.

When the boys arrived at the creek, they mused as to find a way to cross it. On the one hand, each boy could vault over the stream with one gigantic leap, but on the other hand, a jump like that was dangerous with rifles. Plus, the dark, alkali-frosted mud that lined the banks laid in wait for fools to step on it. The soggy ground was one to two feet in depth, and anyone that became entrapped by it would have to sacrifice their boots for their freedom.

Pete motioned Josh and David to where he stood about a hundred yards to the north. The boy had found an abandoned 24" pipe that still spanned across the creek. Josh bounced his entire body weight on the old pipeline and ensured it was still secure enough to walk upon it. Once all three boys made it to the west bank of the creek, Josh again led the way southward toward the opening of Bothwell Draw, but in the back of his mind, he knew that they would encounter the place marked *Thermo* first.

While Josh had stopped to relieve his over-full bladder into a stand of greasewood, David stepped forward another fifteen yards. When he suddenly stopped, Pete almost ran into his back.

In a soft yet stable tone, David called to Josh, "what is this?" as he pointed to a small pond in front of him shaped like a bathtub and about two to three feet deep.

Josh walked up while still zipping up his jeans and looked to where his friend pointed. Then he said, "gentlemen, I present to you the area where Coach Savolt said he collected the *specimen*."

Standing next to David's left hip, Pete suddenly squatted down to get a closer look at the pool.

"Hey, what is that slimy-looking stuff on the bottom and the sides of this thing?" Pete asked.

Josh squinted, and then he saw it himself. "Good eyes Pete. I believe that has to be the *specimen*."

David sneered at the sight of the organism. "But what is it exactly?"

Josh reached up and adjusted his rifle sling and then used the same hand to lift off his hat to scratch his head. He then returned his hat to its previous position on his head.

"I can tell you what it is not. It is not algae, and it is not a plant. So, I think it must be some form of bacteria."

While he knelt, Pete slid one of his gloves off and attempted to reach into the pool with his bare hand. Without warning, David latched onto Pete's arm with an enormously firm grip just an inch from the top of the water. Then, without letting go of his friend's arm, David motioned Josh to follow his eyes toward the trickle of water that filled the pool. The small stream of water flowed directly out of the earthen bank. In doing so, it had eroded a tiny canyon of sorts down to the edge of the pool.

But what David observed was the tendrils of steam that lifted from the trickle of water. "I bet that water is coming from a broken injection well pipe somewhere near here," he surmised.

Pete's face expressed pain since his arm was still in the talonlike grip of David's hand.

"Let go of me, man. You are crushing my arm!" Pete begged.

"Sorry, dude," David said and released his grip on him.

Pete stood up and rubbed his forearm. Then he looked down again at the pool and asked, "why did you do that? Is it acid?"

Josh unslung his rifle and cleared the bullet from the chamber. Then he leaned the weapon against a stout sagebrush branch. In doing so, it freed him up to carefully kneel to peer over the edge of the cauldron. Then he stood up and folded his arms across his chest.

"It's worse than that," and then he kicked a dirt clod into the pool with the toe of his left boot. "If this water indeed came from an injection well, then that would mean it is from the Ten Sleep formation. If I remember correctly, that water is 200 degrees Fahrenheit at its source, or just below boiling."

Pete shook his head in defiant disbelief, but his expression quickly changed to one of gratitude.

"How hot would you say it is here?" David asked.

Josh shrugged. "I don't know without a thermometer. However, I'd guess it is around 150 degrees. If that is true, it means that David just saved your hand, Pete, since third-degree burns at that temperature happen within seconds."

"You mean that water is just like that in Yellowstone?" Pete asked.

David and Josh replied simultaneously with head nods that affirmed the question. Then, still dumbfounded, Pete removed his ball cap, ran his hand through his thick jet-black hair, and refitted his hat.

Josh then held his hand out with the palm down just above the water, and the heat instantly warmed his hand to the point of being hot. As the boys stood around the pool and contemplated what to do next, a thought occurred to Josh.

"Hey guys, do you smell that?" Josh asked.

Pete grinned and asked, "why did anyone fart?"

"Come on; I am serious here. Do you guys smell anything, anything at all?"

Pete and David sniffed the air and then looked at Josh to indicate that they couldn't smell anything.

"Thanks, that is what I thought since I didn't smell anything either." Josh then stood up and moved closer to David. Then he asked, "David, have you ever smelled injection well water that didn't have the overwhelming presence of sulfur?"

He shook his head and said, "no, I can't say that I have, but what does it mean?"

Josh returned his stare at the pool and replied, "I don't know, I just don't know."

When he lifted his head, David had already grabbed his rifle and had begun marching toward the low hill behind the earthen tub.

David stopped and turned his head. "I'm going to try to find an injection well around here."

Meanwhile, Josh removed a sandwich from his pack, and Pete did the same. They both ate in silence as Josh thought about collecting a sample of the mysterious specimen from the scalding water.

"Whatcha thinkin' Josh?" Pete asked.

"I am just trying to figure out how to get a sample of that stuff without burning my hand."

With a mouthful of sandwich, Pete muffled out, "why don't you use that spoon over there," and Josh followed Pete's finger to where he pointed.

Sure enough, a long-handled cafeteria-style spoon made of stainless steel hung on a small branch of sagebrush, not three feet from him. Josh grabbed the oversized serving spoon and held it upright. Then he took out his now empty plastic sandwich bag and placed it over the scoop. After that, the boy carefully dipped it into the water, which partially filled the container with hot water.

Pete observed what Josh was doing and asked, "why did you do that?"

Josh continued to tumble the bag to ensure he rinsed it with the hot water. Then he replied, "I am sterilizing my bag. Now, here, grab this bag by the edge and hold it up, and then give me your bag."

Pete complied and handed it over. Again, Josh repeated the procedure with Pete's bag as well.

Afterward, Josh grabbed the long-handled spoon again and tried to lift a piece of the specimen out of the water. It was difficult because the chunk of bacteria kept washing out of the bale of the spoon.

Minutes later, David arrived back at the pool. After a quick look, he inferred what his friend was trying to accomplish with the spoon.

David then announced, "I walked in a 100-yard semi-circle and didn't see a thing."

Josh uttered a simple "okay" and then pursed his lips in concentration as he lifted out a sizeable piece of the specimen and placed it in the plastic sandwich bag.

He then handed to Pete and said, "try to get as much air out of the bag as possible and then seal it, please," and then began working on getting another sample.

Pete lifted the bag and looked at it, and asked, "Is this like the bacteria that makes you sick? I mean, what if I get this on me?"

Josh let out a chuckle. "No, I don't think it is harmful, but then again, don't get any on you." Then, after a brief pause, he continued, "I think this specimen came from deep within the earth's crust itself."

"But doesn't bacteria need oxygen to live?" Pete asked.

"Wow, you do pay attention in biology class, after all. But, no, not all bacteria need oxygen to grow, and those that don't are called anaerobic."

David laughed at Pete, which was interrupted when Josh handed him the other bag to seal as well, which caused an instantaneous grimace to form on the boy's face. Josh then separated the two samples and gave one to David to carry while placing the other inside his pack.

David asked, "why did you separate the bags?"

Josh shrugged. "I am just cautious, that's all."

The boys shouldered their packs and reloaded their rifles with bullets in the chambers. Then they and resumed their trek to where they had seen the deer. As the boys made their way through the thick waist-high patch of sagebrush at the end of the draw, they first heard and then saw a group of four mule deer does rise out of cover. Instinctively, the boys dropped to one knee, and they watched the deer bound up and over a small hill to the northwest.

The boys then split up with David on the left flank, Josh in the middle, and Pete on the right side, and they half crawled and half walked up to the top of the hill to where they last saw the deer. However, right before they crested over the ridgeline, a shot rang out, followed by two more. The boys waited for a few minutes before standing up because it was foolish to skyline themselves when someone else was shooting on the other side.

David stood up first, and the other two boys followed his lead, and as a group, they walked over the hill and to the other side. What they saw sickened them.

Two does were gut shot. Entrails hung out of their bodies and strung amongst the sagebrush branches like garland on a Christmas tree. The dead animal next to them was just a fawn. The boys did not know what to do and just stood there and watched the helpless deer that looked back at them as if pleading for help.

All of a sudden, a jeep that carried three occupants roared down the hill toward the boys as it bounded over sagebrush and prairie dog mounts. An older man with black hair sprinkled with gray and a substantial bulbous belly stepped out of his vehicle. He wore a red and black checkered flannel jacket, complete with a leather shooting patch above the right shoulder.

The stranger pulled out his pistol, walked over, and quickly dispatched both wounded female deer with a single shot in the head.

Inexplicably, the man then turned to the boys and demanded, "keep your hands off of my deer!" Except that the man's voice dripped with a heavy accent. The man's speech dropped the "r" off the end of the word "deer." Instead, it sounded like the man said, "dee ah."

The boys held their hands up to signify that they were not a threat and backed away a few steps up the hill, except for David.

He chinned towards the downed deer and said to the man, "you mean those three does that you shot?"

The hunter replied, "Ya, they ah my dee ah!"

Josh then asked, "Sir, do you know what hunting area you are in?"

The man was taken aback at the question and then said, "yes, it is area 34."

David shook his head. "No, this is area 31, and the other problem is that neither area 34 nor area 31 are open for antlerless deer. It is bucks only."

The man stood there confused and did not know what to say next when Pete interjected, "Sir, you should also be wearing something with blaze orange on it like we are, which is also required by the hunting regulations."

The hunter turned and walked over to his companions in the Jeep. Likewise, the boys also started to turn away to walk back toward the creek. Then they heard the stranger say something from behind them.

"What am I supposed to do with these?" the man asked as he pointed to the deer.

Josh looked back at him and said, "go back into Midwest and call the game warden and tell him what happened."

"And what if I don't?"

David sneered, "we have your license plate number, which we will provide to the game warden or the area law enforcement officers when we get back to town. I am sure they will believe our version of the events more than you because we live here."

The boys turned their backs and walked back over the hill, except David. Instead, he sidestepped down the hill and kept the man in his sight least the man did something stupid like taking a shot at them.

At the bottom of the hill, the boys passed the hot spring and crossed the creek over steel pipe again. On the other side of Salt Creek, Josh dug out a watch and noticed it was already 11:30, so he insisted to the others that if they wanted to hunt some more, then they would have to hurry. The boys stepped out on their march across the valley and made their way up the gentle slope and tables toward the area that Josh parked his car just above Coal Draw.

As the boys stepped onto the road, their ears suddenly filled with an overwhelming roar. Josh looked over at Pete, who faced north, and he wore a petrified look on his face, so he naturally followed his friend's eyes.

Barreling down upon the boys was a United States Air Force bomber, a B-52 to be precise, at an altitude of about 500' off of the ground.

The sight of the aircraft was not unusual in the area. Over the last few decades, the U.S. Air Force trained its crews, primarily bombers, on low altitude flights along the Powder River, including the Salt Creek basin. The aircraft originated out of Ellsworth, Air Force Base in Rapid City, South Dakota.

As the bomber approached at incredible speed, David ran up onto the road and raised his rifle over his head, and shouted, "Wolverines!" just like portrayed in the movie *Red Dawn*.

Pete and Josh laughed aloud and watched the flying beast whoosh over them toward the southern horizon. While Pete lauded David over the stunt with the bomber, Josh looked up, and his wide grin vanished into a blank stare. His car was gone.

* * *

28

Josh stumbled over to where his yellow Plymouth was once parked and stopped there with his hands extended sideways at hip level. Meanwhile, David and Pete broke off their laughter and joking when they, too, realized that the car was missing.

"Dude, where is your car?" Pete questioned.

Josh offered no reply. Instead, he stared blankly ahead into nothingness.

David nudged him. "Josh?" and then shook him at the shoulders and repeated, "Josh, did you leave your keys in the car?"

The boy slowly turned to David and returned to his faculties. He then uttered softly, "Yes, I left them in the car under the floor mat like I always do. My dad has always insisted that I do so when I am out in the country like this so that I won't do something stupid and lose my keys."

Pete shook his head in disbelief. "Now, what are we going to do?" To which, David answered, "what do you think we are going to do? We are going to walk back to town."

David grabbed Josh by the sleeve of the jacket and led the way.

By early afternoon, the weather had started to warm up, and the air temperature climbed into the low 50's, which forced the boys to shed a layer of clothing. After walking half of a mile, David suddenly warned his friends, "get off the road."

Josh and Pete complied, and, did so without looking to see what alerted David. Instead, they followed him as they sprinted 150 yards up and over the crest of the hill to the east. At the top, the boys panted so hard that none of them could readily speak. Instead, David then motioned with his arm repeatedly that the other two needed to look back over the other side. Still panting, Josh crept back to the crest of the hill, lay down in a prone position, and looked down toward the road.

Confused as to where to look, Josh looked back over his shoulder to David. He then raised his eyebrows as if to ask, "where?"

David scrambled up the hill in a low crouch, looked over the hillcrest, and pointed to a place near the creek.

Then, between pants, "do you see now why we had to get off of the road?"

Appearing below them on the valley floor was a 1970s model dark green Ford F150. It drove slowly along the road that paralleled the Salt Creek. Both Josh and David lifted their binoculars and studied the truck and its occupants.

"I see two men, one a small guy with dark hair, and the other is bigger with wide shoulders and short blond hair," Josh described.

"I agree. That is what I see, too," David said.

Then Pete offered, "that smaller guy has a pointed or weasel-like face."

Josh and David looked at Pete with a mixture of astonishment and amazement. "How in the heck can you see the smaller guy with a naked eye when we can barely make him out with binoculars?" David asked.

Pete shrugged. "I don't know. I just told you what I can see."

Next, the boys withdrew well out of sight on the backside of the ridge.

David stared at his still panting friends. "That truck looks like it is hunting something, and I think that something is us?"

Josh shook his head. "I don't understand? How come it is that every time I am out here, that stupid truck shows up. I mean, how could those guys possibly know when or where I will show up?"

"That's easy," Pete said authoritatively, and David motioned for him to continue. "Someone is watching whenever Josh goes, you know, a spotter."

Before Josh or David openly dismissed his suggestion, Pete continued, "my mom thought that my step-dad was cheating on her. So, she set up a whole network of friends to call her whenever they spotted him going from one place to another. It turned out that he just went from the house to work and back to the house every day…. kind of like that."

David nailed the point home when he asked, "it is just like *Big Brother* always watching us *proles*, isn't it, Josh?"

"What are you talking about, and who is *Big Brother*?" Pete asked.

Josh cast a long gaze on his friend. "It is from that book you are supposed to be reading in English class, you know, *1984*."

Josh then patted Pete on the shoulder, and the boys resumed their trek toward home.

The boys unanimously decided to follow along the ridge to the south toward town even though the ridgeline slightly angled easterly toward Edgerton the closer it got to Midwest. If they calculated correctly, they could emerge over the ridge on the north side of the Salt Creek Golf Course just behind the ninth hole tee box. From there, the boys determined that they could skirt the bottom of the hill and out of sight until they crossed Highway 387 behind the sixth hole tee box.

Josh, David, and Pete walked for another hour, but it was slow and cautious. Every twenty steps, at least one of the boys turned around and looked behind them for the mysterious truck. Finally, Josh rechecked his watch, and it indicated *2:02* p.m. Then he told his friends, "We need to hurry."

Surprisingly, Pete possessed not only incredible eyesight, but his navigation skills proved to be uncanny as well. Pete led the way up to the top of the ridgeline that made a bend toward the east. At the top of the ridge, they looked around. Midwest stood to their right and to the left; the large tank that supplied drinking water to Edgerton sat boldly upon the end of the ridgeline the boys had followed. Then, while looking below them, they saw that they were directly above the green of hole #8.

Peter looked at his buddies and shrugged. "Sorry guys, I was off by fifty yards," and then broke out into his unique and silly laugh.

The boys scrambled over the crest and then kept to the bottom of the slope as planned, which afforded them some cover. However, at the slight rise before crossing the #7 fairway, Pete stopped abruptly.

He tapped David's arm and said, "look," and pointed toward the northwest.

The small rise gave the boys a slight advantage because they could see the beginning of Light Plant Road and the medical helipad just north of Highway 387. Next to the pad sat the mysterious dark green Ford F150 facing north with a full view of anyone that traveled along Light Plant Road.

The boys decisively moved out quickly and crossed over the fairway. Next, they carefully stepped over the borrow pit fence. Then, just as they learned in Hunter's Safety Class, each boy handed their rifle to another while they swung each leg over the barbed wire. They repeated this procedure when they reached the other side of the road.

Just before emerging onto Burke Street, the boys were alerted to the sound of another vehicle that approached them. However, this one was so noisy that Josh instinctively knew who was behind the wheel.

* * *

29

Bill Crooks came to a screeching halt in his Jeep pickup and abruptly told the boys, "Get in now!" Josh, David, and Pete quickly tossed their gear into the bed of the pickup truck and scrambled up the rear bumper themselves. Once the boys loaded, which took only seconds, the teacher pulled away from the curb and turned left down Burke Street, and then made another left onto Navy Row. Instead of stopping in front of the Anderson home, Crooks parked his truck as close to the garage as possible.

Josh collected his rifle and pack from the bed of the pickup. Then, together with David, Pete, and Bill Crooks, they entered the house's side door and noisily went up the back steps and into the dining room.

Meanwhile, Rob Anderson jumped up off the couch, discarded his coaching notes onto the coffee table, and walked back to greet them.

"What's going on, guys, and why are you home so late, son?" The question caused everyone to freeze in place, including Bill Crooks.

Rob looked sternly at his boy. "I thought I made it clear to you about coming home early today? I mean, don't you have an interview today and a game tonight?" he sternly interrogated at a volume just under yelling.

Josh and his friends stood idly by and were petrified. None of them knew exactly where to begin their story. Rob then looked over at Bill Crooks, who remained frozen in place like the boys.

Then Rob greeted him, "Hey Bill," with a significantly softer tone.

Then Josh's mother, Sara, emerged from the back bedroom behind the group. However, her approach was vastly different than her husband's.

Instead, she said, "Hi Bill," and nodded at the two teens next to him and greeted them, "boys." Then she asked, "why don't you all just sit down while I get all of you something to drink because you look like you could use it."

Josh, his friends, and even Crooks found a seat at the dining room table. Sara walked over from a few steps away in the kitchen and set down a large plastic bottle of cola and five glasses. David reached out and began to pour everyone a pop. Only then did Josh start telling his story to his father, who remained speechless ever since his wife's interjection.

"What do you mean someone stole your car?" Rob shouted to his son.

Josh recounted the specific details of where he parked, where the boys hunted, and when he discovered that his car was missing. The boy then told his dad about the mysterious dark green pickup.

Abruptly, Rob stood up from the table and covered his ears in a gesture that intimated that he had heard enough. Then he strode away from the table and walked down the five steps to the back door. Next, Rob exited the opening and walked out into the yard.

Rob paced in the yard next to the house and was completely embarrassed that he lost his temper with Josh. He reassured himself that taking a quick break offered a chance for him to cool down, but he questioned himself why he was so mad in the first place.

Inside the house, Sara served the hungry boys some leftover goulash, which to Wyomingites was a dish comprised of hamburger, any type of noodle, and tomato sauce. Bill Crooks, however, graciously refused the offer of food and instead grabbed his drink and went outside to talk to his friend.

Seconds later, Crooks walked up to Rob and tapped him on the shoulder. It startled Rob, and he turned around with a jerk of his head.

Bill nodded. "Before you say anything, I want you to see something," and he grabbed his friend's sleeve and led him toward the back gate of the yard. Crooks stopped 50 yards beyond the back fence and into the open field. He then dug out his binoculars that were concealed under his flannel shirt and gave them to his friend.

"Take these and look over to the helipad and then just to the left and tell me what you see."

Rob begrudgingly threw up the binoculars to his eyes and slowly adjusted the focus of the lenses. "I'll be darned. A dark green Ford F150 is sitting next to the helipad facing north."

Rob lowered the glasses down and looked at his friend, and from Bill's viewpoint, his friend's face had lost all color and had a wild and surprised look in his eyes.

Bill nodded again. "Your boy told you the truth, didn't he?" Before Rob could speak, Crooks continued. "After our in-service ended at noon, I immediately went out to my favorite roost by Coal Draw to hunt and possibly lend the boys a hand if they had anything down. But from where I sat, I looked down upon the turnout above Light Plant Road. It was then that I saw fresh tire tracks in the dirt. So, I went down, and I could make out Josh's distinctive tire tread from the winter tires that he always rides on, but something else caught my eye."

"What was it?"

Crooks narrowed his eyes. "Rob, there was another set of tires with an aggressive off-road tread that had parked next to Josh's car."

"That doesn't explain someone stealing Josh's car?"

"No, it doesn't. But I have a hunch that whoever drove that other vehicle took your son's car. Judging by the footprints I also saw, I think the boys were somewhere down by the creek, and when they returned, they saw that the car was missing and had turned toward town."

"So, you never saw the boys?"

Crooks shook his head. "No, I did not. But after seeing that truck, I figured the boys had seen it too and were making their way back to town on foot along that ridge to the east of Light Plant Road. I also reckoned that if they did, they would emerge somewhere along the golf course, which is exactly the spot that I spied them."

Rob rubbed his forehead as if his brain had exceeded its capacity to filter and sort the information that his friend had just given him. He then stopped, looked up at Crooks.

"Why is it that you associated that green pickup truck with some sort of danger?"

Crooks dropped his head. He secretly dreaded having this very conversation with his long-time friend. He shuffled his boots and finally looked up.

"Josh confided in me that he has been secretly putting the pieces together about the study that Savolt conducted...."

Rob cut him off. "Why is that news? You know how word travels in this town? I mean, you cannot go to the bathroom around here without everyone knowing whether or not you lifted the toilet seat or not!"

Bill nodded. "Okay, but I think whoever is in that pickup has been hunting your son ever since he started his inquiry. That truck went past him and me while we were antelope hunting just a few weeks back too. It's as if someone is watching your son, and anytime he goes afield, that pickup shows up."

Rob thought long and hard about the enormity of the situation, but he just didn't know what to do next.

"Rob, can I suggest something?"

"Sure," he said curtly.

"Let's go inside and call both Chief Traynor and Deputy Crandall and get them over here to file a stolen car report, and I will witness to it as well. Then, as to Josh, I suggest that he doesn't go anywhere afield unless you or I are with him."

Rob nodded his head that he understood and then turned back toward the house.

Then he teased his friend, "why can't it be something simple with my son? You know, something simple like girlfriend problems?"

Bill chuckled and then pointed down five backyards to the one behind the Flemings. Then he said, "you mean like that?"

The teachers not only saw but audibly heard a fiery argument between Ricky Fleming and his girlfriend, Sheila.

The men turned and smiled at one another. Then Rob suggested, "I guess I should be thankful, huh?"

After re-entering the house, Rob telephoned Chief Traynor. He reported that Josh's car was stolen and requested that he and Deputy Crandall come over to his home. Traynor informed Rob that he and the deputy were together in his office, and they could walk over within minutes.

* * *

30

Deputy Crandall arrived at the Anderson home with Chief Traynor in tow. Josh sat down with both officers at the dining room table and explained the whole story again. Chief Traynor scribbled down the make, model, and the color of Josh's vehicle, although he could do it from memory.

The boy recounted the entire story again that included the mysterious appearance of the green Ford. Pete spoke up and gave his description of the two occupants in the truck. Even Bill Crooks stepped forward to authenticate that the boys did emerge onto the golf course and into town, where he picked them up. Afterward, Crooks then excused himself to take David and Pete home. Still, he promised to return to the house with the U.S. Coast Guard Academy representative as previously planned.

Deputy Crandall and Chief Traynor pulled Rob and Josh aside and assured them that the car would turn up. They also suggested that maybe an oilfield worker became stranded and borrowed the car to get some help. However, neither Josh nor his father Rob believed the suggestion, but they nonetheless thanked the officers for their support.

Just after the lawmen exited the house and before they exited the gate, Josh bounded out the front door and ran up to the lawmen.

"Hey, Chief, I almost forgot, when we got over to Bothwell Draw, we ran into three guys in a red Jeep who illegally shot two mule deer does and one fawn. We told the guy that we would tell you two when we returned to town."

Chief Traynor chuckled, as did Deputy Crandall. Then, Traynor looked at the boy and said, "I talked to the guys you described around noon today when they drove up to my rig at the junction store. It turns out that they were out-of-state hunters from Massachusetts, as you probably detected from their accent. The squat and rotund man said he needed a game warden to report that three teenagers harassed them about the deer they had in the back of their Jeep. So, I called the Game Warden on the radio, and he showed up about 25 minutes later. The Warden took one look in the back of the Jeep, and he cited all three for taking the illegal game and for wanton destruction of animals. He also confiscated their guns until the pending court date."

Josh looked up at Chief Traynor, and all that the boy could say was "wow," before he turned and ran back into the house.

Though, just before Josh reached the porch, Deputy Crandall shouted toward him, "good luck tonight!"

Chief Traynor then looked over at Deputy Crandall and said, "let's go over to the helipad and see if that truck is still sitting there."

After walking over to the office to get into the department Bronco, Traynor turned right off of Navy Row and onto Fitzhugh. When they went over the cattle guard just before the intersection with Highway 387, the lawmen could see that the truck was no longer sitting where the Andersons reported it. Instead, Crandall looked at the Chief and motioned for him to drive towards the helipad anyway.

Next, Traynor parked the Bronco on the side of Light Plant Road. Then he and the deputy exited the vehicle to look around, and the two of them split up to look for any clues that might validate the boys' story.

It didn't take long for Crandall to find the tire tracks where a vehicle had sat. Based on the impressions of the tire tread in the soft soil, it was most apparent that the pickup truck had an off-road set of tires. But, suddenly, Traynor told the deputy to stop and wait while he went to get his polaroid camera from the back seat. When the Chief returned, he took several photos of the tire tread impressions in the soft soil.

"Chief, I see something else here, look!" instructed Crandall while he pointed to the bits of white and brown paper in two distinct and opposing places on either side of the tire tracks.

Traynor walked behind the deputy to see what he had found and then took a pen from his left shirt pocket. He used it to turn the bits of paper over.

"Well, Deputy Crandall, it looks like that the two occupants of the vehicle smoked. These tiny bits of paper are cigarette butts, and I can read the word *Camel* on one of them."

Crandall shook his head. "But why are the butts torn up? I mean, most people drop them out of the vehicle and onto the ground?"

"That is what I thought too. But then I remembered my experience in Vietnam. Our platoon sergeant showed all of us how to field strip a cigarette for fire safety. It also came in handy while we were on patrol in the jungle."

Crandall furrowed his brow. "What do you mean, Chief?"

"What I mean is that troops would carry out their cigarette butts in their pockets, lest the enemy tracked us like a trail of bread crumbs."

After a brief pause, the deputy spoke, "I get it! So maybe we are dealing with a couple of former service members who are still in the habit of field stripping their cigarettes even to this day. Is that what you are thinking?"

The Chief stood up. "Exactly. But I also think this is a fit with other clues like the military-issued .223 bullet casing."

After loading back into the Chief's Bronco, Traynor relayed that the two needed to get back to his office and update the previous all-points bulletin for the Ford pickup. However, this time, they will include the descriptions of the Ford pickup's occupants as provided by Pete LaRoche. Traynor also added that they would need to meet with the County District Attorney's office to discuss where they were at in the Savolt disappearance and potential murder case.

At precisely 4:40 p.m., Greg Domenget and Bill Crooks arrived at the Anderson home as previously planned. When the doorbell rang, Rob warmly welcomed the representative from back east into their humble abode. At the sound of the greeting, Josh came out of his room and shook the representative's hand.

"I am pleased to meet you, Mr. Domenget."

The visitor smiled and said to Josh, "my team had a bye this week, so I took this trip. So, if you qualify for the Academy, Josh, you may start calling me Coach Domenget."

Josh smiled at that prospect and then ushered him to the nearby couch. The coach then asked Josh about his academic progress and achievements. Then he explained the process that Josh would go through if he received acceptance into the Coast Guard Academy. The coach also informed the boy more about the U.S. Coast Guard and its dual role in providing coastal defense and law enforcement actions within United States waters.

Only then did the coach talk about football. "So, what position do you play, Josh?" Coach Domenget asked.

Josh replied, "I play two positions, Sir. Tight end on offense and outside linebacker on defense, and I play on all special teams too."

The coach nodded. "I see, so your coach likes to play ironman football in only putting the best athletes on the field, huh?"

Josh shifted in his seat a little and further explained, "to be honest, Sir, in a school our size, I don't think Coach Fleming has many choices. But, as you will see tonight, our replacements are young and pretty small."

"Well, I like the fact that you are familiar on both sides of the ball, and I am sure we can find a position that we can use you in. But, right off, I think you could make a good safety with your size, and you would get to work with me because I coach the defensive backs. But we will see what you do tonight," Coach Domenget said as he reached over and patted Josh on the knee.

The conversation turned to idle chit-chat about Midwest, the Salt Creek Oilfield, and Wyoming in general. Finally, the guest offered that he was from a small farming community in central North Dakota himself. He credits his deeply rooted small-town values for providing him with a foundation throughout his life.

Suddenly, Josh looked up at the clock mounted on the wall above the television. He then informed the visiting coach that he needed to get to the school and prepare for the game. Coach Domenget stood up, shook Josh's hand, and told him that he would meet him down on the field immediately following the game.

Josh turned and quickly disappeared into his room. He then put on his maroon and white letter jacket, grabbed his gym bag, and exited the house for the quick walk to the school.

Meanwhile, Josh's parents continued to entertain their guests and offered them some more coffee and a slice of apple pie, to which the coach eagerly accepted. In between bites, and sips of coffee, Coach Domenget assured the Andersons that Josh would fit in well at the academy. Moreover, he predicted that once their son graduated from the academy, an exceptional career awaited the boy if he chose to do so. Still, at Josh's five-year point, the boy could decide to exit the service. Meanwhile, Bill Crooks sat silently, and if the living room weren't so small, nobody would have known he was there at all.

After the coach lifted his last forkful of pie to his mouth and then set down the plate on the coffee table, he looked at Josh's parents. Then he re-emphasized that the five-year service commitment after graduation was all Josh had to do in exchange for the excellent education he would receive from the academy.

As if on cue, Domenget and Crooks stood up, and the coach thanked the Andersons for their hospitality and that he would see them both at the football game.

However, when the coach reached the door, Sara stopped him. She then asked, "I am a little curious, coach. How is it that you came to notice my son from the east coast and then travel out here in the middle of nowhere to visit him?"

Coach Domenget recognized Sara's suspicious expression. He replied, "let's just say a little birdy called me and recommended your son and then sent me his academic transcripts and game films."

"But who?"

Domenget winked at Sara and then nodded toward Bill Crooks, who stood sheepishly alongside the coach.

Sara turned toward Bill and threw up her hands around his thick neck to hug him, and said, "oh, thank you, Bill."

Oiler Field

6:20 p.m.

Cars and pickup trucks began to trickle into the stadium's parking lot. Additionally, vehicles lined Ellison Avenue along the cliff edge above the field. From that vantage point, fans had an excellent view of the game and could have a tailgate party if they wished. Soon, the fans watched as 35 Oiler players marched down the hill from the school to the stadium in their maroon home uniforms. Then the boys took the field to warm up.

Yet, from the time Josh arrived in the locker room until he entered the field, the more he retold the story, the more it felt like a fairy tale than the actual truth. Thankfully, both David and Pete were there alongside him to validate the account.

Josh didn't think that Ricky had heard a thing because his friend was so distraught about his sudden breakup with Sheila just a few hours before. Ricky was so outwardly angry that David came up to him before the game and head-butted him, helmet to helmet. He then demanded Ricky to wake up and use that anger on the field.

However, the undefeated Tongue River Eagles were warming up on the other side of the field, who boasted some big linemen. Still, they also had one of the best halfbacks in the entire State. Located in the town of Dayton at the base of the Bighorn Mountains, Tongue River High School was also three times the size of Midwest in student enrollment. Despite the classification difference, the schools continued a long history of competing against one another.

The game began when Brian Agee put his toe into the opening kickoff that traveled 70 yards in the air and bounced off the goal post for a touchback. After that, neither team could move the ball very far on offense, though the Eagles' halfback burst through the line a couple of times for eight- and nine-yard gains, respectively. But by halftime, the score remained knotted in a 0-0 tie.

After the Oilers had a three-and-out possession to open the second half, Steve Otten dropped back to punt and boomed a 45 yarder. Pete LaRoche streaked down the left sideline and blasted the Tongue River return man just as the ball touched his hands. The football rolled freely behind the returner, and Josh recovered the ball. Then the Oilers scored on the next play on a 20-yard run by Ricky on a sweep to the right side. Additionally, Josh caught the two-point conversion that made the score 8-0.

Tongue River came back on their next series and scored a touchdown in only four plays but failed to add a conversion. Then, Tongue River opted for an onside kick by booting the ball into the back of an unexpecting Oiler freshman on the return team on the ensuing kickoff. However, one of the Eagles fell onto the ball, giving Tongue River possession. Making matters worse, the Eagles scored on the next play. Thus, it made the score 12-8 at the beginning of the fourth quarter.

Following the kickoff, the Oilers began a 14-play march of their own. Finally, they pulled ahead when Carlos tucked himself behind David. The latter snowplowed a path through defenders to lead the quarterback across the goal line. Afterward, Chet Harrison scored up the middle for the two-point conversion, putting the Oilers ahead 16-12.

With less than two minutes to play, the Eagles marched into Oiler territory. Then on a crucial third down, the Tongue River halfback broke loose through the line of scrimmage with nothing but open space in front of him. However, Josh sprinted and chased the boy down from behind. As he tackled the runner, Josh wrestled the ball loose and forced a costly turnover. From there, the Oilers ran out the clock and remained unbeaten and untied for the season.

As promised, Coach Domenget made his way to meet Josh on the field after the game. After patting many of the Oilers on the back, the coach finally caught up with Josh.

When Domenget spun the boy around, he said, "Josh, next year, you may be my new starting safety!" But then he continued. "That play at the end of the game, you covered the entire width of the field to chase down that kid. That kind of play, son, is just what we look for at the next level."

Josh profusely thanked the coach again and then walked him over to Coach Fleming, who had just finished talking to the Tongue River coach. He then introduced the coaches, and the two walked off the field, talking about Josh's college prospects.

* * *

Monday, October 8

Josh and Ricky still felt soreness in muscles they didn't even know they had as they climbed into Ricky's car to go to the school. The boys had spent most of the past weekend together to ice sore muscles, plus the fact that Ricky and Sheila had remained apart. But, just like every day since the previous Friday, Ricky's attitude continued to be distant and sullen.

After turning onto Shannon Avenue towards the school to the south, the boys noticed a small gathering of people standing at the junction of Highways 387 and 259. The crowd carried signs, but neither Josh nor Ricky could make out what they said from that distance.

Josh suggested, "let's go over to the junction store so we can see what is going on?"

Ricky replied with a curt, "okay," and turned his car onto Lewis toward the gathering of people and took an immediate left into the store's parking lot.

The boys then got out of the Volkswagen and stood near the rear of the vehicle. From there, they heard a rolling chant from the group: "*No More Oil, No More Oil, No More Oil!*" The boys looked at one another in disbelief, and when they looked back, both of them could now read the signs that the protesters carried.

"*Oil kills?*" Ricky questioned.

Josh nodded. "I see that one, and there is another one that says, *Stop Poisoning Salt Creek!*"

"Who are these people, and why are they here, Josh?"

He shrugged. "I don't know, but I am sure we will know more tonight because look who just pulled up."

A news crew from Casper turned onto Lewis Street off of Highway 259 and crossed over the cattle guard on the edge of town.

A few minutes later, the boys arrived at school, placed their letter jackets inside their lockers, and then went together to their first-period Chemistry class. Once in the lab, the boys overheard two debating students about the protesters at the Junction. Josh and Ricky sat down next to David and listened silently. Soon afterward, Ms. Kowalski entered the room and closed the door. Instead of stopping the students' discussion, the teacher sat on the front of her desk and seemed to enjoy the free talk.

However, Josh became irritated that the talk continued throughout the daily recital of the Pledge of Allegiance. So instead, Josh, Ricky, David, and Scott Merino stood up and faced the flag and placed their hands over their hearts. Other students followed their lead as well.

During the middle of reciting the oath, Ms. Kowalski waved at the standing students to sit down. But, she said, "it is okay, you don't have to do that; we have a great discussion going on this morning."

Undeterred, the four boys remained standing until the end before they sat back down in their seats.

Afterward, Ms. Kowalski stood up from her seat on the edge of her desk and walked amongst the students. Then she turned around and announced, "I have a new class rule. If we are discussing something, we will not be interrupted by anything except a fire alarm. It also includes stopping to recite an obsolete Pledge of Allegiance."

While she said so, Ms. Kowalski batted her heavily mascaraed eyelashes and nodded as if soliciting approval from the students. Josh remained in utter silence and again thought back to what his dad said about correcting others. He foresaw that if he did say anything, another visit Dr. Gaines would await. So, he kept quiet.

However, the usually reserved and introverted Scott Merino pushed away from his lab station and stood up.

Then the boy said without restraint, "Ms. Kowalski, my grandfather died in Belgium with the 101st Airborne during World War II. He died defending the freedoms that all of us enjoy today. I stand every day to honor him and every other hero that didn't make it back home. I think it is the least thing that you or I could do to honor their sacrifices!"

Ms. Kowalski stopped and stared at Scott and briefly did not know what to do. Then she blinked. "You need to go across the hallway to Dr. Gaines' office, and I will be there right behind you."

Scott grabbed his things off the top of his lab station and made his way to the door, though he stopped and cast a harsh glare toward the science teacher. Then he mumbled something.

"What was that?" the teacher asked.

In a loud voice, Scott retorted, "I see I have the right to free speech only if it agrees with your position."

"That is enough, Scott! Get out now!" shouted Ms. Kowalski. Then she turned and challenged the rest of the class. "Is there anyone else that wants to go see Dr. Gaines too?"

Josh and Ricky looked at one another with mouths agape and then turned their faces toward their open textbooks that sat open on the lab table in front of them. Then, as promised, Ms. Kowalski got up and joined Scott Merino in the Principal's office.

However, as she opened the door, she looked over her shoulder and instructed the class, "review chapters five and six. I will be right back."

While the school was abuzz with the news of the protest at the intersection, Chief Traynor sat in his department Bronco outside the junction convenience store. He also silently fumed. Earlier that morning, his call to the District Attorney was not the welcomed advice he sought. Instead, the official told him that all of the evidence collected so far did point to a crime. Moreover, without a body or corroborating witnesses purporting a murder, the case would remain an open missing person's case.

The phone call was nearly identical to the one Traynor had with his friend Ken Hopkins at the state DCI office. The agent sadly shared that the DCI had yet to receive any new information about Tim Savolt. Yet, still, Hopkins cautioned Traynor that "without a corpus delicti," he was at a dead-end in the case.

Suddenly, Deputy Isom opened the passenger door and snaped the Chief out of his brooding, if only momentary. As the deputy stepped inside, he handed Traynor a cup of coffee. But then, almost instantaneously, the vehicle filled up with the smell of a freshly microwaved green chili and cheese burrito.

As Isom took his first bite, Chief Traynor asked him, "how on earth can you eat those things?"

"What?" mumbled Isom through his mouthful.

Traynor pointed at the burrito and then at Isom's belly. He then said, "when that thing starts working there, you will stand outside all day, or you can walk back to your house and come back here in your cruiser. I don't like the nuclear explosions that will come out of you."

Isom quietly finished his burrito, and as he did, he pointed toward the highway junction and asked, "I wonder who that is?"

Chief Traynor saw it too. A red and white Trailways bus with the destination scroll above the front windshield reading *CHARTER* pulled into the parking lot. It came to a stop 20 yards directly in front of the Bronco. The bus door opened, and the Chief counted 37 people exiting and all of them carrying protest signs. The passengers quickly assumed their position alongside the original protesters. Meanwhile, the television news crew captured the entire scene.

Traynor turned to his deputy and asked him to walk home and return with his department cruiser quickly. Isom nodded and opened the door in compliance without a word.

The Chief then got out of his unit and walked over toward the bus, where the driver stood outside to stretch his back, which indicated it must have been a long ride.

The bus driver nodded at Traynor and offered a quick greeting, "good morning." He quickly introduced himself to the driver and then asked, "where did you start from?"

The driver said, "from Denver. I thought I had drawn a good hand when my boss called me last night when he said there was a charter for me into Wyoming. My error was assuming the passengers were a bunch of retirees wanting to go to Yellowstone or something."

Traynor laughed. "Well, you are a long way from Yellowstone."

"Thanks, officer. I've had my fill of sarcasm already this morning after catering to this bunch of wackos."

The Chief nodded apologetically and then asked, "what do you mean by wackos?"

The driver turned coldly toward Chief Traynor and explained how he had to listen to the four people in the front of the bus. Mile after mile, the group ranted at him about diesel exhaust's effect on clean air and how oil and coal were dirty energy sources. Additionally, the driver recalled how the group derided the people of Wyoming by insinuating that only the poor and uneducated live in the state. Then he also recalled how one protestor professed that the entire state of Wyoming should become a national park and kick out all of its residents to Nebraska.

Chief Traynor's eyes danced with curiosity. "Why Nebraska?"

"Good question, and I fell for it too when I asked that woman over there in the tan poncho to explain. She said that Nebraska would be better suited than Colorado for Wyoming refugees because Colorado has evolved from old west conservatism into the model of progressivism, whatever that means."

Traynor stepped back in shock and asked the driver, "she said that?"

"Verbatim," and then the driver added, "though I work in Denver, I was a born and bred in Wyoming, Wheatland actually, and this bunch just pushed me over the edge."

The men turned and watched the crowd walk around in a circle and vocalizing their incessant chant.

The driver spun his body around to the Chief. He asked, "Is there another way out of town other than driving through that bunch over there?"

Traynor smiled. "Why? Is it your intention to leave them?"

The driver nodded. "Absolutely. I will drive back to Denver, and when I get there tonight, I will tell my boss he can have my job. There is no way I will withstand a return trip with that group."

"You are just going to strand them here for me to take care of them?"

"Don't worry, the ring leader has the number to the dispatch center, and she could call for another bus to complete their pre-paid charter. So, officer, is there another way out of this town?"

Chief Traynor nodded again. "Follow me," and he led the bus straight down Lewis Street and on to Fitzhugh and up to the stop sign at the junction of Highway 387. The driver gave the Chief a thumbs-up and turned left onto the highway to link him with southbound I-25.

Just after Traynor turned his truck around and started back for Midwest, his radio squawked, "Chief Traynor, Deputy Crandall."

Traynor lifted the handset off its mount on the dashboard and replied, "Chief Traynor, go."

"Chief, this is Deputy Crandall, and I have located the missing 1969 Plymouth Fury III."

"What is your 20?"

"I am sitting under the Interstate 25 overpass on Old State Road 25 north of 387."

"Roger Deputy, I can be there in about ten mikes."

Josh and Ricky caught up with Scott Merino in the cafeteria at lunchtime and set their lunch trays down next to him.

Josh asked, "so, what did Dr. Gaines tell you?"

Scott dropped his fork back onto the tray that contained a colossal mountain of mashed potatoes and meatloaf. Then the boy looked over toward Josh.

"Dr. Gaines told me that sometimes, it is best to keep my thoughts to myself rather than argue with a teacher in public."

Josh nodded. "I know. That is the same thing he told me."

A few minutes later, while Josh slid his empty tray into a slot on the wash cart, Rob Anderson pulled his son aside.

"I just got a message from Deputy Isom, who relayed that Chief Traynor and Deputy Crandall have found your car. Go to your locker to get your jacket, and then meet me in my car in the parking lot. We will go out there to bring it back home."

"Okay, Dad," Josh said with excitement in his voice.

Josh climbed into his dad's 1980 Pontiac LeMans and left the high school parking lot. However, the father-son duo decided to exit town out the back way as vociferous protestors had all but stopped most of the traffic from entering or exiting Midwest at the junction.

As he entered Highway 387, Rob looked over at his son. He then asked, "what is on your mind

Josh shrugged. "Nothing Dad, I don't get why those people showed up here to protest. I mean, none of them are from around here, so what gives them the right to dictate anything to us?"

Rob searched for the right thing to say to his son but came up absent. So instead, he reached over and patted his son on the knee. Afterward, the two of them rode in silence as Rob turned right onto State Road 25. Meanwhile, Josh looked out of his window and exchanged a stare with a lone Pronghorn buck that watched the vehicle speed by him. Then the boy spotted the pond that used to be the local swimming hole until Pete and Steve found a dead sheep floating on top of the water last May.

Soon, the interstate highway overpass came into view. Rob pulled over to the side of the road behind Chief Traynor's Bronco. Instantly,

Josh exited his father's car quickly began inspecting his abandoned vehicle.

"Rob, Josh," greeted Chief Traynor.

"Is the car alright? I mean, is it wrecked or undrivable?" Rob asked.

Traynor lifted his hat a little and replied, "the good news is that it is drivable. It starts because we found the keys under the seat. But the bad news is that it looks like someone was looking for something. Take a look at the carpeting pulled back and the slash in the backseat. Yep, somebody did that deliberately."

The boy walked up to his car and looked inside. It was just as the Chief described. Josh stepped back from the open window and then turned and leaned his backside against the front fender.

Deputy Crandall addressed the Andersons in informing them that he lifted a couple of fingerprints off the inside of the trunk lid. However, the rest of the car was devoid of prints. He also explained that Chief Traynor was taking the fingerprints that afternoon to the Wyoming Department of Criminal Investigation in Cheyenne.

Rob twisted his mouth in confusion and asked, "why not your department in Casper, deputy?"

Crandall folded his arms across his chest and looked down at the pavement. But, he said, "we have a hunch that whoever stole your son's car might be connected somehow to Tim Savolt's disappearance. The Chief has a friend inside the state DCI to run the prints for identification."

"I hate to question you, deputy, but again, why not send these into the lab in Casper?"

"I know what you are getting at Rob, but I believe that certain people within the county believe the investigation into Savolt is a total waste of time. However, if we get a fingerprint match from what we lifted off of your son's car, we may get a great lead to solving the greater mystery."

Deputy Crandall wasn't lying. Two days ago, Sheriff Doan summoned him to meet him in his office in Casper. First, the Sheriff admonished his deputy for wasting the department's time on a missing person's case. Doan insisted that anybody with common sense would end the case and allow the "Midwest Constable" to handle it.

Then Chief Traynor stepped forward and gave Josh the set of keys to his car and told him, "It okay for you to take your car home," and patted the boy on his shoulder.

Rob turned toward his son. "Okay, Josh, you heard him. We need to get this car home, and I will excuse you from your afternoon classes while you clean up and straighten out everything inside your car, but be sure to make your football practice,"

"Thanks, Dad."

Both of the Andersons turned their cars around and headed back to town.

Meanwhile, Chief Traynor turned toward Deputy Crandall. "I am leaving for Cheyenne right now. But I need a favor."

"Sure, Chief, anything."

Traynor nodded. "Good. Could you hang out around the junction to make sure things don't get out of hand with that protest? Because if it does, I doubt that my deputy can handle it."

"No problem, Chief, I can do that, but why are you leaving so soon?"

Traynor looked skyward and then dropped his eyes toward Crandall. "Haven't you noticed that the temperature has dropped about 15 degrees since we arrived out here? I think we might get a storm that will sock us in for a while."

"Want me to stop by and tell your wife what you are up to?" Crandall asked.

Traynor started to shake his head no, thinking he would call her later, but then thought better of it and said, "yes, that's a good idea, and tell her I will call as soon as I get to Cheyenne."

Minutes later, Josh parked his car in the family's empty garage. Then he began the task of re-setting the carpet, which he had to glue back into place with a lot of rubber cement. Next, Josh cleaned up the mess of loose stuffing from the backseat and then retrieved the old wool army blanket from his trunk and fashioned a seat cover out of it. All the while, he kept a close watch for any hidden clues that might have escaped Chief Traynor and Deputy Crandall, which he did not.

Afterward, Josh got back into his car, started it, and turned the heater on because it was already getting chilly. He left the garage and slowly drove east on Navy Row, and then he spotted something. So, Josh stopped his car, got out, and left it idling in the middle of the street.

He then walked over to the chain-link fence outside the art teacher's house and looked up at the long, thin, grey-colored antenna that rose from the ground to above the gutter line on the roof. The antenna's base extended a small cable that entered the house through a visible, freshly drilled hole in the wall because he spotted bare wood around the entry point. The antenna puzzled him, but he got back into his car and drove back to school for football practice.

As Josh drove south on Shannon Avenue, he looked over toward the junction. He noticed that the protestors were no longer marching in a circle. Instead, they all sat on the ground and huddled up to protect themselves from an icy wind that blew.

Immediately after crossing over Lewis Street and onto Teachers Row, Josh stopped his car once more. He noticed an identical antenna erected next to Pierson's house like the one on the art teacher's home.

* * *

32

Thursday, October 11

Midwest Police Station

Chief Traynor returned home to Midwest three days later. He carried with him two dossiers, which contained added information to the case file on Tim Savolt. Then, after an evening of reuniting with his wife, Chief Traynor called Deputy Crandall in the morning and asked him to meet him in his office.

When the deputy entered the Police Station, he hung up both his jacket and hat on the coat rack, and then filled himself a cup of coffee that resembled liquified tar. He then walked into Traynor's office and sat down in the seat immediately in front of the desk. The Chief looked up at Crandall and said nothing but sported a sly grin as if daring him to ask about the results of the fingerprints.

"Okay, Chief tell me what you found," Crandall said as he took a sip of coffee. He then winched at the bitter aftertaste of the brew.

"My buddy in Cheyenne was able to run those prints that you took off of Josh Anderson's car. They matched these two gentlemen," Traynor said as he handed the folders over to him.

Crandall opened the first folder and said aloud the name, "William E. Pruitt." Then unsealed the second folder and said, "Marvin A. Stiles," and then looked at the pictures of the men that also accompanied the folder.

Traynor interrupted the deputy. "I'll save you some reading. Stiles is 34 years old, six foot one, and has blond hair. He once was a special forces operator who was a suspect of hiring himself out as a mercenary. He also has a standing warrant out in Texas for vandalizing some oilfield equipment."

Crandall lifted his eyes suddenly from the page and looked at the Chief like he couldn't believe what he just told him.

"The other turd, Pruitt, is the same age and also a former special forces operator. I would bet the two of them met while they were in the service and currently work together as hired thugs."

Deputy Crandall sat back and slowly absorbed the information from the files. Then he asked, "Is there any information about Pruitt or Stiles before entering the service. I mean, where is their hometowns?"

The Chief shrugged. "I am not sure, but maybe that is something I can ping my friend at DCI to gather for us?"

Then, finally, the deputy rose and refilled his coffee cup and returned to his seat. After another gulp and a further wince, he said, "let me see if my theory matches yours. So, these two guys were hired to do away with Tim Savolt and then hung around? Why would they do that?"

Crandall paused to look inside his coffee mug but refused to take another mouthful of bitters. Then he continued, "I believe they hung around to make sure that nobody discovers where they stashed Tim Savolt's body. How does that match so far?"

Chief Traynor nodded and intimated for him to continue. The deputy set his mug on the desktop and said, "but, what they never expected was a group of high school kids that would start finding clues left behind. Now, these thugs are trying to find something that they believe Josh Anderson has in his possession that links Savolt's disappearance to a murder. Am I still tracking the same as you?"

Traynor nodded and then motioned with his hand for the deputy to keep going. Crandall obliged, "what we don't know is where these thugs hang out, how they know about Josh finding that evidence, and how is it that every time that Josh and his friends go afield, that the thugs show up?"

Traynor shifted forward in his chair and laid his meaty hands upon the desk. Then he said, "you have come to the same conclusions that I have, and I harbor the same questions. But here is what I think: there are other folks around here involved with something greater that we don't even know about."

"Are you referring to that staged protest?"

"Yes, I mean, why they would come up here from Denver to protest in Midwest of all places? Couldn't they have protested at one of those small oilfields in Colorado? It just doesn't make sense unless someone had organized this thing to come here."

Crandall's forehead suddenly left its furrow and dropped back into its natural place on his face as he deadpanned his response. "Wasn't the tag on that dark green F150 a Colorado plate as well?

Traynor rubbed his eyes. Then he shook his head. He looked up at Crandall and said, "we cannot break this case until we detain and question Stiles and Pruitt or if we find Tim Savolt's body."

"I know, Chief, I am waiting on that break in the case too."

* * *

Friday, October 12

The Oiler football team entered the final stretch of the season and every player, Josh included, focused all attention on the sport. All during that week, homecoming, the Oilers still rode the high after knocking off Tongue River from the unbeaten list the Friday before. However, they now focused their attention this week on the Hulett Red Devils. By now, the team chant of *OFT* became a town-wide phenomenon as the crowd shouted *OFT* following every positive play by the Oilers. *OFT* had even made its way onto posters that littered walls and lockers throughout the school.

The game was a blowout as Midwest built a 36-0 lead over Hulett by halftime, and once again, Coach Fleming removed the starters and inserted the reserves for the rest of the game. But, all week long, David kept talking to the freshmen and reserve sophomores about the solid black helmets of Hulett. He especially emphasized how those helmets would leave a black scuff mark upon the white ones the Oilers wore.

David went too far, though, when he mentioned that obtaining the marking of the other team's helmet your own was a symbol of toughness. Then, during the fourth quarter of the game, the remaining freshmen entered the contest. Standing at five-foot, one inch tall, and 105-pounds, defensive back Randy Masson substituted in. On Masson's first play from scrimmage, he jumped on the dogpile of Oiler tacklers and squirmed his way to the Hulett ball carrier. Then, the boy received a 5-yard delay of game penalty. The infraction? The boy refused to let the Hulett running back regain his feet because he continued to aggressively rub his helmet against the helmet of the Hulett player.

The real scandal of homecoming wasn't the delay of game penalty—instead, Ricky's former girlfriend, Sheila, arrived at the dance with Pete LaRoche. Apparent to everyone, Pete had superseded his two-week rule following the breakup of Sheila and Ricky.

Josh heard all about it from his sister, Cindy. During gym class on Tuesday, she overheard Sheila telling another girl all about in the locker room. The two had been secretly seeing each other since last June. Incidentally, that date aligned perfectly to when Ricky was in Douglas, Wyoming, to attend American Legion Boys' State.

After the homecoming game, Josh talked to Ricky about Sheila and Pete as they walked back up the hill from the stadium to the school. Ricky thanked Josh and relayed that he already knew about Pete and Sheila. That issue was what they had fought about regularly since last summer. Josh decided to skip the homecoming dance and went home instead. He invited Ricky to come over to his house, and the two of them spent the rest of the evening watching videos on the show, Night Tracks.

* * *

Friday, October 19, 1984

A week later, the Oilers survived a scare from another larger 2A school, Moorcroft, during what most remember as one of the coldest games under the lights in Midwest history. The fog from the nearby cooling ponds and Salt Creek flooded the field with a dense cloud that made throwing the football nearly impossible. Nevertheless, Moorcroft jumped out to a 21-8 lead by halftime, which had benefited from Ricky's three fumbles deep inside Oiler territory.

During halftime, David pinned Ricky up against the equipment shed and told him that if he couldn't get his head on straight, he should just walk off the field and let a freshman carry the ball for him instead. It worked because Ricky rebounded with three rushing touchdowns, and the Oilers won 28-21. The win also cemented the 1984 team with the 1980 Oilers as the only two in school history to complete the regular season undefeated and untied.

* * *

Saturday, October 27, 1984

Then, in the following week, the Burlington Huskies came to the Midwest for a playoff game to determine who would go to the State 1A Championship game. This contest was a rematch of a playoff game held in Burlington the previous year when the visiting Oilers dominated the undefeated home team by winning 21-8. Ricky scored two touchdowns in that game, one of which was a 50-yard interception return for a score. But the Huskies had no luck in playing the spoiler role this time as Carlos Mondragon returned the opening kickoff 70 yards for a Midwest touchdown.

Then after the Midwest defense stopped the Huskies on a fourth down and goal to go at the 8-yard line, Carlos scored again off a quarterback sneak. The play was supposed to get a yard or two but turned out to be a 92-yard scamper up the middle. Midwest eventually won the game 54-8, and the team anxiously waited for news as to whom they would play for the state championship.

But what most people would end up remembering most about this particular playoff game was not the 92-yard run. Nor would they recall the five turnovers that the defense took away from Burlington. Nor was it the 54 points the Oilers scored, which was the second-highest total in Midwest history to that point. No, what was remember most were the protesters. Scores of them that lined the highway coming into Midwest chanting *No More Oil*. They even picketed outside the football field fence in the parking lot once the game began.

In response, the fans that packed Oiler Field, and the others who stood shoulder to shoulder along the cliff high above the field, began to drown out the protesters. So loud was the chant that the protestors gave up by the end of the first quarter and went home, wherever that was. The special cheer heard around Midwest and throughout the entire game was *Oil Field Trash*!

* * *

33

Monday, October 29, 1984

Midwest, High School

After arriving at school, Josh took his usual seat alongside Ricky and David in their first-period Chemistry class. Since the exchange with Scott Merino weeks before, Ms. Kowalski refrained from commenting further about the Pledge of Allegiance. Though Scott still held a grudge since he never saw her recite the words herself. Instead, the teacher always remained seated behind her desk with her arms folded across her chest.

Then, oddly, the voice of Dr. Gaines sounded from the speaker. He declared that the school would hold a memorial service for Tim Savolt at 2:00 in the main gym on Thursday. Additionally, he asked students to volunteer, setting up the gym.

From that moment on, all the energy and the excitement over their massive win against Burlington fizzled. Plus, any momentum the Oilers had to overcome the rival Cokeville Panthers faded away like grey-white ash blown from a spent campfire. Hearing Tim Savolt's name publicly again brought out the underlying guilt that Josh had managed to bury deep inside him for much of the school year. Now, he wore the repressed emotion on his sleeve for everyone to see.

Ricky continued his melancholy attitude about losing Sheila, but on that day, he was devastated. The day before, Sheila became Mrs. Peter LaRoche. Pete's parents and Sheila's mother had agreed that the two should marry for a couple of reasons. First, both Ricky and Sheila were 18 years old, and, secondly, Sheila was pregnant. The ceremony was a small and private affair with Pastor Roberts officiating. David had heard about it through the Salt Creek pipeline that Sheila's due date specifically targeted the conception date around the time of Ricky's absence from town last summer.

Football practice later that afternoon was sloppy. It oddly resembled the mediocre attention to detail and execution that the team exhibited when Coach Savolt went missing. Weighing on Josh's mind was the ridiculous notion of memorializing the teacher during this of all weeks. Yet, Dr. Gaines thought it was appropriate as a motivator for the team before they left Friday morning for the state championship game on Saturday.

However, the unintended consequences of the planned memorial reminded the players of their loss of a great teacher and coach. The timing of the memorial service also served as an object lesson that decisions have consequences, both good and bad. It also intimated that even the noblest of intentions might fail due to insufficient forethought.

Tuesday, October 30, 1984

By noon that day, the team had received word that Scott Merino would not travel to or play in the title game. The reason given was simple: he was academically ineligible. It all stemmed one day back in September when Scott's mother checked him out of school and took him to Casper to see an allergy specialist. As expected, the boy went to all of his teachers the next day and received his missing assignments, save for typing class. Instead, Mr. Pierson told him that he could make up his typing test in class at any time. Scott took the make-up exam a few days later and gave it to Mr. Pierson, who accepted it. Yet, the exam remained ungraded for reasons unknown and left a "0" in the grade book.

When midterm report cards came out on Monday, Scott had carried an F in typing. Mr. Pierson maintained that Scott had yet to make up his test and one other assignment, and it was now too late to do so. The

Wyoming High School Athletics policy at the time mandated that each athlete holding a C average and have no failing classes. Scott's failing grade on the midterm rendered him ineligible for athletics.

Ironically, Merino needed only one core class to graduate, and his schedule mainly was elective courses like typing. Scott's parents and Coach Fleming strongly objected to the ruling, but Dr. Gaines informed them there was nothing more that he could do.

Wednesday, October 31, 1984

Before leaving the house that morning, Sheila reported her new last name and marital status to the school district registrar's office. What happened next, nobody could have predicted. Unbeknownst to anyone, Sheila had sparked an archaic school district policy. It prohibited married student-athletes from competing in sports or other school-sponsored activities. Dr. Gaines appealed to the district superintendent, and they discussed the matter. But she refused to make an exception to the rule.

Dr. Gaines was displeased to notify Peter that he wouldn't play in the State Football Championship or any other sports for the rest of the school year. Plus, he had to tell Sheila that she could no longer participate in cheerleading.

Because of the loss of two starting players, Coach Fleming sat his team in the small gym before practice and discussed how they would overcome. He also uncovered the new game plan to compensate.

Thursday, November 1, 1984

During first period, David suddenly felt ill and excused himself to see the school nurse. He later went home a fever and a weird rash. His mother immediately took him to the Salt Creek medical clinic to get checked out by the doctor. Unfortunately, David was diagnosed with chickenpox. It was remarkable that he had never contracted the virus earlier in his life. So, David's mother set up a quarantine unit in her basement. She tended to him over the next week until he showed signs of no longer being contagious.

At lunchtime, Josh sat with Steve Otten and Carlos Mondragon. They talked about what they needed to do now since the Oilers were down three starters on offense and defense. While they schemed, Dr. Gaines walked up and asked to speak to Josh alone for a second.

After Josh got up and walked a few feet away from the table, Dr. Gaines leaned toward his ear. He asked the boy, "would you mind saying a few words about Mr. Savolt this afternoon? I mean, you of all the students in this school knew him the best, and I think it fits for you to memorialize him."

Josh was immediately awash with grief. It was almost like getting clubbed. Then, after a few moments of silence, he eked out a meager response, "okay."

Later that afternoon, the entire junior and senior high filled the gymnasium. First, Dr. Gaines talked about Tim Savolt's life, beginning with his childhood in Thermopolis. Then he spoke of Tim's military service. And then, he finished by talking about Savolt's years of teaching and coaching in the Midwest.

Afterward, on a white screen behind the podium, a slide projector clicked through various pictures of Tim, both in the classroom and on the practice field. Meanwhile, Karen Connelly silently sobbed, while strangely stoic Kandi Kowalski held her hand while trying to console her. Many students, including Josh and his friends, perceived that Connelly had overplayed her histrionics.

Josh then stepped forward on Dr. Gaines' cue and took his place behind the podium. He stood silently in front of his schoolmates, and his face told his silent anguish about what he had to say. He finally cleared his throat and said:

"It is difficult to memorialize a teacher, a coach, and a friend when the nature of his disappearance is still unknown. I wish I could tell you that he is alive and well and living in another place, but I cannot. I wish I could tell you that he met an unfortunate accident along Salt Creek, but I cannot do that either. I wish I could tell you that his life had ended by evil characters, but the lack of evidence prevents me from telling you that either. But what I can do is offer my thanks and appreciation to Coach Savolt for inspiring me and many others to succeed in everything we do, from academics to sports. I also want to thank Coach Savolt for instilling in me the never-ending quest for truth. I am comforted by the verse found in first John, chapter one, that I shouldn't just believe the truth, but that we should live by it as well. So, to my classmates and mentor, Mr. Timothy Savolt, I pledge to live out that scripture by always seeking the truth. Thank you, coach, for your wisdom and your constant caring for all of us here in the Salt Creek community. If Coach can hear me now, wherever he is, I hope he understands the true pride we bear behind the letters O-F-T."

Josh silently exited the podium, and instead of returning to his seat, he walked over to his father. The latter stood against the gymnasium wall next to Bill Crooks. Rob then gave his son a tight and warm hug that proclaimed his pride, and Crooks reacted by patting both on their backs. After the father let go of Josh, the boy nodded at his dad and the civics teacher. Then he turned and went into the locker room to get ready for football practice.

As students filed out of the gym, Dr. Gaines approached Rob Anderson and asked him to come into his office. Crooks had overheard the request, raised an eyebrow, and asked, "what is this about Doc?"

Dr. Gaines turned to him and said, "this doesn't concern you, Bill, but it does concern Rob and his son Josh, so if you don't mind, I...."

Crooks cut him off. "What do you mean it doesn't concern me? Why that boy is my student of mine and my best friend's son. Why wouldn't that make it any of my business?"

Rob turned to Dr. Gaines and asked, "so, what is this meeting in your office all about?"

Dr. Gaines took an exasperated breath, and he let out a long sigh. He looked back up at Rob and revealed, "Doug and Shelly Pierson pulled me aside a few moments ago to protest that Josh quoted a scripture during his memorial speech. They want me to discipline Josh for it. That is why I want you to meet me in my office so that we can sort this out amicably."

Bill Crooks could not contain himself when he protested, "Doc, you know that is a load of BS!"

Dr. Gaines lifted his hands to indicate that he understood Crooks' position and then gently grabbed Rob Anderson to walk away. Rob stopped short and motioned to Crooks to follow, which he gladly accepted the invitation. Dr. Gaines started to object but allowed the inclusion of Rob's friend into the meeting.

Doug and Shelly Pierson were already seated on one side of the small conference room table in Dr. Gaines' office when the group entered. The Piersons acknowledged Dr. Gaines and Rob Anderson, but they showed confusion when Bill Crooks followed into the room and shut the door.

Shelly Pierson asked, "what is he doing here?" while pointing in the general direction of Crooks, who now leaned against the wall because there wasn't a seat for him at the table.

Rob sat forward. "I asked him to be here with me."

Dr. Gaines raised his hands to quiet the faculty members and asked Doug and Shelly Pierson to voice their concerns.

Shelly started the conversation. "Dr. Gaines, I know we all agree that religion has no place in a public school. So, we feel that when Josh mentioned an excerpt from that ancient religious text, it instantly became a violation of the U.S. Constitution. You know, that part about the separation of church from state?"

Dr. Gaines sat back in his chair as he was confused at Shelly Pierson's implication, and he frankly did not know what to do. Finally, he started to ask a question, but Shelly cut him off.

"This type of violation warrants an immediate expulsion from school."

Rob leaned forward once again, but this time his expression turned serious. Then he shook his head. "An immediate expulsion would cause a whole series of negative events. Like Josh not playing in the state championship or even worse, it might dampen his chances of getting into the U.S. Coast Guard Academy."

Doug Pierson looked Rob Anderson coldly into the eye. "I care less about the football team, and I care even less about your son going off to become a warmonger for Ronald Reagan. This issue, Sir, has to do with your son violating a law."

"What law is that, Doug?" Crooks challenged.

"You should know, considering that you teach civics, Bill. Josh violated the U.S. Constitution."

Bill Crooks reached into the back pocket of his slacks. He pulled the small paperback copy of the U.S. Constitution that he always carried on him. He then flipped it toward Doug Pierson, and it landed on the table directly in front of him.

Crooks smiled. "Alright, smarty-pants, open that up and show me where it says that there is a separation of church and state clause?"

Doug and his wife Shelly exchanged glances, and then Doug picked up the pamphlet and began a hasty search for his reference.

Crooks held his hand up. "Stop. I will save us all some time here; you won't find it anywhere on those pages. The actual terminology of separation of church and state stemmed from a judge's decision. He found that no government agency had the right to endorse one religion over another. However, the judge also reiterated that citizens afford the freedom and opportunity to worship and openly speak of their faith."

Crooks paused for effect, then he continued. "Furthermore, it doesn't matter where the worship takes place, even in a government building. Preventing folks from doing so is, in fact, a violation of the First Amendment. But then you could also read Thomas Jefferson's affirmation about this subject in some of his writings."

He let his comment hang in the air like a cloud before he continued again. "Yes, Josh mentioned a scripture from the Bible, but he did not proselytize, nor did the boy declare that his faith was superior over all others. No, Josh only quoted a single scripture that inspires him, nothing more, which is perfectly within his First Amendment rights!"

Crooks thumped his index finger on the table with each point that he made. He then turned to Dr. Gaines and said, "I told you this was a bunch of BS, and now you need to shovel it all out of the barn."
Then he turned to Rob and said, "we are out of here!" and the two of them rose and exited the office.

* * *

Friday, November 2, 1984

Midwest High School, 5 a.m.

The Oiler football team loaded onto the bus for their eight-hour ride to Kemmerer. Once there, they would spend the night and have a quick practice later that afternoon on the Kemmerer High School football field.

As Josh and Ricky took their traditional seat on the bus, the gravity of the missing players hit Josh's conscience full force. Only Steve Otten occupied that last row, and he too felt a little out of place without David, Peter, and Scott sitting beside him. If Chet Harrison felt odd and out of place, the boy did not show it. Instead, he took up his usual role of jockeying the music out of his stereo for the trip.

Fifty minutes later, the bus drove along the outskirts of Casper and then west along Highway 220. Aside from the occasional groups of Pronghorns, it seemed like an endless sea of grass. Josh watched as they rolled past the exit to Alcova Reservoir and caught a glimpse of Pathfinder Reservoir that hid behind the hills to the south. He also noted Independence Rock, the Sweetwater River, Devil's Gate, and the Swan Ranch as the more prominent landmarks on the Oregon Trail. Amazingly, the 150-year-old immigrant trail was still easily seen across the prairie in that remote area of the state.

Later, the bus driver turned onto Highway 287, and they traveled south. When they arrived in Rawlins, the bus pulled into a large truck stop on the west end of town for a restroom break. Coach Fleming used this stop as an opportunity to hand out boxed lunches to the team that was prepared the night before by community volunteers that met at the Community Church.

Josh took his box and thanked the coach, and when he opened it, he found a small white plastic football with small maroon lettering stenciled on the side that read:

MIDWEST OILERS
Wyoming Class 1A State Championship
November 3, 1984
OFT

Josh set the ball aside and began to eat some of the food. While he ate, he looked over the intimidating expanse of the Red Desert. He smiled at the thought that when people drove north from Casper, they thought the area around Midwest was nothingness...the Red Desert was the epitome of nothingness.

Somewhere around Wamsutter, while the bus traveled west along Interstate 80, Josh slipped off to sleep. He later awoke when the bus hit the cattle guard on the exit ramp near Little America. The bus then turned onto Highway 30 that took them through the small coal mining towns of Granger and Opal, which at Josh's first glance, did not look that dissimilar to his home in the Salt Creek oilfield.

Soon, the trip ended outside of a two-story hotel in Kemmerer. As the team exited, each member paused long enough to grab their gear from the storage bins located under the bus. Then in the parking lot, the players were greeted by assistant Coach Jim Orton. He had arrived minutes before the bus in the school's light blue Chevrolet Suburban.

Orton had time to check the Oilers into the hotel, and now he called room captains by name and handed each of them a room key. Next, he called out the players to accompany each room captain. The coach gave Josh the room key to #208, which also came with three freshmen to room with him.

Coach Fleming then announced to the team, "you guys have 30 minutes to get settled into your rooms, get dressed for practice, and be back on the bus by 3:30.

Their practice in Kemmerer was much better than Josh could have possibly anticipated. Everyone seemed to be upbeat and eager to play the Championship game the next day in nearby Cokeville. After completing a drill, Josh looked up and noticed a pair of familiar faces in street clothes and Kemmerer letter jackets standing underneath the goalposts near him.

"Tony Parker, how are you doing?" Josh asked while walking up to the boys.

Josh had wrestled against Parker four times in high school, and they both shared an even split in wins and losses against one another.

"Hey Josh, do you guys think you have what it takes to beat Cokeville? And where is your buddy David Proctor? I don't see him?" Parker asked.

"You don't see him because he isn't here. He is home with the chickenpox."

"You are kidding me. But, man, that is lousy timing just before state," Parker said.

Josh looked away for a second and then looked back at Tony Parker and said, "I know, lousy timing."

Tony Parker and his friend continued to scan the field, and then he asked, "where is Scott Merino? I don't see him out here either?"

Josh nodded. "Merino is at home too because he is academically ineligible because of a teacher that had it out for him. We are also without Pete LaRoche."

"So, what are you guys going to do?"

"Coach Fleming has moved some players around to fill in on the line, and he has brought up a sophomore to replace Pete."

"Man, that sucks, but I have to tell you that when we beat Cokeville this year and gave them their only loss, we pounded them up the middle with our big fullback all game long. But that won't work for you guys without David anchoring your line. But you have Ricky, and he is fast in open space. So maybe you guys should concentrate on running on the edge."

"Thanks for the advice, Tony, but I got to get back to practice. I'll see you later this year on the wrestling mat because we have to break up our tie."

"Count on it," Tony retorted.

The Oilers finished up one of their better practices of the year, loaded back up on the bus, and headed back to the hotel.

Then, at 6:30 p.m., the team walked as a group to a nearby restaurant, where the team remarkably received cheers from Kemmerer residents that passed along the street. What the boys didn't understand was that Cokeville was the town's long-time rival.

Later that night, after meeting with Coach Fleming and with the other starters on the team to go over the game plan one last time, Josh laid down on his bed. It was then that he remembered something. It was the first time all season that he and his friends hadn't met to watch a game film and the movie *All the Right Moves* the night before they played. Josh did not believe in bad omens as it stood juxtaposed to his religious upbringing. Still, to be sure, he lifted a prayer that night to God for favor upon himself and his teammates the next day.

* * *

Saturday, November 3, 1984
State 1A Football Championship game
Cokeville, Wyoming

It was halftime of the State Championship game. Josh sat on a bench, soaked to the bone from the sloppy, wet, and snow-covered field. His toes squished in his mud-covered cleats, and he struggled to untie his double-knotted laces, so he could take his shoes off and put on a dry pair of practice socks available inside his gear bag.

It was an extremely close game and knotted up at 0-0. Midwest's game plan of attacking the edge of the Cokeville defense had worked. However, the two times the Oilers had gotten inside the Cokeville 20-yard line, disaster struck. They fumbled away one opportunity, and Carlos threw an interception when a Panther lineman tipped the pass into the hands of an awaiting linebacker.

But the Oiler defense held stout as it had all season. Coach Fleming encouraged the team to keep up their persistence in the second half, and by doing so, they would be state champs by the end of the game.

The second half started horribly for the Oilers when Cokeville returned the second-half kickoff 75 yards for a touchdown. When Midwest got the ball back, Ricky carried the ball on four consecutive plays for 8, 5, 4, and 4 yards, respectively. But then fullback Chet Harrison was stuffed for no gain, which forced the Oilers to punt. In David's absence, Brian Agee replaced him on the offensive line. However, muddy field conditions mixed with trying to block a three-time All-State nose guard hampered his effectiveness.

Later, Midwest was stopped and had to punt again, and then Cokeville was forced to do the same. Then on a fourth-down punt late in the final quarter, Carlos received the ball on the Oiler 38-yard line and weaved and slipped his way through the mud for a touchdown. It put Midwest ahead 8-6 with three minutes left to play.

Cokeville began their last drive at their 30-yard line. They grounded out three first downs and were at the Midwest 28-yard line with 4 seconds to play. But then the Cokeville quarterback drilled a pass to his tight end in the left flat on that final play. Josh reacted perfectly and immediately tackled him to end the game. However, the screams of the partisan Cokeville crowd told a different narrative.

When Josh put his shoulder into the Cokeville receiver, the boy flipped the ball to a running back trailing behind him. The Cokeville player streaked past the Oiler sophomore cornerback, who had lost his footing, and scampered down the sideline for the deciding score. Cokeville won 12 to 8.

After stopping at Little America for a post-game meal, the team re-loaded up onto the bus for the long trek home. Once the bus merged onto I-80 east, Coach Fleming got up and methodically moved from seat to seat. First, he congratulated every member of the team and thanked them for their effort. Then, the Coach reminded them that sometimes, you lose a game despite doing everything humanly possible to win.

Coach Fleming skipped Josh and Ricky. Instead, he talked privately with all the others around them. Then the coach lifted his head and looked toward Josh and motioned for the boy to follow him to the front of the bus. He looked over to Ricky, who was fast asleep already, and then stood up and followed the coach.

After Josh sat down, Coach Fleming looked at him for a long silent moment. He then said, "Josh, I could not be prouder of you, Ricky, and Carlos for taking over the leadership of this team throughout this last week. I mean, we had Cokeville where we wanted them, and it pains me that we played that game without three cards in our deck."

Josh looked up to his coach and said, "thanks, coach, and I miss having my friends out there too, but I don't think it would have made a difference."

Coach Fleming objected, "but Josh, we could have won with those other guys."

Josh nodded but then added, "Coach, that was the best football team I have ever played. We hit them with all we had. I mean, after losing the championship to them last year, I felt that we could beat them. But, today, I saw how they kept their composure, and they earned that victory. So, I don't want to play the game of what-ifs because, in the end, we still lost, and the Cokeville Panthers are the State Champions."

Josh nor any of the Oilers could have predicted that Cokeville was on the cusp of becoming the most dominant force in Wyoming high school football history. Cokeville's Head Coach, Todd Dayton, would later boast 22 State Championship titles to his credit. Plus, Dayton would become the winningest coach in Wyoming's history, both in winning percentage and total wins. Many would later speculate that many of Coach Dayton's state championship teams would have beaten any of the larger schools in Wyoming during that period.

Coach Fleming picked up his hat and placed it on his head, and said to Josh, "you are right. Again, that was a great team, but you did one heck of a job, and you should be proud, son."

The bus rolled on long into the night toward home, and when it stopped at the truck stop in Rawlins, only half of the team got off to use the restroom and get some snacks. Josh got out and tried to stretch out the soreness of his legs and his arms.

Once inside the truck stop and under the overhead lights, he pulled up his sleeve to see multiple deep purple bruises on his forearms and biceps. They were visible reminders of all the hits Josh had absorbed when filling in for David at middle linebacker during the game. He bought a Coke and a Salted Nut Roll and strolled back onto the bus.

Later, Josh awoke in his seat as the bus drove over the cattle guard at the end of Lewis Street in Midwest. He looked down at his wristwatch, and it read 4:30 a.m., and he yawned and stretched to wake himself up.

He watched as the bus's headlights illuminated the reflectors of at least 50 cars parked on Teachers Row and in the high school parking lot. Then, as the team exited the bus, they were greeted by nearly 100 townsfolk who vociferously expressed how proud they were of their Oilers.

Josh then saw his cheering section that included his father Rob, his mother Sara, and his sister Cindy who congratulated Josh for a fantastic season.

* * *

35

Monday, November 5, 1984

Midwest High School

The end of the football season came to an anticlimactic ending that afternoon when the team stood outside of the equipment room in a single file. First, each player handed over a practice jersey and pants, plus their game jerseys and pants. Next, each player turned in their helmet, hip pads, thigh pads, and shoulder pads. Finally, assistant Coach Jim Orton checked off each item and cleared the players upon returning the items.

Josh remained in the gym afterward since the basketball season started that day with a short practice once all the football gear was turned in and stored away. David was still home in quarantine, and Josh had visited him the day before for about an hour. He recalled nearly every play with exacting detail to his friend. Still, the more Josh talked about the game, he detected the overwhelming feeling of remorse from his friend, who was not able to play. Finally, Josh reiterated what he had told Coach Fleming on the bus ride home that Cokeville was indeed a great team.

But now it was basketball season, and Josh moved to the other side of the gym to shot free throws while waiting for practice to begin. Finally, however, the athletic director rescheduled their season-opening game for the upcoming weekend. It was a practical move since the Oilers were already a week behind all the other teams since their football season extended to the championship. Conversely, Josh looked forward to his upcoming weekend off without another game to play.

Later that night at home after practice, Josh sat at the dining room table and listened to his father's conversation with Bill Crooks when the phone rang. Josh rose from the table and answered the phone.

"Hello," he said.

"It is me, Pete. How are you doing, Josh?"

"I'm okay. How about you?"

"I'm good, but I had to start working after school to support Sheila and the baby, and that is why I am calling."

Josh furrowed his brow. "Okay," and tried to follow Pete's meaning.

"Josh, did you buy a small game license this year?"

"I did. I bought it with you over at the store in Edgerton, remember?"

"That's what I thought, so how about you, Steve, and I go out on Saturday and go rabbit hunting north of town near the old light plant? Those rabbits will go a long way to feed Sheila and me, so how about it?"

"I don't know Pete, let me check," Josh said and covered up the mouthpiece on the handset.

He then looked over to his father a few feet away and asked, "dad, Pete is on the phone and was wondering if I can go rabbit hunting with him near the old light plant on Saturday?"

Rob looked over to his son with hard-set eyes. "I thought I made myself clear about you going out of town and into the oilfield after your car got stolen?"

"I understand, dad, but this will help fill up Pete's freezer with meat. I wouldn't ask unless it was for doing something worthwhile."

Rob felt torn between two positions: on one side, he didn't want to become too overprotective of his son, but on the other hand, he wanted Josh to be safe. So instead of providing a curt on-the-spot answer, he deferred his decision to later when he could think about it more thoroughly.

Meanwhile, Josh stood nearby with the telephone receiver still pinned next to his chest to mute any possible conversation between him and his father.

Rob looked up at his son and said, "Tell Pete that you will have to call him back because I need to think about it."

Josh instantly felt disappointed, reflected in his slouched body posture as he lifted the receiver back to his ear.

He despondently said to Pete, "I will have to call you back."

Then he replaced the receiver into its cradle and walked to his room without any other words directed toward his father.

Bill Crooks took in the whole situation and then suggested to his friend that they go outside. They stood up and donned their jackets since the temperature that late fall evening hovered around 40 degrees. After leaving the house, the men walked over to the garage, and Crooks reached down, lifted the door, and stepped inside.

"What's on your mind, Bill?"

"Rob, I know this isn't my business of how you parent your son, but I know that you want to keep Josh safe, plus I know that you want him to feel normal all the same."

"Okay, I will bite. What would you do if you were in my shoes?"

"First of all, I am not trying to wear your shoes though I do have an option for you if you can accept it?"

"Okay...."

"Since nobody has spotted that dark green Ford in nearly a month, how about you let Josh go and be with his friends. Meanwhile, you and I can trail 10 minutes behind them. We could then pull over near the Sand Rocks and find a position. That way, we could watch over the boys without them even knowing we were there. What do you think?"

"It is a plausible plan, but do you honestly think the boys wouldn't hear us driving down the road in that old truck of yours? I mean, a deaf man could hear that thing coming from miles away?"

"I have thought of that, Rob, so we would have to take your car, but don't worry, the road is well maintained enough for your car to handle it. Besides, I need to patrol some of the BLM lands anyway with my side job. So how about it, want to tag along?"

Rob took nearly a full minute of deep thought before he looked up to his friend and said, "alright," and the men re-entered the house.

Rob went directly to Josh's room and informed him that he could go hunting with his friends, the news of which elevated the boy's mood considerably. Josh jumped up off of his bed and darted past his dad, and picked up the phone in the kitchen.

He dialed the four numbers to Pete's house and waited for the call to connect. When the other end of the line picked up, he said, "Pete, I can go. What time do you want to meet?"

"Good, I will meet you at your place at eight o'clock in the morning, and I will bring Steve with me," and Pete hung up the phone.

Josh replaced the phone into the cradle and walked through the house and into his room. However, this time he sported a huge smile on his face.

By that Friday, David was finally out of quarantine and could return to school the following Monday. While visiting him the night before, like he did every night after basketball practice, Josh invited him to hunt rabbits with Pete and Steve on Saturday morning. David declined and relayed that he still didn't feel well enough to do very much.

Saturday, November 10, 1984

Early that morning, Pete arrived outside Josh's house in his father-in-law's green Dodge Power Ram pickup. Once loaded, they drove back to the junction store for gasoline before going out into the oilfield. Meanwhile, Josh went inside the store, poured a black coffee, and selected a glazed apple pie.

As he moved toward the register, Josh almost ran into the Midwest art teacher, Debra Jansen. It gave him pause for a second because he realized that he rarely, if at all, spoke to her, which was weird. After all, they were practically neighbors.

"Careful, Josh, with that coffee," she said. But then the teacher asked, "where are you off to this morning?"

"I'm sorry, Mrs. Jansen, I didn't see you," Josh said and then answered her question. "I am going with a few friends to hunt rabbits out by the old light plant."

Debra Jansen's face tightened into a wince and her lips slightly curled. "Do you hunt them for fun?"

Josh did not want to get into an ethical discussion with her. Instead, he shook his head. "Not really for fun ma'am, we are hunting them to eat because they make a great substitute for chicken."

The teacher rolled her eyes. "No thanks, I'll stick with meat that is covered in cellophane if I eat animal protein at all."

Josh refrained from further comment and let the teacher walk away. Then he paid for his stores and exited the door to join his buddies in the truck.

After taking his seat, Josh asked, "Pete, before we go out to the light plant, could you drive your truck down by the creek where we walked across over on that old pipe casing?"

"Sure, we could do that, but what do you have in mind?"

Josh shrugged. "I just want to go see that hot spring we found and see if it is still there, that is all."

Twenty minutes later, Josh stood over the bathtub-sized hole in the ground that once held the hot springs containing Savolt's *Specimen*. Josh looked around and surmised that the leak from the unidentified injection well must have been fixed. By now, all that was left behind was a small pool of water clouded with a thick gray particulate. Josh kicked at the crusted snow from the rim onto the top of the gray soup. Then he let out a long sigh. Thankfully he had a specimen of his own safely tucked away in his room and that David still had the other one stashed in the loft of his garage.

Josh climbed out of the crater and walked toward Pete and Steve, who were trying to flush out rabbits along the slopes of Bothwell Draw. Josh whistled at them, and his friends reemerged from the bushes.

Then he asked, "are you guys ready to go?" and without a word, the trio made their way back to the awaiting pickup and drove further north to the light plant.

By late morning, the boys had harvested ten rabbits, but Pete wanted just a few more. The boys separated themselves briefly but then began to meander closer together. Josh cradled his favorite .22 pump action rifle in the fold of his left arm, and when he caught up to Pete, he lowered the gun to point his barrel toward the ground.

Pete stopped and moved his iron-sighted .22 magnum bolt action rifle to his shoulder as if standing in a military parade. Soon afterward, Steve came down from the hillside near them and joined in on the huddle.

"What do you think Pete, should we move back down south along the creek because I am not seeing anything moving around here?" Josh asked.

Pete scratched his three-day-old growth of whiskers on his chin and shrugged his shoulders, and said, "why not."

Steve reached down and grabbed the string of rabbits and carried them back further down toward the creek without a word.

A few minutes later, Josh stopped in his tracks with a jerk when he saw the infamous dark green Ford F150 parked just 200 yards away, but he did not see the occupants.

The boy pointed out the truck to his friends and said, "let us get out of here," and the boys turned left and started to run for their pickup parked near the Sand Rocks, a rocky outcrop adjacent to Light Plant Road.

While the boys weaved in and around sage and greasewood, they heard a short *PA-TING* sound followed by two more. Steve was running in the lead, and his down-filled coat exploded into a cloud of feathers that caused him to drop the string of rabbits as he fell.

Josh sprinted a few yards and slid to the ground alongside Steve, who remained motionless on his back. He then moved his friend's gloved hand and found that blood had already soaked through his shirt and into the hole in the jacket. On the other hand, Pete was on the ground a few feet away in a prone position and frantically tried to spot their attackers.

Utter silence enveloped the boys, and though Steve was wounded, he had yet uttered a single sound. Then, suddenly, Pete's head jerked to the left as he identified the sound of a dry sagebrush branch breaking. He then turned back toward Josh and motioned for him to take up a position to his left, to which Josh did quietly.

Josh peered through the sagebrush and saw two men about 50 yards away walking cautiously in their direction. The man on the left was taller than him, had broad shoulders, and sported a short blond colored haircut, while the man on the left was shorter by at least four inches. Additionally, the small man had a narrow face and jet-black hair. Each of the men carried a rifle that Josh had only seen in the movies. To him, the weapons looked like a military-style M-16. Except these guns had a suppressor affixed to the end of each barrel and an unknown type of scope.

Then a strange thing happened. Josh recalled how rifle silencers didn't make much noise in the movies. But, in real life, the suppressor merely muffled the sound into a tin-like *PA-TING* popping sound.

Pete whispered to Josh, "take the man on the left, headshot only. I'll get the guy on the right."

Josh nodded and knew that his .22 lacked any real power to stop a determined person. Still, he also understood that a properly placed bullet could enter the skull but not go all the way through and would cause devastating damage to the brain. So, he took his aim, clicked off his safety button, placed his finger on the trigger.

KA-BOOM thundered a shot from above and to the right of the boys. Instantly, the boys observed the little man's chest blossom into a cloud of red mist and fall lifelessly onto the ground! The blond-haired man fell and grabbed something out of the downed man's back pocket and grabbed the extra rifle, and then disappeared into the brush behind him.

"Boys! Grab Steve and get back to your truck now!" thundered a voice from above and behind them.

Josh looked at Pete and said, "that is Mr. Crooks, just do what he said, now!"

The other two boys helped Steve to his feet, and Josh steadied him while Pete picked up Steve's .410 shotgun and the string of rabbits and followed in behind. The trio quickly made it across the open ground to where they parked the old Dodge pickup

Josh half walked, and half carried Steve to the truck's rear and leaned him against the open tailgate. Above them, the boys spotted Bill Crooks laying prone on a sandstone ledge behind his .308 caliber scoped rifle that rested on a tripod. Without taking his eyes off his field of view, he instructed the boys to get into their pickup and get Steve to the clinic. Then they needed to get Chief Traynor and Deputy Crandall out here on the double.

"Mr. Crooks, I can't leave you out here by yourself," Josh protested.

"Josh, I will be fine, but I have to stay here in case that big guy circles around across the creek and back towards his truck. If he does, I will have him too, now GO! That is not a suggestion."

Another voice lifted out of the rocks, but this one was Josh's father, Rob.

"Son, do what Crooks demanded. We will be okay, now please go."

"Yes, Sir," Josh said and complied by getting into the bed of the pickup with Steve, and Pete sped back to town.

Pete pulled up outside the clinic, and lucky for Steve, it was still open. While Pete and Steve went inside, Josh ran over to the small Police office behind the Town Hall.

When the boy threw the door open, he found Deputy Isom sitting quietly at his tiny desk, reading the newspaper.

"Deputy Isom, get Chief Traynor on the phone and quick."

Isom dialed four numbers on his phone and took a look at Josh and the dried blood down his side.

"Hello Chief, this is...." but Josh snatched the phone out of Isom's hand and said, "Chief, this is Josh Anderson. Both Bill Crooks and my dad are out at the Sand Rocks next to Light Plant Road near the plant itself. Mr. Crooks has downed one man from that green Ford pickup and is waiting for the other man to show himself."

"Josh, stay right there. I am on my way. Tell Deputy Isom to radio Deputy Crandall to see if he is in the area for backup."

The boy replied, "yes, Sir," and hung up the phone. He turned and relayed the Chief's instructions to Deputy Isom. However, the deputy overheard the conversation was already talking to Deputy Crandall on the radio.

Isom hung up the microphone and told Josh, "You best stay here unless you are hurt, which then you should go over to the clinic."

Josh nodded that he understood and watched the deputy rush out of the office with a rifle in hand.

Two hours later, Chief Traynor arrived back at his office with Bill Crooks and Rob Anderson in tow. He instructed Josh, Crooks, and the elder Anderson to write out statements. When they had finished,

Traynor looked over their accounts and determined they were a spot-on match.

The Chief then looked over to Rob Anderson and said, "the perp that Crooks drilled through the heart is the man I believe him to be William E. Pruitt. His face matches a picture I have in a dossier with that same name. But forensics will do a match of his fingerprints since he didn't have any identification on him."

Josh looked over to Chief Traynor and asked, "what happened to the other guy?"

Traynor sighed. "Unfortunately, Josh, the other guy, who I believe is Marvin A. Stiles, is still on the run. He never made a move back toward his truck, or Mr. Crooks here would have drilled him too. Deputy Crandall is out there now with some other deputies he called in from Casper, and they are conducting a man-hunt right now."

"Where are they looking, Chief?"

"They started at the creek where you saw him and then westward across the BLM land to the Mondragon Ranch. They are also working south toward Highway 387. I have also placed an all-points bulletin on the guy as well, so don't worry, we will get him."

Josh suddenly reflected upon the gravity of the situation and looked over to Crooks and said, "but you are now in trouble for shooting that guy."

Chief Traynor laughed out loud and said, "hardly." He looked over at Josh. "Your teacher is also a law enforcement officer with the Bureau of Land Management and has been for over ten years now."

The boy's face flushed red, and he turned his head toward Crooks. "Is this true?"

The teacher smiled and pulled his wallet out of his back pocket. Then he produced a U.S. Department of the Interior shield for Josh to study.

"I have been doing this job part-time job after school, on weekends, and during summer breaks. It provides me with a little extra income. Even your dad didn't know about this until the other day."

"Why all the secrecy?"

Crooks smiled at Josh. "My supervisor and I agree that it is best for the community if they feel the public lands are open and free to use. However, we don't want people feeling regulated, so that is why I went undercover."

Josh remained motionless and had no clue what to say next.

Traynor rose and readjusted his hat. Then he turned to the men and said, "why don't you take Josh home."

Rob escorted his son out of the Police Station with Bill Crooks a step behind them. It took them only a few seconds to walk the empty lot next to C Street. But when they reached the curb at Navy Row, Debra and Lucas Jansen sped by them in their silver Datsun B210. They continued down Navy Row to Fitzhugh, where they turned right toward Highway 387.

Rob mused, "I wonder what they are doing?"

Bill looked up and said dryly, "what, the Jansen's? They probably have a case of the munchies after what they've been smoking."

Once they entered the house, Rob recalled every detail to his wife. Sara didn't say a word throughout the retelling of the story, and when her husband finished speaking, she got up and gave her son a big hug and a kiss on the cheek.

* * *

36

The manhunt lasted for three long days, and the Salt Creek area residents were encouraged to stay at home with their doors locked. Even the school was closed for a couple of days.

At the angst of Chief Traynor, his nemesis, Sheriff Doan, once again held the spotlight on the evening news throughout the ordeal. But after no further sightings of Marvin Stiles coupled with no new leads, the full-scale investigation into Savolt's disappearance was called off by Doan and left unresolved.

The rest of the school year lacked any of the excitement that the first part had provided. Since the blond-headed man was still on the loose, Josh was remanded strictly at home throughout Thanksgiving and Christmas holidays. Just as most high school graduates felt when they looked back to their senior year, Josh was stunned at how fast his senior year sped by, as if he woke up one day and his high school days were over.

The 1984-1985 Midwest boys' basketball team fell precipitously short of last year's team that finished with a school record of 19 wins and three losses and a trip to the state tournament. Instead, the squad finished with an even number of wins and losses. They also missed out on a repeat trip to the state tournament. Josh played well, though, and he received Conference Honorable Mention honors at his forward position to go along with his First Team All-State football honors.

Josh was also invited along with David Proctor to play on the North Team in the annual Wyoming Shrine Bowl. The game featured the best high school players regardless of classification against one another. Unfortunately, Josh declined the invitation, but Ricky Fleming became his replacement.

The reason Josh declined the honor that most Wyoming boys only get to dream about was that he received a phone call from the Coast Guard Academy. Just before his Shrine Bowl selection, Coach Domenget had phoned the Anderson home. The Coach told Josh that he was selected to attend the Academy in the next freshmen class. Additionally, the coach informed the boy that he would receive a packet of material, but verbally instructed to be on campus by July 5th for cadet orientation. Coach Domenget also stated that he welcomed Josh to the football team and promised him a fair chance to earn a starting position as a freshman.

Josh then followed basketball season right into wrestling. Midwest was an anomaly in that it had shortened basketball and wrestling seasons rather than having both teams competing at the same time. By separating each sport into separate seasons allowed small schools throughout Wyoming, like Midwest, to field two competitive teams. Otherwise, basketball and wrestling occurring at the same time would deprive each group of quality athletes.

Unfortunately, Josh's wrestling season never happened because while in gym class, he fractured his ankle when he landed on Steve Otten's foot while playing volleyball. So instead of wrestling and running track, Josh concerned himself with rehabbing his ankle throughout the rest of the winter and spring to be ready for football camp later that summer.

Steve Otten had fully recovered from the gunshot wound within eight weeks and could use his arm fully. He was lucky that the bullet avoided any bone and ligaments; instead, it tore only through the muscle.

Both Pete LaRoche and his bride Sheila graduated early after the first semester. Pete went to work full-time for MERP driving a vac truck. Then, in April of 1985, Sheila gave birth to an 8-pound, 3-ounce baby girl.

However, during the first week of February 1985, Midwest had two scholarship signings for football. First, Ricky Fleming signed his intent to attend and play football at Weber State University in Ogden, Utah. Ironically, Ricky didn't send the college an application. The other signing was David Proctor, who accepted a full-tuition scholarship with Carroll College in Helena, Montana. Josh was also seated at the table. In front of him sat a U.S. Coast Guard Academy Bears hat to celebrate his already announced acceptance.

Oddly though, ever since the shooting by the old light plant, the protesters quit coming around as well. Whether it was attributed to the winter or somehow connected to the mysterious passengers of the green Ford F150, but no protests had occurred since the fall. Even better for the entire community, Marvin A. Stiles never showed his face around Midwest again.

The only break in the Savolt case came when Deputy Crandall stumbled upon the location where the two mystery men had hidden out during their time in Midwest. Crandall had received a call from Henry Parson, who oversaw the Miller place west of Midwest near the old cemetery. The Millers occupied their ranch in May, June, and July from their permanent home in Canton, Georgia. During their absence, they hired Henry to conduct a weekly check upon the house. However, Parson recently uncovered that the unused barn had some recent activity.

After receiving the call, Deputy Crandall went out to the Miller ranch to investigate the barn. He found a neat set up of a twin burner camping stove, a refrigerator run by an extension cord with a three-way splitter that originated in the tool shed. The deputy also found a television and two heavily worn twin mattresses with blankets folded in crisp military-style hospital corners. Additionally, Crandall found tire tracks with an aggressive tread pattern perhaps belonging to the infamous Ford pickup.

The thing that intrigued the deputy the most was the tall, grey, and slender antenna that extended upward along the back wall of the barn and out of sight from the corrals. Crandall tracked the feeder line back inside the barn to a table. Then under a tarp, he found a relatively new Motorola base radio that allowed the barn trespassers to communicate with others.

Josh and his friends graduated in late May of that year. Along with David, Ricky, and occasionally, Pete, Steve, and Carlos, the boys spent as much time together as possible until the end of June. It was then that Josh and his family planned to drive out to New London, Connecticut, for his cadet orientation.

Then on the day before leaving home, Josh met with his friends one last time. They decided it would be fitting that they put together a time capsule of sorts inside an old cracker tin. The boys passed the container around and even turned their backs while secretly placing their keepsake inside. Then they gave the metal box to the next person.

Once filled, the boys decided to bury the capsule in the one place in Midwest that would always be there, the Post Office. In the shadow of an old Elm tree, the friends dug a small hole next to the southeast corner of the building. Then they lowered the time capsule and refilled the opening with dirt. Finally, they each made a pact to return and open the box together one day.

Then, suddenly and dramatically, came the realization for four of the six boys that their youth was over. But, as fate would also have it, each boy had someplace else to go.

The boys didn't exchange any long, drawn-out goodbyes with one another. Instead, as each one of them turned to leave, they offered one another their usual, "see ya," and walked away.

* * *

37

November 4, 2018

Tampa, Florida, 34 years later

Josh Anderson got out of bed and went to the kitchen to get a cup of coffee. Then, he picked up his smartphone to see if he had any messages. It was the same routine that he had held for most of his career after being required to carry a cellular phone as part of his job.

He had completed all four years at the Coast Guard Academy. As promised by Coach Domenget, Josh started as a cornerback for the Bears as a freshman. Then, in his sophomore year, Josh switched to strong safety. During his junior and senior years, he earned first-team honors at his safety position in the New England Football Conference.

At graduation, Josh also earned a bachelor's degree in marine and environmental science. With prior authorized permission, Josh submitted his senior thesis that completed the work done by Tim Savolt four years before. His paper was published and distributed throughout peer-reviewed journals. His work proved without a doubt that the Salt Creek was neither worse nor better off than it was in its natural state before man arrived in the area. But one curiosity that Josh could not explain was the water sampling results from the location just downstream of the hot spring that Savolt had found. The multiple samples taken there showed nearly no trace of either sulfur or petroleum.

Afterward, Josh received a commission as an Ensign. Surprisingly, he received orders to attend a 21-week school in Georgia. There he learned his new job as a Special Agent in the U.S. Coast Guard Investigation Service. Josh had forever attributed that selection to another one of Bill Crooks' phone calls to one of many connections.

While on his first assignment in Florida, he met and married his wife Katie, and they had two children, a daughter named Sara and a son named Timothy. Josh served out his five-year active-duty commitment by investigating fisheries and environmental crimes. At one point, he explored other criminal matters about drug trafficking along U.S. Coastal waters.

But in 1994, Josh left the Coast Guard. Instead, he received acceptance into that year's new crop of Federal Bureau of Investigation (FBI) trainees. His first assignment was in Texas after graduation from the FBI Academy, located in Quantico, Virginia. Later, he took other positions in Florida and California, respectively. Finally, he retired from the FBI in early 2016 because of two things: one, he had already served over twenty years; and two, he and other agents began to sense that some of the agency's senior leaders in Washington D.C. operated on their own accord, and the hard work of regular field agents, like himself, was often ignored.

Josh studied his phone and selected the message icon. Then, he opened the message that he received at 11:54 p.m. the night before from 307-437-9891, and it read:

Josh, Pete here. Give me a call ASAP

He took a sip of coffee, looked over the microwave oven, and saw that the clock indicated 8:00 a.m., and Josh knew that Pete was two hours behind, which made it 6:00 a.m. Wyoming time. So, instead, he decided he would call in an hour or so to see what was up with his life-long friend.

While Josh got dressed, he thought of all of his buddies from high school. Pete LaRouche had remained in Midwest and was still happily married to Sheila, and together, they had five children. Pete eventually became a custodian at the school. In addition, he drove the travel bus all across Wyoming for Oiler teams on away games. Pete also assumed the head custodian position ten years ago when Reed finally retired.

Reed was allowed to live in his maintenance shop bungalow for a monthly rent of $10. Sadly, the man died two years ago of an unknown ailment. Still, when school officials entered his apartment, they found that Reed had made a museum of sorts of hundreds of discarded items. They found things like a lone football cleat that he found in the locker room, which Reed wrote *1984* on it and the season record of *9-1*. School officials then turned his place into a school museum, and it was open to the public when each day school was in session.

David Proctor had graduated from Carroll College and became a lawyer and still served as the district attorney in Weld County, Colorado, where he lived with his wife. Yet, sadly they did not have any children.

Steve Otten chose to remain in the Salt Creek community. He married a young woman from Kaycee immediately after high school graduation. He now owned a backhoe business in Edgerton and lived west of Midwest near I-25. His daughter had also attended and graduated from Midwest High School.

Carlos Mondragon had graduated from Western State College in Gunnison, Colorado, where he played football on a scholarship. After graduation, he moved back to the Mondragon Ranch and took over operations from his father. He transformed the ranch into a premier vacation lodge. It also boasted a rustic and authentic feel, complete with horseback riding, nightly chuckwagon suppers, and a cattle roundup.

Ricky Fleming and Josh had remained incredibly close throughout their adult lives. They made it a habit to call each other every Sunday to exchange news. During football season, they talked during Denver Broncos football games. Fleming had graduated from Weber State and was a three-year starter at running back. In addition, he earned a degree in education. Ricky then accepted a teaching position as a social studies teacher and followed in his father's footsteps as the head football coach at a small town in south-central South Dakota.

Sadly, Ricky died four years ago when he suffered a heart attack. While riding his bicycle, Ricky came across a disabled car of teenage girls that sat directly over a set of railroad tracks. With a train barreling down at full speed, Ricky used his physical strength to push the car out of the path of the train. Almost immediately afterward, he felt a sharp pain in his chest, and he collapsed. By the time medical responders arrived, Ricky was dead from an apparent heart attack.

Josh, David, and another former teammate, Scott Merino, had attended Ricky's memorial ceremony together. At the conclusion, they lowered Ricky's ashes into a small concrete interment outside the west end zone of the football field and the stadium that was re-dedicated in Ricky's name.

Josh wiped away a tear from the corner of his eye because he still missed his best friend today.

Lastly, Scott Merino had a long and decorated 25-year career in the U.S. Air Force and now taught Civics and coached football in Midwest. Moreover, Scott and Josh were closer as friends than in high school since the invention of email allowed them to remain in consistent contact with one another.

At 9:35 a.m., Josh picked up his cellphone and called the number provided by Pete.

"Hello," Pete answered.

"It is Josh. You said to call ASAP."

"Hey, buddy, good to hear your voice."

"Same here, Pete. What can I help you with?"

"Josh, you won't believe it, but our Oilers are playing in the state 6-man football championship here in Midwest this upcoming Saturday."

"That is great news, Pete. Tell Scott Merino and the boys to go get 'em for me, will you?"

"Josh, you can tell them yourself. The community has asked me to contact members from the 1979, 1984, and 1991 teams come back to Midwest for a huge pep rally this Friday night."

Josh was a little confused by the invite. "I don't understand, Pete. The 1979 and 1991 teams won their championship games. So why are we from the '84 team invited? I mean, why not invite '83 and '89 teams too?"

"Josh, you just don't get it. Folks around here consider our '84 team as one of greatest, so can you make it?"

Josh smiled to himself. Then he said, "well, as luck would have it, I was planning to fly into Casper on Friday morning to spend the weekend with my folks and go to take my dad to a Broncos on Monday night. So yes, you can count me in."

"Great, I can't wait to see you! I will text you with more details soon."

"Hey, Pete, who else is coming?"

"Well, me, you, Steve, and Carlos because they live here, but I don't have David's number."

"Don't worry about David because I can call him. So, tell the others that I will see them at the pep rally on Friday night and then Saturday morning, let's dig up that time capsule. What do you say?"

"It sounds like a plan, Josh, and again, I can't wait to see you. But one more thing, nobody knows how to get a hold of Coach Fleming; I called his house phone in Idaho, but the phone is disconnected."

"Pete, I hate to tell you this, but Coach Fleming is in a nursing home. He was diagnosed with Alzheimer's disease ten years ago, and immediately after Ricky's death, he lost all lucidity."

"Oh man, that stinks. I would have liked to see the man that used to work us near to death once again. But, hey, do you remember when he made me, you, and Ricky run laps on the track until, as he instructed, one of us puked?"

"I do, and we were lucky that Coach didn't see you put your finger down your throat to do it on the sixth lap," then they both shared a laugh.

"Well, it was good talking to you, Josh, and I will see you soon," Pete said and hung up the phone.

After setting his phone on the kitchen counter, Josh informed his wife that he had a slight change of plans in Wyoming and asked her if she wanted to go too. She deferred because she would rather spend time with their daughter.

Josh and Katie had already planned to fly together from Tampa to Minneapolis on Thursday to visit their daughter, Sara, and Bret, their son-in-law. They lived in the nearby city of Minnetonka. Then, he had planned to stay Thursday night with the kids and fly to Casper the following day.

Josh grabbed his phone again and looked up his speed dial for David. He then called his buddy to relay the news about the current Oiler football team and that their 1984 team would be honored during the prep rally.

* * *

Friday, November 9, 2018

Minneapolis-Saint Paul International Airport

Josh sat in a chair outside the small gate to board a Canadian Regional Jet to Casper. His smartphone suddenly alerted to indicate that he had received an email. He touched his email icon and saw a new message from his former FBI partner, Special Agent Dale Grisby.

Josh opened the email, and it said simply, *read the attached report- Griz.*

He then downloaded the attachment and read about two high school-aged boys who found a skeleton in an abandoned mine entrance in Oregon. The report stated that the body was hidden from view and had a broken right femur with a bullet still lodged in the bone. In addition, the skeleton had a perfectly round hole in the upper sternum that resembled another bullet entrance point.

The report named the body's identity as a man that went missing in 1995 while conducting an environmental impact study on the effects of logging operations within the spotted owl environment. On the lap of the researcher, investigators found a journal. Inside the notebook was a detailed summary of the man's research. Plus, it contained what investigators described as a list of dying wishes and declarations.

Josh stopped reading and closed out the report on his screen, and dialed up his friend.

"Hey, man! Did you read the report I sent you?" Griz asked.

"I did, but I'm unsure what you want me to do with it. I mean, do you want me to review it or something?"

"Nope, not all, buddy, but do the circumstances seem eerily familiar to you?"

After a beat, Josh said, "do you think this is like the Savolt case?"

"I do, but when I tell you the details of what is in the man's notebook, I know I will have your attention."

Griz provided the information gleaned from the journal plus a sworn statement of someone already in custody. Josh listened and furiously scribbled down notes. When Griz read off a list of names connected with the researcher's demise, Josh almost dropped his pen. However, he regained his composure enough to write down the list, nonetheless.

"Josh, the Oregon authorities have issued arrest warrants for the names on that list, and believe it or not, they all live together in a small community in the Oregon mountains."

"Thanks, Griz, for the information, and coincidently, I am about to catch a flight to Casper. When I get off the phone with you, I will call the Natrona County Sheriff and schedule an appointment with him this afternoon."

"Do you know the Sheriff out there?"

"I do, and his name is Eddie Crandall."

Josh hung up with his former partner and did a web search on his smartphone for the phone number to the Natrona County Sheriff's office. Once he found it, he selected the embedded link that connected his call. Josh spoke with the sheriff's assistant and secured a 2:00 p.m. office call with him, and when the assistant asked for his name, he said, "Special Agent Anderson."

In-flight, Josh looked out of his window and watched as the Black Hills came into full view on the horizon and felt the plane bank slightly toward the southwest. He mused that this time of year was his favorite because the once vivid green prairie took on a deep golden hue. Then Josh saw bands of cottonwood trees along the waterways that still held onto a few golden leaves that refused to concede to winter.

The cottonwood's presence always meant that he was home and away from the heat and the population of Florida. However, he did not have the same affinity toward another tree or plant for the cottonwood in his lifetime.

The plane made another course adjustment and placed it directly to fly over the Salt Creek valley. He then saw the snaked outline of the Salt Creek and watched as the familiar oilfield began to show itself. Next, the town of Midwest emerged in his window, and he could pinpoint his old house on Navy Row, but a town park of some kind had replaced the vacant lot. He could also see Edgerton that rested just over the hill to the east. Lastly, Josh saw Teapot Rock from the air. The monolith looked much different from above, which displayed the years of erosion.

Josh's reminiscing was interrupted when the pilot announced that they were on final approach to Casper over the intercom. Ten minutes later, the plane landed on the runway and had arrived at the gate a few minutes ahead of schedule. Josh retrieved his carry-on suitcase and walked through the gate area, through the security checkpoint, and through the terminal doors to find his mom and dad waiting for him at the curb.

* * *

Josh drove his parent's car back to their home situated near Adams Park in the center of Casper. The Andersons had purchased the house in 1987, shortly after their youngest child, Cindy, had graduated from Midwest High School. The prospects of an empty nest initiated a thought that Rob and Sara had never owned a home. Instead, Rob resigned from coaching and teaching in Midwest and took a similar position at a junior high in Casper. Likewise, Sara also found work as the head administrator for an elementary school. Both Andersons retired in 2015.

He pulled into the driveway of his parent's home and parked the car in the garage. Josh then carried his suitcase to the room he usually occupied at least once a year on his regular visits home.

Over lunch, the Andersons sat down at the kitchen table. Josh then carefully unfolded the new information that his former FBI partner had given him. His father dropped his fork onto the plate, and his mother's eyes welled up in tears when he revealed the names of the suspects that were implicated in the death of Tim Savolt 34 years before.

Later that afternoon, Josh arrived at Sheriff Crandall's office 10 minutes early and took a seat in the small waiting area next to the desk of a busy assistant. The Sheriff opened his door and looked over at Josh, and his face flushed red and flashed a wide smile simultaneously.

"Well, if it isn't Josh Anderson!" The Sheriff then admitted, "when I saw my assistant's notes about a meeting with a Special Agent Anderson, I didn't think much about it. But, now, I see you sitting in that chair. How are you, Josh?"

Josh rose from his seat in the chair and shook the Sheriff's outstretched hand.

He replied, "I am doing great, Sheriff. I apologize for using my former title, but I knew that if I used it, then your office would see me immediately." Josh then added, "I retired a year and a half ago from the FBI."

The Sheriff continued to smile and motioned Josh into his office, and he shut the door behind him.

"How many years has it been Josh, ten or eleven?"

"It has been 17 years, Sheriff, when I consulted with you about a potential domestic terrorist group operating here in Natrona County."

"I remember doing that; it is a case that I wish I could forget. So, are you in town to go to the big game in Midwest tomorrow? I rarely miss a game if I can't help it. Yeah, sure, Natrona County High School has won their host of championships, but I prefer to watch the Oilers since I still live out there. But, you know, once *OFT* always *OFT*."

Josh shook his head. "I can't believe that *OFT* is still en vogue, but yes, I will be there, but coincidently, there is another matter to attend to as well."

"What is that?"

His face faded into a serious expression, and he asked, "do you remember the Tim Savolt missing person's case?"

Crandall dropped his smile as well. "Do I?" He then reached down and opened the bottom drawer of his antique oak desk and retrieved an aged, worn, and tattered folder, and placed it square upon his desktop in front of him.

The Sheriff pointed to it and said, "yes, I do. Some of these are from my file mixed with the original notes from Chief Traynor, who gave me his when he retired. Did you know he still lives in Midwest like me?"

Josh shook his head. "No, I didn't, though I have only been out to Midwest a couple of times since I left for the Coast Guard Academy. When I went out there, I didn't call any friends like Pete, Steve, or Carlos. Instead, I just walked around and took in a few sights. It just hurts too much to be out there without Ricky alongside me too. You know, it just doesn't feel like home anymore."

Crandall replied dryly, "I know what you mean. I get the same feeling every time I am in Glenrock too."

Josh then opened his briefcase and extracted his notebook. He laid out all the information he had just received from his former partner. Josh then took out a pen and a piece of scratch paper and copied down the suspects' names. He handed the note over to Crandall. His reaction upon reading the surnames of the suspects was much like Josh's parents. Yet, instead of dropping a fork and shedding a few tears, the Sheriff simply dropped his pen.

"But why Josh? What were these folks involved in?"

Josh moved his right hand to his shirt pocket and pulled out a folded piece of paper. Then he handed it over to the Sheriff. "They were all charter members of this."

Crandall slowly unfolded the aged paper and revealed the same flier that Josh had retrieved out of the vacant land behind Doug and Shelly Pierson's house all those years ago.

"I found that paper at the start of my senior year in Midwest."

Crandall opened the Savolt file and found a similar piece of paper, and turned it around for him to see it.

"Chief Traynor found this just east of Teachers Row too, but what does this mean?"

Josh explained, "As you know, after 9/11, I investigated potential domestic terrorist groups, and that group listed on the paper in front of you rose to the top of our watchlist."

He further explained that *LEAF* was an acronym for the Leave Earth Alone Foundation that had established a nationwide network of chapters starting in the late 1970s. *LEAF* chapters had rooted themselves in the fabric of many universities that supported enlightened liberal thinking and politics.

Then he provided examples of *LEAF* in action. First, Josh cited the bombing of a Texas oilfield company building that killed three men.

Then he discussed the details of a breached Louisiana oil pipeline that caused a massive oil spill. And lastly, Josh described how *LEAF* members spiked trees to prevent logging in the Northwest.

"Sheriff, I have long known what LEAF is and that they were operating in Midwest. In addition, I've long suspected that the group may be responsible for Tim Savolt's disappearance. Still, I had no confirmation of the members' names until this morning to tie this thing together."

Sheriff Crandall leaned back in his chair and twisted his thick mustache with his right hand, and left the conversation for a moment of thought. Then, he sat forward and removed a map of the Salt Creek area from his desk drawer and spread it out onto his desk.

"Josh, the problem we have is that there is no corpse, and I was hoping you could look at this map with me and help pinpoint where you think they hid Savolt's body."

Josh stood up and moved in behind the Sheriff. Then he placed his right index finger precisely on one of the area's most famous landmarks and said, "here, I know it is here."

"Why do you think it is there? I mean, I checked out that place myself?"

Josh nodded. "But did you look everywhere inside and outside it?"

While the Sheriff scratched his head to think, Josh reached into his briefcase and produced the architectural plans for the building and placed it over the map.

Then, he asked the Sheriff, "did you look here exactly?" and Crandall looked to the point that Josh indicated on the paper.

"Well, no. I pulled up and looked around, but I hadn't seen any tire tracks or any other evidence that anybody had been around the place. But you are certain the body is there?"

"I do, Sheriff because it just makes sense. You and I both know that most criminals are not as smart as they think they are, and these guys needed to hide Savolt's body quickly. But my experience also tells me that culprits will often stash things in plain sight because to thinking people like you and me, we will overlook the obvious."

Josh stood up and walked around to the other side of the Sheriff's desk. Then he recalled, "about ten years ago, other agents and I exhumed a dead body from four inches of pond water. Additionally, the body remained hidden within a hundred yards from the suspected crime scene."

"But how does that case give you a clue to this one? I mean, I don't see a connection here, Josh? And how is it you theorize that Savolt ended up in this place?" Crandall asked as he tapped his finger repeatedly on the structure identified on the map.

"Do you remember the dark green Ford F150?"

"Of course, how could I forget?"

"The key to this whole thing rests in the locations that Ford showed up. First, it showed up when I was close to the place where I found Savolt's backpack. Then it showed up for the last time...."

Crandall cut Josh off. "I get it now."

Josh continued, "I have waited over half of my life for enough evidence to surface to obtain a search warrant for that building since it sits on private land. Do you think you can get an order together and signed by a judge?"

"I can, but it will be dark before we can get out there today, so how about tomorrow morning?"

"Sure, how about I meet you there at 9:00 a.m. to allow you to get your team and all the gear ready. Sound like a plan?"

Sheriff Crandall lifted his eyes to Josh and said, "you bet. Then, afterward, how about I buy you a Coke at the game?"

Josh nodded. "Sounds like a deal."

* * *

39

Later that Friday afternoon, Josh parked his father's pickup on the parking pad outside of the same Proctor home that he had spent much time during his high school days. He noticed that many of the houses seemed the same on his way into town, though others looked poorly kept and in disrepair. He also noted that the red-white-blue painted Centennial Pump Jack no longer greeted visitors at the Junction. Instead, it rested on the golf course.

When Josh stepped out of the truck, he drew a deep breath through his nostrils, but he noticed a glaring absence of sulfur that used to envelop the town. He turned and closed the truck door, walked up onto the porch's steps, and knocked lightly upon the door.

Immediately, the door swung open, and Toni Proctor greeted him and gave him a warm hug. David came up from the basement where his former room was and bear-hugged Josh with enough force that he almost broke bones. David had added another thirty pounds to his impressive high school physique and looked like he could still don football pads and play a game.

The reunited friends spent the next hour talking and catching up with one another. Then they walked easterly up Stock Street and entered the school's rear door just down from the office. Once inside the hallway, the men stopped at the trophy case. They noticed that many trophies were missing and that only a dust ring remained to signify their placement. Beyond them, townsfolk were already filing into the main gym from a line that must have started in the high school parking lot.

When David and Josh entered the gym, they were greeted immediately by Pete, Steve, and Carlos. The trio had waited for them to show up. After many handshakes and a few manly hugs, they all took their seats in an area reserved for the 1984 team. Josh noted that only four members of the 1979 team were present, while ten members of the 1991 team sat in their designated section.

Josh turned and greeted his other former teammates, and his 1984 team boasted the biggest turnout for this homecoming. But, when Josh turned back around to face the gym floor, he saw a row of chairs behind the podium assumed for the football team. But, then, the missing trophies noted earlier were on full display on the table in front of the stand.

Pete walked up to the podium and took over as the master of the ceremony. First, he welcomed the crowd that had filled the bleacher sections on both sides of the gym. Pete started by having the audience members focus on all the trophies on the table and insisted that one was missing: the one that their Oilers would win the next day.

He then announced the members of the 1979 championship football team. Next, Pete began calling out individual names, causing the former players to stand and wait for an acknowledgment. Next, Pete announced the 1984 team, and David and Josh both stood in respective turns. Lastly, Pete began introducing players from the 1991 team.

However, Pete also made an interesting point that in the three years from 1978 to 1980. Those three Oiler teams amassed 22 wins and four losses while averaging over 25 points a game and allowed just less than ten. Next, Pete highlighted the 1991 team's accomplishments of becoming the last near-perfect team during the previous 27 years. He noted this team boasted winning the first tie-breaking three-way round-robin playoff game to determine which two conference teams entered the playoff bracket. The 1991 Oilers then bested Burlington in regionals and beat long-time rival Big Horn in the state championship.

Pete then acknowledged his bias for talking about the 1984 team last because he was a proud member of that team, which brought the gym into a roar of laughter. He pointed out that the group was perfect in every way and came within a miraculous game-ending play of winning a state title. He also recalled that they played the game while missing three key starters.

But Pete also provided some additional facts about the Oiler teams from 1984 to 1986. First, he noted that those teams also sported a 22-4 record, scoring a perfect 15-0 against the larger 2A schools. It was a feat never before achieved or ever matched since. Then, finally, Pete boasted about the 1984-1986 teams scoring over 26 points a game while only allowing their opponents a meager six points a game.

Pete then introduced each of the fifteen members of the current squad by name and read off their positions. Josh and David noted that each boy came out wearing their home maroon and white jersey. However, the modern look of the material was much better than what Josh and David remembered wearing. Then Pete announced Scott Merino, a former player from 1982 to 1984 and current Oiler head coach.

The event concluded with every member in attendance shaking the hands of the football players and ended with Pete leading off the chant *O-F-T*, which echoed out of the gym.

Afterward, Josh got a chance to talk to both retired Chief Traynor and retired teacher Bill Crooks, who sat next to one another on the old wooden bleachers. Josh spoke of his travels and his retirement but then drew the two men into a close huddle and made a request of them, to which they both nodded their agreement.

Josh also got a moment with Scott Merino. As briefly as possible, Scott informed Josh that he wanted to speak to him about an unrelated matter. Josh promised his friend that he would call sometime that weekend after the football game.

Later in the evening, Pete, Carlos, Steve, Josh, and David met up again at the Proctor's house for a quick chat. They shared a beer along with many laughs with one another in the backyard around the firepit. Additionally, everyone told each other about what they had done in their lives and what they still planned for themselves in the future. They reminisced, and they joked and told funny stories like Pete timing Steve taking a leak at the rest stop on the way to Guernsey.

Suddenly, Pete set down his beer and excused himself to the rear of the yard and into the Proctor's garage. When he returned, he carried a shovel and came back to the firepit.

Steve swallowed his sip of beer and then wiped his mouth with his sleeve. He looked at Pete and said, "what are you going to do with that?"

Pete started giggling just like he did in high school and said, "how about we go dig up that time capsule?"

Five grown men, each carrying a beer in their hand, laughed and talked the short distance to the post office and went around to the back of the building. Pete removed four shovels of dirt exactly where they had buried the canister and stopped when he felt the presence of tin against the blade. Josh bent down and gently broke the container free from the soil and handed it up to David.

"I think we should go back to the firepit where we can see and open this thing up," Josh suggested, and the others agreed.

Back at the Proctor house, David carefully opened the rusted lid. To everyone's surprise, it opened instead of breaking apart. He squatted above the light grey concrete patio bricks around the firepit and slowly poured out the container's contents.

Pete spotted an unopened can of Copenhagen and said, "That is mine. I wonder if it is still good?" Then he used his thumbnail to tear the seal and opened the tin. Then he placed a pinch of the aged dry tobacco in his lip. He shook his head from side to side and said with a puckered face, "it is okay but just dry." Everyone laughed.

Next, Josh picked up the stack of papers that constituted another copy of Tim Savolt's notes. At the time, he thought it was as good of a place as any to store them for safekeeping.

Then Steve retrieved a small key chain that he made in a crafts class, and Carlos retrieved an envelope that held a stack of Polaroid photos of him and the same friends standing around him.

David lifted an old sandwich bag that contained what amounted to a teaspoon full of gray dust. He handed the bag to Josh and asked, "do you remember what this is?"

He nodded. "I do, but there is a lot I have to explain to you guys about that stuff."

However, Pete noticed two things left unclaimed, and he reached down and picked them up. In the light of the fire, his outstretched hand held a matched set of rings.

Josh reached out and patted Pete on the shoulder. "Those are the promise rings that Ricky had bought for him and Sheila during our sophomore year."

Pete's face flushed with embarrassment. "I will take them. I am sure that Sheila would like to have them considering what happened to Ricky."

The men huddled together and offered a toast in unison, "to Ricky." However, nobody wanted to admit how much they missed their lifelong friend.

Josh then held up his hand as if to make another announcement, to which all talk suddenly ceased.

"Guys, what do you have to do tomorrow morning around 8:30?"

The other four men looked at one another, and nobody expressed that they had any pending plans.

Josh reached over to the plastic bag in David's hand and took it from him, and held it up.

"Meet me at the junction store tomorrow morning at 8:30, and I will lead you to a place that will reveal what this stuff is and why Tim Savolt had disappeared.

* * *

40

Saturday, November 10, 2018

Midwest, Wyoming

Josh turned off Highway 259 like he had many other times before and crossed over what looked like the same cattle guard there 34 years earlier. He turned his father's truck into the junction store and parked outside. Josh then exited the pickup and stepped inside the store.

To his delight, he noted that the place had transformed over the years from a simple convenience store to a first-rate roadside truck stop. It offered fuel, hot food from the grill, and other typical consumables like canned food, milk, and bread.

He filled up a large cup of black coffee and selected a sleeve of cocoanut frosted mini-donuts, and took them up to the counter to pay for them. Josh then stepped back outside and set his coffee on the hood of the pickup. He pulled the sleeve back on his left wrist and studied the time on his watch. He was still 10 minutes early.

Bill Crooks arrived first with Chief Traynor seated next to him in the same old beat-up Willys pickup that he owned years before. Josh walked over to the driver's side window and motioned for Crooks to roll it down.

"Hey Bill, I see you are still driving this beast. But you've must have had some work done on it, or else I would have heard it from your house in Gas Plant." His statement incited Traynor into a belly laugh.

"Go ahead, laugh it up, you two clowns. I love this truck. I've replaced the motor twice, the transmission three times, and had a complete exhaust overhaul too. However, it is bought and paid for and still out climbs any of these modern 4x4s driving around today," Crooks replied.

Traynor shifted in his seat and asked Josh, "so, you think you've located Tim Savolt's remains?"

Josh nodded. "I do. Sheriff Crandall will have his crew already in position when I lead our caravan out there."

Crooks squinted due to the reflection of the sun in his side mirror and looked up at Josh. "Where are you taking us?"

Josh smiled. "The old electric plant?"

The old teacher furrowed his brow. "Have you been working on this case all these years? I mean, I talk to your dad all the time, and he has kept me up off all the stuff you accomplished over the years, and I might add, he is proud of you, son. But really, you have never given up?"

Josh looked coldly into Crooks' eyes. "Do you remember the scripture that I referred to during Savolt's memorial service?"

"Vaguely, though I remember the Pierson couple getting their underwear in a bunch over it, though."

Josh looked at both men and recited his exact words: "In first John, chapter one, verses five through seven, we shouldn't just believe the truth but should live by it as well." He paused for a second and then continued. "You see, I have always believed that God gave me the talent to seek the truth to help others. It began in high school, and it perfected itself during my service time and with the bureau. But in my spare time, I have always crunched on the Savolt riddle, and today, the truth will set us all free from this thing."

A noise from behind him caused Josh to turn his head. There, he saw David and Carlos riding together through the west entrance to the Junction. Meanwhile, Pete and Steve arrived together through the east exit. They all parked in a line along in front of the store.

Josh led the caravan out onto Highway 387, away from town, and turned north onto Light Plant Road. Along the way, Josh noted that trails off of the familiar track changed over the years, but he knew where he needed to navigate. The caravan soon traversed over the now treeless Coal Draw and passed by the Sand Rocks, where Bill Crooks saved his, Pete's, and Steve's life. It was also one of two places that held the names of hundreds of Midwest alumni, Josh included, who had carved them into the rock over the years.

A little further down the road, Josh parked next to one of the two remaining cottonwood trees that once outlined the streets of an abandoned oilfield camp. He got out of the truck and saw the dozen or so Sheriff's Department vehicles parked in a long line.

After waiting for everyone else to get out of their vehicles, Josh looked up at the aging hulk of the light plant. He then pointed to it for his contingent of followers.

Then Josh announced, "I think Savolt is in one of the turbine pits inside the electric plant."

Sheriff Crandall walked over to Josh, shook his hand, and gladly greeted his former mentor, Chief Traynor, and his friend, Bill Crooks.

"I hope you don't mind, Sheriff, but I have brought out with me all the folks who were a part of the Savolt mystery. Some even shed some blood like Steve over there," Josh said.

The Sheriff nodded. "No, I don't mind as long as you guys give my folks room to work. I don't see any harm with you on the scene."

"Are your folks ready, Sheriff?"

"Yep, I have two guys rigged up to rappel down into the first pit and then dive into it if need be. I was waiting for you to arrive before we began."

"Okay, guys, let's follow the Sheriff," Josh said as he looked toward his contingent of friends.

Once inside the dilapidated plant, Josh looked around the interior concrete walls. He quickly deduced that it was still a lasting youth memorial. Josh spotted his highly faded spray-painted initials near the northeastern corner. Ricky and David's names were still visible high and bold, and he pointed up to it and gave David a wink.

The group stopped ten yards from the precipice of one of the two long-empty turbine pits and watched as two deputies lowered themselves down. After repelling 25 feet, the deputies hit bottom. Next, they shouted topside that the water was only an inch deep. The mud underneath it made it seem as if it was an endless dark abyss.

In response, two other deputies on the ground floor began lowering two shovels into the pit on a rope. Seconds later, Josh and the other heard the distinctive sound of mud shoveling into a pile.

Ten anxiety-filled minutes later, everyone's jaw dropped when one of the deputies in the pit shouted, "Sheriff, we have a skeleton!"

Everyone moved forward and observed the two deputies gently pick up the remains of a body in a tattered t-shirt, jeans, and leather boots. Additionally, a heavy logging chain was still covering the body.

"Wow, look at how little water is in the turbine pit!" exclaimed Pete.

Steve noted the water level as well. "Look at the watermark stain on the concrete. That would make it, what, five-foot deep normally?"

"Agree, maybe the drought that everyone keeps talking about actually helped us here," Josh surmised.

The men below unfurled a black necroscopy bag and placed the skeletal remains inside it. While the two deputies gently raised the bag, two others helped extract the men out of the pit. Then, Sheriff Crandall motioned for Josh and his friends to join him outside.

Sheriff Crandall walked to one of the old concrete steps to a non-existent house and sat down away from the light plant. Then he took out a piece of gum from his pocket and placed it in his mouth. Pete took out a fresh can of Copenhagen and took a dip, to which Josh and others refused. So instead, Josh sat down next to Sheriff Crandall, and the others formed an arc around them.

Josh looked at Crandall. "Sheriff, I am 100% positive that when you run a DNA sequence on the remains, you will find an absolute match to Tim Savolt."

"Oh, I am sure we will find DNA, but how do we match it to Savolt?"

"I will be right back," Josh said as he got up and walked over to his dad's pickup. Once there, he reached through the window and grabbed the gallon-sized and sealed plastic bag from the passenger seat. Then he sat back down to Sheriff Crandall.

Josh handed the bag to Crandall, who took it. Inside it, the Sheriff saw an old, faded, red King Ropes hat with a once white-colored rope that stretched across the brim.

"Sheriff, this is one of Tim Savolt's old hats that was inside a box full of papers that Reed gave me 34 years ago. After working on crime scenes with the FBI, I knew that I had to seal it up to prevent further cross-contamination. Still, I am certain that there is enough of Savolt's hair fibers to run your sequence," Josh explained.

The Sheriff drew a deep breathed and asked him the critical question, "what was this all about anyway?"

Josh recalled for everyone's benefit that Tim Savolt accomplished two things. First, his study proved that Salt Creek was not the ecological monster that the environmentalists had labeled. Second, he recalled publishing Savolt's results as a part of his senior thesis.

"Also, Savolt found this!" Josh said as he held up a sandwich bag with grayish powder inside.

"What is it?" Crandall asked.

"This, gentlemen, is the dried-out remnants of a thermophile. It is a special form of bacteria that occurs naturally in hot springs. But, only three places on earth support these organisms, and Yellowstone is one of them. So, that hot spring that I found using Savolt's notes also held a huge quantity of this stuff."

Chief Traynor shook his head. "But what is so important about this stuff, Josh?"

"Thanks, Chief, for that exact question." Josh then explained that a Montana State professor discovered thermophiles in Yellowstone, which he labeled *tag polymerase*. He further described how researchers found that certain types of thermophiles consume sulfur and petroleum products in water.

He looked back at Crandall. "But the ironic thing is that when you do the DNA sequencing, Sheriff, the sequencing medium is a thermophile too."

Steve interjected, "you mean that thermo, whatever you call it, could have applications in the oilfield like consuming sulfur and waste oil."

Josh nodded. Then he said, "yes. A thermophile might have led another boom in the Salt Creek area if Savolt's puddle hadn't dried up. I suppose if someone researched to replicate the same conditions in that accidental hot spring back in 1984, the thermophile might avail itself again."

Steve nodded. "Josh, I have some engineers that I want to talk to you about this. Can I have them call you?"

Josh shrugged. "Sure, but we need to get back on subject here. All this means, guys, is that someone murdered Tim Savolt to keep his greatest discovery from coming forward. However, I believe the findings of the study ran contrary to a certain environmental group's messaging. I know Savolt mentioned his preliminary results to someone because his notebook annotated as much and specifically called the person a *colleague*."

Josh looked again at Sheriff Crandall. Then he asked, "do you have that list of names I gave you yesterday?"

The Sheriff reached up and pulled the paper from his shirt pocket and handed it to him.

Josh started at the top of the list, "Doug and Shelly Pierson were the ring leaders of an underground eco-terrorist group called *LEAF* or Leave Earth Alone Foundation. While in the domestic terrorism office with the FBI, I discovered that the Piersons are possible connections to hundreds of accounts of vandalism in Texas, Louisiana, and even here in Midwest. Still, there was not enough direct evidence to charge them."

Bill Crooks interjected, "Josh, did you know that the Piersons left Midwest a year after you graduated?"

Josh nodded. Then he revealed how the Piersons showed up in another small oilfield town in Texas, which was the location of more vandalism and even a bombing. After that, the couple left Texas and surfaced again in Oregon in 1994 near an area that loggers began to find spiked trees to prevent them from logging.

"I found out from my former partner yesterday that the Piersons were responsible for the death of a researcher on snowy owl decline back in the early 1990s. The scientist was about to publish that the owl's decline wasn't due to just logging. Instead, it was a multitude of factors."

Josh looked up to Crandall. "Sheriff, I will have my buddy at the FBI supply you with a copy of the journal found on the body of the deceased researcher."

Josh took a deep breath and continued. "Next on the list is Karen Connelly." He looked around and saw the mention of her name had astonished the men surrounding him. Josh then explained that Karen's involvement was the hardest to connect.

Crooks spoke out again, "Incredible, I just now remembered that Karen had left Midwest in 1987, which was the same as the Piersons."

Josh nodded in reply. Then he hypothesized that Karen's job was to get as close to Savolt as possible, including pillow talk, if necessary. She would then extract information from him about his findings and report them to Doug and Shelly Pierson.

"I also know that Karen had a key to Savolt's apartment because he told me so," Josh said.

Chief Traynor cleared his throat. "Yes, that would make complete sense. I always felt that since there wasn't any sign of damage on Savolt's door, meaning that whoever tossed his place must have had a key."

A few moments later, Josh continued, "I clearly remember the argument between Doug and Shelly Pierson in the hallway outside of my class. I came to understand later that their spat was over the missing Savolt files, which I came into possession."

"Wait a minute, Josh. So, you had the files?" Traynor asked.

"Yes, Sir. The box was left at my doorstep one afternoon during the fall of 1984."

"Who left them?" Sheriff Crandall asked.

He shrugged. "I don't know, but I have always assumed it was Reed."

"Why do you think it was Reed?" Chief Traynor asked.

"Chief, only Reed could have accessed those files whether the box was in Savolt's apartment or his classroom. What most people didn't know was that Savolt and Reed were pretty good friends. So, it makes sense that he took the material and gave them to me. Additionally, the mailing label was addressed to the custodial staff."

"But why didn't Reed give the box to the Chief or me?" Sheriff Crandall asked.

"My theory is that Reed feared his disappearance if someone caught him with the files. Plus, if he did give the files to law enforcement, then that study would never have been completed by me or anyone. Savolt's valuable findings would have just collected dust in some case file warehouse," Josh explained, and a quiet hush enveloped the men.

Pete broke the awkward silence when he interjected, "Wow, am I glad I didn't sleep with her!" He then looked around to a team of unbelieving faces.

Pete then pleaded, "no, really, Ms. Connelly invited me over into her apartment in early September that year. She wanted me to redo the spaghetti dinner that I messed up on and had received an F." Pete looked up to see if he still held an audience before he continued. "I went over to her apartment, and when she opened the door, it was lit only by candles, but then her telephone rang, and she whispered to me that we would have to reschedule."

"It must be true because Pete would have told us if he had gotten anywhere with her," Steve said and looked around, "am I right?"

Josh chuckled but got the other's attention again when he cleared his throat and continued.

"The other members on the list, Debra and Lucas Jansen, and Kandi Kowalski, all went to college with Doug and Shelly Pierson. I firmly believe it was there that they joined as members of *LEAF*. Furthermore, I think they were used as lookouts to notify Stiles and Pruitt to chase anyone that ventured too close to either Savolt's kill site or his resting place. I pieced the last part together when I remembered that these same people had identical antennas on their houses. So, I now suggest that they used a radio to communicate with the Stiles and Pruitt, who operated that mysterious Ford pickup. Plus, Chief Traynor told me nearly 25 years ago that Sheriff Crandall here had found their suspected hideout in the old barn on the Miller place."

Chief Traynor interrupted, "but Josh, Kandi Kowalski did not live in a house with the other teachers on Navy Row?"

"That is true, Chief, but she did live in that small trailer on the corner of Navy Row and Fitzhugh."

Everyone looked around at each other as if they finally understood his implication.

Then, after taking a long drink of coffee, Josh continued.

"But as to why they targeted my friends and me, I can only reason that the LEAF members thought we all knew too much and tried to take us out on that one day in November of 1984. They would have succeeded if Crooks hadn't drilled one of the perps."

Josh stopped talking momentarily and took another breath.

"Here is the kicker: every person on that list is still living. They are in another small town but in Oregon this time. I know the local authorities rounded all of them up yesterday, including Marvin Stiles. He worked at the same school with the Piersons in the cafeteria, although under an alias."

Josh spat onto the ground. Only then did he look over at Sheriff Crandall. He said, "Sheriff, I think I have given you enough information to put together an extradition order for all the people on that list."

Sheriff Crandall stood up and excused himself for a moment and talked to one of his Deputies to provide him some instructions. He then walked back to the group and sat back down upon the step.

"Josh, what I don't understand is how you can sum up this case; I mean, what kind of proof is there?" the Sheriff asked.

"Good question. Aside from the entries in the notebook found on the dead Oregon researcher, the key link came from the testimony of one of the *LEAF* members himself."

"Who was that?" the Sheriff asked.

"In that report that is being sent to your office today, you will find a sworn statement from Lucas Jansen."

During the pause, Josh then heard a collective gasp emit from the group. Then he continued, "Lucas was apprehended last week while trying to sneak across the Mexican border in Arizona with 5 pounds of fentanyl in his backpack. You know, that stuff causing overdose deaths? But, when the border agents questioned him, Lucas asked for leniency in exchange for information about a missing researcher in Oregon and a missing teacher in Wyoming."

Every face looked toward Josh after that revelation. Finally, he recounted how his former partner in the FBI, who now runs the domestic counter-terrorism department, was called in to interview Jansen. The new information also corroborated with the evidence found in Oregon.

Josh said, "My friend then called me. But that left finding Savolt's body as the last step in this investigation."

Once again, Sheriff Crandall stood up and stretched. Then he reached up to his other shirt pocket and took out a mini-recorder, and pressed the stop-record button.

He smiled and looked up at Josh. "I learned this little trick of using a pocket recorder from a game warden friend of mine near Sheridan. I hope you didn't mind my recording your summation? At any rate, the recording sure saves me the hassle of writing everything down."

Crandall then looked over to David and asked, "so, David, since you are a prosecutor, do you think there is enough evidence to get a conviction in this case?"

David quickly professed, "yes, I believe so based on the evidence the FBI has collected. But the crucial part is linking the corpse you found today with Tim Savolt. Even if DNA is no longer viable due to age, I think the circumstantial evidence will overwhelmingly prove a criminal conspiracy that led to murder. I would also throw in other stuff like illegal entry to Savolt's apartment and trespassing on the property here at the old light plant. How is that for assurance, Sheriff?"

"Your opinion suits me fine, David," he said.

Pete stood by and rubbed his head. Then asked the one question nobody had asked, "but why, Josh? Why would they resort to killing at least two people because they want to preserve nature? I just don't get it, buddy?"

Josh thought for a second. "Maybe this bunch of people was ahead of their time in carrying out their passion for a cause. Take the environment; for example, I believe that we all should be good stewards of the land, as spelled out in the Book of Genesis. But using vandalism and murder to further the cause is disgusting to me. Look around you, gentlemen; today, protestors block roads, engage in rioting, and cause all kinds of mayhem.

Then consider what the nation went through with Judge Kavanaugh's supreme court nomination. All the talking heads on both sides kept bullying people to see their point of view. I am not even talking about the merits of the accusations lobbed at the man. It is a scary world."

"It reminds me of the book *1984*," Pete suggested.

Josh nodded his head. Then he added, "we are living in a precarious bubble that could pop at any time. Anyone with a cause may use physical violence as their default means to be heard by other people.

Bill Crooks finally spoke up. "Good speech, son, now maybe you should run for office?"

With a quick retort, Josh said, "not on your life. Do you know what the press would do if they looked into my yearbook and saw what my friends wrote? I mean, who could explain the entry of Steve's record-breaking urination?"

A cacophony of laughter erupted from the group who crowded around Josh and congratulated him for finally solving the mystery. Most relieved was Chief Traynor, who expressed his gratitude for putting all the pieces together that had eluded him for so many sleepless nights.

Three hours later, Josh, David, Pete, Steve, and Carlos sat abreast in the stands and watched their beloved Oilers play in the championship game. Though this was the first time that both Josh and David were at the field and not participating in a contest.

The friends yelled "*OFT*" along with the crowd. Plus, they cheered in unison and with passion when the final seconds ticked off the game clock, and the Midwest Oilers had won its third state title since football began in the small town in 1923.

Outside the field and out in the parking lot following the game, the guys stood around talking. They repeatedly remarked how they all need to get together more often. Finally, after a while, Pete looked down at his watch. He announced that he needed to go back up to the school and lock it up, which initiated the need for others to leave likewise.

As they had as kids, the friends didn't exchange any long, drawn-out goodbyes with one another. Instead, as each one of them turned to leave, they offered one another their usual, "see ya," and walked away.

THE END

AFTERWORD AND ACKNOWLEDGEMENTS

The Wyoming towns of Midwest and Edgerton depicted in this story are real. They are the last townships within the Salt Creek Oilfield that once held the World's Largest Light Oil Producing Field title. Another truth is that Midwest High School was the first high school in the United States to host and play a nighttime football game under a lighted field. Lastly, the Salt Creek Oilfield continues to produce millions of barrels of high-grade crude. In many respects, the Salt Creek community carries the principal responsibility for the growth and development of neighboring Casper along with the State of Wyoming. Indelibly, the oil from this small region continues to fuel this nation.

The schedule, the opponents, the final scores of games, and any history depicted about the 1984 Midwest Oiler football team are factual. However, the game highlights within this work are the fictional insights of the author.

Photos: All photos are by the author. The location of the front cover's depiction of Salt Creek is just south of the football field. The image of the author is on the porch of his childhood home located at #10 Navy Row in Midwest, Wyoming.

Additionally, the author thanks his wife, Nancy, for inspiring him to write this story that he has carried inside him for over 30 years.

Lastly, the author invites readers to follow his website for news related to upcoming book releases and ordering of published novels. See phillemaitreauhor.com

OTHER BOOKS BY THE AUTHOR

EARLY DAWN: A Salt Creek Novel
BITING WIND: A Salt Creek Novel

Phil LeMaitre

ABOUT THE AUTHOR

Phil LeMaitre is a former resident of Midwest, Wyoming, and graduated from Midwest High School in 1986. LeMaitre is a 29-year active-duty veteran of the U.S. Air Force and now serves as a Christian Life Coach. Other works include *Biting Wind: A Salt Creek Novel* and *Early Dawn: A Salt Creek Novel*. The author lives in Florida with his wife and their three youngest children.